THE
GOOD
ONES

THE
GOOD
ONES

A Novel

POLLY STEWART

HARPER

An Imprint of HarperCollinsPublishers

THE GOOD ONES. Copyright © 2023 by Mary Stewart Atwell Schultz. All rights reserved. Printed in the United States of America. No part of this book may be used or reproduced in any manner whatsoever without written permission except in the case of brief quotations embodied in critical articles and reviews. For information, address HarperCollins Publishers, 195 Broadway, New York, NY 10007.

HarperCollins books may be purchased for educational, business, or sales promotional use. For information, please email the Special Markets Department at SPsales@harpercollins.com.

FIRST EDITION

Designed by Kyle O'Brien

Library of Congress Cataloging-in-Publication Data has been applied for.

ISBN 978-0-06-323415-4

23 24 25 26 27 LBC 5 4 3 2 1

To Keith

THE
GOOD
ONES

Prologue

The last time I saw Lauren Ballard, she was scraping a key along the side of a new cherry-red Chevy Silverado.

The newspapers and media reports never showed this side of her. They liked to use the photo of Lauren leaning against a stone wall in a gown encrusted with a thousand hand-sewn crystals, or the one where she posed in a field in a long white dress with her train rippling behind her and a butterfly perched on her wrist. The problem was that the pictures were fakes, relics of the summer she spent modeling for the wedding boutique downtown back in high school. Her own wedding had been small and not particularly joyous, the swags of white tulle decorating the pews hanging limply in the August heat.

It was a familiar small-town story; the girl whom everyone expected to move away and make something of herself had been caught instead, locked down by the familiar forces of inertia and an unplanned pregnancy. The guests seemed puzzled by how things had turned out, and I guessed that no one knew what I knew: that Lauren had gotten knocked up on purpose, having flushed her birth control pills down the toilet in her senior year of college.

What followed was so predictable that I could have written it myself. Lauren and her new husband bought a starter home on Blue Ridge Road, and he went to work for his father's realty company. After their daughter, Mabry, was born, Lauren got her real estate license and worked part-time. From the outside, they looked like a family in an ad for cereal or stackable washer-dryers. After Lauren disappeared, the police and the media saw what they wanted to see: a young, beautiful wife and mother who had married her high school sweetheart and settled in their hometown. She should have been cable news catnip, the pretty white girl from a good family whom viewers could ogle and pity at the same time.

But this is what I've learned: the dead or missing girl is never the subject of the story. Sometimes she's not even the object. She is the circumstance, the accident, the nexus through which vectors cross. No one really knows her, not even the people who were closest to her in life. She becomes a stranger when you realize that her last moments were incomprehensible, an abyss you can't fathom.

This is not a story about a murder. It's not the story of what happened to Lauren Ballard in the early-morning hours of August 10, 2001. I can't tell that story, because even all these years later, I still don't really understand the events of that night. All I know is what was left behind: broken glass, a trace of blood on a wet washcloth, tire tracks in the grass.

These details are what matters, whether they're in photos on a true-crime blog or lying neglected in a police evidence locker. I've arranged them every way I can think of, but it's like trying to play a board game with pieces missing. It's like a dream when you're walking down a familiar street and suddenly you're in a different city, staring at your reflection in a plate-glass window, trying to remember what brought you here.

THE HEAT THAT MORNING WAS THICK AND DAMP, THE KIND THAT MAKES you sweat in the crease of your neck and behind your knees. After breakfast, I dragged the two dusty gray inner tubes out of the shed, loaded them into the bed of my truck, and met Lauren at the outfitters by Horseshoe Bend, where we paid a guy ten bucks to take us upstream to the boat launch, packed in with half a dozen out-of-towners who oohed and aahed at every mountain vista like they'd never seen a tree before. Lauren's husband had taken the baby to visit his parents for the weekend, and we'd decided to spend it like deadbeats, floating the river with a cooler of beer. We waited until the tourists had paddled downstream, busily plying their oars to one side and then the other, before we waded the tubes out to the middle of the current.

There's no good way to get into an inner tube in moving water. I tried to slide carefully into the doughnut hole while Lauren flopped into hers butt-first. Six months after the birth of her daughter, she was running four miles a day and her body was back to its usual sinewy thinness. Today she wore tiny pink shorts over an old blue racerback suit that she wouldn't have been caught dead in if there were guys around, her hair swept up in an untidy dancer's bun that allowed a few curls to escape and trail down the side of her neck. Even early in the morning, we were already sweaty, and the keloid scar on her arm from a childhood bout of chicken pox gleamed, tight and shiny as balloon skin.

We held hands and lifted our feet, and I let my head fall back against the smooth side of the tube. The river was flat and wide enough that I was pretty sure we could float halfway to the county line without bothering to steer. "Nachos," I said.

Lauren turned her head to the side, giving me a deadpan look. "That's not even a name."

"It's a great name," I insisted. "Then every time you went outside and called him, people would think you were just hungry. It's a conversation piece."

"I swear we didn't have this much trouble naming the baby," she said, her foot brushing mine as the tubes bumped. "Warren wants Lucky."

Of course he did, I thought; Warren Ballard was the luckiest person I knew. Back in the day, he and Lauren had been the king and queen of Tyndall County, their cutesy rhyming names a guarantee of their rightness for each other even if their looks hadn't matched them as high school royalty: Warren a dead ringer for Rob Lowe in *The Outsiders;* Lauren with blond hair and perfect posture that made up for the fact that her features weren't entirely regular, the nose and mouth a little too big, the eyes too far apart. Senior year, she'd had the second-highest GPA in her class, a fraction of a point behind a boy who would go on to study robotics at MIT.

If she'd been notable only for being pretty and smart, she might have been despised, but she was likable too, at least some of the time. Instead of trying to minimize her accent, as another ambitious girl might have done, she had leaned into it, and her drawl was loud enough to carry from one end of the hall to the other. She had a catalog of expressions that sounded as if she'd picked them up from a chain-smoking beautician or a charming one-eyed hustler in a biker bar, and if I hung around her long enough, I'd find myself talking like her, dropping my *g*'s and calling everybody *sugar.*

Our fingers loosened as the tubes spun away from each other. "Do you want to spend the night at our place?" she asked. "Warren won't be back until lunchtime tomorrow."

I shook my head. I'd spent the week rotating between my mom's and Lauren's, but I'd told my mom I'd stay in tonight. "I could come over in the morning," I said. "We could do breakfast."

She shrugged, tugging me toward her again. "Maybe, but not before ten. I want to sleep." Our feet tangled, and Lauren ran a toe up the side of my leg before they broke apart. "We should have a party before you go back to Fletcher."

"I hate parties."

With my head back against the side of the tube, I could sense but not see her rolling her eyes. "Sean is down in North Carolina, you know."

"I'm not afraid of Sean Ballard."

That was a lie, and Lauren probably knew it. The last time I'd seen Warren's younger brother had been at the wedding last summer, and the meeting had been so awkward, with both of us nearly breaking our necks to avoid eye contact, that I was sure everyone had noticed. "Then why don't you talk anymore?" she countered. "Is it because you don't want him to know that you're a lesbo now? *Nicola likes giiiii-irls,"* she sang out across the water.

"Fuck you," I snapped, and let go of her hand at the same time I kicked her tube away with my heel. We spun out in different directions, and when I raised my head, I saw that she was looking back at me across half the span of the river, eyes wide. Lauren loved to get a reaction; she couldn't help herself, even with people she supposedly cared about, like me.

She didn't apologize, and I sulked all the way down the river as the sun climbed higher and I trailed my fingers in a loose V, the contrast between the cool water and the heat on my legs just stimulating enough to keep me awake. The bottle between my thighs stuck to my skin, and I took a last sip before swapping it out for a fresh one. Arching branches of tulip poplars and sycamores slid overhead in a shifting screen. When I heard shouts, I raised my head just as we passed a trio of sunburned rednecks drinking on the beach below a mudbank. Hooting, they raised their beers and mimed hip thrusts. One waded into the shallows and made a grab for my tube, but Lauren pulled me away in time.

In the end we overshot the path to the parking lot and had to bushwhack through a quarter mile of undergrowth, the tube banging awkwardly against my body while I cinched the handle of the nearly empty cooler in the crook of my elbow. Cicadas droned in the thicket, and mosquitoes nipped at my shoulders and the backs of my knees. I was still mad at myself for not calling Lauren out. Telling her to fuck off wasn't strong enough, but if I brought it up now, she'd tell me that I was being too sensitive and *lesbo* was a term of endearment, like *bitch.*

Lauren was ten feet ahead when we got to the parking lot, and I heard her groan, "Well, damn it all the way to hell" before I saw the problem. A brand-new red truck had parked kiss-close to her BMW, the back end angled out so far that she'd need to drive over the berm and execute a three-pointer to get out.

"Maybe it was more crowded when he pulled in," I replied, but I couldn't convince even myself that this was a plausible explanation.

The angle of the truck seemed malicious, as if the driver had seen Lauren's 7 Series and decided to make a point.

She circled the truck with her hands on her hips. The look in her eyes made me nervous. "Someone ought to teach him a lesson."

"You can pull out. Don't be psycho about it." Sweat slid into my eyes and I flicked it away with the back of my wrist.

Lauren was still staring at the pickup. "Can you give me back my key? If you're staying at your mom's, you won't need it."

I slid it off my keychain and turned to walk to my car, but I saw in the corner of my eye that Lauren wasn't moving. She was holding the key between her thumb and forefinger, and suddenly I knew what was on her mind. "You're going to get your ass arrested," I said. I thought of the rednecks we'd passed upriver and glanced over my shoulder, half afraid they might be sneaking up behind us.

Lauren shot me a wink and drew the key along the length of the Silverado, the sound of metal on metal flushing a flock of birds from the oak at the edge of the lot. "What the fuck!" I shouted, pressing my hands to my ears. "Please stop. How many people around here have a navy-blue Beamer? Either he'll come after you or the cops will."

"Like I give a shit," Lauren said, moving to the other side.

"I'm leaving." I waited a minute. I hoped that my disapproval would give her pause, but she kept going, scoring in another line below the first one. "Do you know how much it's going to cost to get that painted over?"

She didn't answer. I circled the back of my truck, deciding that I would pull onto the shoulder on Route 131 and wait until I saw her car safely exit the parking lot. I wanted her to know that I disapproved, but I also wanted to make sure she didn't get stuck between the damaged vehicle and some half-drunk hillbilly who probably owned special microfiber towels to wipe down the polish without scratching the paint.

I looked back one last time. One strap of her bathing suit had fallen down her shoulder, but she ignored it, just as she ignored the mosquito that had landed between her shoulder blades. That was Lauren,

I thought; when she set her mind on something, she really committed. She would do as much damage as she possibly could.

THE RAIN STARTED AS SOON AS I GOT BACK TO MY MOM'S HOUSE—SLOW AT first, spattering the concrete patio outside the back door, and then harder, hammering the tin roof with so much force that we had to shout to hear each other. Until late yesterday evening, the forecasters had predicted that Hurricane Gayle would turn after landfall and take the usual route up the East Coast, but instead the storm had rolled up the spine of the Appalachians, conserving the five to ten inches of rain she was projected to drop on the valley overnight. My mom had ordered pizza, and we ate in front of the TV, watching an old miniseries about a college kid who murdered his stepdad while Mom made grim projections about power outages and flooded roads.

I woke at ten the next morning, sweaty and disoriented, the sun shining straight through the living room window into my eyes. Sometime during the night, Mom had thrown a yellow afghan over me, snugging it up under my chin.

It must have rained all night. The backyard was flooded, the brown water that rose over the tops of the grass wobbling like a mousse. On the way to Lauren's, I saw that River Road was blocked off by barricades. Early on a Saturday morning, the streets were all but deserted, and the world had that uninhabited look that used to make me wonder if the Rapture had come while I was sleeping.

On Blue Ridge Road, a For Sale sign marked the fence where I turned from the main road onto the long gravel driveway. Lauren had told me that she and Warren had just put a down payment on a house on Lovell Avenue, in the nicest neighborhood in town. "You know how it goes," she'd said. "Wedding, small house, baby, bigger house. I don't know what comes after that. Divorce, maybe." I didn't know if that was a joke.

When there was no answer to my knock on the kitchen door, I hesitated and then knocked again. She was home, I knew that much; her BMW was in its usual place, the back left tire mired in a puddle that was nearly two feet wide. I rattled the door and then knocked a third time, but there was no response. "Lauren," I yelled, cupping my hands to the glass. No lights were on in the kitchen or the living room. Maybe she was still asleep.

Finally I tried the knob, and to my surprise, it turned. I stepped over the welcome mat into the kitchen. There was an odor in the air, a faint must that reminded me of sweaty college house parties. Broken glass was scattered over the living room floor. Later the police would ask why a detail like this hadn't made me suspicious, and all I could say was that it wasn't impossible to imagine Lauren dropping a glass on her way to bed and then deciding she'd clean it up in the morning. Like a lot of beautiful people, she was a secret slob.

A framed picture of the two of us from the time she'd visited me at college sat on the end table, and I stopped for a closer look. People sometimes said we looked like sisters, both blond and passably pretty, though I always wore my hair long, almost down to my waist, while Lauren never let hers grow past her shoulders. My eyes were hazel, hers blue; I wore glasses and she didn't; but the real difference was in our expressions. As a child, I'd gotten in the habit of smiling at strangers to compensate for my mother, whose moods ran the spectrum from brusque to ornery. By the time I got to grade school, I smiled so often and so readily that teachers regularly complimented me on my pleasant disposition. Last year a friend of Erika's had told me that I smiled too much to be a lesbian—meaning, I think, that I smiled to placate men, though that wasn't necessarily true. I smiled to placate everyone.

Lauren rarely smiled. She didn't have to, since people gravitated toward her without her doing a thing to draw them in. She was a firecracker, Sean said once, and it was more than just an expression. She could light up the night, or you could end up with singed eyebrows and the taste of gunpowder in your mouth.

There was a soiled washcloth lying at the bottom of the stairs, and I picked it up and threw it in the laundry room before I started up the stairs to the bedrooms. The door to the master was ajar. I knocked gently before pushing it open with my fingertips.

The bed was empty.

I snapped the switch, the light confirming what I thought I'd seen in the dark. The California king bed was vacant, the sheets and duvet folded neatly as a hotel turndown. Could she have fallen asleep in the baby's room? It seemed unlikely, since Mabry was with Warren at his parents' house, but I told myself I ought to check just to make sure.

I nudged the door across the hall with my foot. The walls had been painted shell-pink, white letters spelling out MABRY hung on the wall by the crib. The rocker swayed gently, displaced by the breeze from the open door. In the interest of thoroughness, I checked the closet and then the bathroom across the hall.

My heart was pounding now, and my throat stayed dry no matter how many times I swallowed. I went back outside, half hoping that I might recognize someone driving by and flag them down. This time I noticed the tire tracks in the grass. Another car had been here, and it had driven halfway up in the yard, as if the driver were either distracted or drunk. It must have happened overnight; the tracks were deep and muddy, grass lying in clumps like wet confetti.

I walked down the driveway to the main road and looked back. From this distance, the house could have been abandoned. The porch sagged, the rain gutter hanging at an odd angle. The paint was peeling, and trumpet vine had grown through the latticework that hid the crawl space. No wonder they wanted to sell.

I stood still, breathing in the scent of last night's rain. I should call the police, I thought. No, I should call Warren first, and then Lauren's mother. Surely there was some explanation, some innocuous reason for her absence, that I simply hadn't thought of yet.

I heard gravel crunch behind me, and relief surged through my body before I realized that it was Warren driving the Range Rover his parents had bought him when he graduated from UVA. Mabry was sleeping in her carseat in the back, her thick brown hair mussed into a baby Mohawk. "Hey there," Warren called through the open window as he rolled to a stop.

Though it almost certainly wasn't the right moment, I felt the

familiar shiver up my spine. Before Lauren locked him down, Warren
Ballard had been the catch of Tyndall County. In high school he'd
played football, sung in the choir, even acted in the school plays. Junior
year, he'd given an uninspired but diligent performance as Henry II in
a performance of *Becket*, egged on by an ambitious drama teacher who
would decamp to a school in northern Virginia with higher property
taxes and a budget for the arts. Lauren played Eleanor of Aquitaine,
and when they came out for the curtain call, Warren kept his arm
slung over her shoulder, meat jewelry.

I'd wondered then if he'd fallen for Lauren because she was the only
girl who didn't get flustered at the sight of his cheekbones and *Tiger
Beat* grin, instead looking him straight in the eye, secure in her belief
that she had a God-given right to his regard. Back then he'd looked at
her as if she were the last beer in the cooler, but since I'd come home
this summer, I'd noticed that something was off. It had long been my
habit to stare at Warren Ballard when he wasn't looking, and my experience with the gradations of his expressions told me that the easy
charm had dimmed a bit. When he talked or smiled, it seemed to cost
him an effort, like a man trying to walk through water up to his knees.
It seemed likely that the tension between them had to do with what
had happened back in June, when Lauren was almost arrested for child
endangerment after leaving their daughter in a parked car in ninety-
degree heat. My mom had told me the family managed to hush it up
and keep the details out of the papers, but if Warren was still mad, I
wouldn't have blamed him.

I didn't speak, but something in my face must have alerted him.
"Are you okay?" he said, bracing his elbow on the car window's ledge.
"Nicola. Hey. What's going on?"

WARREN'S FAMILY HAD PLENTY OF FAVORS TO CALL IN, AND NEWS VANS
from Charlottesville and Roanoke showed up that same night. Police began the search, combing the mountains and valleys of Tyndall
County. Volunteers in orange vests knocked on the door of every home

within a square mile of Blue Ridge Road. Though the police told me to get some sleep, I made sure that I was one of those volunteers, a tote bag stuffed with flyers slung over my shoulder. We searched for three days, but there was no trace of her, not in the woods or in the river, which they dragged with a dive team before the week was out.

Rumors spread: Lauren had committed suicide; she'd run away to Florida with a secret boyfriend; she'd been murdered by drug dealers who buried her under the new tennis courts at the city park. At the daily news conferences, I waited for the police to debunk these stories, but they never did. Every lead would be investigated, they said. Tips from the public were welcome and would be followed up on. They sounded as baffled as the rest of us. Tyndall County hadn't seen a murder in five years, and no one had ever disappeared as far as anyone could recall.

A few details came out, either because of the cops or in spite of them. A cast-iron doorstop was missing from the living room. They'd found fingerprints on the light switches and door handles, but it was only whom you'd expect: Warren, Lauren, their mothers, a couple of his football friends and his brother, and me. When she saw me looking at the Missing flyer, a woman in line behind me at the grocery store told me that the police were looking into the disappearance of a little girl from Ewald County, believing that the two cases might be connected, but that didn't make sense to me. What kind of weirdo would take both a twenty-four-year-old woman and an eight-year-old girl?

I NEVER TOLD ANYONE ABOUT THE RECURRING DREAM IN WHICH I AGREE TO go home with Lauren that night. In the dream, I'm there when a man shows up at her door. He's faceless, a hulking shadow in a black raincoat, standing just out of the glow of the porch light to hide his eyes.

At the heart of that nightmare was a question: would I have become another victim, or would my unexpected presence have thrown a wrench in her abductor's plan? Perhaps he had only enough rope for one, and having to improvise would have caused some hesitation, a flash of self-doubt that we could have used to our advantage. In my dream, this is always how it goes: he's thrown off his game, and in that moment of uncertainty, I manage to dial 911 or run down the road and call for help.

When Warren arrived that morning, I tried to tell him that it was my fault. "I should have been here," I said, following him as he paced through the empty rooms with the sleeping baby pressed to his shoulder and the phone to his ear. "I should have protected her." He patted my shoulder in a distracted way, and for a moment I wondered if I was being insensitive, taking on a role that was his by rights. Warren should have been the one breaking down, but he didn't seem to need comforting—not yet, anyway. His wife was gone, and I could tell from his face that he couldn't get his head around it. How could a person be here one minute and then vanish the next?

When the officers arrived, I showed them the broken glass I'd swept into a dustpan and the washcloth I'd picked up at the bottom of the stairs. They interviewed me twice in the days that followed, and for a time I wondered if I might be a suspect, but nothing ever came of it. I'd never been in trouble in my life, and I had an alibi. My mom and I had eaten dinner and watched a movie together, and she swore that she'd checked on me every hour during the night.

Before the police asked us to leave, I caught a glimpse of Warren staring out at the driveway, Mabry clasped to his chest, his expression unreadable. Like me, he'd probably never conceived of life without Lauren in it, and I wondered if he felt the same little jolt of excitement, stronger in that moment than either fear or grief. It was a shameful feeling, but I couldn't repress it. It was as if a mountain on the horizon had vanished, and suddenly I could see the view.

1

My mother had taught me that the fangs of a decapitated copperhead could still bite. After I'd struck with the machete, I stepped back to what I thought was a safe distance, but my heel banged into the lawnmower and I fell hard, landing on my palms before scrabbling backward like a crab, as the snake gave one final hiss that made my chest constrict.

I scrambled to my feet and dusted off the seat of my jeans, looking around discreetly to make sure that no one had watched me fall on my ass. Though there were neighbors on both sides, neither house could be seen from this vantage point. The yard was empty, the scent of honeysuckle mingling with the sour reek of the trash can my mom had always kept on the back patio.

My heartbeat was just beginning to slow when Warren Ballard rounded the corner of the house. He saw the machete in my hand and stopped short. "Snake," I said, moving the blade behind my back. "I got it, I think."

Warren kept a cautious distance. He was wearing outdoorsy pants in some kind of wickable material and a green chambray shirt, which seemed weird for a weekday, though maybe you could get away with that sort of thing in real estate. "I was going to go in for a hug, but I think I'll wait until you put that down," he said, nodding at the ma-chete. "Can I see?"

I swept my free arm in front of my body like an usher, and he moved closer, prodding the dead snake with his foot. "You'll want to make sure there's not a nest under the house," he said. "I have a friend who does wildlife management. He books up months in advance, but I'll text him and see when we can get him out here."

This was worse than I'd thought. "I assumed it came from the woods," I said, but Warren looked skeptical.

"You've got gaps in the foundation," he said. "Probably lots of good things to eat under there, if you're a snake. If you're going to sell, I'd have somebody check it out."

I was glad he was taking charge, since I worried that beheading the snake had made me look misleadingly competent. The truth was I knew nothing—about wildlife management, for starters, but also about selling houses. That was why I'd called Warren in the first place.

Though we hadn't seen each other in sixteen years, I'd kept up with him online, in the way you do with high school friends who aren't really friends anymore. In pictures he looked like an age-progressed version of the guy I'd known back then, with the broad frame of an ex-athlete and dark hair grown just long enough to fall on to his forehead in a boyish way. A few wrinkles scored the skin at the corners of his eyes, and he'd grown a close-cropped beard that had come in half a shade lighter than the hair on his head. He didn't look like a movie star anymore. He looked like a movie star's unfamous brother, with five or ten extra pounds around the waist and a suggestion of mild impatience in the set of his jaw.

He knew about my life too, or at least the bare outline: college in eastern Virginia, graduate school at Yale, then a smattering of teach-ing jobs around the country. "I looked you up," Warren confessed as we leaned against the side of the house. "I knew you'd do something special."

I felt a warm glow at the thought that our cyberstalking had been mutual, but then I felt the weight in my left hand and realized I was still holding the machete. I tossed it into a patch of weeds, and Warren cleared his throat. "Want to show me the house?"

It had been built in the 1940s in the Craftsman style, but it looked nothing like the cute updated bungalows I'd seen on real estate websites. "Two bedrooms, two baths," I said as I opened the front door. "Pretty standard starter home, I guess."

I caught a glimpse of myself in the mirror over the fireplace and looked quickly away. I was wearing an ancient pair of overalls over a ratty tank top that read *Forty Fuckin Niners*, liberated from the lost-and-found box in the laundry room of my last apartment. I'd been an athlete in high school and college, and running and yoga had kept me in decent shape, but all I could see were the differences that Warren would surely notice—the smile lines around my mouth and the black-framed glasses that had looked cute on the model but that I was now afraid made me look like Jeff Goldblum.

If Warren noticed me checking myself out, he didn't let on. "Did your mom own the house outright?"

"Yeah, there's no mortgage. I guess I could just hold on to it and rent it out or something, but—" I stopped, fingering the tassel at the end of the green velvet curtains that had always made me think of Scarlett's dress in *Gone with the Wind*.

He finished the thought. "You don't want to."

"I don't plan to be here for more than a few months," I admitted. "I'm sure it's a great place to raise kids and all."

"I get it," he said over his shoulder as he headed down the hall to the bedrooms. "I probably would have moved away too if it weren't for Mabry."

I nodded, but I didn't believe him. It was impossible to imagine Warren anywhere other than Tyndall County.

He ticked off the renovations that ought to be made. A new front door. New light fixtures. New double-pane windows. New carpet. New countertops and appliances in the kitchen. "You'll have to get a roofer and patch the drywall," he said, pointing to a brown spot on the ceiling of my mom's bedroom. "That'll be the biggest cost, along with the exterior paint. Boiler looks fine. How old is the roof?"

I had no idea. "What if I did the renovations myself?" I asked. "Some of them, anyway."

I was grateful when he didn't smirk and ask me what I knew about patching drywall. "It would save some money," he said. "But don't you have something to get back to?"

"Not really." I considered explaining that my last two-year teaching gig had just ended and none of the jobs I'd applied for had panned out, but I wasn't ready to reveal myself in that way.

In the pause that followed, I realized with a start that Warren was looking me over with the same evaluative gaze I'd turned on him. I could feel myself flush, and I wished I'd washed my hair this morning instead of spritzing it with dry shampoo. "What kind of asking price are we talking about?" I asked, just for something to say.

He squinted, calculating in his mind. "Without the renovations, you could ask about one fifteen. With the added value, you could go a lot higher, maybe one seventy-five."

"That's it?" I'd forgotten that houses could sell for so little.

"At least it's likely to sell quick. We get a lot of commuters now, and this is a desirable neighborhood—close to the elementary school, close to downtown, and there's a playground down the street."

I bit back a smile at the thought of how my mom would have snorted to hear our block called a *desirable neighborhood.* "Have you talked to Sean?" Warren asked, leaning on the wall as if he planned to stay a while. "They're always looking for substitute teachers."

Of all the changes that had come about in the sixteen years since I'd left home for good, the most remarkable had to be Sean Ballard's transformation into the principal of Tyndall High. "So he's okay now?" I asked, suddenly tentative.

Warren knew what I meant. "Yeah, he's good. His wife left a few years ago and took the kid, but he's stayed off the hard stuff." He opened the door to the left, stepping back for me to enter first. "Was this your room?"

He'd been right to use past tense. The room looked the same as it had the summer before eighth grade, when Lauren had picked out the paint—midnight blue—and helped me move in the double bookshelf and a window air conditioner we'd found at Goodwill. That was the summer I'd gotten my braces off and grown boobs, and Lauren had applied herself to polishing my image, including changing my name from Nicole to Nicola, since she claimed that Nicola was classier.

Warren looked uncomfortable, and I couldn't tell if it was the low ceiling or the faint echo of those long-ago girls that seemed to linger in the air. "I think that's it," he said. "I'll make a list of everything we talked about, and you can tell me what you think."

There was no bench or porch swing, so we sat side by side on the top step. "I'm sorry about your mom," Warren said, looking up from his clipboard to show that he was sincere. "When did she die?"

"Two months ago," I said. "Pancreatic cancer. She hated doctors, so by the time she found out she was sick, she only had a couple of weeks left. When I got here, she was already in hospice."

I looked away, afraid that Warren could see on my face how hard those days had been, sitting in the plastic chair at my mother's bedside while she moaned in a dream she would never wake from. We hadn't been close. On the rare occasions when she'd visited me in Providence or Tampa, she'd complained that there were too many people speaking languages she didn't understand, and once she'd had to sit beside a man wearing a turban on the plane. He could have had anything in there, she insisted; for all she knew, he'd been carrying a bomb on his head. I'd tried to argue with her, but she'd only raised her eyebrows and told me I was brainwashed. Talk radio had convinced her that I was a Left-Wing Coastal Elite, and nothing I said could be trusted.

In those last days, women from the Baptist church brought food and flowers, but none of them stayed long. Mostly I was alone, flipping through magazines on nutrition and gastroenterology and wishing it was over. I had good reasons to be angry with her, and I stoked the feeling, knowing that anger would keep me from feeling anything else.

But Warren would know all about that, I thought—about loss, and how regret could thicken the air you breathed. "How are things with you?" I asked. "Any updates?"

He shook his head. "The lead detective retired. We have a new one now, a woman."

"Is she any good?"

"As far as I can tell, she thinks the same as the last guy. Dale Westcott did it and he's dead, so there's nothing to investigate."

"What do you think?"

He shrugged. "I don't know. If the police think it was Westcott, I guess they're probably right."

This was what I'd expected—what I'd gathered myself from the updates on Lauren's disappearance that I'd sought out over the years. As far as I knew, there had only ever been one suspect. Dale Westcott had motive and a criminal history that made it no great stretch to believe that he would kidnap and murder the girl who had wronged his family. Facts, rumor, and speculation fit together neatly as a dovetail joint. No wonder Warren was content to leave well enough alone.

But Warren didn't know everything. He didn't know what I'd done to Dale Westcott's daughter back in high school. He saw me as an old friend come home after a long absence, but if he knew the truth, he'd never speak to me again. After all, I might be the reason his wife was dead.

THE SKY HAD CLOUDED AND IT FELT LIKE RAIN. AFTER I'D WATCHED WARREN drive away, in a black Range Rover that was clearly an updated version of the vehicle he'd been driving when Lauren disappeared, I went in and treated myself to a heavy pour of red wine. A woman had been abducted, probably murdered, and no trace of her had ever been found. How did you tell a story with an ellipsis at the center? How did you make sense of that sort of absence?

Before Lauren's disappearance, she'd been a constant presence in my imagination, looking over my shoulder and judging every decision I made. Knowing that she would scorn any attempt at imitation, I never tried to become her, but I did try to be someone she would approve of. In the way I talked and dressed, in my choice of eyeliner and pink shimmer lip gloss, even in my relationship with Erika, I thought about how Lauren would evaluate my choices, and made the subtle course corrections that I thought would ensure her regard.

The first week after she went missing, I hardly slept. I lay in my childhood bedroom with an open box of Kleenex on the extra pillow and the shades drawn and tried to reread the books I'd loved as a child, but I could get through only a page or two before my mind circled back to the questions that obsessed me: Where was Lauren? Who had taken her? Was she being hurt, or was she already dead? I knew things were bad when my mother, who belonged to the suck-it-up-and-stop-crying school of parenting, began making special meals to try to tempt me out of my room. Would I like fried chicken, or meatloaf, or the good kind of frozen pizza with the cheese that really tasted like cheese? Finally she lost her patience and told me that she was sorry I was sad, but if I didn't get up and take a bath in the next hour, she was going to take the sheets off the bed with me still on them.

The grief and panic didn't go away, but they faded into the background until it was like listening to a whispered conversation from another room. As I came back to life, I remembered the feeling that had come over me when I watched Warren at the window. I could see now that Lauren's absence was also an opportunity. Freed from the inhibition of judging by her standards, I could do whatever I wanted to do.

And I'd followed through. It was too late for Erika and me by then, but now that I was released from the burden of wondering what Lauren might think of my choices, I could date anyone who caught my fancy. I had a fling with a visiting assistant professor who drove a Vespa, and spent four months with an Irish exchange student who told me I looked like a Pre-Raphaelite painting. After college I'd moved to New England for graduate school, where I lived in an apartment above a hair salon and lost fifteen pounds because everything tasted like ammonia. In the summers I traveled to Morocco, where I left my passport in a taxi, and Greece, where I fell in love with a yoga teacher in Mykonos and seriously considered never coming home.

Not all these experiences were good, but all of them felt like mine: my decisions, my mistakes. From time to time I could hear Lauren's voice asking why I wanted to live in a place where winter lasted six months and why would I waste my time getting a Ph.D. when I could have been making an actual salary, but I always managed to tune her out.

I looked Warren up on Facebook once or twice a year, and I knew he'd never remarried. He'd said today that his daughter had been his reason for staying in Tyndall County, but I had my doubts about that. The Ballard family was at the top of the social hierarchy, and even a missing wife hadn't been enough to tarnish Warren's prospects. At forty, he was exactly the man he would have been if Lauren had never disappeared: a little weathered but successful, handsome, competent; still eye candy for the aging soccer moms who probably batted their eyelashes when they ran into him around town.

From a distance, I'd felt a vague scorn as I clicked through his pictures of Rotary dinners and church picnics, but now I wondered if we were really so different. All this time I thought I'd been following my inclinations, but what if I'd simply posited what Lauren would have done in any given situation and done the opposite?

Back home in Tyndall, I couldn't avoid the fact that I'd been shaped by the loss of Lauren more than I cared to admit. What choice did you have, after all, when the person who had stood at the center of your sense of self wasn't there anymore? You grew around that damage like a tree wrapped in barbed wire. You let it bite into you. You shaped yourself to the new reality, until it was hard to tell what was you and what was the hole she'd left.

2

It was as if that afternoon with Warren had made me visible again.

In the first few weeks I was home, no one had seemed to recognize me, and even the people I thought looked familiar passed without a glance. It happened so often that I usually decided I'd made a mistake and the woman who looked like a graying, wrinkly version of my tenth-grade math teacher was probably a stranger after all.

After Warren, people I knew were everywhere, at the bank and at the grocery store. *Hey, I know you*, the men would say, and then look nervous, worried I might think they were flirting. *You look gre-eat*, the women would say, drawing out the last word as they looked into my cart that held no milk or individually wrapped lunchbox snacks, just salad greens and wine and maybe a package of chicken thighs that would be my dinner for the next two days.

On one trip to pick up cereal, I made insipid small talk with a girl who had peed in her pants at a fourth-grade sleepover and a boy who once tried to stick his tongue down my throat in the weedy smoking area behind McDonald's. Once I ran into Susan Kyle, Lauren's mother, who kept me there, holding both my hands in her own as she told me how sorry she was about my mother's death. Susan was tall, with a strong build, but somewhere along the way she'd been taught to make herself smaller, hunching her upper body and taking dainty steps that made me think of the elephants doing ballet in *Fantasia*.

"I went to see her," she said, gripping my hands so tightly that I nearly winced. "I brought a pot of orchids. Did you see them?"

I remembered the gift, a ceramic pot spilling over with mouth-shaped blooms in humid shades of pink and purple. There was no card, and it hadn't looked like something the Baptist ladies would send, but it had never occurred to me they might be from Susan. "Thank you," I said, working to tug back my hands like Houdini sliding out of a pair of cuffs.

The mere fact of her presence made me uncomfortable. When I was growing up, Susan had been my mother's closest friend. They'd met when I was a baby and my mom moved to town to take a job at Kyle Plastics, but even after Mr. Kyle died and the plant closed, the strange friendship between his widow and a woman he'd paid ten dollars an hour to put the handles on plastic bins had survived. For most of my life, they were on the phone several times a day, and Susan came over almost every Friday to play cards and drink the bourbon that my mom kept in the cabinet over the sink. They'd insisted that Lauren and I spend time together too, though she'd more or less ignored me until I got my braces off.

On one level, the relationship made sense; they were both outsiders in a small town, my mother having moved from West Virginia and Susan from somewhere up north. If this hadn't been enough to draw them together across the boundaries of class, they also shared a common awkwardness, a blunt head-on approach to the world that even I knew would never go over well around here.

But something had gone wrong. When I'd come home after my freshman year of college, they were no longer speaking. After Lauren disappeared, I'd asked my mom if she was going to call Susan or go to any of the vigils, but she'd said she didn't want to talk about it.

I had no idea what had happened between them, but my mom's refusal to let bygones be bygones had struck me as unnecessarily cruel, even in a woman who'd made a practice of cutting people out of her life. After all that, I was surprised that Susan had cared enough to bring a fifty-dollar flower arrangement to my mother's deathbed. She said something about me coming over to the house for tea sometime, and I made polite but noncommittal noises as I pushed my cart in the opposite direction.

That was bad enough, but the next week I was cornered in the paper goods aisle by Stephanie Gilliam, now Stephanie Mack, Lauren's best friend from high school. The sight of me hit her so hard that she had to tear open a box of tissues right there in the store, sniffling that Lauren had been a bitch on wheels but she still couldn't believe she was gone. When she'd finished whimpering, she filled me in on her news, making sure to work in that she'd bought a gigantic Victorian on Alexander Street that probably cost a cool half-mil.

With Stephanie, and with the other classmates I ran into on the street or on a trip to the library, I tried to keep the conversations short. Sometimes people told me about their own family—this child in the gifted program, that one a field hockey star—but I offered no follow-up questions, and things tended to trail off. I could tell that I made them nervous. A classmate moving home at this stage of life, without husband or family, was vaguely worrying, like an unexplained plume of smoke on the horizon.

The fact was that I had been gone too long. I had missed too much. When we reached the inevitable uneasy silence, the women always leaned in and said, *I heard you're back in touch with Warren. You must have* so *much to talk about.*

"DID YOU EVER THINK THEY'D FOUND HER?" I ASKED.

"Once or twice," Warren said. "They pulled a woman out of the Campbell River, or parts of a woman—an arm and a leg, remember?"

I nodded. In the years after Lauren's disappearance, there was an article every now and then about a Jane Doe who might be relevant to the case. That was how the police always put it: *might be relevant to the case,* not *might be Lauren,* and the language had seemed vicious in its impersonality, its refusal to recognize that these arms and legs once were attached to a human being. "Whatever happened with that?" I asked.

"They identified her," Warren said. "She was a runaway from Richmond. Some guy was convicted for it eventually."

He'd made a chicken tagine with lemons and olives, and we were eating outside on a wrought-iron table set with fat-bottomed candles. The house at 507 Lovell Avenue was a four-bedroom brick Colonial with black shutters and neatly clipped boxwood framing the front door. Driving past the neighbors' well-kept yards tonight, I'd had the sense that I could see into the homes I passed as if they were dollhouses. My mom had worked as a house cleaner, and I'd accompanied her to work often enough to know that the Turners had an extensive and varied porn collection, and sweet Mrs. Levin on Alexander Street kept a loaded handgun with the safety off in her underwear drawer.

Of course, I had no way of knowing if the owners were the same as when I was a kid. The town was changing, or at least thinking about changing. Warren had told me that he'd gone in front of the City Council to argue for renaming the streets christened after Confederate generals, though apparently nothing had come of it yet. Now new people were moving in, commuters and retirees. The mailbox two houses down said *Srinavasan*, a name I didn't recognize. In the directions he'd given me, Warren had told me to look for the statue of a cat on a pedestal in the front yard, which the family dressed up in costumes to commemorate different holidays. Tonight it was wrapped in bunting for the Fourth of July.

Peering at the numbers on the mailboxes, I'd felt a pit in my stomach at the thought of how little I'd made of my life. I'd always known that I didn't want kids, but I'd had vague intentions of getting married someday. I should at least have a long-term partner. I should own a house. How could I be thirty-six years old and back in my hometown, when most of my friends from graduate school had waltzed right into the lives they saw as their birthright?

For a long time, I thought I'd at least learned to impersonate a successful adult. I knew to say that I went to school in Connecticut instead of saying Yale. I knew that job interviews went better if I appeared in a tailored suit with great shoes and a nice bag, even though the search committee must have known that I made forty thousand dollars a year and had no occasion to wear a suit in real life. I knew what to talk about at dinner parties and how to give an elevator pitch and how to make my way in a foreign city with nothing more than a phone and a credit card, but what had it all added up to? The tenure-track job I'd been promised had never materialized. I'd spent the past seven years bouncing around the country, moving in and out of cheap one-bedroom apartments, jumping on and off the same dating apps, feeling more like I was on a treadmill than a road to a brighter future.

Lauren would have understood. She'd known my mom. She'd sat in our tiny kitchen with the lightbulbs that flickered no matter how many times you changed them and the framed picture of Jesus on the cross, fat drops of blood spilling down his temples. To the untrained eye, I might look like I was doing all right, but I sometimes thought that the poverty I'd grown up with lingered on me like the odor of cheap detergent.

But maybe I wasn't the only one trying to let go of the past. On a brief tour of Warren's house, I'd seen enough to know that he'd kept nothing from the house on Blue Ridge Road where Lauren had disappeared. That house had been decorated like a showroom, with a big mahogany bed and a leather sectional that barely fit in the space. Warren's furniture looked as if he'd chosen each piece at an antique store or yard sale and restored it himself, polishing with linseed oil to bring out the grain.

In the yard, I could glimpse an outdoor fireplace and a little outbuilding that Warren had told me was his workshop, before the lawn ended at a cedar fence hung with strands of glimmering white lights. The photogenic gloss of it all made me feel slightly off-kilter. How could we be discussing floating body parts when I felt as if I'd stumbled onto the set of one of those home-improvement reality shows?

"Did you ever hear anything about Opal Yarrow?" I asked. "She was the girl who disappeared from Ewald the year before Lauren. There was a rumor going around that they were going to connect Westcott to that one, but it always seemed like a stretch to me."

Warren whistled and the dog, Lucky II, ran up from the garden and bumped his head against his master's knee. "To be honest, I don't pay much attention," Warren said, reaching down to scratch Lucky II behind the ears. "Mabry has a Google alert on her mother's name, and she checks those Jane Doe databases every couple of weeks to see if she can find one with a chicken pox scar on the arm. I tried to discourage it at first, but in a way, it's better for her to know if anything comes out."

"That makes sense," I said. I thought it might be in bad taste to point out that after sixteen years, the skin on Lauren's arm would be long gone.

He speared an olive with his fork. "Last year I found a list in Mabry's drawer of all the supposed sightings. We had a talk about that. I don't want it taking over her life."

I'd seen the same reports. People claimed to have seen Lauren at a grocery store in Albuquerque, a gas station in Richmond, a post office in the Upper Peninsula of Michigan. None of them had been confirmed by law enforcement, and I thought they were all bullshit. If Lauren had somehow planned her own escape, she would have headed straight for Hawaii or the Virgin Islands.

Warren refilled my wine, and I thought about asking if he could show me a picture of Mabry on his phone. The last time I'd seen her, she'd been a modified feminine version of her dad, with the same thick brown hair and strong chin. They were equally camera-ready, and I couldn't count how many issues of the local paper I'd seen with their faces on the front page. *Grieving husband Warren Ballard*, the papers had called him, so often that it began to seem that the description was part of his name.

But Mabry was seventeen now and spending the summer at a ballet camp in the Adirondacks, which meant that Warren and I had the house to ourselves. He opened another bottle. Sunset lit the sky behind the screen of oaks at the edge of the yard, and then it was night. I turned my gaze to the windows on the back of the house, little blocks of gold superimposed on the darkness. Lauren never lived here, I reminded myself. There was nothing of her in this house—no floorboards that remembered the weight of her footsteps, no vanished reflections hiding in the depths of a mirror.

Warren scooted his chair closer. "You know, I had my eye on you in high school," he said. "I always thought you were the prettiest girl in town."

I made a raspberry sound. "I did," he insisted. "You weren't flashy or anything. You didn't show off, but you had this sweetness about you. This wholesomeness. You probably think I sound like an idiot."

Although it was hard to tell in the low light, I thought he might be blushing. "I always thought of you as the one who got away," he went on. "Not from me, specifically. From the town."

I narrowed my eyes, but I could tell that he was sincere. He'd made up a story about me, and in that story, I was the girl who evaded his grasp by leaving Tyndall County. The truth was that I would have been only too happy to stay if he'd shown the slightest sign of preferring me to Lauren, but he'd had no way of knowing that.

And wasn't it the same for me? Warren added to his classic good looks all the qualities that your stereotypical American woman wanted in a man: he was loyal, reliable, skilled with his hands. The problem was that I had no idea who he was under the surface. Even back in high school, I hadn't really known him that well.

"I talked to Sean," I said. "One of the English teachers is going on maternity leave this fall. He said the job is mine if I want it."

I couldn't read his expression. "Are you going to take it?"

"Might as well. I don't want to go through my savings."

"Good. I'm glad you're sticking around for a while." He leaned closer. Pins and needles began in the bottoms of my feet and moved up the inside seams of my legs. "Sean always talked about your dimple," he said. "He always said he wanted to stick his finger in it. Do you mind?"

"Are you serious?" I asked, but I wasn't going to stop him from closing the distance between us and touching his pinkie finger to the hollow in my left cheek.

As a child, I'd been self-conscious about the dimple. Lauren had told me it made me look like a baby. Later I'd been afraid that it made me seem too pliable, like a girl who'd be easily pleased. Now I was grateful for it, if it gave Warren an excuse to let his arm settle around my shoulders and bend his face to mine.

But as our lips met, I felt a flicker of nausea that might have been too much wine or might have been something else—the first signal of the guilt that I'd managed to repress until now. "I have to go," I said.

Warren pulled back. For a moment I thought he was going to argue with me, but then he whistled for Lucky II, who padded along behind us on our way to the door. "Let me know what you decide to do about the house," he said. "I can recommend some contractors. Or I could help out if you really want to do the work yourself."

I checked his face to see if he meant it. It was one thing to invite an old friend for dinner hoping you might get laid, but offering to renovate her kitchen was another level of commitment altogether. "I'll text you," I said.

IN THE WEEKS AFTER LAUREN WENT MISSING, MY MOM HAD DUTIFULLY repeated the rumors she'd heard at church or in the houses she cleaned. People said Warren's car had been seen in town on the night Lauren disappeared, when he was supposed to be at his parents' beach house in North Carolina. They said the police had found traces of blood on the dashboard. A girl who worked for State Farm went all over town telling people that Warren had taken out an insurance policy just before Lauren disappeared, though that turned out to be untrue.

Clearly the town gossips had seen enough movies to pick up a few tropes. The husband was always the focus of suspicion, and there was no escaping it in this case, when everyone knew he'd had a motive. I wasn't the only one who'd noticed that the marriage was on shaky ground. Someone said they'd seen Warren and Lauren fighting outside the hardware store the week before she went missing. A woman who worked at Mabry's daycare swore that Warren had slipped her his number with a wink, whispering that she'd make a great stepmom.

I'd never believed the rumors, and not only because I knew Warren wasn't stupid enough to broadcast his plans to kill his wife to all and sundry. He and Lauren belonged to each other, matched for eternity. That was the only possible explanation for why he hadn't remarried after all this time.

At my mom's house, I flopped on the futon and ran my fingers over my lips, feeling a sudden nonsensical urge to call Lauren and apologize. But maybe she wouldn't have been mad. Maybe she would have understood that Warren and I had come together out of a shared need. Neither of us had the life we'd planned for, and now here we were, two middle-aged people stuck in their hometown with nothing to look forward to but more of the same. Would it really be so terrible if we offered each other some kind of comfort? When I closed my eyes, Lauren's face swam before me, looking just like her picture on the Missing poster, Photoshopped to plastic perfection. Just before I dropped off, she seemed to be about to speak.

3

The day after my dinner at Warren's, Susan called. Though it was nearly noon, my head was pounding and my stomach in knots, and the sight of her name on the caller ID made the guilt I'd felt the night before flare up like an old injury. Did she know that I'd kissed Warren? Had someone seen my car at his house and called her with the news? In my paranoid state, it made sense that Susan would be the one to avenge my betrayal of her daughter. She was the one who had wanted Warren for Lauren before it had ever occurred to Lauren to want him for herself.

But Susan hadn't called to chastise or berate me. She had something for me, she said. Something from the house on Blue Ridge Road.

I'D LEARNED EARLY THAT THE FARTHER UP THE MOUNTAIN YOU LIVED, the more money you had. My mom and I lived in the floodplain, just blocks away from the factories along the Campbell River, including the now-defunct Kyle Plastics. A bit higher in elevation were the streets named after dead generals, inhabited by the lawyers and professors who commuted to Charlottesville, but the real money was outside the city limits, in the subdivision called Laurel Heights where both Warren and Lauren had grown up.

I knew that Warren's parents had retired to the beach in North Carolina, but I couldn't stop myself from doing a drive-by of their house, slowing to five miles an hour to peer up at the sprawling French Provincial set on so much acreage it might as well have been a golf course. Warren's family went back generations in Tyndall County. His grandmother had owned a legit estate even farther up the mountain, and his dad had started the real estate firm that Warren now ran. Back when Sean and I were friends, I'd come over occasionally to watch a movie and fill my half-empty Coke bottle from his dad's bourbon collection. I'd never felt at home there, in the cavernous basement rec room with the big TV and pinball machine and upright Space Invaders game just like the one at the arcade, and Sean's mother's habit of opening the door suddenly to see if we were making out certainly didn't help.

The sun was setting behind the pines by the time I made it to Susan's house. When I was a kid, I'd thought of it as The Mansion, more impressive in some ways even than Bearwallow, the Ballard family estate out in the county. The pile of gray stone featured crenellations along the roofline and even a turret, and there was a fountain in the middle of the circular driveway with two bronze dolphins cavorting in a basin. Once the basin had been lit from inside, but the lighting system had malfunctioned and now let off an eerie muted glow that made me think of radiation poisoning.

Susan met me at the door. When I was growing up, she'd always been impeccably put together, making my mother look drab in comparison. She wore the same giant diamond earrings every day, even with tennis clothes, and I used to wonder if she knew that everyone was calculating the price of all those carats. Today she wore a filmy green ankle-length dress with a sunflower motif. As usual, she'd added too much jewelry—big knobbly rings, a gold bracelet, and the familiar pair of oversize earrings. "Nicola," she said in a breathy voice that made her sound as if she'd run up the stairs. "So kind of you to stop by. Do come in."

If Warren's house looked like a set for HGTV, The Mansion was straight out of those magazines that you see in the checkout line—*Woman's Day* or *Family Circle*—with lace doilies spread like coasters on the side tables and a line of seasonal decorations marching across the mantel. Today it was decorated like a village square celebrating the Fourth of July, with flagpoles and houses hung with swags of red, white, and blue. An animatronic Uncle Sam stood in the center, waving and nodding at the empty living room. I remembered my mom hauling boxes of decorations out of the basement, then replacing them with a new panorama after the holiday had passed. At Christmas, it had taken the two of them days to decorate the tree, which had a different theme each year, and which Lauren and I were never allowed to touch.

I wondered who it was all for. Surely not Mabry, who was well past the childhood-wonder stage. Did Susan have friends who piled in to fill up the two enormous couches and eat the cookies piped with fireworks in royal icing? Somehow it was hard to imagine. "I like the decorations," I said finally, when I could tell I'd been silent too long. "Really colorful."

But Susan wasn't looking at Uncle Sam or at the cookies. She was looking at me, and I realized that she'd been sneaking glances ever since I'd come in. "You look different," she said. "Why aren't you wearing your glasses?"

I reached up as if to adjust the missing frames. "I have contacts."

I didn't need to explain myself to her, I reminded myself as she bustled off to the kitchen, murmuring that she'd be right back with our tea. Then I caught a glimpse of myself in the mirror over the couch, and I realized that Susan was right: I did look different from when I'd run into her at Kroger. I'd been eating better and taking daily walks, and now I could see that my face was less angular, my hair thicker and shinier, the dimple in my left cheek more pronounced. I'd covered the tattoos on my upper arms in deference to Susan, and it occurred to me now that I wouldn't stand out among the Tyndall soccer moms. On the contrary, I might appear to be one of them.

By the time Susan came back, carrying a tray with two glasses, my armpits were damp with sweat, my head buzzing. "Homemade iced tea," she said, clunking the tray on the table. "Mabry loves it. I make hers without the whiskey, of course."

I'd already taken a drink before she got to the word *whiskey*, and I had to inhale through my nose to keep myself from spitting it out. It tasted like something I would have scooped out of a trash can in college.

Susan didn't seem to notice. "I want you to have this," she said, setting a box by my plate with the half-eaten cookie. "I'm embarrassed to say how long I've held on to it. I should have sent it to you years ago."

It was a cardboard jewelry box, the kind with cotton in the bottom. Susan had said it was something of Lauren's, hadn't she—some kind of memento?

But I'd gotten it wrong. It was a necklace spelling out my name, *Nicola*, with a rhinestone at either end. The gold was shiny, as if someone had cleaned it with a toothbrush, carefully massaging the bristles in and out of the hollows. I tried to still the tremor in my hands. "Where did you get this?"

"I found it when Warren and I cleaned out the house on Blue Ridge Road. You must have left it there when you stayed over."

I lifted the necklace out of its bed of cotton and held it to the light. Tears pricked the corners of my eyes and I blinked them back, embarrassed. "It's from your mom, isn't it?" Susan asked.

The softness of her voice startled me. "I remember when she bought it for you," she said, watching me closely as I fastened the clasp. "She had it on layaway for months. She was going to get *Nicole*, but I told her if you'd decided you wanted to be called Nicola, she should respect that. She saw my point eventually. She just wanted you to be happy."

My throat felt like it was closing up. What Susan had said was true, I knew, though it was only half the truth of my relationship with my mother. "Thank you," I croaked. "Do you mind if I use your bathroom?"

Even after so many years, I remembered the layout of the Kyles' house, and I knew that even though there was a half bath on the first floor beside the kitchen, Susan didn't like anyone to shake out the hand towels or smudge the perfect eggs of soap nestled in their dish. She wouldn't think twice if she saw me head for the stairs to the second story.

At the landing, I paused to look at the family portrait hanging above a drop-leaf table: Lauren, Susan, and Richard Kyle, posed against one of those marbled gray backdrops that all photography studios used back in the eighties. I hardly remembered Lauren's dad. In the picture, he was a big man with an easy smile and high color that seemed to hint at the heart attack that would kill him before Lauren was a teenager. I knew almost nothing about him—where he'd grown up or how he'd gotten into plastics manufacturing or how he and Susan had met— though I had a vague sense that he was the source of Lauren's sense of humor, along with the country accent she played up for laughs.

In the portrait, Susan looked happier and more relaxed than I'd ever seen her, standing beside her husband's chair with her hand settled proudly on his shoulder. Lauren must have been eleven or twelve, an age when nobody looks their best, and she was dressed in a high-waisted pink dress that Susan had probably chosen from the Laura Ashley catalog. Hairspray had poufed her bangs to a gravity-defying height that made me cringe on her behalf.

Down the hall, I bypassed the bathroom and let myself into Lauren's old room. Susan had pushed the huge bed into a corner and brought in a fancy little desk with pigeonholes, but other than that, everything was exactly the same as when Lauren lived here, down to the pinkish-violet paint and the collage of high school photos hung beside the closet door. I leaned in and ran my finger over the faces—Lauren and Warren on the beach at Nags Head; Lauren and Stephanie in heels and formal dresses; Lauren and me at McDonald's, our arms around each other's shoulders.

I remembered that day. It was one of the first times that Lauren had let me tag along with her and Warren after school, and I had felt enviably mature as I swung my legs from the back of Warren's Jeep, sipping a milkshake spiked with vodka. Lauren was leaned back in the passenger seat smoking a Capri 120, and when a boy from school had come over to see what we were doing, she'd turned her eyes to him without moving her head. "Not a thing, sugar," she'd said in the drawl that sometimes made her sound like a cross between Dolly Parton and Mae West. "Just smoking, drinking, being somebody."

I'd loved the phrase so much that I'd repeated it in my head as if it were a spell that could bring back Lauren at her best. I knew even then that it wasn't just her beauty that had made Warren fall head over heels. It was a brightness about her, something that made you want to be near her even when she was doing nothing more interesting than smoking a cigarette in a parking lot on a Thursday afternoon. If her case had become a staple of true-crime shows, like a Jodi Huisentruit or a Tiffany Sessions, the host would have said she "lit up a room," and, in Lauren's case, it would actually be the truth.

But I didn't believe Susan about the necklace. If Susan had found it in the house on Blue Ridge Road, it wasn't because I'd left it there. It was because Lauren had taken it, probably when she visited me at college. She couldn't have wanted it for herself—you couldn't wear a necklace with another girl's name on it—but I'd hurt her back then, and she might have felt that she had the right to hurt me too.

Suddenly I noticed that the picture frame angled out a little from the wall, as if something kept it from lying flat. I lifted it and ran my fingers over the back, sure I'd find a folded-up twenty or a baggie of dried-out shake. There was nothing, and I was just about to hang it back on the wall when I noticed a message painstakingly inked on the plaster underneath. FUCK YOU, Lauren had written in tiny capital letters.

Not to Susan, surely. She'd always said she had weak eyes, and it was hard to imagine her noticing the faded print even if she'd thought to move the frame. To whom, then? Perhaps Lauren had seen the future and somehow known that sixteen years after her disappearance, I'd be back in Tyndall County, making out with her husband and eating cookies with her mom.

I had a pen in my pocket, one of the blue ballpoints I liked to use for grading papers. I braced my elbow with my other hand while I composed my reply: *well fuck you too Lauren.*

4

The summer I turned thirteen, my mom looked at me and said, "If anybody ever hurt you, I wouldn't just want him dead. I'd flip the switch myself."

Lauren was over at our house that night. Susan must have had some sort of function, a political fundraiser or a gala at the country club, and though Lauren was sixteen by then—more than old enough to stay home by herself—sometimes she chose to have her mother drop her off with us instead. I saw these visits as a kind of advanced tutorial in the art of being a girl, and took mental notes on the way Lauren sat, the way she moved, even the way she held her chin in her hand as she leaned forward in the blue glow of the TV.

We were watching a tabloid show about a girl who had been murdered by some creepy older guy she'd met at a pool hall. I'd already been thinking that she looked a bit like me, and now I knew that my mom had seen it too. Like me, the kidnapped girl had a round chin with a dimple and eyes that were too big for her face—*E.T. eyes*, Sean Ballard had said once. She was the kind of girl who would be called cute, not pretty, the kind of girl boys would wink at in passing and then immediately forget.

"I think kidnappers look for a certain type," Lauren said. "Somebody mature. Experienced. I don't think Nicola is in any danger."

Though the comment stung, I felt that Lauren was right. I was and was not like the victims on those shows, the ones who were never seen again and the ones who were found in landfills or locked in the trunks of cars, bloodied and burned, heads cut off and organs removed. I imagined that they, like me, had grown up with single moms, in houses so ugly that kids laughed and nudged one another when the school bus pulled up at the curb. But I didn't wear tight shirts that showed my belly button or talk to grown men I didn't know. My mom had always been fiercely protective. Though she'd trained me to be a rule follower, she sometimes fretted that I was too compliant, and she'd told me once that if a man ever made me uncomfortable, I should kick him right in the nuts.

"Well, nobody would want to kidnap you either," I said, but the rhythm was off—I'd waited a beat too long—and even I knew that the insult didn't make sense. Everyone wanted Lauren. She was the main character, the one the camera followed in ever tighter close-ups, mimicking the heat of the killer's obsession.

My mom shook her head and reached for her cigarettes. "You girls don't know what men are like," she said. "You have absolutely no idea."

I KNEW THAT MY MOTHER WAS TRYING TO WARN ME, NOT SCARE ME, when she told me what she'd want to do to my hypothetical rapist and murderer. I suspected even then that she'd had a lifetime of fearing terrible men.

She'd been born on the other side of the mountains, in a place she referred to, elusively, as *up the holler*. She never told me anything about her family, but I knew that my father had been a truck driver named Charlie Smalls, whom she'd met while working at a convenience store in Fayette County, West Virginia. They'd known each other only a few weeks, and she swore she didn't have any idea where he was or have any information that would help me trace him. Years later, Google searches would turn up lots of hits on the composer of *The Wiz*, but none on a white guy who had lived in Fayette County in the early eighties.

Sometimes I wondered if she'd made the whole thing up. Was I the love child of some forbidden romance? Certainly I didn't look anything like my mom, who had thick, square hands like a man's and freckles on every inch of exposed skin. Maybe I was adopted, or maybe she'd stolen me, like a witch in a fairy tale.

Once I went through her drawers, looking for letters or a diary that would give up her secrets. I didn't find what I was looking for, but I did find some other interesting things: a little ceramic pipe in a velvet case, and a picture of a bunch of people on a riverbank with all the boys' heads cut out. I picked out my mom, prettier and younger than I'd ever seen her, but I couldn't identify any of the faceless boys, all wearing variations on the same high-waisted eighties jeans and snap-button shirts. It gave me a sour feeling in my stomach, and after a minute I put it back.

"I don't know what to do with you girls," Mom said after the show had ended and Lauren had gone home. "Lauren doesn't have a clue how the world works. She thinks as long as she has good manners and gets straight As, she can do whatever she wants." She shook her head, tapping the table the way she did when she wanted a cigarette but wouldn't allow herself to have one. "You're almost as bad," she said. "You think you have to be nice to everybody. It scares the shit out of me."

But I knew then that there was something about me that my mom didn't understand. She didn't know that the stories of victimhood didn't frighten me; they excited me. I had to hide from her how my breath quickened when I saw a headline about a girl who'd left the house to meet friends at the mall and was never seen again. Their loss cast a rare glow on those mundane moments, elevating them to the status of clues. I longed for my life to have that burnish, that sense of significance. Maybe, I thought, something terrible had to happen for your life to matter to anyone but you.

◆ ◆ ◆

SEAN HAD SCHEDULED A FACULTY MEETING ON FRIDAY MORNING. I HAD TO rush to get out of the house on time, and as I took a sharp right around the side of the old Armory Building, I knocked the passenger-side mirror off my car.

For a minute I just sat there. The students parked on the other side of the school, and the other teachers were already in the meeting. No one had witnessed the accident, but now I would have to make an even bigger fool of myself by walking in late with everyone's eyes on me, and I thought briefly about packing up the few things I cared about at my mother's house and just taking off for some random dot on the map.

All through that sweltering summer, I'd worked on the house. I'd carted most of the furniture to Goodwill and torn out the old carpet in the bedrooms. I'd watched YouTube videos on how to replace windows, and one afternoon I'd driven all the way to Charlottesville to get a deal on a used dishwasher. Apart from the Internet, Warren was my only resource, and I called him at least once a day to get his opinion on bathroom finishes or how to swing a sledgehammer. Last week he'd talked to his snake guy, who was on a kayaking trip in Baja. The snake guy had said he'd check in when he was back in town, but in the meantime, I should be on the alert for the smell of snake poop, which smelled like regular poop, only worse.

After the first few calls, Warren got in the habit of stopping by in the evening. We worked mostly in silence, stopping now and then to mop our foreheads with paper towels or pass a bottle of water wordlessly between us. Twenty years had gone by since his days as a varsity athlete, but he was still strong enough to lift a gutted kitchen cabinet over his head, the muscles in his back standing out in relief against the thin fabric of his T-shirt.

He didn't try to kiss me again, and we never mentioned Lauren. I didn't tell him about going over to Susan's or about the necklace that Lauren had stolen. I didn't tell him I'd looked up the woman he'd mentioned, the one who'd been pulled in parts from the Campbell River. Her name was Jessica Lacey, and she'd been just about to turn seventeen when she ran away from a group home in Petersburg. Six months later, her torso had been found floating less than a mile from Horseshoe Bend, where Lauren and I had gone tubing the day she disappeared. It was an intriguing connection, but Warren was right: Jessica's stepbrother, a boy named Eugene Dawkins, had been convicted of the murder. Rather than providing any clues to Lauren's disappearance, Jessica Lacey's case seemed only another object lesson in how dangerous it was to be a girl.

After I'd tried and failed to reattach the side mirror, I shouldered my giant book bag and headed for the gym. I managed to open the big doors quietly, and only a few people looked up as I slipped in and took a free seat on the bleachers. Sean stood on the basketball court with a microphone, going over the fall football schedule.

"And our job is to make them feel that support," he said. "I want these kids to know how committed we are to our Lions family."

A few people clapped halfheartedly. He paced down the line of bleachers, still talking, and I let my eyes drift to the yellow and blue banners fluttering overhead:

Girls Volleyball
State Champions
2005

Football
State Champions
1994

It was the first time I'd been in the gym since I'd come back to Tyndall, and something about the smell—dust, ball sweat, the special polish they used on the court—hit me like a jab to the ribs. Lately the past seemed to be coming at me from all angles.

I'd seen Sean for the first time two days ago, when I stopped by his office to sign my contract. He spread his arms before he took a step toward me, so at least I was prepared when he wrapped me in a bear hug, the first time we'd touched in nearly twenty years. "Shit, look at *you*," he said. He directed me to a chair, holding my elbow as if I were an old lady he was helping to cross the street. "Can you believe we all ended up back here? Well, Warren never left, I guess."

"The only thing I can't believe is that you're a high school principal," I said, and he laughed so hard that his receptionist looked up from her computer in the outer office.

"You and the rest of the town. I'm pretty good at it, though," he went on. "I care about these kids. I do my best for them. That's why I hired you," he said, flashing another grin that was almost flirtatious but not quite.

Did he know that I'd been spending time with Warren? I wondered. In the old days, Sean had always tried to compete with his brother, though Warren rarely seemed to notice. Now Sean's professional affability gave the appearance of friendliness without revealing anything about his actual feelings, which suited me just fine. The last thing I wanted was to be some kind of prize in the lifelong competition between Warren and his brother.

Our eyes met across the gym, and I thought Sean shot me a quick wink before turning away. Then I thought maybe I'd imagined it, but the woman to my left had noticed too and gave me a quick assessing glance.

"Before we move on, I know there are still a lot of questions about what happened back in July," Sean said. "I want you to know that the police were called, and they're taking this very seriously. They don't look at this as a prank or harmless fun. It was a crime, and it's going to be dealt with accordingly. Questions?"

He had my attention now, but when he opened the floor, people wanted to know about standardized tests and college advising. I felt a prickle on the back of my neck and turned to find that the woman to my left was still watching me. She was probably in her early forties, a little heavy, with long graying hair, leather-bag wrinkles, and what looked like a permanent half frown.

I looked back to Sean, and then it hit me like a punch to the ribs. It had been nearly twenty years, but I would have known her anywhere. Just my luck, I'd picked the seat right next to Jessi fucking Westcott.

After the scattered applause at the end of the meeting, I thought about grabbing my bag and hauling ass before she could speak to me, but our eyes met again as we stood up from the bleachers, and I had to make myself feign surprise. "Oh my God, *Jessi*?" I asked, my voice rising to something like a shriek. "What are you *doing* here?"

"I work here," she said, adjusting her bag on her shoulder. "I'm the assistant guidance counselor."

We were blocking traffic, and the people streaming toward the double doors glanced at us curiously. "Assistant?" I said, my voice somehow still at a nails-on-a-chalkboard pitch. "Does that mean Coach Nye is still around?"

"Alive and kicking." She patted the pocket of her bag and came up with half a soft pack of Marlboro Lights. "Good to see you, Nicola." Before I could lie and tell her it was good to see her too, she started walking, saying over her shoulder, "Don't feel bad that you didn't recognize me right away. I've been up with my kid for the past three nights. I know I look like shit."

WHY HADN'T WARREN OR SEAN TOLD ME ANY OF THIS? THAT JESSI WORKED at the high school. That she had a child. That she was different now— not just older but harder, fiercer. In high school she'd been a pushover, but now she seemed like somebody you'd think twice about messing with. If she knew what I'd done, I thought, she wouldn't be this friendly. She'd probably pop me in the nose.

The smart thing would be to avoid her. Nothing good could come from Jessi and me spending time together. Still, I found myself looking up her office number in the school directory during my free period. Most days I'd been eating lunch alone in the teachers' lounge, and seeing Jessi had made me long with a new acuteness for the days when I'd had real friends.

Before school had started, I'd put a lot of effort into my classroom. I'd hung the walls with prints of Rembrandts and Vermeers instead of inspirational posters, and lined spider plants and ferns along the windowsill. I wanted it to feel like the college classrooms where I'd sat on the floor, a copy of *Walden* or the *Collected Poems of Emily Dickinson* open on my thighs, warming in the sunlight that filtered through high windows, but as it turned out, you couldn't re-create that atmosphere at a Podunk public school. No matter how many plants I brought in, the room was still a charmless box with industrial lighting and a plastic floor painted to look like tile.

It didn't matter anyway. No amount of effort on my part could transform the children of Tyndall County into the students I longed for, eager and bright and well prepared. Some were smarter than I'd expected, yet even they seemed to regard me with a veiled but implacable hostility. Teaching college, I'd been able to defuse this sort of reluctance with jokes, but that didn't seem to work here. They knew I was a one-semester sub. There was no point in trying to please me when they'd barely have time to learn my name. One day I'd gone out to the parking lot after school and found a note folded in half under my windshield wiper. It was written in red pen, the letters slanted and distended to look like dripping blood: *NO ONE WANTS YOU HERE*. I took a photo of the note and reported it to Sean, but I didn't expect the school to actually do anything about it. I'd already known that my students found my presence superfluous; seeing it written down didn't make it any worse.

I was only passing through, and everyone could see it. I felt a longing to be around someone who really knew me, and maybe that was why, after the last bell rang, I fought the tide of students streaming out of the building until I found Jessi's office.

I could see her through the window, typing on her laptop with a pen clamped in her mouth, and she waved me in. "Welcome to the Pit," she said. "That's what the students call it."

The office was small, maybe eight feet by twelve, the walls covered in cheap wood paneling that made it look even smaller. With her eyes on the screen, Jessi pulled out her cigarettes and dropped them on the desk between us. "Do you still smoke?"

"Not for years," I said, hoping it didn't sound as judgmental to her ears as it did to mine.

"Good for you." She squeezed out from behind the desk, and I pressed myself against the wall to allow her access to the window, which was already cracked. Now that I was looking for it, I thought I could sniff out the odor of old cigarettes, barely masked by a layer of Febreze.

"I was surprised to see you," I said. "I didn't realize you'd moved back to town."

She shrugged. "I never really left. I took homebound classes and eventually got my GED. Then I went to community college over in Logan County and got my certification. I taught special ed for a while, and then this position came up." She shook a cigarette into her hand. "So what's it like to be back?" she asked, thumbing her lighter.

I sat in the chair reserved for students. "The weirdest thing to me is how many people we knew back then have kids in high school. I ran into Stephanie Gilliam at Kroger a few weeks ago, and I guess she's married to Jason Mack? I have their son, Connor."

"They've divorced, Stephanie and Jason." Jessi tapped her ash neatly into a Coke can she seemed to keep on the windowsill for that purpose. "Jason's a financial analyst or some shit like that. Stephanie spends all her time trying to be queen bee, just like in high school. The kid's a piece of work, no surprise."

"I picked up on that," I said. Connor Mack was a junior, a smirking frat boy in training who did well on the reading quizzes but looked at me with dead eyes whenever I asked him a question. When I'd tried to be the cool teacher by showing the class Franco Zeffirelli's *Romeo and Juliet*, setting up cushions on the floor and inviting them to find a spot around the DVD player, Connor had leaned forward and pressed pause just as Juliet's naked chest came on the screen.

Jessi bent to the window and exhaled. "Did you know he used to date Mabry Ballard?"

"No, really?" I felt a vague sense of disappointment. Mabry wasn't a great student, but she was smart and self-possessed, and I was sure she could have done better than Connor Mack.

"They broke up over the summer. Mabry has big plans, you know."

I didn't reply. I knew from Warren that Mabry was eschewing college to apply to the most prestigious conservatories in the country, but I didn't want to reveal that to Jessi. Of all the off-limits subjects between us, none was more dangerous than Warren and Lauren.

I took a cigarette from the pack on the desk and tapped the filter against my palm. I didn't really want to smoke, but it gave me something to do with my hands. "Hey, do you know what Sean was talking about at the end of the assembly? About the police being called?"

The fluorescent light above us gave a loud pop, but Jessi didn't turn a hair, and I figured she was used to it. "Somebody broke in over the summer and smashed up the trophy case by the front stairs. That's why all the trophies are on a folding table."

"Do they think it was a student?"

"It's always a student, isn't it?"

Suddenly this topic of conversation felt just as dangerous as talking about the Ballards. If Jessi and I got on the subject of high school pranks, who knew where it might lead? "I have to—" I began, but then Jessi's phone rang inside her battered purse.

"Hold on," she said. "My lighter's in the inside pocket if you need it." She pressed the phone to her ear. "Hello? Yes, this is she." I squeezed myself against the wall again so she could get to the door, her shoulders hunched as if she'd already prepared herself for bad news.

As I twirled the cigarette between my fingers, I realized I could picture the trophy case, a big glass box that used to sit in the front hallway just below the county seal. It was hard to believe that someone would be both angry and brazen enough to break in and methodically smash it to bits, but then again, it wasn't the first act of malicious vandalism in the history of Tyndall County High. I could still picture

Jessi's locker as it had looked the morning after—the vent dented, the letters *S-L-U-T* spray-painted down the front at a slant.

I pulled Jessi's purse on my lap and rummaged inside. I didn't see the lighter, but there was a wallet insert full of photos, the kind that no one carried now that we all had phones. I tugged it out and flipped through the plastic pages: school pictures of a brown-skinned boy with big ears and a lopsided grin from kindergarten up to third grade. One of Jessi on a beach, her arms around a tall man with dreadlocks. I wondered if he was her son's father, and if so, where he was now. I hadn't noticed a wedding ring.

The last photo was an old one. It was a family shot, the group gathered at what might have been a birthday party or a picnic. The image had the orangey tinge that made me think of my own childhood photos, carefully pasted by my mom into a leather album, and I was feeling pleasantly nostalgic until I noticed the figure in the back row. It was a big man in his late twenties or early thirties, smiling broadly, his hand resting on the shoulder of a little girl in a daisy-print dress. It was Dale Westcott—Jessi's father, and the only named suspect in the disappearance of Lauren Ballard.

5

The rumors about Dale Westcott started a few weeks after Lauren disappeared. Word had gotten around that he was the one driving the shiny red Silverado that she'd keyed in the parking lot at Horseshoe Bend, though it actually belonged to his son, Matt, who was stationed with the army in Germany. Dale drove the truck once a week to keep the engine in good shape, and that afternoon he'd decided to take it down to the boat launch and float the river with a group of men from his church.

I knew Jessi's dad, though not well enough to recognize his vehicle. He was a huge man with a black walrus mustache and a big gut who drove a wrecker and liked to sit on the front porch listening to the Redskins on the radio. He and Jessi were close, and sometimes when we were kids he'd take us for ice cream in the big truck with the crane on the back. I'd felt a pinch of jealousy now and then, as I often did in the company of friends with present fathers, but I'd never had an opinion about him as a person. I was at the age when any conversation with adults was an embarrassment.

When Jessi stopped coming to school in the spring of ninth grade, we'd fallen out of touch, and I didn't think of Dale Westcott again until the whispers started after Lauren's disappearance. People said he'd been beside himself when he saw the ruined paint job, not only because of the damage but because of the insult to his son. They said he'd spent the half hour before the police arrived pacing the parking lot, rubbing his mustache and muttering to himself. One of the men later claimed that Westcott had said, "I'll kill the son of a bitch," though the rest of them swore up and down they'd heard no such thing.

From what I remembered of Dale, I had to wonder if the bad parking job that had enraged Lauren might have been an accident. Lauren and I had assumed that the driver was a redneck, the kind of preening, strutting cock of the walk who would have intended the angle of his back end as a sort of vehicular fuck-you. Dale Westcott had never seemed like that type of guy to me, much less the type who would murder a woman for keying his truck.

In the first days, people defended him. Westcott insisted that he'd had no idea who had caused the damage, and if he had known, he would have told the police, not gone after her himself. That seemed reasonable enough, but then someone leaked his police report to the press. In his early twenties, he'd been charged twice with aggravated assault and once with robbery. In one of the incidents, he'd apparently swung a tire iron at a man's head, just missing killing him and dislocating his shoulder instead. Maybe he was that type of guy after all.

And Dale Westcott might have had other reasons for wanting revenge on Lauren Ballard. After all, people whispered, Lauren had practically destroyed Jessi Westcott's life back in high school. It wasn't hard to imagine that these two offenses against his family could canker in a man's heart and make him do things he'd never be capable of under normal circumstances.

But it was hard to say if Westcott ever would have been charged in Lauren's kidnapping, because two weeks later, he was dead. He'd been out on a lake in Ewald County when he capsized and died with the top of his head less than an inch from the surface of the water. It looked like an accident, but people who knew him said that Dale Westcott had never upset a boat in his life—certainly not in good weather on a lake smooth as a fresh-made bed. I'd heard that a tox screen showed he'd taken enough sleeping pills to euthanize a horse, but I never knew if that part was true.

My mom sent me a clipping about his death. There was no card or note, just the cutout newspaper article folded in thirds in a business envelope. Though Erika and I had broken up by then, I went straight to her off-campus apartment, used the key under the mat to let myself in, and finished a half-bottle of chardonnay I found in the fridge. When she got home, she found me drunk on the couch with the column of newsprint spread across my chest. "It's my fault," I sobbed. "All of this is my fault."

Erika nudged my foot with her knee. "Look at you. You're a fucking mess."

I started crying again. She sighed, then half carried me to the bedroom and tucked me in under the comforter with the pattern of sprigged violets. When I woke the next morning, the article about Westcott's death was folded in my hand, black letters printed on my skin.

"I JUST DON'T SEE THE POINT OF STIRRING UP THAT OLD SHIT," SEAN SAID.

Though I'd had the same instinct when I first saw Jessi, I found myself wanting to push back. "Why?" I asked. "Don't you think Warren and Mabry want to know what really happened?"

He took a last bite of his chicken leg and chewed thoughtfully. "Mabry's doing great," he said. "Jessi and Warren too. If you start bringing up Lauren, it's only going to fuck them up, and we'll end up right back where we started."

When Sean had asked if I wanted to meet up at the Hideout for the Sunday-night fried chicken platter, I'd convinced myself that it was some kind of professional development exercise. Perhaps, as principal, he invited all the new teachers out for Sunday dinner. I decided I wouldn't drink, but when I arrived, Sean was already at a table with a pitcher of Miller Lite. "Can you believe they still do dollar pitchers?" he said with such enthusiasm that I couldn't refuse the frosted pint glass he slid across the table.

Back in high school, the Hideout had been our dive of choice, the

kind of backcountry redneck bar where the jukebox listed the All-
man Brothers next to Joan Jett and they weren't too particular about
checking IDs. The building looked like an old railroad shed, the roof
made from sheets of corrugated tin that sounded like a conga line
when it rained. Inside was just one big room with a sticky dance floor
and pinball machines that were usually on the fritz. Though it was
only September, tinsel had been draped around the mirror, and a few
wilted-looking crepe paper decorations shaped like ornaments hung
from the ceiling on fishing wire.

The bartender was a young, muscled biker type, not the old bald guy
with navy tats whom I remembered from long ago, but still, the smell of
vinegar from the jars of pickled eggs and pigs' feet lined up on the bar
made something twist in the pit of my stomach. It wasn't exactly pleasure or even nostalgia, more a feeling of recognition, like realizing that
a stranger you just passed in the street wore your ex's cologne.

"It's kind of weird that her disappearance didn't get more coverage,"
I said, pushing a plastic fork through what was left of my coleslaw.
"There was some around here, obviously, but now you Google Lauren
Ballard and it's like one podcast episode and a few blog entries from ten
years ago."

Sean gave me a strange look, and I wondered if I'd revealed more
than I'd meant to. My interest in missing and murdered girls went all
the way back to those tabloid stories I'd watched with my mother back
in middle school, but Lauren's disappearance had developed my secret
taste into a full-blown hobby. I didn't necessarily want Sean to know
that I'd scoured the Internet for every bit of information about Lauren,
every supposed sighting and off-the-wall conspiracy theory. I certainly
wasn't going to tell him that I'd been the one to start her only Reddit
page, r/LaurenBallardDisappearance, which saw approximately three
hits a month.

And it wasn't only my obsession with the case that he'd find peculiar.
People online had a particular way of talking about crime. They aped
the language of TV cops, talking about blood splatter and trace DNA as
if they existed apart from human bodies. Cultivating that distance was

what allowed you to view a murder as a puzzle, just a bunch of pieces you could move around until they fit. I wasn't sure I wanted Sean to see that side of me.

He knocked back the last of his beer. "I still say it's better not to dig up the past," he said blandly. "You ready to head out?"

I thought we'd say goodbye at the door, but he leaned against the plywood beside the entrance, apparently in no hurry to move. His nerdy little Corolla was parked just in front of us, close enough for me to put my foot up on the bumper. Back in high school, I'd teased him for the way his license plate had bent nearly in half from hitting parking stops. "I should have asked for coffee," he said. "Got to sober up a little before I get in the car."

I fingered the necklace that lay flat against my collarbone. "So it's okay for you to drink?" I asked tentatively, wondering if I should have broached this question earlier.

He scoffed. "It was two beers. Anyway, I'm in NA, not AA."

"I was just asking," I said. "Erika's in recovery, and last time I talked to her, she said she didn't even smoke weed anymore. I guess I thought that was the rule."

I was drunk too, and had the hot-faced feeling I got when I talked too much. "So were you always into girls?" Sean asked. "Sorry if that sounds ignorant. Like do you think you were born that way?"

A drop of water hit me on top of the head. It was coming through the awning, I realized. "Are you asking if bisexuality is a real thing?" I said. "Yeah, I'd say that's pretty ignorant, Sean. Do you think I was in a delusional state when I slept with women and then reverted to my normal condition of straightness?"

"I'm sorry," Sean said immediately, and I got the sense he meant it. "You were in a relationship with me right before Erika, and I've always wondered, that's all."

I didn't say anything. I wouldn't have called what we'd had back then a relationship, and I was surprised that Sean would use the word. He was looking at me with a tenderness that made me want to pull my hood up over my head and hide until he went away.

"Could things have turned out differently with us?" he asked. "If I hadn't been such an asshole?"

I scrambled for a way to dodge the question. "Well, I didn't really see you after high school," I said. "It seemed like whenever I came home, you were at the beach house."

"Yeah." Sean leaned his back against the wall. "Well, that was kind of the way I wanted it at the time. Did I ever show you the tattoo I got down there?"

As he rolled up his sleeve and positioned his arm under the glow of the lights, I felt a sudden urge to say, *No, I do not want to see your tattoo.* I was expecting a naked lady or a skull and crossbones appropriate to the drugged-out dumbass he'd been at the time, and it took me a minute to puzzle out the form of the word scripted down his bicep in Gothic letters: *Resurgam.* I knew the reference immediately. In *Jane Eyre*, it was the word that Jane has carved on her best friend's tombstone after she dies of tuberculosis: *I will rise again.*

I couldn't keep myself from reaching out to touch it, tracing the curved letters with the tip of my finger. "You loaned me that book a long time ago," Sean said. "I don't think I ever gave it back. I liked it, though. Obviously."

I'd believed that nothing he could do would soften me—I was sure I was far too wary for that—but as I traced the letters, I felt a warmth in my chest like a shot of bourbon going down. "It's beautiful."

Sean stepped away, rolling down his sleeve. "Lauren used to say she and Warren would come down and get one from the same guy, but they never did."

I couldn't imagine Lauren with a tattoo. When I'd wanted to get a bird on my hip to mark my high school graduation, she'd made fun of me so relentlessly that I'd put it off for nearly a year. "What tattoo did she want?

"Fuck if I know. Something dumb like a butterfly, probably."

Wind hit the side of his face, and I pushed myself off the wall, but Sean didn't move. "Things changed for me after she went missing," he said. "Seeing Warren go through that, I realized I needed to keep myself in line if I wanted to be there for anybody else. That's why I try to stay on the straight and narrow now."

"And that's why you're a good principal," I said. "By the way, aren't you worried about being seen out at a bar on a Sunday night? Could be scandalous."

He shrugged. "The school board loves me," he said. "I'm untouchable."

I knew he'd meant to sound cocky, but there was enough truth in the joke that my old rancor returned. What would it be like to have that kind of confidence—to know that as long as you stayed among the small circle of people who had known you and your father and your grandfather before him, you could never really fail?

"I'm going to head home," I said, but as I turned toward the parking lot, the toe of my boot caught on a crack in the pavement, and I stumbled toward him. Sean caught me by the shoulders and pulled me to his chest, and I didn't pull away.

"When I think of you, it's like we never stopped being close," he said. "I understand that it's not like that for you."

I could smell him now, the dry warm scent of his skin and the faint minty odor of Irish Spring soap. It *was* like that for me, I wanted to say. All these years later, there was still some old familiarity drawing me back in spite of myself.

He kissed my hair and then released me. "I don't mean to put you in a spot," he said. "I want to seize my moment, that's all. Last time you left, you were gone for sixteen years."

6

Sean didn't know that I'd already kissed his big brother. From his perspective, I was entirely unattached, and it must have seemed as good a time as any to say what he needed to say.

But he'd hurt me back then. At one time, everyone we knew had assumed we'd end up together, our union nearly as much of a foregone conclusion as Warren and Lauren's. Senior year, I'd secretly planned to lose my virginity to him sometime around prom, or maybe beach week, when our classmates would be distracted by their own potential hookups, but by the time spring rolled around, we weren't even speaking. Even after all the years away, getting close to him again felt like stepping into a hot tub: I could feel my body shrinking back even as I tried to convince myself to move forward.

With Warren, it was easier. It was true that the friends I'd made in grad school and in the college towns where I'd taught would have viewed him as unbearably basic, but I liked to think that he was more than the boring catalog hunk they would have taken him for. He would have known better than to ask Sean's dumb question about my sexuality, and then there was the way he made me feel—the unsettling energy that always kept me a little on edge, a little dizzy, as if I'd just pounded a glass of good champagne. Maybe he's been waiting for the right woman, I thought, and then couldn't shake the giddy feeling that maybe the right woman was me.

THE RAIN HAD BEGUN BY THE TIME THE HOUSE CAME INTO VIEW. JUDGING by how long it had stood empty, I'd thought that Bearwallow might be a wreck, but it looked the same as it always had, a redbrick Colonial Revival with white columns and dark green shutters, so genteel and old-fashioned that you might expect a butler to greet you at the door. Of course people said it was haunted. Warren had told me that some teenagers had sneaked onto the property a few years ago and driven their car into a tree, panicked by the certainty they'd seen a ghostly woman in white peering out from an upstairs window.

When we'd parked, Warren came around to open my car door. He'd never done that before, and I wondered if he was feeling the house's influence. "Did you and Lauren ever talk about moving up here?" I asked.

He gave a short laugh. "You know Lauren. She never would have lived in the country. She couldn't stand being alone."

This made sense, though I wanted to point out that being with your husband wasn't quite the same as being alone. "And it's just been sitting empty all these years? Why don't you sell it?"

"I'd sell in a heartbeat," he said. "It's a money pit, and it doesn't make any sense to let it sit empty. But Sean's name is on the deed, and he won't let me put it on the market."

This surprised me. Sean was paying child support; surely he could have used the money. "Why not?"

Warren shrugged. "Sentimental attachment, I guess." He led the way up the steps to the green-painted porch, the boards creaking under our feet. "I have to grab something from upstairs. Do you want to sit out here or have a look inside?"

"I'd love to look around," I said. I followed him into the house and opened the first door on the right, stepping into what Mrs. Ballard had called the parlor. The furniture was gone. Maybe that shouldn't have been a surprise—she'd been dead for more than twenty years—but it made me melancholy to see the rooms empty, wallpaper hanging off in strips. It was clean enough, at least; Warren had told me that he paid a housekeeping service to come up once a month.

Warren knew that my mom had been his grandmother's house-cleaner, but I'd never told him how much time we'd spent together when I was in fifth and sixth grades. I'd never told him how Mrs. Ballard had made a point of seeking me out while I sat in an old wrought-iron chair on the side patio, reading as I waited for my mom to finish the dusting. She'd ask questions about my books, undeterred by my one-word answers. I'd already read *Anne of Green Gables* and *Rebecca of Sunnybrook Farm*, but she gave me *The Secret Garden*, *A Little Princess*, *Pippi Longstocking*, and when I came back for more, *Wuthering Heights* and *Jane Eyre*. I liked *Jane Eyre* the best because the cover had a picture of a house that reminded me of Bearwallow, a dark, looming mansion backlit by the moon.

Ever since I'd been secretly proud of my association with the house, as if the time I'd spent there had given me some kind of ownership stake. But when I'd tried to explain this to Erika, not long after we'd started dating, it hadn't gone well. "Bearwallow was a plantation," she'd said.

No, I told her, already frustrated; it couldn't have been a plantation because there was no farm. There had never been large-scale agriculture in Tyndall County; the terrain was too mountainous and too hard to clear. "But it was built by slaves," Erika interrupted. "It must have been. In 1830? Don't tell me that some rich guy went out to the back end of nowhere and built a big house all by himself."

I'd faltered, unable to come up with a good answer. In my imagi-nation, Tyndall belonged to the Ballards and the Mabrys because they had always been here, since before the county even had a name. It had never occurred to me to wonder who had hauled the stones for the foundation up the mountainside, who had mortared and stacked the bricks.

But I felt certain now that Erika had been right. I went back out and walked around the side of the house, running my hand along the pitted bricks. The rain was steady but not cold. It pattered on the dirt as I looked up to a diamond-shaped third-floor window, the glass paled by the reflection of the clouds. The window was smaller than the others and spaced oddly apart—a maid's room, maybe.

Before I turned the corner, tires crunched on the pea gravel and a truck pulled up, the left front tire bumping into an overgrown flower bed. This was where the hired help—my mom, and the cook, and the gardener—had always parked, as opposed to the family, who left their cars on the circular drive at the front of the house.

But the figure that stepped out wasn't the workman I'd expected. It was Sean, wearing jeans and a baseball cap with an American flag patch that I thought I recognized from high school. "What are you doing here?" he asked.

The tone wasn't unfriendly, but when I let him lean in for a hug, we only grazed each other, his palm barely brushing the back of my shoulder. "I'm with Warren," I said. "He's upstairs."

"Oh," Sean said. "Like a date?"

"N-no," I stammered. "He just asked if I wanted to see the house."

Sean looked away, clearing his throat. "I came to get the lawn-mower from the shed. Mine died all of a sudden."

Warren opened the kitchen door. When he saw Sean, he managed a smile, but it seemed forced, the skin around his eyes never moving. "What's up," he said. "Nicola, ready to get going?"

"Stay a while," Sean protested with a grin. "Don't we still have some beers in the fridge from Dad's birthday party?"

From the tilt of Warren's head, I could tell that he'd caught the faint edge of hostility in Sean's voice. "Can't do it, man," he said. "We've got plans tonight."

In the car, he switched on the radio, turning it up loud enough that I would have had trouble making conversation even if I'd wanted to, which I didn't. I'd planned to ask about the history of the estate and what he knew about the enslaved people who might have lived there, but I was distracted now, staring out at the pines and thick snarls of rhododendron.

From long experience, I knew that Sean was far more invested in their sibling rivalry than Warren was. For Warren, things were easy. If he wanted me, it was because he wanted me, not because I had once been his little brother's almost-girlfriend. The simplicity appealed to me. If I had to choose between the Ballard brothers, I would choose the one who saw me as a person and not a trophy in a lifelong competition. What I'd felt for Sean that night at the Hideout had been nothing more than a dollar-pitcher buzz and a nasty case of nostalgia, and now it was time to move on.

I slid over to Warren. "Why did you tell Sean we had plans tonight?"

"I don't know," he said, the corners of his mouth lifting. "I was hoping you might want to grab dinner or something."

I moved my hand to his lap, lightly touching his leg. "Mabry is out tonight, right? Let's skip dinner and go back to your house."

He looked at me. "You sure?"

Instead of answering, I guided his hand between my legs, grateful for whatever buried instinct had led me to wear a skirt today. "Okay, then," he said softly, and it took him only a moment to find a rhythm that let me relax against the headrest.

The road down the mountain was full of curves and switchbacks, but Warren seemed to know what he was doing, and I suspected this wasn't the first time he'd fingered a girl in the car. I closed my eyes and pretended we were back in the days before children and responsibilities, before Lauren went missing, when, whether I knew it or not, the whole world had been laid out before me like an all-you-can-eat buffet.

7

In the middle of the night, I woke to Warren turning me on my back. The streetlight outside the window lit up the tattoo on his shoulder, bike gears in an interlocking pattern, and sweat shining in the hollow of his throat.

Afterward he reached to unwind a quilt trapped between our legs. "It wasn't like this with her," he said.

I thought about pretending to be asleep. The last thing I wanted was to hear about his sex life with Lauren. "You were young," I said finally. "Nobody knows how to have sex until at least their mid-twenties."

He paused, and I thought for a moment he was going to tell me that he'd known how to have sex just fine, thank you very much. "What did you think of me back then, anyway?"

I laid my chin on his shoulder and spread my fingers across the bones of his rib cage. "I thought you were gorgeous—both of you—and totally in love."

"You didn't know me very well."

"Are you saying you weren't in love with her? Or that you weren't gorgeous?"

"I was in love with her." He shifted, displacing my hand. "But it wasn't what people thought. She was complicated."

I heaved what I'd meant to be an inaudible sigh. I would have talked about Lauren's disappearance all night long, but I didn't want to talk about her personality quirks or their pet names for each other or how she always left the towel on the floor after she got out of the shower. Those details would only remind me that I was fucking my dead friend's husband, and I wanted to avoid that subject if possible. "I never understood why you got married so young," I said, more to myself than to him.

Warren laughed. "It was kind of an accident, believe it or not. She'd accused me of cheating on her, and I said something like, 'You don't think I love you? I'd fucking marry you right now.' I'm not sure we actually would have gone through with it, but then when she got pregnant, it was pretty much a done deal."

I considered whether I should tell him about Lauren flushing her birth control pills down the toilet, but what would be the point? It wasn't like he could do anything about it now. "Who did she think you were cheating with?" I asked.

"Jessi Westcott."

After all these years, I was surprised to find myself feeling hurt, even a little jealous. "And did you?"

"No, of course not." He turned to me, and I could tell that he was trying to make earnest eye contact, though the ambient light left his face in shadow. "I'm not perfect, but I'm not a cheater. I'm not built that way."

I believed him. As much as I'd enjoyed my fantasy on the car ride home, I knew that Warren wouldn't have slipped around back then. He'd been too much in love, and again I wondered whether I should tell him all I knew about Lauren. I was pretty sure that she'd cheated on him when she visited me at college, and she'd done other things too. "Did you know she drank during her pregnancy?"

I thought I saw him wince. "No, but it doesn't surprise me, the way she drank the rest of the time. You know what she did to Mabry, right?"

I knew the outline of the story, but I let him tell me anyway. How Lauren had come home drunk in the middle of the day and left the baby in the car. How the mailman had stopped by a few minutes later and happened to see Mabry asleep in her car seat with the windows rolled up. How, when he knocked on the front door, he'd found Lauren on the couch, dead to the world. "Are you sure she did it on purpose?" I asked.

Warren folded his arms behind his head. "I don't know," he said. "I don't think she liked being a mother. She wasn't a warm person, and Mabry never seemed to take to her. I think if Lauren could have pressed a button and made her disappear, she probably would have done it."

The harshness of his tone surprised me almost as much as the words. I would have liked to defend Lauren, but even I had noticed the way she fussed over the baby's accessories—the giant bows and monogrammed bibs trimmed with rickrack—more than the actual baby. "Do you think she had postpartum depression?" I asked. "I wish I'd talked to her about it. I definitely knew that something was off, but I was pretty self-absorbed back then."

"It wouldn't have done any good," Warren said. "I took her to the doctor, and they did the screenings, but she always said everything was fine."

That sounded like Lauren. Admitting that she needed help would have meant acknowledging the cracks in her perfect life, and she would have avoided that at all costs. "Who was she with that day?" I asked. Implicit in my words was another question: *Who let her drive drunk with a baby in the car?*

Warren's eyes met mine as he said, "Sean."

HE WENT BACK TO SLEEP, BUT I DIDN'T. WHAT WOULD IT BE LIKE TO COME home from work to find that your wife had gotten plastered with your brother and almost killed your child? He'd said that Lauren would have pressed a button to make Mabry disappear, and I had to wonder now whether he would have done the same to Lauren. Warren wasn't a murderer any more than he was a cheater, but it was possible that he hadn't been entirely sorry when his wife was no longer around.

As far as Sean and Lauren went, I had to admit that none of it surprised me very much. Sean and I had more or less lost touch after Jason Mack introduced him to coke, but I knew that he'd spent most of those post–high school years going back and forth between Tyndall and the family beach house, partying and working part-time jobs when the monthly checks from his trust ran low. I was certain that Sean never would have laid a finger on Lauren, but would he have gone out drinking with her in the middle of the day, knowing that she had a small child to care for: sure, why not? They were united in their thoughtlessness, and in the fact that they never seemed to suffer any consequences.

Until they did. Less than a year after Mabry almost died, Lauren had gone missing. A few months after that, I'd heard that Sean had checked in to rehab for the first time.

Considering all that Lauren had done back then, I had to ask myself if sleeping with Warren was really such a terrible thing. In high school I'd been careful to keep my long-standing crush on him a secret, knowing that if Lauren had gotten the smallest inkling of it, she would have pitied me. Everyone knew that the two of them were made for each other, matched in heaven by some fathomless cosmic algorithm. Still, here I was.

And she was gone.

WHEN I WOKE, I FOUND A NOTE ON THE BEDSIDE TABLE. *HAD AN APPOINTMENT. Back soon.*

I showered and put on the same skirt and blouse I'd worn to Bearwallow. It was wrinkled, and there was a red wine stain near the second button, and I wondered what Warren would think if I brought a change of clothes and a toothbrush that I could leave in his medicine cabinet. It didn't have to mean anything beyond the fact that I didn't want cavities.

Downstairs I made coffee in the big sunny kitchen. Warren had left the radio on, playing a Bach cello concerto. Lucky II wagged frantically at me through the glass door to the yard. I let him in, and he went straight to his lumpy bed in the corner, sinking down with a grateful harrumph.

While the coffee brewed, I fingered the glass jars of spices, things I'd heard of but had no idea how to use: ras el hanout, za'atar, saffron. There was a stack of raffia placemats on the counter, and a jar of home-made hot sauce that seemed to be fermenting. The windowsills were covered with ferns and ficus. Warren was probably the kind of guy who talked to them while he made dinner.

I had to wonder how a man like him had managed to stay single all this time. Even a missing wife shouldn't have been enough to keep the women of Tyndall County from a hot dad with a successful business who cooked, gardened, and loved nothing more than heading up to the Blue Ridge Parkway on the weekend for a fifty-mile bike ride. Even to me he sometimes seemed unreal, as if he'd just stepped out of a J.Crew ad, smiling as he hefted a beat-up leather messenger bag on his muscled shoulder.

While I turned over the boxes of tea—manly stuff: Assam, Russian Caravan—I considered my options. *Back soon*, the note had said, as if he expected me to wait.

If Warren had been anyone else, I would have taken these empty hours as an opportunity to snoop. I would have told myself that it was a safety issue; I had to check for weapons, drugs, and weird pornography simply as a precaution. When you got involved with someone new, going through drawers and closets was a kind of due diligence.

But this was different. If I wanted to poke through Warren's stuff, it wasn't because I was afraid of him or even wary. It wasn't possible to imagine him with a dark secret. I was simply curious, and curiosity could have consequences. If I got caught, he'd peg me as a nosy bitch with no respect for privacy, and he'd be right.

The trick, in that case, was not to get caught.

I started with a circuit of the living room, running my finger over the surface of the mahogany desk, the spines on the bookshelf. Though it had warmed up again after a few days of rain, the woodstove and the fleecy woolen blanket folded over the back of the couch gave the room a cozy vibe, and I thought that I would have been happy to take down the five-hundred-page biography of Ernest Shackleton and curl up to doze away the rest of the morning. I cast a longing look at the leather club chair, but it was almost eleven thirty, and I didn't know how much time I had left.

In the drawer of the end table, I found a picture of Lauren and Warren holding Mabry. It must have been her christening, because she was wrapped in a white embroidered blanket with lace on the hem. Warren and Lauren looked impossibly young, skin as smooth as the After shots in an acne wash commercial. At first glance, they seemed happy, but Warren's smile had a tightness to it, as if he'd been holding his jaw in the same position for too long.

I ran my finger around the edge of the frame. Maybe it had been out on the table for a while and then Warren had shoved it into a drawer. Maybe it was too painful for him to look at Lauren's glowing face, her eyes brighter than I remembered, as if they'd been tinted to that uncanny shade of green.

Upstairs, the first door I opened turned out to be to Mabry's. Even though I saw her in class every day and knew exactly how old she was, somehow I'd been picturing her nursery, with the rocker by the crib and fabric-covered cutouts of the letters of her name stapled to the wall. This was a typical teenager's room, with blinds pulled down and piles of clothes in the corners. I spotted an Xbox that looked as if it hadn't been used in a while beside a pile of textbooks tipped on its side.

In the dim light, it took me a moment to notice the giant framed wedding portrait. Lauren stood beside a waist-high garden wall, a long lacy train draped over the grass. The dress was cringeworthy, endless billows and puffs of white satin, but Lauren looked exquisite, her skin as fresh as the lilies in her bouquet.

When I looked closer, though, something seemed off. Lauren and Warren had married in August 2000, but in the picture her face was less defined, more like a teenager's. The dress was wrong too, with its bumps and poufs in unflattering places, and I was pretty sure the lilies were fake. The longer I looked, the more convinced I felt that this wasn't Lauren's wedding portrait at all but an advertising photo from when she'd modeled for Emmeline's Boutique back in high school. Did Mabry know? After a minute or two, Lauren's unfocused gaze began to freak me out, and I shut the door quickly behind me, circling back to Warren's room.

Immediately my eyes traveled to the bed—a king with a snowy white comforter, heaped with pillows. It would feel so nice to sink down onto that crisp white duvet, and what was the point of snooping, anyway? Warren and I hadn't seen each other in a decade and a half, and already I could read his thoughts as if they were written on his forehead.

But some piece of Lauren was in this house—I knew that instinctively, and finally, on the top shelf in the guest room closet, I found what I didn't even know I'd been looking for.

It was a silver Nine West box that probably once held boots. Inside was a dried-out prom corsage and a messy pile of three-by-five snapshots, less favored versions of the photos I'd seen in the frame at Susan's house. I flipped through picture after picture of Warren and Lauren, Lauren and Stephanie Gilliam, Warren and Lauren and Stephanie and Sean, laughing beside the river or at somebody's party, holding red Solo cups and cigarettes. Jason Mack was in a few of the pictures, and so was I, lurking uneasily in a corner of the frame. I didn't like the way I looked in those pictures. I was trying to please everyone in those days, and the strain of the effort was visible in the set of my shoulders and the stiffness of my smile.

Except in the one photo of me by myself, lying on the grass behind the weight room in my soccer uniform. My long hair was loose, and I looked sullen, my chin jutted toward the viewer. I felt my stomach drop and removed the picture from the pile, laying it facedown on the floor beside me.

Most of the photos had clearly been taken by Warren, and it wasn't hard to see where his priorities were. There was Lauren sitting cross-legged on the lawn by the picnic tables where the seniors ate lunch; Lauren in his Jeep, her elbow braced against the window; Lauren in a powder-blue formal, smoking and laughing into the camera. Only a besotted boyfriend, already talking marriage at seventeen, would have cared enough to document the shades of her expression with such enthusiasm. In most of the group shots, she looked older than the rest of the group, and I wondered if this trend would have continued—if the enviable maturity of adolescence would have translated, post-forty, into early-onset middle age, drooping breasts and saddlebag wrinkles. For a moment I let myself indulge the fantasy, and then I came back to earth: Lauren would have gotten Botox.

In the pictures it was evident that she was conscious of being observed and that she had arranged her face in a certain way for Warren's sake. I couldn't say exactly *how* I knew—it was a certain slant to her eyes, an angle to the head that was not quite natural. It was one reason that she hadn't succeeded in modeling; she looked fake, as if she could just manage pretending to have a good time but not actually having one.

Below the high school photos was a handful of snapshots from the wedding and reception, held at the country club. I was in a few of these too, standing awkwardly at the edge of the group in a blue dress I'd borrowed from my roommate, the cat's-eye glasses I'd affected that year slipping down the bridge of my nose. I hadn't been asked to be a bridesmaid, something that had hurt me at the time. I was three years younger than Lauren and we'd never been besties, but I'd thought of her as almost family—someone I was connected to even when I didn't want to be—and I'd assumed she'd felt the same.

Just below the wedding photos, I found a birth announcement for Mabry Elizabeth Ballard, born February 18, 2001. You could hardly call it a shotgun wedding when the groom practically sprinted to the altar, and I knew that no matter what Warren said now, back then he'd thought the sun shone out the crack in Lauren's ass. Getting married and having a baby were hardly going to faze him. He would have jumped off the Campbell River Bridge if she'd told him to.

Under the wedding photos was something I hadn't expected—a stack of eight-by-tens, taken on a good-quality camera and probably developed in a darkroom. A series of portraits of Lauren dressed up as various characters: on an elevator, gazing through the open doors with a startled look; in a parking lot, glancing over her shoulder as if she'd heard someone call her name. In others she leaned against trees or applied lipstick in a visor mirror, looking generically pretty and winsome. In the one I liked best, she was sitting on a park bench wearing a neat dark suit as if dressed for a job interview, but her pantyhose was ripped, makeup smeared around her eyes and mouth. Was she on her way home from a rough night, or was this supposed to be the aftermath of an assault?

These photographs had something that Lauren's modeling work never had. In these images, she was fully present and wholly absent at the same time, as if, rather than playing a character, she'd melted into her. The series had been made in clear imitation of Cindy Sherman— derivative for sure, but still, more skillful and well thought out than one would expect from student work. If Lauren had taken these pictures, she'd had a lot more artistic talent than I'd ever realized.

In the lower-right corner of each image, a word had been printed in light blue pen: *T-E-E-V-E-E*. Maybe it was the name of the series.

When I lifted out what I thought was the last photo, I saw that there was one more stuck to a corner of the box. It didn't look like the ones Warren had taken, and I spotted faded red numbers in the bottom left corner: 8 17 96. The image showed Lauren beside a girl I didn't recognize, leaning against a brick wall and squinting into the sun.

It was the other girl who interested me. Lauren, like most snobs, had always taken care to surround herself with attractive people. I guessed now that she'd allowed me into her group not because of our tenuous family connection but because by high school I was acceptably pretty, not a rival by any means but cute enough not to embarrass her while setting her own beauty into relief. This girl was downright ugly, wide-mouthed and skinny as a rail, with stringy black hair and prominent teeth. Based on the date, the picture had been taken in Lauren's freshman year of college. But I thought I'd met all Lauren's friends when I visited her in Richmond, and I knew I would have remembered a face like this.

I took the picture of me and the one of the unknown girl and tucked them into my bag. Then I returned the box to the top shelf, taking care to push it all the way back against the wall.

I'd just made it downstairs when I heard the front door creak. I grabbed a book from the nearest shelf and dived onto the living room couch, arranging my face into what I hoped was a plausible where-has-the-time-gone expression. Now that it was too late, I wondered if I'd made a mistake in assuming that Warren would want me here when he got back.

I shouldn't have worried, because the figure coming through the door wasn't Warren after all. It was a teenage girl with long hair tugged into a low ponytail, wearing sunglasses and carrying an overnight bag. Mabry stopped and stared, a small smile tugging at the corner of her lips. "Hey, Ms. Bennett. Is my dad home?"

I stammered something about the appointment and how he'd probably be back soon. "I came to borrow some books," I said, holding up the one I'd grabbed, which turned out to be a guide to building your own cabin. "I should get going."

Mabry nodded as if she believed me, and I felt a tiny sliver of hope that I could get out of this without embarrassing myself further. "Can I ask you something?" she said. "Could you look over my college application essays? Like help me edit them? Actually it was Dad's idea."

"Oh." I'd been prepared to dash out the door at the first opportunity, and now that it was clear that she wanted to have a conversation, I couldn't figure out whether to stand or sit. "Not today, but sure."

"Cool, thanks," she said in a tone that suggested she'd already lost interest. "I'm going to make tea, do you want some?"

I didn't want tea, but I found myself telling her that would be lovely. She was back in less than five minutes, carrying an enameled tray with a clay pot and a set of handle-less cups. Living in this house must be like living in a Pottery Barn, I thought.

She poured me a cup and offered sugar. It was green tea, hot and strong, and I studied her while I pretended to sip. She still looked like Warren, but a feminine version, the lines of the chin and angles of the cheekbones scaled down and softened. In my class she was the kind of student who did all the work and turned everything in on time with absolutely zero enthusiasm. I had watched her take notes, writing down my exact words—*The first line of* A Tale of Two Cities *is meant to be not contradictory but complementary*—so she could repeat them back to me later in short, neat, uninspired little essays that made it precisely to the recommended word count and then stopped, once in the middle of a sentence. Working with her on college applications would be about as pleasurable as unclogging a shower drain, but considering the role I might have played in her mother's disappearance, I felt like I owed her that much.

"Does my dad know you're here?" she asked. "You didn't break in or something, did you?"

I almost dropped my cup. "What? Of course not."

"Well, it doesn't bother me that you're fucking him, if that's what you're worried about. It's about time he had a girlfriend."

Mabry took a quick glance at my face, and I willed myself not to blush. I knew teenage girls. They found the idea of their teacher having a sex life both hilarious and somehow unseemly, and I could already hear the smothered giggles that would follow me down the hall if this got around at school. "So he didn't have girlfriends before?" I asked, trying to sound like I was just making conversation.

"I mean, sort of," she said. "Nobody super-long-term. How well did you know my mom, anyway?"

I took a gulp of tea, scalding the roof of my mouth. "Pretty well, I guess. Our mothers were friends, and then we got to be friends too."

"Do you think my parents were happy together?" she asked, cupping both hands around her tea as if to warm them.

"When I saw them together, they seemed happy." That was only half the truth, but I certainly wasn't going to tell her what Warren had told me last night.

She turned her eyes to the picture window, watching a cardinal flutter at the birdfeeder. The longing on her face was so naked that I couldn't help wishing myself elsewhere. I wondered if she knew about the time Lauren had locked her in a hot car and how close she must have come to death.

"My grandma says they fought a lot," Mabry said. "But you never know what a marriage is like from the inside."

This sounded like something she'd read somewhere, and the crack in her I've-got-it-all-figured-out persona made me warm to her for the first time. "That's true," I said.

"What do you think happened to her?" she asked, with no more inflection in her voice than if she'd asked what I'd had for breakfast. "Do you think that Westcott guy murdered her or what?"

"Well, some people thought she ran away," I said, stalling. "I guess I wanted to believe that at one point."

It wasn't really an answer, but Mabry didn't seem to notice. "That's what my grandma thought," she said. "She said my mom and dad had been having problems, and she thought that my mom just ran off to Florida for a week or something."

I let myself picture this: Lauren speeding down I-95 in a top-down convertible with a Britney CD in the stereo and a roadie beer snugged into the cupholder. She could have holed up at some mom-and-pop motel in Panama City, flirted with the college boys, come back tanned and hungover, the inside of her suitcase reeking of coconut oil. It might have been a scandal at the time, but no one would even remember it now.

"People always act like it was this terrible thing that happened to me," Mabry said. "But how can it have happened to me when I literally don't remember any of it?"

She was looking down, pointing and flexing her bare feet on the carpet. Light outlined the curve of her cheek, and she looked exquisite, like a Flemish girl in one of the paintings I'd hung in my classroom. If things had gone differently, she might have fallen asleep in her carseat one hot afternoon and never woken up. Surely Warren had imagined this scenario—how he might have come home to find her unresponsive and Lauren on the couch sleeping off her lunchtime hangover. Surely when he looked at his daughter's lovely face, he imagined another life he might have lived: how Lauren might be here, and Mabry gone.

I probably should have felt sorry for her. Like other kids with less dramatic backstories, she probably hadn't realized how fucked up her family was until she got to be a teenager. It was clear that Warren didn't talk to her about her mother or what had happened to her, and she would leap on anyone who would offer her information, whether it was her grandmother or her substitute English teacher.

But I was wary of getting too close, because I knew I could never tell Mabry the real story of how I felt about her mother. I had never told anyone that story—not the police, not even Erika. I couldn't possibly explain the combination of jealousy, fear, and crushing guilt I'd felt back then, and how it had led me into places I'd never expected. Lauren had been a manipulative bitch sometimes, but I was something worse than that. I was a wrecking ball.

8

'd always hated going to work with my mom, and not just because of the dread of seeing a kid I knew from school at one of the houses she cleaned. The rich wanted their homes spotless, but they would have preferred the cleaning to be done by robots, or maybe the birds and squirrels from *Snow White*. If the lady of the house swanned in laden with bags from Thalhimers and Pappagallo and found me doing my homework at the kitchen table, she'd inevitably give a sniff as if she'd just caught a hint of the great unwashed.

In revenge, I rarely stayed where I was supposed to. I waited until Mom started running the vacuum and then sneaked into the living room, picked up knickknacks, and shook out the sheet music. I read mail sitting out on counters. In the bedrooms, I opened women's drawers and ran my hands over their slips. I never stole, though I'm not positive if it was because I knew it was wrong or because my mom was sure to find out. Probably the latter, since I was certain she would make me wish I'd never been born, while God seemed less predictable when it came to punishment.

Tuesdays after school, we drove up to Bearwallow. Mrs. Ballard went to the beauty parlor while my mother cleaned, which meant I was free to roam the house and grounds with no fear of being interrupted. I named the bedrooms based on their furnishings: the Map Room; the

Blue Room; the Turtle Room, where I'd found a figurine of a turtle on a nightstand; the Boys' Room; and the Fancy Room, which was the only one I didn't feel comfortable snooping in. I could feel Mrs. Ballard watching me from the big portrait on the wall, her eyes tracking me as I tried out different facial expressions in the mirror.

In the other rooms, I opened drawers and took out old tins of face powder, old-fashioned bobby pins with jewels on the end, loose batteries, a handkerchief folded around a bunch of old seashells and a scattering of sand that hissed away between my fingers. I had favorite things that I came back to again and again, as if they were friends: a gold glass-topped jewelry box on little legs that held what I was pretty sure was a diamond bracelet; a mirrored perfume tray with an array of ancient half-full bottles giving back their glittering reflection. Once I dabbed Shalimar on the inside of my wrists. I only used a little, but on the way home, Mom said I smelled like a church full of old ladies.

The Blue Room was my favorite, and sometimes I sat on the edge of the four-poster bed and stretched as if I'd just woken from a nap. I could tell from the silk bedspread and the paintings of primroses on the walls that a girl lived here once. I'd found a lace scarf in one of the drawers, and sometimes I'd drape it around my shoulders, pretending it was a party dress. I was standing on one foot on the pink and blue Persian rug, carrying on a half-whispered conversation with an imaginary prince modeled after Warren Ballard, when I caught a flash of movement in the mirror.

It was Mrs. Ballard. She was wearing a blue silk dress with a floppy bow at the neck and blue-tinted glasses with octagonal frames, and her hair looked as if a hurricane wouldn't move it. "What are you doing, child?" she said, her voice rusty, as if she hadn't spoken for days.

I was startled enough to tell her the truth. "I'm pretending to be Nicole of Bearwallow."

"Nicole of Bearwallow," she repeated, unsmiling. "I see."

Petrified by embarrassment, I was newly conscious of the fact that I didn't look the least bit like a princess or a heroine. I had grown three inches that year and gained so much weight that the doctor said I was clinically obese, though he also told my mother not to worry, that my body would change when I went through puberty and grew into the "woman's shape" he sketched in the air with his hands. "She won't look like a teddy bear forever," he'd said as tears pricked the corners of my eyes.

And it wasn't just that I was fat; I was weird too. Lauren refused to acknowledge me if we passed each other in the hallways of the middle school. My fifth-grade teacher was always calling my mom in for conferences because, as he said, I *hid behind books*, using them as a shield to keep other children at bay. My only friend was Jessi Westcott, who was also weird and spent recess drawing horses in her notebook.

I saw that version of myself reflected in the mirror and withered with shame, but Mrs. Ballard didn't seem to notice. "Don't let me interrupt you, Nicole of Bearwallow," she said as she turned to leave. "Please carry on."

AFTER THAT DAY, MRS. BALLARD MADE A POINT OF STOPPING TO SAY hello if we met in the house, which caused me agonies of embarrassment. I'd never had practice talking to adults other than my mother and teachers, but Mrs. Ballard kept asking questions about the books I was reading, no matter how many times I tried to put her off with *pretty good* or *fine.* "I was a reader too as a girl," she said once. "I used to hide in the Flower Room with a book when my father was in one of his rages."

It thrilled me to know that she had nicknamed the rooms, just as I had. For the first time, I didn't want to run away. "Which one is the Flower Room?" I asked.

I thought maybe it was the one I'd called the Blue Room, where she'd caught me pretending to be Nicole of Bearwallow. "On the third floor," she said vaguely. "I haven't been in there in years. It must be frightfully dusty."

Frightfully: I repeated the word in my mind as she offered me the tray of tea cakes iced with pink frosting. I loved the way she talked, precise and old-fashioned, almost British, like one of the characters in my books. I had never been happier, but on the way home that afternoon, my mom said, "I don't like you spending so much time with that old woman."

My heart beat fast. Had Mrs. Ballard complained that I was bothering her? But she was always the one who came to find me. "Why?"

"She looks down on you," she said. "They all do—a family like that."

I never went back. The following Tuesday, when Mom asked if I wanted to come with her to Bearwallow, I said I'd rather stay home by myself. I told myself that she was right about the family, and stopped thinking about Mrs. Ballard until, years later, I saw the obituary in the paper: *Margaret Mabry Ballard, 1899–1995.*

I'd never known much about Mrs. Ballard's life, and some of the details surprised me. She'd graduated from St. Catherine's School in Richmond and then received a BA from Radcliffe. After that she'd lived in New York City, where she'd worked as the secretary for something called the American Youth Congress. I'd occasionally heard rumors that she was a Communist, but I'd chalked them up to dumb hick-town gossip. Now I wondered if maybe it was true.

Before I could mention Mrs. Ballard's death to my mom, she brought it up. "I got a call from a lawyer," she said on the way to school. "That old lady left you something in her will."

I imagined a check written in a spidery hand, a jewelry box overflowing with old-fashioned necklaces and rings. "What is it?" I asked.

"He said it's a box. Probably just some old junk. I thought for a minute she'd left you the house, but no such luck." She winked at me as if she'd made a hilarious joke, and I scowled and slid down in my seat.

As usual, she was right. Mrs. Ballard had left me a bunch of old children's books I'd never heard of: *Betsy-Tacy, Elsie Dinsmore,* plus a few Brontës and some paperback mysteries by Agatha Christie and Dorothy Sayers. The *Betsy-Tacy* books were all right, but *Elsie Dinsmore* was god-awful. I read ten pages and shoved the whole box in my closet.

◆ ◆ ◆

I HOPED THAT LAUREN AND THE BALLARD BROTHERS HADN'T HEARD about the books. Though Sean and I had been in the same class since kindergarten, I avoided him whenever I could. In elementary school, he'd been the kind of boy who drew cartoons of the teacher in his notebook and shouted out the latest *Saturday Night Live* catchphrase to make everybody laugh. Once he'd refused to be my partner for square dancing in PE because my hands were too sweaty. It was like shaking hands with a fish, he said, and all the other boys said *eeeww* and backed away, stuffing their hands in their pockets. After he decided I had E.T. eyes, the other boys spent the rest of the year holding up their hands to their ears and telling me to phone home. To punish Sean, I'd refused to give him a valentine, even though the note sent home by the teacher stipulated that we had to make one for every member of the class.

I would have been happy to avoid him forever, but one day as I was crossing the school parking lot, I heard footsteps behind me. "Hey," said a voice that made me tuck in my chin and hunch my shoulders. "Where you going?"

It was Sean, wearing a Tyndall Lions sweatshirt with the sleeves cut off, the fabric across his chest dark with sweat. "Nunya," I said, and kept walking. I hoped my rudeness would do the trick, but he trotted along beside me toward the exit.

"I heard my grandma left you something."

I stopped walking. "How did you know about that?"

"When I visited her in the retirement place, she asked if I knew you. She said she wanted to give you a present."

I could feel my face turning red. If Mrs. Ballard had talked about me to Sean, she'd probably also mentioned that my mom had been her maid. "Sorry for your loss," I remembered to say, and then turned and started walking again.

He was still behind me, the soles of his sneakers slapping the asphalt. "Slow down, girl. Damn, where's the fire?"

We'd reached a block of split-level ranches just beyond the school property. Someone had left a hose draped over their fence, and I picked it up and doused my head and the back of my neck. When I stood up and threw back my wet hair, Sean was staring. "What?" I asked.

He shook his head. "Nothing. Gimme that."

I handed him the hose and he soaked himself, blowing air through his nose like a horse. "Shit," he said. "I like you. You have good ideas."

He was treating me as if we'd never met—as if the square-dancing incident, the E.T. eyes, and the missing valentine had never happened. I couldn't abide such hypocrisy, and I decided to tell him the truth. "My mom used to clean your grandma's house," I said. "She knew I liked to read, and she wanted to give me some books."

I steeled myself for proof that my mom was right about the Ballards. There was meanness in Sean; I'd always known it, even when the rest of the class doubled over at his impression of the earth science teacher, who walked with his feet turned out and his rear end stuck out like a duck's.

He crossed his arms over his chest, a drop of water running down the side of his nose. "What kind of books?"

"Kid books." Now I worried that he might lay a claim to them on behalf of the family. Maybe they'd argue that old Mrs. Ballard hadn't been in her right mind and that any bequest should lawfully come to them. "They're not valuable or anything."

Sean was still staring at me. Maybe I was wrong about the books not being valuable, I thought. Maybe the family knew that Mrs. Ballard had hidden something between the pages of *Elsie's Holidays at Roselands*—an amended will or the key to a safe-deposit box—and Sean had been charged with getting it back. "Do you want to go to the funeral with me?" he asked.

"You want me to bring the books back, you mean?"

"What?" He looked at me the way Lauren sometimes did, as if I were a few cards short of a full deck. "No, I don't care about the books. I just thought that since she liked you, you might want to come to the funeral. It's a memorial service, I guess—she was cremated. Maybe your mom would want to come too."

"No," I said immediately. I had no idea whether my mom would want to come, but I knew I'd rather be drawn and quartered than walk down the long red aisle of St. Philip's Episcopal a half step behind her. "I can probably make it, though. When is it?"

"Two o'clock Saturday," he said, and insisted on writing the time on the inside of my wrist with a ballpoint pen. Lying in bed that night, I rolled up the cuff of my pajamas to read the number, already a bit faded, and press my thumb to the spot where, just for a moment, his thumb had rested.

AT THE SERVICE, I SAT ALONE SEVERAL PEWS BEHIND THE BALLARDS: Warren, straight-shouldered in a navy suit; Sean, his flaming red hair easily identifiable even in the dim sanctuary. I didn't see Lauren or her mom. I didn't know when to stand and when to kneel, and when I saw Sean's mother glance my way, I understood that my one black dress, bought off the sale rack at JCPenney, was somehow frumpy and slutty at the same time. A woman I didn't recognize was sobbing loudly into a handkerchief. On the way out, I dipped my fingers into the little bowl of water by the front door. I had no idea what it was for, but everybody else seemed to be doing it.

Sean caught up with me on the steps, where I stood wondering if there was some sort of reception I was supposed to go to or if I should just head home. "You showed up," he said, with such undisguised delight in his voice that I began to think this hadn't been such a mistake after all. "She would have been glad you were here," he went on. "Most of these people didn't even know her."

"Really?" I turned to watch the men and women filing out of the church. They were mostly middle-aged white couples, the men in suits, the women wearing silk dresses in black or navy with single-strand pearl necklaces. Some of them stopped to talk to the guy in robes and others with the family, who stood in a cluster at the top of the steps.

"They came for my dad," Sean said. "To impress him or whatever. It's a bunch of bullshit, if you ask me."

He kept a smile on his face, and after a moment of confusion I realized that it was for the benefit of his mother, watching us from the top of the steps. She didn't have Sean's red hair—that came from the Ballard side—but she had the light eyes and square bruiser's chin that gave him that odd air of pugnacious sensitivity. "Well," I said, "you probably have family stuff to do. See you at school."

He nodded as if acknowledging this truth, but when I turned around, he put his hand on my arm. "We're having a Halloween party on Friday," he said. "Up at Bearwallow. Warren and Lauren will be there. I can pick you up if you want."

"No, thanks," I said. "I can get a ride."

At that moment, Warren glanced over and met my eyes. His hair had been slicked flat for the occasion, instead of ruffed up like he wore it at school. His lips were full, with a slight pout that I found irresistible. He grinned and tipped his head toward me before turning away.

Sean didn't seem to have noticed. "Cool," he said, scuffing the concrete step with his heel, a goofy smile twitching at the edge of his mouth. "See you then."

IT WAS MY FIRST REAL HALLOWEEN PARTY. NOT THE KID KIND, WITH BAGS of candy corn and bobbing for apples, but the high school kind, with black eyeliner and fishnet stockings. Jessi and I got ready in her downstairs half-bath, jittery as we slicked our lips with Bonne Bell Lip Smackers, Jessi leaning in to the mirror to spackle a rash of zits with her mother's concealer. We were both dressed as witches, but I was wearing the standard black robe and peaked hat, while Jessi had on a tight black dress with sequins sewn around the low-cut neck. It looked more like an ice-skating outfit than a witch's costume, but I didn't want to be the one to tell her.

At Bearwallow, we parked on the side of a narrow road made muddy by recent rains. I was wearing a coat, but Jessi hadn't wanted to cover her costume, and I could feel her shivering as we walked toward the lights and noise, a bass beat pumping in the background.

We'd gotten a ride from a senior named Luke Barlow, a basketball player who was apparently Jessi's new boyfriend. He'd spent the drive rapping along with a Dr. Dre tape, mean-mugging his own reflection in the rearview. "What if somebody calls the cops?" I whispered.

Luke turned and walked backward. "Cops don't come up here," he said. "They don't mess with the—"

I shrieked as I saw a figure leap into the road behind him. It wasn't shaped like a person; it was wider and taller, and the proportions were all wrong. I heard Jessi scream and tried to echo her, but it was as if my throat had been frozen. Then we heard the laughter. The figure was bent double in the middle of the road, and his head seemed somehow to have slipped to the side.

The boyfriend pulled a flashlight from his jacket pocket and I saw that it was Sean Ballard, wearing a costume that looked like a bunch of twigs and leaves sewn or stapled on black trash bags. "Oh my God, that was the funniest shit I've ever seen," Sean gasped, staggering back. "Luke, you should have seen your face."

"What kind of costume is that?" I asked, trying to steady my quavering voice. Branches formed a kind of wreath around his face, every inch of his body so immersed in foliage that I couldn't imagine how he sat down. "You look like the Green Man."

"What's a Green Man?" he said, still grinning. "I'm a tree."

I couldn't tell from his face that he was drunk, but I could hear it in his voice—a slipshod quality to the vowels. "You're a fucking idiot, Sean," Luke said, his voice still raw with fear. He stalked off toward the noise of the party, and Jessi scurried after him.

Sean and I looked at each other, and suddenly I felt like laughing too. I could see that he'd gone to a lot of trouble. There seemed to be some kind of frame under the plastic to keep it in the right shape. "What's Jessi doing with Luke Barlow?" he asked, using one of the twigs stapled to his arm to scratch his nose. "That guy's a dickhead."

Now that Sean had said it, I felt that I could trust my own judgment: yes, Luke *was* a dickhead. The story was that he had waited for Jessi beside her locker and asked if she wanted to go to McDonald's before he even told her his name, an approach that she'd found thrill-ingly confident but struck me as both arrogant and lazy. "Tell me about it," I said. "He wouldn't even come in to meet her parents."

Sean paused as if he'd considered a reply and then thought better of it. "You want a beer?" he asked, turning back toward the gravel driveway. "This party kind of sucks, I'm not going to lie. Right now it's mostly the football team and the sluts they hang out with." He wet his lips, and I could tell he hadn't missed the flinch that I'd tried to pass off as a shiver. "Sorry," he added immediately. "I didn't mean Lauren, obviously."

"Do you have punch?" I asked. I walked toward the music, Sean moving as close to me as he could without bumping me with his branches.

At the end of the drive, we came in sight of the house, which looked gloomier than I remembered, only a few of the downstairs lights switched on. "There's a pool over there," Sean said, pointing to his right. "Warren told everybody to bring suits, but it's too cold to swim."

I knew before Sean had mentioned it that the boxwood hedge screened a spring-fed pool. I'd longed to swim in it since my mom had first brought me to Bearwallow, but tonight the ice slicks sloshing on the surface weren't the only problem. The pool was filthy. It looked as if people had been throwing in cigarette butts and red Solo cups all night, mingling them with crumbling dead leaves and patches of green algae.

A big guy dressed as a vampire grabbed Sean and pulled off his headdress, tossing it onto a deck chair. "Seaniiiiie," he crooned, rub-bing his knuckles over the top of Sean's head. "Who's this, your new girlfriend? You know she's too hot for you, right?"

Sean tried to push him away but couldn't move him. He was a mountain of a man—tall and sloppy-fat, his stomach straining at the fabric of his black T-shirt. His name was Jason Mack, though everyone called him Truck. I'd heard Stephanie Gilliam say that he'd be cute if he'd lose weight, but I didn't know how she could tell.

Finally he let Sean go and turned to me with a leer that exposed a set of plastic fangs. "Sean's got good taste," he said. "How's it going, *Nicola*?"

He'd read my necklace. I flushed and adjusted my costume, pulling the collar up around my throat. "Aw, don't do that," Jason protested. "It's cute."

"I'm cold." I glanced around for Jessi or Sean, but they had disappeared.

Jason took a step closer. "You know Sean Ballard is a piece of shit," he said. "He'd get his ass stomped on the daily if it weren't for his brother, and you're too pretty to give it away to a freshman. Time to trade up, girl."

"Fuck off, Truck." Sean appeared at my right with his headdress back on and a six-pack of Natural Light under his arm. "Come on," he said to me, "I want to show you something."

I squeezed past Jason and followed Sean into the house, where I stepped nimbly around the furniture, the shapes familiar even in the dark. Sean led me up to the third floor and, at the end of the hall, opened the window onto the gable roof. He stuck one leg out, the plastic rings of the six-pack gripped loosely in his free hand. "What?" he said.

"Nothing," I said, and trailed him out the window. From here we could see down the slope to the glimmering pool. Warren and Lauren were there now, talking to a group of seniors by the diving board. I watched her toss her thick blond hair, a gesture I was sure she'd copied from shampoo commercials.

More guests had arrived, and I could tell that the party was about to take a turn toward mayhem. An hour from now, people would be throwing up in bushes and sneaking into the empty bedrooms. "What would your grandma think about you having people over right after she died?" I asked.

"She wouldn't care," Sean said. "My dad told me she was wild back in the day. She had a bunch of affairs before she married my granddad. Famous politicians and some actor I'd never heard of."

"Oh," I said. I was about to ask for names, but Jason Mack gave a rebel yell down by the pool. He'd pulled off some girl's bikini top and was twirling it above his head.

"Fucking idiot," Sean said. "God, I hate that shit." It wasn't clear to me whether he meant the rebel yell or the sexual harassment, but in either case, he didn't seem to intend to do anything about it.

My mind went back to what Jason had said a few minutes ago: I was too pretty to *give it away,* meaning sex. Why would he assume that Sean and I were sleeping together? Was everybody doing it except me? "Do you think Warren and Lauren are having sex?" I asked, my breath coming out in a thin cloud of smoke.

Sean blushed and took a long swallow. "I mean, I assumed, but Warren wouldn't tell me one way or the other. He's weird about stuff like that."

I angled my knees so I could see him better. The tree costume had been a good choice, I thought. His finely featured face had been made to peek out of that wreath of green brambles. Still, I knew he wouldn't be flattered if I told him he looked like an adorable elf.

He put a hand on my knee, and for a few moments we both stared at it. I'd imagined kissing him before, and in my mind it had always been seamless, melting, like a movie kiss, but it wasn't like that at all. The twigs around his face kept getting in the way, poking me in the eye whenever we tried to find a better angle. His tongue was in all the wrong places, thick and insistent, and finally I used the loud voices coming from the pool as an excuse to pull away. "What's going on down there?" I asked, wiping my mouth discreetly on the back of my hand.

It was Warren and Lauren. Someone had turned off the music, and I wondered if it was on purpose so we could hear them better. As far as I knew, Tyndall County High's golden couple had never had a fight in public before.

"You're making a big deal of nothing," Warren said. He was wearing a Joe Montana jersey that didn't even look like a costume.

"Oh, right, nothing," Lauren scoffed. "You think I'm a damn idiot? She looked like she was about to start licking your face."

Her head swiveled, and it was as if she'd noticed for the first time that they'd drawn a crowd. Most were boys, Warren's friends, and perhaps she sensed, as I did, a barbed edge of hostility in their manner—a distaste for the picture she made at that moment, makeup smeared, hair wild around her face.

"Throw her in and she'll cool off pretty damn quick," Jason Mack called. He was reclining in a pool chair on the other side of the deck, wearing sunglasses and holding a red cup.

"Shut the fuck up," Sean shouted, but nobody even glanced in our direction.

Lauren dropped her head and turned to say something to Warren, and I assumed the drama was over. The hum of voices around the pool swelled, people turning back to their own conversations. Warren was talking to her in a low tone, but Lauren didn't seem to be listening, and suddenly she was pulling her costume over her head. She'd come to the party as a hippie, in a long flowered dress that peeled easily from her thin body. In a moment she'd stripped down to her underwear and was standing on the diving board.

The sight of the most desirable girl in the senior class one thong away from buck-naked made the crowd fall abruptly silent. Her body was perfect by Tyndall County standards, full in the right places and stick-thin everywhere else, but what I saw was her pale skin, probably mottled by goosebumps, and the arrogant smile that tried to hide her chattering teeth.

Warren, who had been standing back as if this scene had nothing to do with him, now stepped forward. "Don't be an idiot," he said. "You're going to freeze your ass off."

Lauren shot him the finger, and the crowd oohed in a tone mingling delight and contempt. She bounced a few times on the balls of her feet, but I thought I saw a flicker of hesitation cross her face. You don't have to go through with it, I thought, just as she gave one more bounce and jumped, her body splitting the layer of ice like a stroke of lightning, like the bravest thing we'd ever seen.

THE PARTY WAS OVER AND EVERYONE KNEW IT. SEAN AND I CLIMBED down from the roof in time to watch Warren carry Lauren into the house, her face pale and waxy as funeral flowers. No one seemed to know if an ambulance had been called, but if the EMTs came, it was likely the police would show up too, despite what Luke had said about the Ballards' special status.

In college, I would see guys do plenty of stupid things at parties—take a sip from the dip cup or run around the room with their dicks flopping like windsocks. I even took some dumb dares myself. Once, after Erika and I had broken up, I folded down the top of my shorts to show a roomful of frat boys the bird tattoo on the back of my hip, and I wondered then if the perverse thrill I felt might be what Lauren had experienced that night at Bearwallow.

With the perspective of distance, all that seemed pathetic to me, the inadvertent exposure of a not so secret willingness to give up self-respect for attention. Like me, Lauren had wanted to turn everybody on and at the same time let them know they couldn't touch her. She'd been just as mixed up as the rest of us, but what impressed me even now was the physical courage it must have taken for her to arrow down into that dirty water, the cold and the shock of it, and how her heart and lungs must have paused before breath flooded into her body.

9

Back then I'd seen only the grand gesture, not the fear and insecurity behind it. No matter how far Lauren went, what chances she took, I found a way to make excuses for her. Even when she hurt other people, I told myself that she was special, Tyndall County's Daisy Buchanan, at once captivating and dangerous. A keen sense of risk management was the price of her company, and it was a price I was willing to pay.

Even when she started in on the underclassmen on the soccer team, I never thought to call it hazing. Hazing was something boys did, in fraternities and in the military. They branded and humiliated the recruits, made them chug ten beers or piss off the back of a pickup truck going thirty miles an hour. Girls weren't like that. Girls had standards, and they helped each other meet those standards. That wasn't hazing. That was mentorship—even, if you looked at it in a certain light, empowerment. At least that was what Lauren said.

At the first practice after the Halloween party, she ordered the freshmen to line up in the locker room so she could inspect our uniforms. "It's my responsibility as team captain," she said primly, and so accustomed was I to falling in line that I didn't object, not even when she told us to roll down the elastic waistband of our shorts and lift our T-shirts up just below our bras.

I'd been on the team for three weeks. I'd made up my mind to go out for soccer after the only gym teacher I'd ever liked, an excessively tanned woman with thick muscled calves and a Northern accent, told me that I had a *natural athleticism*. I'd been the fastest kid in relay races since second grade, and in dodgeball I was always getting in trouble for accidentally throwing the ball too hard and walloping someone in the face, but it had never occurred to my mom to sign me up for extracurriculars, and I probably wouldn't have thought about it myself if Ms. Beale hadn't pulled me aside after class. On the first day of practice, Coach Scott told me not to get my hopes up because freshmen never played in actual games, but he changed his mind after I dribbled past three midfielders and shot up the sideline to score. He gave me a look I would learn to recognize on men's faces—disbelief with a shadow of annoyance, as if, by doing something he hadn't believed I could do, I had somehow offended his pride.

The latch on the window above the lockers was broken, and a gust of cold air raised goosebumps on my bare arms. Lauren didn't seem to notice as she paced the rows. From what I could see, she hadn't suffered any ill effects from her midnight swim. She'd shown up at school today looking perfectly put-together, as usual, and no one dared mention what had happened at Bearwallow.

Suddenly she pointed at a girl named Melissa Green and made a gagging noise. "Oh, *God*," she said to Stephanie, averting her eyes from Melissa's stomach. "It's the Pillsbury Doughboy."

One of the other girls snickered. Melissa's face was red, and the corner of her mouth jerked as if she might cry, but she kept her shirt lifted even when Lauren strolled over and jammed a finger into her belly. Melissa let out a soft *oof*, and one fat tear wobbled down her cheek. I felt sorry for her, but she was the kind of girl who would be mocked by any group she found herself in. Probably she was used to it.

"Ten pounds," Lauren announced, and moved down the line. A girl named Caitlin was told to lose six pounds. Lauren passed by me as if I weren't there and then reached Jessi Westcott, pausing so long that I could tell she, like Melissa, was going to be a target.

It wasn't the first time that Lauren had singled Jessi out. At first I'd thought it was because she was a county kid who lived in a small house so far out in the sticks that she had to get up at six to catch the bus. She wasn't poor, at least not compared to some of the kids out there, but her backpack was the cheap kind from Family Dollar that looked like a pink bag with drawstrings, and her favorite shoes had a hole in the toe that she'd tried to hide with a sticker. I knew from experience that Lauren had an eye for these kinds of details. She always zeroed in on whatever anyone else was at most pains to hide. She wouldn't have cared that Jessi's mother was an Eastern Band Cherokee married to a white man, but she would have known that Luke Barlow had refused to come in and meet Jessi's parents when he picked her up for the Halloween party. She would have known that the kids on the bus called Jessi Squaw and did war whoops when she passed them in the aisle, and she would have filed that away as another possible source of ammunition.

Lauren must have heard the senior boys talking about Jessi the way they talked about all the freshmen—rating between 1 and 10, speculating on who might do what on the first date. From years of sleepovers, I knew that Jessi wore a 34D bra, and because her mom bought her clothes by the bag from Goodwill, her shirts were often a little too small. At fourteen she had the body of a grown woman, and her thick dark hair and strong features made her stand out in a crowd. Once when we'd taken the bus into Charlottesville to shop on the Downtown Mall, a grown man had followed us from store to store, asking Jessi where she was *really* from and telling her she ought to model, he knew some people, she should take his business card and give him a call.

And it wasn't just creepy old men who'd noticed Jessi. Warren Ballard had too. A girl in my geometry class had told me that Jessi was the girl Warren had been talking to at the Halloween party before Lauren lost her shit and jumped into the frozen pool.

Jessi looked at the floor as Lauren took hold of the rind of skin at her waist and squeezed, leaving a bruise that would still be there when we changed for practice the next day. "Fifteen pounds," she said.

Melissa Green quit the team before the end of the week. Caitlin stayed on but said that her parents wouldn't allow her to attend any of the sleepovers or other after-school events. Years later I would look them up online, hoping for reassurance. As far as you could tell from pictures, they seemed to be living happy lives, and I told myself that it was all right; no one had been permanently scarred by what Lauren had done. I didn't know why I cared, but I did.

LAUREN WAS NEVER THE BEST ATHLETE ON THE FIELD, BUT SHE WAS FUN to watch. She'd dive for a ball even when it was clearly a hopeless case. She'd go up against an offensive player twice her size and worry the girl's ankles like a mean lapdog. I suspect that for her, soccer was less about the game than about the chance to fuck up someone's shit in a socially sanctioned manner. She would grab a girl's jersey in her fist and pull, or stick a cleat in somebody's calf if the ref happened to look the other way. Once we were playing six on six and she did it to Jessi, just put her foot out and stuck her and then jogged off the field.

"Foul," I yelled, but it was a breezy afternoon, and the wind seemed to carry my words away. I caught up to Jessi as she hobbled toward the sidelines. "What was that about?"

Jessi winced and leaned a hand on my shoulder while we inspected her leg. I could see the indentation of Lauren's cleat, angry red spots on golden skin. "It's nothing," she said. "It was probably an accident."

I knew it wasn't an accident. As Jessi limped toward the gym, supporting herself on my shoulder, the door to the weight room banged against the brick wall and the football team trotted out. Sean was first in line and waved his helmet at me as he passed. Behind him was Warren. He winked at Jessi and she looked right through him, waiting until he was out of sight before grabbing my hand and squeezing so hard that my knuckles ached.

"What are you doing?" I said, looking over my shoulder to make sure Lauren hadn't seen. "Are you fucking suicidal?"

I wasn't jealous, or if I was, it was only in the down-deep achy way that I'd learned to tolerate as a condition of existence. Far more pressing was my concern for Jessi's mental health. Anybody with a quarter of a brain knew better than to flirt with Lauren's boyfriend.

But Jessi turned on me fiercely, mouth set and thick eyebrows drawn together. "How is it my fault if some guy decides to wink at me? Jesus Christ, Nicola. And you call yourself a feminist."

She was right: as far as I knew, Jessi had done exactly nothing to seek out the attention from Warren. She'd told me that she was sitting alone on the lawn at the Halloween party when he came up to ask if she wanted a beer. They chatted for a few minutes about our history teacher, whom Warren said could be easily distracted from the lesson if you asked him about his days working as a roadie for a hippie band called Bad Habit. That was it, and she had no idea how a harmless five-minute conversation could twist Lauren's panties in such a bunch that she was ready to start World War III.

Then somebody left a half-eaten tuna sandwich in Jessi's locker over the weekend. Someone egged her parents' house late on a Saturday night. Finally I talked to Sean about it. I thought maybe he could intervene and tell Warren to stop winking and smiling at random freshmen, but Sean said he was going to stay the hell away from that one. "Tell Jessi to stand up for herself," he said. "It's not hard. I don't know why everybody talks about Lauren like she's the Great and Powerful Oz."

AT THE TEAM SLEEPOVER, STEPHANIE TOLD US THAT HER DAD WAS THE volunteer prop master for the Tyndall County Opera Society. "It's not a real opera company," she explained, shrugging. "They just pay people to come down here and do a one-night performance. But that's why we have all this crap in our basement." She waved at the boxes set against the basement wall, spilling a froth of lace masks and pirate hats. That spring, the society was doing *Naughty Marietta*, which Lauren said sounded like a porno. She clapped a pirate hat on her head and dangled a plastic sword between her legs, waggling it lewdly.

The sleepover had turned out to be just Lauren and Stephanie and the freshmen. The rest of the upperclassmen had stayed away, and I'd wondered if they knew something that I didn't, but so far not much had happened. A carful of boys had pulled into the driveway and yelled for a while, but after Stephanie had gone out to talk to them, they'd driven away. We ordered pizza (none of the freshmen dared to eat more than a slice) and watched *Jeopardy!*, which I knew was Lauren's favorite show. She was good at it, shouting out answers before I could be sure I'd understood the question. By the time Vicky Marshall found the boxes of costumes from the opera, I'd actually started to relax.

Lauren pulled a long gold scarf from the box and made an *ooh* sound. "You could tie it around your tits and do a striptease for Jason," she said to Stephanie.

Stephanie studied the scarf critically. "It's too thin," she said. Then her face lit up, and she cupped her hand around Lauren's ear.

The scarf had dropped to the floor, and I longed with every bone in my body to pick it up. It was real silk, you could tell—a deep rich gold with spangles cascading along the hem. I wanted to lay my cheek against it, as I used to with department store lingerie when I was too little to be left alone in the car. Once, while my mom was looking at shoes, I'd crawled into a circular display of satin slips, where I'd rubbed them against my skin and put my thumb in my mouth. The next thing I knew, a man in a uniform was pulling me out and handing me to my mom, whose face was white as the slips. I expected her to start yelling as soon as we were out of the store, but she didn't. She cried all the way home, in that snuffly way grown-ups do when they don't want you to know they're crying.

When Lauren wrapped the gold scarf over my eyes, I found my anxiety mixed with a strange kind of gratification. The fabric was as soft as I'd predicted, and I couldn't help feeling lucky. Surely the other girls coveted it as much as I did.

When we were blindfolded, the lights began to flicker. "New girls," screeched a voice that I was pretty sure belonged to Stephanie. "It's time for you to experience the ancient initiation rite of our tribe. After tonight, we will be sisters in the truest sense of the word. Drink now from the cup of friendship."

My heart beat faster. Lauren and Stephanie would get us drunk, and then what? Would the boys come back? I thought I heard footsteps, and I imagined that they were already here—Warren, Sean, Jason Mack, snickering and pointing. What if we were made to take off our clothes and the boy gave us a thumbs-up or thumbs-down? Jessi was the prettiest, if a little too skinny now that she'd dropped over half the pounds Lauren had told her to lose. I couldn't compete with her, but I thought I would probably come out better than Charity Gross, who had knock-knees and thick thighs.

The lights continued to flicker, and I smelled melted candles. When someone put a hand on my shoulder, I jerked, already antici-pating the sting of hot wax on my skin. Instead they put a cup to my mouth, pressing it hard against my teeth.

I was so prepared for the taste of alcohol that at first I convinced myself that this was whiskey—first the burn, and then the sour wash of acid. But the inside of my mouth tasted salty and sharp, almost like seawater, and for a brief second I thought they had handed me a cup of pee until I realized a seed had lodged between my teeth. As I worked at it with the tip of my tongue, I identified the taste: pickle juice.

"New girls, you have each tasted of the cup of sisterhood." Stephanie had begun in her normal voice, but then she remembered and switched back to the high-pitched screech. "Stay in this sacred space and medi-tate on the privilege of membership."

The phrase *the privilege of membership* sounded familiar, and finally I figured it out: it was the inverse of the American Express slogan, *Membership has its privileges*. The tension in my shoulders eased. This was an improvisation, not part of some grand plan to mortify us before an audience.

"You forgot something," Lauren said. What could she have planned for us now? I wondered. Maybe we would be pushed outside blind-folded. At least it wasn't cold.

Suddenly I felt hands cup my shoulders. "Receive the kiss of sisterhood," she whispered.

Her lips were smooth and a little tacky, as if she'd just put on ChapStick. I was too shocked to pull away. I felt her tongue prodding at my lips, and I kept them clamped tightly together. She tried once or twice more, then patted my shoulders briskly and moved away.

I strained my ears to listen as the procedure was repeated on Jessi and Charity. What did the pat mean? Had the whole thing been some kind of test? Was I supposed to open my mouth or wasn't I?

One thing was clear: Lauren was not worried about what we could do to her. She must have considered the possibility that one or all of us would talk about what she did, and—either because she planned to deny it or because she felt immune from scandal—she simply didn't care. She could call Erika Callaghan a fuzz bumper just for wearing an Indigo Girls T-shirt, but no one would ever call Lauren a name like that, no matter what she did.

Or perhaps, I thought, she somehow knew that we would never have the courage to tell anyone about the kiss, each of us trapped forever in the privacy of that moment. If that was what she'd counted on, she'd guessed right. I never even knew if the other girls had opened their mouths.

10

That night in Stephanie's basement wasn't the first time I'd kissed a girl.

It started in fourth grade, not long after Jessi and I became friends. We'd found a *Cosmopolitan* magazine in her mother's dresser drawer, and Jessi decided she wanted to try out the four kinds of kissing described in an article titled "Exercise Your Tongue." We left the magazine open on the side of her bed while we got into position, facing each other with our legs wide and Jessi's knees hooked over mine. She put her hands on my shoulders, leaned in, and I felt her lips—soft at first, like kissing the inside of your own wrist.

We had no idea what we were doing. My Baptist upbringing had led me to think that kissing girls was even worse than reading horoscopes, but I reasoned that practicing for kissing a boy probably didn't count. By the time we finished, the collars of our shirts were wet with spit, the corners of my lips so chapped they stung. "Maybe it's different with a guy," Jessi said, smoothing out the magazine.

After the disaster of that first attempt, I didn't think she'd want to try again, but for the next few years, nearly every time I spent the night at her house, I'd roll over in the night to find Jessi's face inches from mine, eyes shining in the dark. I told myself that I'd wait for her to move, but usually I was the one who bridged the distance between our pillows and pressed my lips to hers. We never did anything but kiss. We angled our hips away like partners at a middle school dance, as if we'd agreed that what we were doing didn't count if no other part of our bodies made contact.

Years later, when Erika asked if I'd made out with a girl before, I never mentioned Jessi. I had known even at the time that she kissed me for research purposes, not for fun, and if I felt more than that, I knew better than to ever let her guess.

ALL THROUGH FRESHMAN YEAR, I'D SOMETIMES CATCH A GLIMPSE OF Warren and Jessi together, talking outside the library or at the door to the senior parking lot. Jessi told me that she was only being nice. He kept coming up to her, she said, and what was she supposed to do, tell him to fuck off? It had been months since anyone had locked her in the girls' bathroom or left a bag of dog shit on her doorstep. Lauren was probably over it, anyway.

By then spring had come, and the picnic table where we waited for practice to start was in a strip of shade that seemed to get narrower by the minute. When I tried to look out into the parking lot, the sun off the asphalt dazzled my eyes.

Jessi was picking at the outside of a banana as if she had no intention of actually eating it. Lauren had spread out a magazine flat on the table, and I could see the pictures upside down if I craned my neck. In one, a guy seemed to have been surprised by the camera in the act of removing his button-down shirt. Another stared at the viewer with a startled look, a flat palm pressed to the plane of his stomach.

"Oh my God, what *is* that?" Jessi said, poking me with her elbow as she leaned closer. She'd tried to Nair off the light brown hair on her arms after Lauren had made fun of it, and now the skin was peeling off in patches, the space between stippled with pink blisters. Today, though it was nearly eighty, she'd worn the long-sleeved soccer jersey.

"It's Coach Scott's," Lauren said. "I found it on his dashboard."

"Really?" Jessi giggled.

"No, sweetheart, I bought it," Lauren said, looking at me as if she wondered how Jessi put on her pants in the morning. "I was curious. I'd never seen a *Playgirl.*"

She flipped the page, and I studied the upside-down form of a man leaning against a brick wall, jeans unbuttoned and folded to show the dark triangle of hair below his navel. I was troubled by how little I felt when I looked at those pictures. I might as well have been looking at a display of soup cans in the grocery store. Shouldn't I have been turned on, even a little bit?

The door behind us crashed open, and four boys in workout clothes jostled out. Warren was one of them, and I watched Lauren pretend not to notice until he'd come up behind her and planted a kiss on the back of her neck. She flipped the magazine shut and slipped it onto her lap.

"We're going to McDonald's," Warren said into Lauren's ear. "Come with us."

"You know I can't," Lauren said with a pout, but the next moment, Warren whispered something in her ear that made her cheeks turn pink with pleasure.

I felt it now—that thing I'd been waiting to feel when I looked at the *Playgirl.* It was the boys, the smell of them, the sweat in the crease of their necks. Or not the boys, plural; it was one boy, Warren. He sat down with one leg on each side of the bench and slid his arms around Lauren's waist, and I realized with a feeling of recognition that I wanted him to do the same to me. I wanted him to take my hips in his hands and move me like a doll. I wanted to lean back against his chest and feel his stubble against my skin as he kissed my neck. I couldn't look at his face straight on, so I looked at other parts instead: the coarse hair on the backs of his wrists, which no one would ever tell him to remove. His lips, full and soft. I felt something twist in the pit of my stomach.

I've always believed that Warren must have sensed what I was feeling that day. I was sure he'd somehow picked up on the heat he'd generated in me, and that was the reason, as he stood up to follow his friends, he looked at the rest of us for the first time.

Jessi looked beautiful, as usual. The humidity that had made me sweaty and cranky had left her dewy and glowing. Lauren had been following the direction of Warren's eyes, but at first she showed no reaction beyond a slight thinning of her lips. She waited until the boys had climbed into Jason's black Lexus before she turned to me and said, "Nicola, lie down on the grass."

"What?" I said, stalling.

"Be a darling and lie down in the grass," she repeated. "I have an idea for a photo."

She was the candids editor for the school yearbook, so I did what she said. She took a camera out of her bag and began giving directions: put your arms behind your head; look like this; no, not like that, like this. I felt awkward and stiff, but when she lowered the camera, she looked pleased. "Amazing," she said. "You look like you're about to give the world's best blow job."

Jessi shrieked with laughter, and I cringed. "What's so funny?" Lauren asked, flipping her hair over her shoulder. "Haven't you ever sucked dick before?" Before Jessi could answer, Lauren grabbed the banana from the picnic table and held it out to her. "Here. Show me how it's done."

Jessi slid a few inches down the bench. "I haven't," she said. "I haven't ever done that."

"Bless your heart," Lauren said. "Then show me how you *would* do it."

I sat up, pushing the hair out of my eyes. "Stop it, Lauren."

She gave me a look of bland disinterest before turning back to Jessi. "Peeled or unpeeled. Your choice," she said, waggling the banana at her again.

Jessi took the banana, her mouth widened as if she were trying to avoid touching it with her lips. I heard Lauren's camera click, but then Coach Scott's green Subaru pulled into the place vacated by the Lexus, and I sighed with relief. Lauren turned away from Jessi and moved closer, taking one more shot of me leaning back on my elbows in the grass. "I love how mad you look right now," she said. "Like you're fixing to get up and punch me in the face."

BUT I DIDN'T PUNCH HER IN THE FACE. I'D ALWAYS BEEN ABLE TO PUSH THE boundaries with Lauren, but I never flat-out said no to her. If I did, she might tell everyone I smelled like fish, like she'd done to Olivia Novak when Olivia challenged her for captain. She might plant a dime bag in my locker and get me kicked off the team. I knew she was capable of all that and more, and the fact that I couldn't be sure what my punishment would be only gave her more power.

Two weeks after the banana incident, we were on the bus coming back from a game. We'd won, and it hadn't been easy; Galloway Christian played dirty, and Joelle Hancock, our best midfielder, was home with the flu. I could feel a new bruise developing at the side of my ribs, and I kept touching it secretly, prolonging the ache.

Lauren and Stephanie were whispering at the front of the bus. Jessi was asleep in the row behind, head tilted back. From across the aisle, all I could see was her throat, the skin shining as we passed by a row of neon signs. It was like the cover of a vampire novel, the swooning victim languishing in Dracula's arms.

In the ghostly light of the emergency exits, I saw Lauren lean over the back of her seat and poke Jessi on the shoulder until she started up, head jolting forward. "Hey, Westcott," Lauren whispered. "I showed Jason those pictures I took of you, and he was really impressed by your skills. He said Luke told him that you were very talented with, you know—*bananas*."

Jessi turned and met my eyes, but I made my face blank. I had already tried to save her once, and it hadn't done any good. What was the point of stepping in now? "Do you know about the party up at Bearwallow on Saturday?" Lauren asked.

Jessi nodded cautiously. The party was for the boys' basketball team, who had made it to the state semifinals. So had the girls, as it happened, but the party was not for them. "I was thinking that you could do a little demo," Lauren said. "For everybody who didn't get to see you on the banana. Jason volunteered to be the test subject. We think it would be instructive."

Jessi looked dazed. The side of her mouth was shiny with drool, and I wondered if she understood that Lauren had just made a plan for her to blow Jason Mack at a party in front of everybody. "He's really into you. Like for real," Lauren said, and Jessi whispered, "Okay."

I caught up with Jessi as we lugged our gear into the locker room. "You can't go to that party," I said.

"I don't think she means it," she said, her voice muffled by the hair falling over her face.

"Yes, she does," I insisted. "Tell her you're grounded or something."

"I don't know." Jessi hitched her duffel on her shoulder. "I feel like that would just make her mad."

I could already see how this would go: Jessi would wait at the end of the driveway for Lauren, standing alone under the dark waving pines by the Westcotts' mailbox. She would travel obediently to the party, where, if she was not forced to do what had been described on the bus, some alternate penalty would be exacted for being the prettiest and weakest girl within Lauren's reach. To make it stop, all Jessi had to do was refuse, but she didn't know how.

I'd been making excuses for Lauren for months—years, probably— but all that was over now. My mom had always told me that I could do anything I set my mind to, and for the first time I believed that she was right. If Lauren could come up with a devious plan to administer the public humiliation of someone she hated, then surely I could do the same.

11

The plan to save Jessi from having to blow Jason Mack came to me while I was setting the table. I'd been worrying over it for two days, trying to figure out how I could strike back without drawing Lauren's attention to me. I considered putting a block of the stinky blue cheese my mom loved in Lauren's duffel, but that was kid stuff. I had to hit her hard enough that she wouldn't have the time or energy to worry about who was responsible. Whatever I did, it had to be big.

I was setting out the knives and forks when Mom brought in the dish of Stouffer's lasagna and laid it on the threadbare tablecloth. "Are you going to your women's group on Thursday?" I asked.

She made a face. We'd attended First Baptist Church my whole life, but my mom had never been a joiner, and we'd never been involved in what the pastor called *the life of the church* until this year, when she'd been drafted as the notetaker for the biweekly women's prayer group. She complained about it every time but always came back in a better mood, usually with half a box of leftover doughnuts. "I guess I don't have a choice," she said. "Can you get your own dinner that night?"

"Of course I can." She hadn't asked me what I was doing, and that meant I didn't have to lie. The idea of lying to my mother terrified me, not only because I had rarely done it, but because she was so good at seeing through me.

Even now, she seemed to sense something. "You're a good girl," she said. "I worry sometimes that people might take advantage of you, but I'm glad you've got such a sweet nature. You don't know how it eases my mind to know that I can trust you."

I took time unfolding my napkin so I wouldn't have to look at her. I didn't need to feel guilty, I told myself. What she'd said was true. I *was* a good girl.

THE WOMEN'S PRAYER GROUP ALWAYS ENDED BY TEN O'CLOCK AT THE latest, so I'd need to be back by nine thirty. As soon as I saw my mom's car turn at the corner of our street, I put on dark sweatpants and a sweatshirt with my oldest pair of sneakers, wound my hair in a tight bun, and stuffed it under a baseball cap. I took two cans of black spray paint I'd found in the garage, left over from when my mom tried to smarten up some lawn furniture.

But my plan to break into the school had some holes in it. For instance, I hadn't thought about how I'd get up to the broken window in the first place. In my imagination, the plan had started with me ninja-ing into the girls' locker room, but I hadn't considered the fact that the window was at least seven feet off the ground, while I was only five-five.

Luck was with me: I found an oil barrel that had been used as a trash can beside a bench dedicated to the class of 1979. The barrel was empty and smelled of ketchup and fermented grape juice. As I upended it below the window, I felt a jagged piece sticking up from the rim scrape along my palm. I stopped to suck the warm blood that tasted like metal, wondering if I'd just given myself tetanus.

The tennis courts along the west side of the school provided enough ambient light for me to get a good look at the locker room window, which had been left cracked, the broken hasp dangling uselessly. I held my breath as I used both hands to shove the window open as far as it would go, then pushed my backpack through the opening and heard it thump to the floor. Now all I had to do was lift myself on the ledge and turn my body so I could slide in feetfirst. "Okay," I whispered, but as I pushed up, my right foot slipped and banged against the top of the oil barrel, and it rolled onto its side with a clatter that seemed to echo in the still night.

Bent double on the windowsill, I braced myself for the sound of alarms and sirens. Maybe I could call it off and run home. But my backpack was already inside, with my name written in black Sharpie on the tag. Being generally known as a rule follower and straight-A student gave me a lot of leeway with the teachers and administrators, but there was no way I could explain a backpack full of spray paint lying on the floor of the girls' locker room.

I took a deep breath and let my body drop. For a moment I felt like I was falling into nothing, but then I landed in a crouch, feeling the impact in the soles of my feet.

Coach Scott had told us to put padlocks on our lockers, but few people actually listened. No one kept anything of value in the locker room, and what was the point in locking away a mismatched sock, a dirty sports bra, and half a stick of caked Secret deodorant? I retrieved my flashlight from the backpack and walked among the rows, stopping to pocket half a pack of Ice Breakers from Joelle Hancock's locker and a glittery pink barrette from Katie Rush's. This must be what it was like to be a grown-up, I thought. As long as nobody was looking, you could do whatever you wanted.

Lauren's locker was the last in the second row. She had a padlock, but I knew she never locked it; probably she'd forgotten the combination. I plunged my hand into the darkness of the top shelf, feeling for the pictures I'd seen her stuff in there last week. Panic surged in my chest, but then I straightened my elbow, and my fingertips brushed against the crease of the Moto Photo envelope shoved under an empty CD sleeve. Here were the images that Lauren had talked about on the bus: Jessi with her mouth around the tip of the banana, her forehead beaded with sweat that could have been from heat or mortification. I was in the background, my blurred face blank as a plate.

As much as I hated Lauren when I looked at those pictures, I hated myself more. For not speaking up. For believing that eventually she would move on to tormenting someone else and the whole thing would just go away.

There were six copies in all. If I put up just one, it was likely that a teacher or a janitor would get to it before gossip spread, but chances were good that they wouldn't find all six. Besides, I had the spray paint.

The school at night was like a place in a nightmare, familiar and yet wholly strange. Light through the big windows made yellow pools on the floor, and computers glowed behind frosted glass windows. The smells I inhaled every day without noticing were now unavoidable—disinfectant, sweat, sour milk, and the cigarettes the rednecks smoked outside the double doors, with a slight tinge of the sawdust the janitor threw down when somebody puked. The floors were smeared with black shoeprints, the walls of the stairwell scribbled over with misspelled graffiti. *Lindsay Howell is A Hoe. I fucked youre mom.*

I tacked one of Jessi's pictures to the bulletin board outside the French and Spanish classrooms, and another outside the teachers' lounge, under a poster of a cat in a tree that said, *Hang In There!* Things were going so well that I felt myself begin to relax. As long as I was out of here by nine fifteen, I had free rein. I could check all the lockers to see who hadn't bothered to spin the combination lock. I could sneak into Mrs. Morris's classroom and find out once and for all whether she really kept a whiskey flask in the top drawer of her desk.

I was crossing the front hall when the wall above my head lit up with the sweep of headlights. I froze and then hit the floor.

The lights steadied on the trophy case, and I heard the slam of a car door. I crab-crawled toward the safety of the dark hallway and made it just in time, looking back to see a man's face pressed to the glass. His uniform didn't look right for police, so likely he was a security guard hired to make a circuit around the school every few hours.

If I heard the key in the lock, I'd have about five seconds to get to the emergency exit by the art room. My fingers curled around the strap of my backpack, breath shallow in my chest. I heard a noise and my whole body tensed, but it wasn't the key; he was just jiggling the door handles. Then I heard footsteps moving away, and a few moments later the headlights swung around the circular drive.

I dropped my head back against the lockers. Sweat slicked the skin of my ribcage, my palms, even my neck. I had escaped through bare luck, and I realized now just how stupid the plan had been from the beginning.

There was no way I was sticking around to poke through the classrooms and offices. I tacked up the last photos on the closest bulletin boards and then circled back to Jessi's locker, where I uncapped the paint can and shook it the way I'd seen my mom do, listening to the rattle. My thumb hit the button, and I felt something wet seep through the toe of my shoe.

I looked down, incredulous. The spray paint had stained the top of my right sneaker and the skin up to the ankle. My heart was pounding again, but I had to be out of here in fifteen minutes; I didn't have time to worry about my shoe. I printed the word *SLUT* in a vertical line down Jessi's locker, then added an exclamation point for good measure:

S

L

U

T

!

It wasn't enough. I had to do something with the energy buzzing through me, so I aimed a roundhouse kick at the *U* in *SLUT*. It felt so good that I kicked again and again, the impact traveling through my body as my heel slammed into the metal. I stopped only when I'd done so much damage that I worried the word wouldn't be readable anymore. I thought of what Lauren had said when she took the picture of me lying on my back in the grass. All this time, I really *had* wanted to punch someone in the face.

AT HOME, I SCRUBBED THE STAINED SKIN OF MY FOOT WITH AN OLD WASH-cloth before wrapping the shoes, the washcloth, and the cans of spray paint in a plastic bag and carrying them out to the trash can at the curb. A few days later, when my mom asked what had happened to my old sneakers, I said I'd lost them. She gave me a look but didn't press it.

By then the fallout was mostly over, both what I'd anticipated and what I never could have predicted. Teachers found and removed several of the photos before school began, but they didn't get them all, and they couldn't do anything about Jessi's locker. That afternoon, the principal called everyone to the gym for an assembly, where he ranted in red-faced fury about lack of respect for other people's property. It was clear that the administration was mad not about the insult to Jessi but about the damage to the school. Girls had been called sluts before and would be called sluts again, but those lockers were supposed to last twenty years.

I poked my tongue into the side of my cheek, tasting blood. A girl I barely knew was whispering rumors in my ear, and it took all my concentration to gasp in the right places. I kept my shoes tucked under my seat on the bleachers, as if someone might see through the leather to the faint black stain marking the skin of my foot.

THERE WERE A LOT OF THINGS I'D NEVER THOUGHT ABOUT—THE NIGHT janitor, for instance. According to the paper, I'd missed him by about twenty minutes, which explained the smell of disinfectant. I also hadn't known that the school had installed surveillance cameras the year before, though luckily they weren't turned on that night. The assistant principal who was in charge of changing the tapes received a formal reprimand, as did the maintenance staff who had never repaired the broken window in the girls' locker room. The security guard I'd seen shaking the door handles was fired, since it turned out that he was supposed to walk through the school and not just check the outside.

His name was Michael Michaels, and years later I'd try to look him up online. On Facebook, I found a Mike Michaels who worked for a construction company in Lynchburg. His profile picture showed a grinning man with a big belly giving a thumbs-up from a tube on the James River. Good, I thought. That was one person's life I hadn't ruined.

JESSI WESTCOTT LEFT SCHOOL AT NOON ON THE DAY THE PICTURES WERE discovered and never came back. I realized then what an idiot I'd been to imagine that my classmates would jump straight to speculating about the culprit. They didn't give a shit who had done it, at least not at first. All they cared about was that Jessi was an all-caps slut who could probably deep-throat an entire banana. In trying to fix Jessi's Lauren problem, I had made her life appreciably worse.

By the end of the week, rumors far exceeded the facts. Jessi had done a train with the football team. She'd sucked off Coach Scott in the back of the bus before the game against Ewald. Everyone knew that Lauren and Stephanie had been called into the principal's office several times in the days following the incident, and so people went to them for the truth of the rumors. Stephanie said that she hadn't done anything and didn't know anything, but Lauren sailed through the crowds with her usual above-it-all look, neither confirming nor denying.

Then I was called into the office, along with Charity Gross. Charity told them almost everything—about the uniform inspections and the bullying and the plans for the Bearwallow party, though not about the kissing at Stephanie's sleepover. "Now, I know y'all understand how serious this is," the principal said, leaning back and folding his hands behind his head. "These are real crimes we're talking about. So if something comes to you that you think might be important, you come straight to me, hear?"

I felt like throwing up, and it wasn't just because leaning back made Principal Lee's too-tight pants bunch up around his crotch. What I'd thought of as a silly prank was being referred to as a crime, or *crimes* plural: vandalism, harassment. It was known that the Gilliams had hired a lawyer. What if Stephanie and Lauren went to jail?

On the way out, Charity chattered while I kept my eyes on the floor. "I tried to call Jessi, but her mom said she wasn't up to talking. I think that just makes it worse, don't you? You can't stay home forever." At the end of the hall, she turned right, toward biology, but I kept going, right out the double doors. "Hey!" I heard her yell, but I didn't turn around.

It was the first and only time I skipped school. I walked all the way to the park, where I found an oak tree out of sight of the paved paths and made daisy chains until I checked my watch and saw that it was safe to go home.

I didn't get in trouble for leaving that day, and as far as I knew, no one even called my mom. My family might have been one step above trailer trash, but I had big eyes in a baby face, and I'd gotten perfect grades all my life except for that one B+ in world history. I probably could have burned down the school and stood outside with an empty gas can in my hand, and everyone would have pointed at someone else—some girl marked out for bad luck from birth, like Jessi Westcott.

Lauren had been protected too, in her case by wealth and her own natural-born sense of authority, but now the school could smell blood in the water. At first it was just the expected whispers: had she done it, or did she know who had? Then a rumor went around that she and Warren had broken up, and the gossip turned vicious. They said that UVA had rescinded Lauren's acceptance. They said that Lauren and Stephanie had gone after Jessi because she'd refused to take part in a three-way. A boy in my geometry class swore up and down that he'd seen them making out at a party, and I wondered if it might be true, thinking of the sleepover, Lauren's tongue probing insistently at the seal of my lips.

It turned out that the whispers about UVA were true as well, or at least partially true: Lauren had been dropped from contention for the Jefferson Scholars program. She could have enrolled anyway and paid tuition—surely Susan could afford it—but the next I heard, she had decided to go to Burwell College instead. For a while it looked as if Stephanie's admittance to William & Mary was also in peril, but the Gilliams pulled some strings—if the rumors were accurate, it involved both the threat to sue and a sizable donation to the capital campaign—and after that, things settled down.

In Tyndall, everything went back to normal, sort of. I tried to forget what I'd done, but I knew I was responsible for everything that followed. If Lauren had gone to UVA like she'd planned, she might have met someone else—some prep-school finance major from Greenwich, Connecticut, who would make Warren Ballard look like the small-pond big fish he was. Then she wouldn't have been at the house on Blue Ridge Road when things went to shit, and now Warren would not have to wonder, daily, if his vanished wife was sunk in a bag at the bottom of a river, stuffed in a barrel at the dump, buried in the woods under a layer of pine duff. Lauren's mother would not have to rewind mental pictures of her daughter suffering, at the mercy of a psychopath to whom the life inside her meant nothing more than the air inside a balloon.

Had Dale Westcott been that psychopath? Was he the ruthless killer the police believed him to be? I didn't know the answer, but I did know one thing: if he'd killed Lauren, it was what I'd done to Jessi that had set it in motion. Lauren keying his son's truck had dug into the old wound and he'd struck out, and that meant the whole thing was my fault. It was no wonder that now that I'd come back to Tyndall, I found it impossible to move beyond the dramas and heart-breaks of those years. I had made Lauren's death possible, and I'd be paying homage to her memory every day, every hour, for the rest of my goddamn life.

12

On the morning of my thirty-seventh birthday, I woke with the worst hangover I'd had in years, the bottle of Malbec I'd killed before bed rolled over on the floor beside my futon mattress. I'd poured the last glass hoping that it would help me get to sleep, but now I was sure it had made my sleep worse, restless and crowded. I'd had nightmares, confusing ones—heavy rain pounding the roof of a car that wouldn't start; a child backed into the corner of an empty room, screaming with terror. The floor was sticky with wine and the remains of the tomato I'd eaten for dinner, juice and seeds dried in a pattern like blood spatters.

I was painting the bedrooms that week, so I'd moved everything I needed to survive into the den. I kept the books I'd stolen from the library at my last teaching job in a stack under the window, and since the kitchen was also out of commission, I kept a Yeti cooler with microwave pizzas and individual packs of tuna salad beside my bed. I was embarrassed to buy my sad dinners at the local Kroger now that I'd realized one of my students, Malik Walker, worked there after school, so I drove twenty miles down the road to buy them from the IGA in Marlborough Springs instead.

I'd planned to clean out my mom's room today, but I couldn't make myself get up. When twenty minutes of staring at the dust motes floating in the light that fell through the slatted blinds did nothing to improve my state of mind, I grabbed my phone and opened Instagram. I had a few birthday messages from former students and out-of-state friends, but I didn't respond, instead mindlessly scrolling past books arranged by spine color and beautiful women in iridescent yoga pants doing splits by the rim of the Grand Canyon. One of my favorite podcasts had posted a new episode on the case of Christelle Varner and Monique Brown, and I clicked the play button, half listening to the tink-tink of the weirdly cheerful intro music.

I knew the details of the story by heart. After high school, Christelle had gone to work for her family's roofing business while Monique took a job at a local nursing home. One night they made plans to meet friends at a party but never showed up. The next day, Christelle's red Honda was spotted in the lot at Walmart, and Monique's house key was found stuck in the lock of her front door. Theories ranged from them running off together to a drug deal gone bad.

They were presumed dead when, ten years after their disappearance, a woman walking down the sidewalk in a rundown part of town saw an arm reaching through a hole in a window blocked by plywood. It was Christelle. She and Monique had been held captive in that house for the past ten years by a man named Larry Graves, who'd worked as a custodian at Monique's church. In that time, both Christelle and Monique had given birth to children, who were found with them, malnourished and traumatized but alive. The women said they had kept each other going by telling stories of the old world: Thanksgivings and Sunday barbecues and eating Popsicles on the front porch. I'd seen clips from a news conference they'd given a couple of days later. Though their answers were composed, their eyes were as wide and frozen as the eyes of flushed deer.

Cases like that were anomalies, I reminded myself. Kidnapping victims had a short shelf life; statistics told us that if they weren't found within forty-eight hours, they were likely dead. Would it be a blessing or a catastrophe if Lauren turned out to be one of the exceptions, kept locked in a room for sixteen years, starved and beaten and chained to a wall? How did a victim who had survived that sort of scarifying torture ever reenter the world?

But aside from the statistics, there were differences in the cases that made it unlikely Lauren had suffered the same fate. Christelle and Monique were Black women in a town with a police department under investigation by the state. The detective quickly labeled them missing by choice and never even bothered impounding Christelle's Honda. Within three years, the DA would be disbarred for destroying evidence and the sheriff indicted for taking bribes. Neither the disappearances nor the corruption in the police department had been national news stories. Christelle and Monique were just ordinary women, whose sudden vanishing meant little outside their own communities. In a society where even crime victims were judged by race, socioeconomic status, and perceived attractiveness, they weren't the kind of victims who grabbed headlines.

But Lauren was, or could have been. In the hierarchy of missing women, she could have been one of the favored few—photogenic and upper-middle-class, as easy to love and to resent as all the other girls who briefly obsessed the national consciousness. But she'd disappeared shortly before 9/11, and her case was overshadowed by the massive impact of that event. Beyond that, the Ballards had leveraged their influence to keep Warren's name out of any local coverage except as a grieving spouse. Dale Westcott's connection to Lauren was too tenuous to make him a juicy suspect, and none of the rumors about a stranger abduction had ever panned out. Still, I had to wonder how things might have been different if Lauren had been like those other girls, plastered on the cover of *People* magazine for weeks at a time.

I opened Reddit and browsed a few threads on unsolved cases before clicking on r/LaurenBallardDisappearance, surprised to see a few new comments after nearly four months of inactivity:

TENDER_MEDUSA
Do y'all realize that a little girl went missing the year before Lauren

Ballard about ten miles away and there's not a single post about her
on here? Just another case of Missing White Woman Syndrome smh.

BLUEFOOT1092
I hate it when people say shit like that. Like nobody should be looking
for white people? How is interest in Lauren's case taking away from
that girl?

TENDER_MEDUSA
https://en.m.wikipedia.org/wiki/Missing_white_woman_syndrome

I knew before I read any further what the original poster was
referencing: the disappearance of Opal Yarrow from Ewald County.
Opal, an eight-year-old Black girl, had been playing hide-and-seek
with her twin sister when she ran down the road behind her parents'
house and disappeared. Over the years I'd gone back and pored over
every article from the local paper for the slightest suggestion that her
disappearance might have been related to Lauren's. The victims were
different enough that it seemed unlikely that a serial killer would go
after them both, but it wasn't impossible. I'd read about a rapist in
Florida who had attacked first a fifteen-year-old girl and then a sixty-
three-year-old grandmother coming home from her job at the post
office. Some criminals were opportunists for whom chance loomed
larger than any other consideration.

I thought about responding to the thread, but I didn't have anything
to say except that the original poster was right. Lauren's case hadn't
received anywhere near as much media focus as the women who were
usually cited as examples of Missing White Woman Syndrome—Maura
Murray, Kristen Modafferi, Jennifer Kesse—but she'd still gotten more
coverage than Opal Yarrow.

I closed the browser and tried to burrow into the covers. Other true-
crime junkies might drop into the thread now and then to speculate on
where her body had ended up, but the only obsessive on the scene was
me, stuck on the events of August 10, 2001, turning them over and over
in my mind. I wanted to see Lauren's life and disappearance laid out in
a narrative sequence that depended on causality rather than recursion. I

wanted someone to make sense of her life and, by extension, make sense of mine.

WARREN HAD TOLD ME TO BE THERE AT FIVE, BUT WHEN I ARRIVED, I couldn't find him. Though his car was in the driveway, there was no answer to my knock, and finally I walked around back to his workshop. He was standing by the space heater, sanding a long, slender piece of wood. "What's that for?" I asked, flopping into the plaid armchair that he'd told me he'd moved out there just for me.

"That house on Rucker. I couldn't find a bathroom shelf that was the right shape, so I decided to make one." He blew on the edge he'd sanded and then leaned over the workbench to kiss me. "Happy birthday."

He was wearing a faded long-sleeved T-shirt that read *Diogenes Brewing*, his dark hair hidden by a Nationals cap that I sometimes borrowed when I didn't feel like taking a shower, a pair of safety glasses obscuring his blue eyes. Why hadn't anyone ever made an HGTV show about Warren? I wondered. He was every basic bitch's fantasy, the hot dad who could tear down a wall in one scene and painstakingly craft a little girl's dollhouse in the next. Then again, any show about Warren would have to include Lauren's story, and you didn't need to be a producer to know that the target demographic might look sideways at a man whose wife had disappeared under mysterious circumstances. "Where's Mabry?" I asked.

"On a date."

"Who with?"

"She wouldn't say." He frowned at the bathroom shelf. "She's been pretty tight-lipped lately."

"That's normal." I stretched out my legs, angling them toward the glow of the space heater. Warren took off his safety glasses and sat on the floor. He pulled off my shoes and began playing with my toes, tugging on each one in turn. I tensed. "What are you doing?"

"What do you think I'm doing? Foot massage," he said, moving to the tender place above my instep. "I made brisket. And I've got a pie in the oven."

"I saw Susan at Lauren's bench today." I waited for Warren to react, but he said nothing, instead digging his thumbs harder into my heel.

Stopping by Lauren's memorial bench had become part of my Saturday routine. I got a coffee from the new place next to the wedding boutique, cut through the park, and wound my way through the hedges until I found the stone bench at the end of the reflecting pool with Lauren's name and the dates of her birth and disappearance etched in the seat. Beside her name was a Bible verse: *Blessed are the pure in heart, for they shall see God,* with a design of vines and flowers encircling the script. I ran my fingers over the delicately slanted letters, thinking of how Lauren would have smirked to hear herself called pure in heart. Literally any other verse would have been more appropriate—some curse from Deuteronomy that threatened your enemy with scars and boils, or a prohibition against riding your neighbor's donkey.

I was ready to move on when Susan stepped out of the hedge of boxwoods that framed the memorial on three sides, holding a bouquet of lilies cradled in her arms like a baby. "Nicola," she said, her voice higher and more girlish than usual. "I didn't expect to find you here."

I hadn't seen Susan since the night she'd returned my necklace, and I hoped it wouldn't occur to her that it was my birthday. The last thing I needed was to remind her that I kept getting older while her daughter was permanently stalled at twenty-three.

We hugged awkwardly, and Susan squatted down to place her lilies by the water. She balanced with one hand on the edge of a planter, her shoulders drooping as if her grief was a kind of apology. After a moment, she wiped her eyes on the back of her hand and sat on the other end of the bench. "I'm glad you came," she said. "I'm glad to know that it gives people some peace to be able to come here and think of her."

"It's beautiful," I said. "Lauren would have loved it."

But she wasn't looking at the memorial anymore. "I like your sweater," she said with a strange edge to her voice. "That's an attractive color on you."

I glanced down at my chest. It was an ordinary cashmere sweater in a shade of pale blue that the website had called Morning Mist. "Thank you."

Susan turned back to the reflecting pool. "I read something you wrote the other day," she said. "I looked you up on the computer. It was about *Jane Eyre*. I can't say I understood all of it, but it was very interesting."

"I appreciate that," I said, feeling both grateful and uneasy. As far as I knew, my mom had never read a single one of the essays I'd published, though I'd dutifully sent her the links. "I'm working on a book," I went on. "It's about narrative erasure in the Victorian novel. Women specifically, and how they're written out of their own stories."

I didn't expect her to see the connection to Lauren, but then I noticed her large eyes had filled with tears. "People just stopped caring, didn't they?" she said. "I guess I expected more sympathy."

I could have explained the problem if she'd been willing to listen. Susan hadn't grown up in Tyndall. She didn't have the soft and conciliatory manner of Southern women, who could cut you off at the knees and smile while they did it, and she'd never behaved the way people expected a grieving mother to behave. She hadn't wept quietly into a handkerchief, surrounded by a protective circle of ladies from her church. She hadn't made Lauren's room into a shrine and spent her days on her knees, slowly fading into a ghost. She'd called the sheriff at home. She'd buttonholed the editor of the newspaper while he was watering his roses. She'd done her best, but the powers that be weren't about to go against the Ballards, who had more clout in this county than Susan ever could.

In her mother's place, Lauren would have managed better, I thought. She'd absorbed the mores of Tyndall County at an early age. Not only would she have gotten everyone to do what she wanted, but she would have made them think it was their idea.

When I looked over, I saw that Susan was really crying now. Even worse, she didn't wipe her face, allowing the big wobbly tears to roll unimpeded down her cheeks. "I've even thought about selling the house and going back to Delaware, but I don't have family there anymore," she said. "Besides, what if she came back and I wasn't here?"

Until then I'd been feeling cold as a walk-in freezer in the face of her grief, but the tears wrenched my heart and I found myself patting her shoulder, my fingers grazing the plank of muscle under the thin fabric. It seemed to startle her, and she turned to me, blinking the tears away. "If only your mother were here," she said with a strangled laugh. "She'd know what to say, wouldn't she? She'd tell us to get off our duffs and do something useful."

I'd laughed too, but the turn in the conversation had made me even more uncomfortable. I knew that if they'd been close when Lauren disappeared, my mother would have taken on Susan's loss as her own. She would have taught herself how to do a grid search and spent every weekend in the woods up at Bearwallow, sifting through the dead leaves for a button or a bone. Then, when my mother got sick, Susan would have dragged her to the doctor. She would have harassed the insurance company until she got a referral to the best oncologist in the state. Even if the cancer couldn't have been stopped, at least my mother would have had a friend with her in her last days.

Neither of us had anything else to say, and after another minute or two I'd left Susan there, hands folded in her lap, staring at the sunlight glinting off the crinkled plastic of her bouquet.

When I finished the story, Warren didn't respond, rubbing his thumbs in a circular motion from the ball of my right foot down to the arch. "What did she mean about my sweater?" I asked. "She said something about me not wearing glasses the last time I saw her. It's been sixteen years. Why wouldn't I look different?"

Warren nodded, moving from the right foot to the left. I didn't get the sense that he and Susan had ever been close, but they'd clearly found a way to coexist, even alternating custody of Mabry for major holidays. I'd never gotten the impression that she blamed him for her daughter's disappearance, though it was a simple fact that if he'd stayed home that night, Lauren might be here today. "Do you really want to hear this?" he said.

"Hear what? What are you talking about?"

He looked up at me. "I think she means that you look a little bit like Lauren. Like the sweater—it's something she might have worn."

"What the hell?" I felt my foot jump in his hand. "What do you mean, I look like Lauren?"

"I doubt she meant it in a *Single White Female* type of way. Not like you're trying to turn into her or anything. There are some resemblances, that's all I'm saying."

But now that he'd made the reference, it was all I could think about. What if Susan did think I was trying to turn into her daughter? I still had no idea if she knew about me and Warren, but she'd always had an uncanny ability to keep up with community gossip.

"Don't worry about it," Warren said. "It's your birthday. Don't worry about anything." Kneeling beside my chair, he took my hips in his hands and slid my body toward him. My skin broke out in goosebumps and I shivered, though I couldn't tell if the tingle in my fingertips was desire or a dread I couldn't name.

WE FUCKED TWICE THAT NIGHT, FIRST IN THE WORKSHOP AND THEN, MORE leisurely, in the big bed that always made me think of a ship at sail. I was on my back and then on my knees, Warren holding my hips as he drew a ragged breath and then put his hand to the back of my head and pushed my face down into the pillow, hard, until I couldn't get a breath and came with a series of muffled screams. He never stopped to ask what I wanted or whether this or that was okay, and this tendency worried and excited me to such equivalent degrees that I never raised the subject even when our pants were on. What was real between us happened in the dark, and it seemed like he was always trying to maneuver us back there, to the place where he was in control.

We were catching our breath when Warren said, "Do you think you want kids someday?"

My hand went reflexively to my lower stomach, as if I could tell by feel whether my diaphragm was in place. "What?"

He rolled over on his side. "I didn't mean with me, necessarily. Just whether you see yourself having them at some point."

"I don't think so," I said. "I mean, I'm too old, for one thing. Or almost."

"You're thirty-seven. That's not old, but you don't want to wait too long."

"Ticktock, ticktock," I said in a singsong voice. "Way to bring a girl down on her birthday, Warren."

"Sorry," he said mildly. "I didn't mean it that way."

He switched on the TV and we watched in silence. A few minutes later I looked over and saw that he was snoring, the fine wrinkles around his eyes smoothed out in sleep. I got up and let the dog out and let him in again, then went back to bed and lay there, trying to convince my brain to stop thinking. I heard Mabry come home, but I didn't move, not even to put on the pajamas I left in the dresser.

When I finally slept, I fell into a dream of walking Lucky II through the streets of a city I'd never been to in real life. The sky was a peculiar pale orange, as if lit by the haze of a distant wildfire. I was walking along a canal path, and people passing on bicycles leered at me as if they knew something I didn't. Then my mother was beside me, lecturing me about something, the wind blowing in my face muffling her words. I felt a bone-deep certainty that I ought to turn around and look behind me, but when I tried, I couldn't make my body move. It was as if I were stuck on a roller coaster, pushing me forward against my will.

Then I was sitting up in bed, fumbling in the sheets for the pajamas I wasn't wearing. I reached over to Warren's side of the bed, but I was alone, breathing fast, my chest vibrating with panic. I grabbed for my glasses. The dog was barking hysterically, a high, tense yip I'd never heard from him before.

At once I knew what had woken me. It was the sound of breaking glass.

13

The police said no to coffee, so I poured myself a cup, more for something to do with my hands than because I really wanted it. It was 2:36 in the morning and I felt jittery enough without caffeine.

"Could you walk us through the incident?" asked the male officer, addressing Warren. Officer Grant was white, with arms like hams, and had already told us that he'd played lineman at Tyndall High from 2008 to 2011.

Warren sighed and rubbed his face as if he could use his hands to put his thoughts in order. "My girlfriend and I were in bed," he began, glancing at me. "I heard a noise. I thought it might have been my daughter coming in—I didn't realize how late it was. I started down the stairs, and from the landing, I could feel a chill, like a door had been left open. I switched on the lights, and the cinderblock with the letter was lying on the floor. Then I opened the door and saw the cat."

Officer Grant was making notes. "And the cat was deceased?"

Warren raised his eyebrows as if he couldn't believe the stupidity of the question. "Well," he said, "you saw it."

I hadn't seen the cat, but I had smelled it as soon as I came downstairs—a thick, rank smell that even now I could taste at the back of my tongue. Warren had told me that it had been left in a banker's box just outside the door, but he'd refused to let me look at it.

"Actually this isn't the first time Nicola's gotten a letter," he said, looking at me.

"Do you still have the first one?" Officer Kearney asked after I'd explained. She was Black and probably in her late twenties, with hair so short I could see the shape of her skull.

"It's in my purse," I said. "I'll get it."

On the way upstairs, I stopped to look at the cinderblock lying on its side on the floor of the living room. It had skidded across the hardwood, leaving an ugly yellow scar. I'd seen the letter tied to it only briefly before Warren had handed it to the police, but I knew that the message was exactly the same as the first one: *NO ONE WANTS YOU HERE*, the words written in red pen and scripted to look as if they were dripping blood.

When I stood in the foyer, the smell of decomposition was even thicker, like a stomach-turning version of the swampy canal water in my dream. The cat was still out there, waiting for the officers to bag it as evidence. I eased the door open and there it was, curled like a parenthesis in the banker's box. It must have been dead for a while—weeks, maybe months. It had been a calico once, but the fur had been eaten off, along with most of the flesh. Its head was turned to the side, eyes missing, teeth exposed in a terrible grin.

Someone had left this for me to find. Someone hated me, or both of us, enough to want us to wake up to this. I covered my mouth with my hand and waited for the gagging sensation to pass before I went back inside.

When I came downstairs with the first letter, Mabry was at the table, fully dressed. She'd been in pajamas when the police arrived, but now she had on jeans and her Juilliard sweatshirt, and I felt relieved. The last thing we needed was Officer Grant ogling Warren's half-dressed teenage daughter. He looked like the type who couldn't be subtle about a thing like that.

Officer Kearney slipped on a pair of plastic gloves and unfolded the letter. "Have you had any confrontations lately, ma'am?" she asked.

"Can you think of anyone who might have a reason to play this kind of a prank on you?"

"No," I said. "Nobody."

"One of your students, maybe?"

Mabry looked up, her gaze meeting mine and then shifting away. "I can't imagine," I said. "How would they even know I was here?"

Kearney nodded, and after a few more questions, the police went back to the foyer to take pictures of the broken window. They tramped out to the flower bed, but there was no hope for identification there, since whoever had thrown the cinderblock had kicked up mulch to obscure their shoe prints.

At three thirty, they packed up their equipment and told Warren he could patch the hole. Mabry had already gone back to bed. "I'll call a glazier in the morning," Warren said to me. "Homeowners' should cover it." I could tell the thought made him feel better. There were a lot of things outside his control, but a broken window—that was something he knew how to fix.

I leaned against the wall. "Your snake guy is coming tomorrow— today, I mean. I'm supposed to meet him at my house at eight."

Warren yawned behind his fist. "Text him and tell him you need to reschedule."

I didn't want to do that. I was almost ready to put the house on the market. If I had a snake problem, I needed to know sooner rather than later.

Warren wanted me to come to bed, but I said I was going to read. Drinking coffee had been a mistake. I took my book to the living room couch and piled my legs with blankets, but I could feel cold seeping around the cardboard over the window. It felt menacing, like the outside trying to get in.

I couldn't concentrate. The words twisted on the page, and after a few minutes I laid the book facedown on my lap and closed my eyes. Warren had told the police that he was in bed beside me when he heard the sound of breaking glass, but I remembered reaching out and pressing my hand to the cold sheet, feeling for his body. He'd lied, and I didn't know why.

◆ ◆ ◆

WHEN I GOT BACK TO MY MOM'S HOUSE LATER THAT MORNING, A RED PANEL truck with *Western Virginia Wildlife Management* printed on the side was already parked in the drive. I'd pictured a beast of a man who could wrestle a bear out of a trailer, but the guy who got out was short and heavily muscled, with a pointed face and black hair to his collar. "I already snuck a peek in the crawl space," he said after I'd introduced myself. "I don't see any evidence of a nest, but I'll poke around just to make sure."

He pocketed his sunglasses and smiled. He seemed very relaxed—so surprisingly mellow for someone about to crawl under a house in search of snakes that I leaned closer, searching for bloodshot eyes or a telltale whiff of weed. While he dressed in protective gear and sorted through his equipment, he told me about the calls he'd been on this week: bats in the chimney, baby raccoons under the hood of a car, a bear camped in an old barn.

Finally he army-crawled under the house and disappeared from view. I whiled away the time picking up brush from the edge of the yard. I'd half expected the snake guy to compliment me on the house—the new exterior paint and new shutters had transformed it into a trendy bungalow that would have made my mother turn over in her grave—but then I remembered that he didn't know what a dump it had been before.

I'd finally gone up to bed at four thirty, only to be woken at seven. Warren had brought me a glass of water and sat on the bed while I sipped. He was wearing his weekend uniform of jeans and a long-sleeved T-shirt from some local brewery, the gym muscles in his arms outlined against the thin fabric. When I reached out with my toes, I could feel my panties from last night bunched up with the top sheet at the foot of the bed. "Don't forget you told Mabry you'd look at her application essays tomorrow," he said.

That was when it came back to me: the broken window, the dead cat. I felt again the chill of the rancid air and shivered, pulling the comforter to my chin. "Officer Kearney was probably right about the vandalism," I said. "It could be a student. Someone who's mad because I gave them a D."

Warren ran his hand along my leg, outlined by the sheet. "I thought you said you were an easy grader," he said, stressing the word *easy*.

I looked down at his hand resting on my upper thigh. I knew that if I smiled at him the right way, he'd strip off his jeans and get back in bed with me. But even though the police had taken the cat as evidence, I swore I could still smell it, as if the odor and taste of decay had gotten into my teeth. "I need to get up," I said.

On the way to my mom's, I'd tried to convince myself that there was no way Warren could have sneaked out of bed, left the dead cat on the doorstep, thrown a cinderblock through the window, and then made it back upstairs before I got out of bed. I knew that I'd bolted up the moment I'd heard breaking glass, and I'd met him on the landing only seconds later. He hadn't been in a hurry or out of breath. It was his posture that had unsettled me—the way he'd moved close to the big square window that looked down on the driveway, as if he was waiting for someone.

I'd told him that I accepted the officers' theory that the letters, the cinderblock, and the dead cat were just a prank, but something wasn't sitting right. Officer Kearney had said there was no way to know if the cat had died of natural causes or been killed, but in either case, someone had put it in a banker's box and left it to rot. Someone had prepared it like a gift for Christmas morning, and the malevolence of that gesture surely went beyond the giggly spitefulness of a mere prank. No one wanted me here; the dead cat was word made flesh, the physical manifestation of the malevolence I'd felt ever since returning to Tyndall County.

Connor Mack, I thought. I had nothing approximating proof, but I pictured his blank eyes and little smirk and thought that he was exactly the sort of person who would kill a cat and leave it on somebody's doorstep.

After fifteen minutes of waiting for the snake guy to emerge, I ran out of brush and moved to pulling the weeds in the mulch by the front steps. When he finally slid out from under the house, I braced myself for the news that he'd seen dozens, hundreds, twining and unknotting mere inches below the floorboards. "Nope, nothing under there," he said as he stripped off his plastic suit. "No evidence of activity."

I should have been relieved, but instead I felt a return of the roiling nausea that had plagued me ever since I smelled the cat. "Oh, I did see a bag," the snake guy went on, his voice muffled as he pulled the top part of the suit over his head. "It's wedged between two cinderblocks to the right of the porch steps. I couldn't get all the way back there in this getup, but I could come back with my assistant if you want. Or you could probably get it yourself."

I stared skeptically at the dark space. "Is it safe? I mean, for someone who's not trained?"

He shrugged. "You'll get dirty is all. Bring a broom to help to nudge it out."

"What kind of bag is it?"

He was already turning away, folding his suit into a plastic box in the back of the truck. "Like a grocery bag, I think," he said. "I couldn't tell, it was all dusty. Probably been down there for years."

I COULD CALL WARREN, I THOUGHT. HE WOULD RETRIEVE THE BAG FOR ME with no questions asked, but if it turned out to be trash left by the previous owner, I'd look like a fool. Besides, I didn't want him to think of me as the kind of woman who had to call a man to do a dirty job. I was renovating a whole house almost by myself. I didn't need to be scared of a crawl space, especially now that the snake guy had told me it was safe.

But as soon as I'd actually gotten down on my hands and knees and stuck my head under there, I had second thoughts. The ceiling—the floor, I corrected myself—was lower than I'd expected. Though my eyes had adjusted, I couldn't see well, everything backlit by the sunlight streaming down on the far side of the house. I stopped and reached down to make sure that I could feel the outline of my phone in the pocket of my jeans.

It turned out the best way to move was to scrabble with my fingers while alternately flexing and pointing my feet. Breathing through my nose, I inched past concrete supports and mounds of dirt that looked as if they could have been made by termites. The snake guy would have told me if I had termites, wouldn't he? Or had I only paid for snakes?

I was beginning to wonder if there really was a bag when I saw something: an object wedged between two cinderblocks, just as the snake guy had said. The space was even tighter here. I barely had room to bring up the broom at my side and nudge it—once, twice, until I angled the bag toward me and could reach out to grab the handles tied in a double knot. Inside was something bulky that shifted when it moved. I wasn't going to stop to examine it here. A spiderweb drifted into my mouth and I stopped to spit, working my lips and tongue like Lucky II when he got a mouthful of plastic wrap.

On the way back, I decided to take what I thought was a short-cut. Even though the passage looked narrower than the one I'd come through, I calculated that it was worth the risk, but I made it less than a foot before I realized my mistake. I was stuck, my face smooshed to the right, my arms pressed so flat to the sides of my body that when I tried again to feel for my phone, I couldn't reach; it was wedged under my leg, useless as a gun in a safe. I thought of a documentary I'd seen about an explorer who got stuck in a cave in northern England, trapped between two boulders. Eventually he'd asphyxiated and been buried in the shaft, his body sealed in by rockfall.

I could feel my heart thumping in my chest. Maybe I should scream. Mr. Vargas next door was a grumpy retired sanitary worker whom I avoided whenever possible, but surely he had enough neighborly feeling to call the police on my behalf. Would they get here in time? What if the snake guy was wrong about the snakes? What if they'd simply melted away from the beam of his headlamp, waiting for the right moment? I could almost feel the cold scales on the bare skin of my ankle and the back of my neck.

My breath tight, I tried once more to push forward with my toes, and this time there was a little bit of give, just enough to convince me to try again. Inch, repeat. I abandoned the broom. I could turn my head to look forward, and then with a last push I freed myself and scrambled out into the air, hauling the bag after me.

I coughed, retched, braced my hands on my legs, and breathed deep. I checked to see if the neighbors were watching, but there was no sign at the Vargases' house, not so much as the flicker of a window blind. This street wasn't a *desirable neighborhood,* no matter what Warren said, but people here did know how to mind their own business.

I was filthy, but I didn't care. Not bothering with the tight double knot at the top of the bag, I used my fingernails to dig into the plastic and tear it open, wondering if I'd gone to all this trouble for what would turn out to be the remains of a workman's lunch.

But it wasn't a Styrofoam container or burger wrappers or a bunch of smaller bags stuffed into a bigger bag. Inside were two empty cans of spray paint and a pair of stained shoes.

I recognized the black circle on the toe of the sneaker where I'd tried to test the spray paint and accidentally sprayed myself. My mom must have dug them out of the trash can, sealed them in the bag, and hidden them under the house. I could see the logic in it. Tyndall was a small town, and our neighbor was a garbageman. If the can had happened to fall over, someone might have put two and two together.

I'd thought I had to be perfect for her, so she'd never have to be embarrassed or ashamed of me. But she'd never thought I was perfect. She'd known all along what I was, what I'd done, and she'd protected me. And I had never tried to know her at all.

14

That night I tore the house apart looking for the picture of the men with the cutout faces.

I started under the bed in my mom's room, pulling out long plastic containers of winter clothes and boxes of tax returns from the nineties. Almost everything went into the trash. For Goodwill I set aside a few pairs of barely worn jeans and a sweater with the JCPenney tag still hanging from the collar. My mom's tastes had tended toward the utilitarian, and I wasn't surprised to find that she owned the same sweatsuit in three different neutral colors.

I'd known all along that she'd pared her life down, wanting nothing and even taking a kind of pride in it. The only pleasures she allowed herself were a finger or two of bottom-shelf bourbon on Friday nights and the annual weekend trip to Virginia Beach with the women from her prayer group. One of the legs on the old armchair by her bed had been broken for years, and as far as I knew, she'd never even tried to have it fixed. Every time I bumped into it and had to screw the bad leg back on, I got irritated all over again.

But surely the version I'd seen wasn't the whole of her. Women always hid the messy parts of their lives from their children; it was part of the contract of motherhood. They probably made it through by promising themselves that someday they'd be able to relax and be their real selves, but my mom and I had never gotten to that stage. She'd been only fifty-four when she died. Surely, if I looked hard enough, I could find the woman underneath—the woman who must have desired something, dreaded something, yearned for something.

I sorted through a dusty box of Christmas ornaments and another of my elementary school artwork. I checked behind the radiators and ran my hand along the underside of closet shelves. I flipped through a box of old cassette tapes in the closet—John Denver, Billy Joel—and another of the mass-market mysteries she bought by the half dozen at yard sales. On the top shelf, I found file after file of painstakingly annotated correspondence with Medicaid, documenting every trip to the doctor in the last months of her life. By the time they approved the referral to the oncologist, she was already on a morphine drip and barely able to lift her head from the pillow. That was right around when she called me, and I booked a red-eye from Seattle that got me home just in time to watch her die.

It was tempting to set down the suffering of her last days to poverty and heartless federal bureaucracy, but I knew that even if she'd had private insurance, it wouldn't have made a difference. My mom was stubborn; it was her defining characteristic, as much a part of her as her tight gray ponytail and surprisingly dainty size-five feet. Even if she'd had a gold-plated health care plan, she would have put off a consultation for months, reasoning that a doctor would order a bunch of unnecessary tests and that a good night's sleep and a cup of ginger tea would have her right as rain.

I kept searching, becoming more careless as I went, throwing a whole pile of corduroy pants into the trash pile without even shaking them out to see if they'd been worn. I didn't remember which drawer I'd found the photo in all those years ago, only the feeling that had come over me when I held it up to the light, the bedside lamp shining through the holes where the men's faces had been. I sorted through piles of T-shirts and jeans and a jumble of old-lady underwear. Finally I took everything out of the drawers and peeled up the painstakingly applied scented liners, but there was nothing underneath except fuzz and a desiccated ticket to a five p.m. showing of *When Harry Met Sally*. I couldn't find the ceramic pipe in the velvet case either, and began to wonder if I'd imagined it.

My mother's unknowability went beyond a parent's customary desire to keep the details of adult lives from young children. While I'd spent my teenage years trying to hide from the eyes so sharp they could see inside strangers' houses, she'd been hiding from me too, and I still had no idea why.

That was one thing that Mabry Ballard and I had in common: we were both the daughters of unknowable women. Maybe that was why, when Mabry asked me to take her to the house where Lauren had disappeared, I hesitated only a minute before I said yes.

IF MABRY HADN'T BEEN WITH ME, I PROBABLY WOULD HAVE MISSED the driveway, choked with goldenrod and chicory sprouting out of the cracks in the asphalt. After negotiating the tight turn from Blue Ridge Road, I positioned my old Toyota in what I thought was the middle of the track and held the steering wheel as if going through the car wash. Not wanting distractions, I turned off the music on my phone, leaving us in silence except for the faraway rush of traffic.

From a distance the house didn't look too bad, but the closer we got, the more I felt as if I were driving onto a postapocalyptic movie set. The steps had fallen in, and the porch sagged on the ends like a downturned mouth. The paint, which I'd remembered as a pretty slate blue, had blistered and peeled in strips, leaving the walls gray and weather-beaten. Swallows had nested in the eaves, and I could hear them twittering in the long grass as I opened the car door. "I wonder who owns this place now," I said.

Mabry picked up a shingle blown off the roof, cradling it in her hand like a seashell. "My grandma owns it. She was afraid that a developer would buy it and tear it down, so she convinced my dad to sign it over to her. She thought the police might want to come back and search again."

I climbed the steps to the porch and cupped a hand around my eyes to peer through the window. Despite Susan's intentions to preserve the scene for future investigations, it was clear that the place had been ransacked. The light fixtures had been pulled down, and one window had been shattered. After the vandals had their way, nature had come in: piles of leaves had drifted around the table legs, and the plants growing through the cracks in the floor were powdered with fine white grains that I guessed had come from the ceiling tiles.

I stared at the spot where I'd picked up the bloody washcloth. What had happened here all those years ago? Clearly someone had hit her on the head—probably with the doorstop, since that had disappeared too. But why wipe blood off someone's face when you were in the process of murdering them? And what about the broken glass on the floor? Had Lauren dropped it when she glimpsed her killer at the window? I saw again the shadow man I'd dreamed about for years, his bulk filling the door.

Triggered by our footsteps, a shower of dust shook loose and sifted down on the floor. "I'll be right back," I said.

THE PLAN HAD BEEN FOR MABRY AND ME TO LOOK AT HER COLLEGE APPLI- cation essays over lunch at Rio Bravo. I'd asked her to bring a finished draft, but the paper she'd pushed across the table had only three lines. *Creativity is important and meaningful for every life. Corporations such as Google value creativity. Since the beginning of time, people have tried to be creative.*

I'd taken a swig of the ice water at my elbow, wishing it were a margarita. "Maybe you should try a different approach," I suggested. "For example, you could challenge the question. Why does something beautiful have to be good in the sense of useful? Could it just be good for its own sake?"

Mabry looked up, her face shuttered by a flat disinterest. "I don't understand why I have to do this. I'm going there to dance. Why do they care if I can write an essay?"

I fought the urge to tell her that I was helping her only as a favor to her father, and if she didn't get her ass in the game, I wasn't going to do it at all. Instead I picked up a tortilla chip from the basket and tapped the sharp end against the tabletop. "I looked up the stats for Juilliard. They admit seven percent of applicants. Do you really think you're such hot shit that you can afford to blow off the rest of your application?"

Mabry looked both annoyed and halfway persuaded. "But I don't actually believe in creativity," she said. "It's just a dumb buzzword. Talent is what counts."

I didn't want to admit that I agreed with her, so I looked away, out to the park, where a bridal party was taking pictures. The bridesmaids were in chartreuse dresses with ruffles down the front like fancy baby bibs. I thought of the portrait of Lauren on Mabry's bedroom wall, the poufy dress and unsettling eyes.

"I'm never going to get married," Mabry said. "I don't even like boys. Not as in I like girls instead," she clarified. "I'm attracted to boys; I just don't *like* them."

I tried to take a neutral stance. "They get better over time. Some of them, anyway."

"Right, maybe when they're like thirty," she said, rolling her eyes.

Maybe she was still on edge about the broken window, I thought. She'd seemed calm enough sitting in the kitchen with the police at two in the morning, but that could have been a pose. "We could come back to the essay another time," I said. "It's been a stressful couple of days for both of us."

Mabry shrugged. "You shouldn't take it personally. Last year people kept pasting maxi pads to Mrs. Moore's door—not used ones," she added, seeing the look on my face. "I'm just saying that kids do dumb pranks sometimes."

"But to kill a cat?" I pressed, my voice rising in spite of myself.

"You don't know that they killed it," she pointed out. "Cats die of natural causes."

She was right, though I wasn't sure that made it any better. "Mabry, if you know who was involved, you have to tell me. You have to tell the police. This is serious."

"I don't know anything. It wasn't Connor, if that's what you're thinking." Mabry took a sip of water and rolled the ice in her mouth. "He's an asshole, but he's not that kind of asshole."

I was surprised that she'd guessed my theory, and for a moment I felt self-conscious, wondering if my dislike of Connor was as evident to the other students as it clearly had been to her. "What do you mean?" I asked, playing dumb.

She picked up her phone. "If I show you something, will you promise not to tell my dad?"

I knew I ought to say no. If she confided in me about drugs, or pregnancy, or assault, I would have to tell Warren; I wouldn't have a choice. If it was bad enough, I might even have to call the police. Then I would have betrayed both of them, Warren by promising to keep the secret and Mabry by failing to keep that promise. Before I could find the words to refuse, she handed me her phone.

On the screen was a blurry, ill-lit nude taken in front of a bathroom mirror. Though the upper half of the girl's face was blocked by the glare of the flash, her mouth was visible, distorted into what she probably thought was a sexy pout. "Connor sent it to me," Mabry said. "It's some girl from Logan County he's been messing around with. I think her name is Karli."

"Why would he send this to you?" I asked, studying the photo.

Mabry sighed dramatically. "We got back together for a while. I didn't want to tell my dad because he never liked Connor. Then we had a fight and he sent me this, just to be hurtful, I guess. He collects pics and shares them with his friends or posts them online. It's pretty gross."

Poor Karli, I thought. Whatever she'd thought she was doing when she took this picture, she'd surely never imagined it being shown to her boyfriend's ex-girlfriend's English teacher. "I think you should delete that," I said, handing the phone back to Mabry. "Kids have been arrested for having pics like that on their phones."

She slipped it into her bag. "He doesn't have any photos of me, by the way. Actually the whole reason we had that fight was because I wouldn't have sex with him."

I tried to keep the surprise from showing on my face. "Not that we *never* did it," she went on. "Just not lately. Isn't there some Greek play where the women won't have sex until the men stop a war or something?"

How did she know about *Lysistrata* when she couldn't be bothered to read a single sonnet for my class? "Something like that," I said. "What did you want Connor to do?".

"Be a decent boyfriend. Consider my needs. Nothing crazy."

I still felt uneasy. "Does Connor's mother know that girls send him nudes? And that he shares them?"

"I have no idea," she said, popping the last bite of taco in her mouth. "He doesn't have a password, so maybe. He's literally such an idiot. Sometimes I can't believe I was ever in love with him."

It surprised me to hear her talking about being in love with Connor Mack, when I'd thought of her as largely disconnected from high school drama. I suspected that she'd kept the secret about Warren and me not because it was embarrassing to admit that her dad was sleeping with her English teacher, but because she didn't care enough to gossip about it. Mabry had the confidence that Lauren only pretended to possess at her age. She knew she was going places and was more than ready to jettison anyone who might keep her from getting there.

Our eyes met, and I realized that she was watching me too, her gaze cool and clinical. "You're not the kind of woman I ever pictured with my dad," she said.

I sorted through the chip bits in the plastic basket, feigning indifference. "What were his other girlfriends like?"

"I don't really know." Mabry wrinkled her nose. "They weren't the kind that stayed for breakfast, if you know what I mean. He said he always wanted me to know that I was the most important thing in his life. I used to think that maybe he'd end up with Ms. Westcott after I went to college, though."

"Really?" I asked. "Why is that?"

"They used to hang out a lot when I was little. You know about her son, right?" she whispered, leaning forward. "He goes to a special school for kids with behavior problems."

Suddenly a handful of details that had puzzled me seemed to click into place. That day in her office, Jessi's manner had changed the moment she looked at her phone and said she had to take a call. In the months since then, I'd noticed the strain on her face whenever we stopped to talk in the hall, and I'd interpreted it in the most egotistical way possible, assuming she'd thought back on everything that had happened and decided that renewing our friendship wasn't worth the trouble. Now I saw that I'd failed to even consider the possibility that Jessi had sources of stress in her life that had nothing to do with me.

But I also wanted to know more about why Mabry had imagined Warren and Jessi as a couple. Did she know that they'd flirted in high school? Had she heard the rumors about Dale Westcott? Did she know that the police had believed—maybe still believed—that Jessi's father had murdered Lauren? "Did they ever actually date?" I asked. "Ms. Westcott and your dad?"

"Not that I know of. Like I said, I was little. I just thought that when I was out of the house, maybe they would."

I didn't like how easy it was to picture this. I knew better than anyone that there had been something between Warren and Jessi back then, agitating beneath the surface. Lauren had sensed it, and I suspected that she'd only made things worse by targeting Jessi the way she did.

I decided to change the subject. "You're applying to other schools too, right?" I asked. "Please tell me you're not counting on Juilliard. No matter how talented you are, that's not smart."

"I know that." Mabry listed off the other possibilities—conservatories in Boston, Los Angeles, San Francisco. "The West Coast would be cool," she said, and added almost shyly, "Dad said you used to live out there."

I nodded. "I lived a lot of places. Washington State, Nebraska,

Rhode Island. Anywhere I could find a job. College towns are pretty much all the same."

Mabry's mouth pursed, and I could tell she didn't believe me, any more than I would have believed a grown-up who told me that all places were more or less alike. "Dad said you dated women," she said. "Like in college or whatever. So are you gay or bi or what?"

The words *none of your business* were on the tip of my tongue, but then I reconsidered. She was only asking questions, after all. "I fell in love with a woman in college, but we broke up after a year," I said. "She's married to someone else now."

"Why did you break up?"

Though I'd just pledged myself to honesty, I wasn't ready to tell her about the role her mother had played in the end of my relationship with Erika. "I was scared," I said. "I was afraid of what people in Tyndall would say if they found out. If I could go back, I'd do it differently."

The look of uncertainty on Mabry's face brought her mother back so sharply that for a moment I felt almost breathless. Maybe it was because hesitation or doubt had been so unusual for Lauren that this combination of cues—the chin dipped to the side, eyelashes fluttering—had a unique ability to revive the past, as if the girl in front of me were a hologram of her lost mother. "Did my mom know?" Mabry asked finally, curling a piece of hair around her finger.

"That I had a girlfriend? Of course."

"And she was cool with it? I'm not saying she shouldn't have been," she added quickly. "I'm just asking because of my grandma. I mean, she's pretty conservative."

This wasn't news to me. I had no idea if Lauren had told Susan about my relationship with Erika, but if she had, Susan surely would have disapproved. "Your mom was her own person," I said. "If she knew that she and her mother would disagree about something, she kept it to herself."

Or lied. I didn't say the words out loud, but when I looked up, I could tell that Mabry had read them on my face. As permissive as

Warren was in some ways, chances were good that she knew plenty about lying to parents. "I feel like I don't know anything about her," she said. "I look at her pictures, and it's like I'm looking at somebody in a magazine."

"I know what you mean," I said, though I was thinking of my mother, not of Lauren.

Mabry stuck the last chip in the dish of pineapple salsa. I didn't know exactly when or how it had happened, but something had shifted between us. "Hey, are you in a hurry to get home?" she asked. "Because if not, could we go see the house where she disappeared?"

SEE THE HOUSE WAS A PHRASE THAT COULD HAVE MULTIPLE MEANINGS. Mabry could have been asking simply if we could drive by Warren and Lauren's old home, something she probably didn't often have occasion to do, since there was no reason to come to Blue Ridge Road unless you were going to the John Deere dealership. I was the one who had interpreted *see* as *go inside and look around*. I'd tried to convince Mabry to wait outside, but I already knew that I wasn't going to give up the plan if she insisted on coming with me.

Even as I forced open the window to the living room and climbed over the dusty sill, I knew that breaking and entering was a bad idea. After over a decade of neglect, the roof probably wasn't in the greatest shape, and I had no idea what had been living in the walls. I made my way down the hall and peered into the kitchen, which was dark and dirty, small shadows scurrying away at the sound of my footsteps. When I pulled out my phone to turn on the flashlight, there was a new Reddit notification, and I accidentally pressed it instead of the light.

There had been a surprising amount of activity on the r/LaurenBallardDisappearance page in the past couple of days, as if the comment about Missing White Woman Syndrome had sparked new interest.

VARIATION_OF_HUMANITY
I just keep wondering about the body. I know there's lots of woods

around there but it seems like some sign would have been found after all this time.

HYPOCRITE_ALLIGATOR
Does anybody know if her car is missing? Maybe she faked her death.

NUMBER.1.LURKER
Police reports say car was parked outside.

TRIVIALENTHUSIASM342
How is it possible that there isn't more on this case. I know it's a backwater but damn.

CHAMPIONDREAMS4091
Maybe they didnt try that hard. The police thought they had their guy pretty early on.

CHEESEAGENDA
I looked around and found a possible match. "Average build, medium length blond hair, healing rib fractures." Does anybody know if the husband hit her?

TRIVIALENTHUSIASM342
There's no mention of abuse in the reports.

TRIVIALENTHUSIASM342
Also that sketch doesn't look like the photos at all.

CHEESEAGENDA
The sketch is from skeletal remains, it's not going to look exactly like her photo.

BLUEFOOT1092
I think the husband killed her and hid her body in the house.

TENDER_MEDUSA
That's literally impossible. It's a regular house, not a medieval castle. I don't think it even has a basement.

TENDER_MEDUSA
I'm not saying the husband didn't do it, just that he couldn't have hidden her body in the house.

BLUEFOOT1092
How would you know

TENDER_MEDUSA
I grew up around there.

I clicked on the profile for Tender_Medusa, whose avatar was a little faceless alien in a pink baseball cap. She didn't post much, but she'd commented on a lot of true-crime threads, including several I followed. Impulsively, I opened a private message:

u/Tender_Medusa:
Subject: Tyndall County?

Message:

Hi, my name is Nicola Bennett. I saw that you said you grew up in the Tyndall County area, and I'm just wondering if we know each other?

Before I could change my mind, I pressed send. Mabry had just climbed through the window, and I wondered suddenly if she might have been the poster, but the phone in her pocket didn't buzz.

"I guess I'll just look around," she said uncertainly, wiping her palms on her leggings.

"Be careful," I said. "I'm going to check out the upstairs. We shouldn't stay long."

At the top of the stairs, the first door on the left opened into what had been the nursery. The letters that spelled MABRY were black with mildew but somehow still stapled to the wall, the Y swinging sideways in the breeze I'd made when I opened the door. I was grateful that Mabry wasn't behind me. No matter how tough she thought she was, no child could be indifferent to the sights and smells of that long-abandoned room.

I closed the door and let the flashlight guide me across the hall to the master. The other rooms had seemed strange, dark and unfamiliar, but in Warren and Lauren's bedroom, I remembered exactly how it had looked before, with the California king bed and the two matching mahogany dressers. They'd filled the room with furniture intended for the larger home they would buy when they had the money, but none of those pieces had made it into the house where Warren lived now.

Working in real estate, he would know that furniture had a personality just like people, and everything here had been Lauren's.

The closet was half open, a rectangle of shadow falling on the soiled carpet. Incredibly, a few pieces of Lauren's clothing lay on the floor, as if someone had raided her wardrobe and left the rejects behind. With my fingertips, I picked up a blue Gore-Tex parka that I remembered her wearing when she visited me at college the summer before she disappeared. It was dirty, but the fabric was intact, and I fought the urge to slip it on over my sweater.

As I turned with the parka draped over my arm, the flashlight illuminated a stain on the carpet so like the outline of a body in a police procedural that I had to bend down to reassure myself. Looking closer, I could see that what had appeared to be a head was just a dark half-circle marking where rain had blown in through the broken window. This was the root of the problem, after all: there was no body, no answers, and here I was again, picking through what was left like a scavenger, trying to make a story out of bits and pieces.

I'd just made it back to the hallway when I heard Mabry's voice. "Oh," she said from downstairs—not to me but to herself.

It was the sort of *oh* that could have meant a lot of things: surprise, or disappointment, or a disaster whose effects hadn't yet been fully measured. I raced for the stairs, but I'd made it only halfway down when Mabry intercepted me. She had a stripe of dust on her left cheek, but otherwise she seemed fine.

"Look," she said, holding out her hand. "I found it in the living room."

The metal was dull, tarnished and smudged by years of dirt and grime, but I knew right away what I was looking at. It was a diamond earring, a perfect fit for the pair that Lauren had worn almost every day of her life.

15

When I walked into Warren's living room, Detective McRae was sitting on the couch. She was younger, prettier, and smaller than I'd imagined, five-two at most, with a short blond ponytail and a gold cross peeking out from the collar of her light-pink blouse. My hopes sank. She reminded me of girls I'd known in college—girls who didn't even have the self-awareness to be grateful for their easy lives.

"It's so nice to meet you," she said. Her voice too was discouraging, chirpy and overly upbeat, as if we were making plans for a sorority mixer. When she smiled, I noticed a lipstick smear on her teeth.

"I was hoping to talk to Mabry," she said to Warren, taking a pocket-sized notebook from a cheap leather bag beside her. "Could you ask her to join us?"

"Why?" I was the one who asked, but I could see from Warren's face that he was wondering the same thing.

McRae's smile stayed fixed just a moment too long, letting me see that she'd made note of my reaction. "She was waiting outside, right?" she asked. "While you went into the house?"

That was the story that Warren and I had agreed on in the parking lot of the police station that afternoon. There was no point in bringing Mabry into it when I could claim to have found the earring myself. "She went over to a friend's tonight," Warren said. He'd brought out a bottle of wine and poured me a glass without asking. "She was upset, understandably. Should I call and ask her to come home?"

When Warren tipped the third glass toward her, McRae shook her head. "No, we can go on without her," she said. "Nicola, could you start by telling me why you and Mabry decided to visit the house?"

"Well, it was Mabry who suggested it." So far, at least, I was telling the truth. "I hadn't been there since just after Lauren disappeared, so I was curious, I guess."

"Did Mabry say why she wanted to go?"

"I didn't ask." I looked at Warren, who was fiddling with his watch and wouldn't meet my eyes. "I thought she might want to ask me some questions about her mother."

"But once you got there, you separated."

"Yes," I said. "I mean, we separated so I could go inside. I thought I'd just poke my head in and get right out again."

The detective smiled agreeably, but her next question made me wonder if she believed anything I'd said. "How exactly did you find the earring? From the reports I've seen, the police searched the house pretty thoroughly."

I'd had the same thought. A few days after Lauren had gone missing, I'd returned to the house hoping to pick up some clothes I'd left and found it swarming with cops and lab techs. They told me they'd gone over every inch, and I believed them. It seemed unlikely that an earring would simply appear in a crack in the floor sixteen years later, but then again, what other explanation was there? Was McRae implying that I'd planted the earring at the scene so I could "find" it in the presence of a witness?

I recited what Mabry had said when I'd asked her the same question. "I was shining my flashlight across the floor. I thought it was a piece of glass at first, but then I picked it up and saw that it was a diamond—or a rhinestone, maybe. I can't tell the difference, but it looks just like the earrings that Lauren used to wear. Her mother has a pair that are similar."

Detective McRae nodded and took a photograph from her bag,

passing it first to me and then to Warren. It was the earring, nearly black with dust, laid on a white background. "I want you both to take a good look," she said. "I don't want to make any assumptions here. Are you sure this is Lauren's earring?"

"Who else would it belong to?" Warren asked with a hint of annoyance.

McRae turned in his direction, crossing her legs and leaning forward with what struck me as excessive solicitude. "I understand this is frustrating," she said. "Do you have any old pictures where she's wearing the earrings? It would be helpful if we had something to compare it to."

Warren said he had a box upstairs somewhere. As soon as he'd left the room, I realized he'd gone to look for the Nine West box that I'd discovered a few weeks ago, and I felt a light trickle of sweat run down between my shoulder blades.

To cover my nervousness, I tried to make small talk, but McRae responded with the shortest answers consistent with common politeness. Without Warren in the room, she'd reverted to her no-nonsense posture, feet firmly on the floor and hands resting on the knees of her wash-and-wear black slacks. Since she clearly wasn't interested in chatting, I entertained myself by making up a backstory for her. She was probably from a wealthy background and had gone into law enforcement to prove something. Maybe she'd had a tough dad, a military type or a football coach, who told her she was just as good as the boys. Maybe she'd taken the entrance exam on a dare and learned she liked the sense of power that came with a gun and a badge. Maybe she liked being the only woman in a roomful of men, and now she'd been handed a case that meant absolutely nothing to her beyond an unexpected chance to flirt with Grieving Husband Warren Ballard.

Though I knew I'd invented every bit of this biography, and though I knew it was sexist and unfair, it was plausible enough to feed my resentment. I sipped my wine until Warren returned, setting the box triumphantly on the coffee table.

McRae found several photos of Lauren wearing the earrings and put them aside. "Who took this?" she asked, holding up one of the prints from the Teevee series: Lauren in a kitchen wearing a flowered dress so short I could see the tops of her thighs.

Warren said he didn't know. "I found them after she disappeared. I figured one of her friends took them, or maybe she made them herself. She was always interested in photography."

I tried to look curious and a bit puzzled, as if the pictures were new to me too. I was the only person who knew that two were missing—the one of me lying in the grass beside the school picnic table, and the one of Lauren leaning against the brick wall with the girl I didn't know. I was counting on the fact that Warren wouldn't have a clear memory of the box's contents, and he showed no signs that he'd noticed anything amiss. "How do you think the earring came off in the first place?" I asked. "Does that seem like evidence of an assault?"

"We can't speculate at this point," McRae said as she replaced the lid on the box.

I was about to say that it had been sixteen years and seemed as good a time to speculate as any, but she was still talking. "I saw there was a report from this address from a couple of days ago," she said. "Something about a broken window?"

Warren launched into an explanation, though I was sure McRae already knew all about it if she'd read the report. "Do you have any idea who might do something like that?" she asked when he'd finished.

"Well, it's not connected to what happened to Lauren," I put in. "I mean, is it? Do you think it is?"

Warren frowned so hard that I wanted to lean across the table and wipe off the lines between his eyebrows like a mother swabbing a milk mustache. "Oh, I don't have any reason to think so," McRae said, again with that wide sorority-girl smile. "It is interesting, though, isn't it? The two of you start spending time together, and suddenly there's glass breaking in the middle of the night."

Warren and I looked at each other blankly. McRae slid the photo of the earring into her bag, and after we'd shaken hands, Warren walked her to the door, where I heard her saying the expected things: she'd be in touch and we should let her know if we remembered anything that might be relevant. When the door closed, Warren sat heavily on the couch.

"What the fuck was that about?" I said. "Is she implying that somebody doesn't want us to be together? Maybe she's the one who threw the cinderblock through the window. She's got hot pants for you, that's for sure."

He didn't say anything, and I got the feeling he was listening for McRae's car backing down the driveway. "Do you ever wonder if maybe Westcott didn't do it?" he said finally.

"I asked you that months ago," I reminded him. "I asked if you thought Westcott was guilty, and you said if the police thought he killed her, he probably did."

He looked up. "What if nobody killed her?"

"I don't get it." But then, all of a sudden, I did. I thought of the comment on the Reddit thread: *Maybe she faked her death.*

"Remember when you asked why I didn't post much on social media?" he said. "I have this vision of her, wherever she is, trying to follow my life online and not being able to. I guess that gives me some kind of satisfaction. She doesn't deserve to know what she left behind."

I could see it, I thought—an older version of Lauren pulling out her phone in Chicago or Portland or Rome, searching for the family she'd abandoned. I decided not to remind him that they would not actually be hard to find, since Mabry posted on TikTok approximately every five minutes. "That doesn't make sense," I said.

He closed his eyes. "I just get this feeling sometimes that she's still out there. It's like an itch on the back of my neck."

I moved over and rested my head on his leg. His mood tonight had unsettled me, I didn't like this new unpredictable Warren. *I* was supposed to be the unpredictable one. He was the guy who washed his car on alternate Saturdays and filled the coffeemaker with fresh grounds every night before bed.

Maybe, I thought, he was still mad at me for taking Mabry to Blue Ridge Road. Before McRae had shown up, he'd let me have it, telling me that Susan could have me arrested for trespassing and that if I was going to act like a fucking idiot, I better leave his daughter out of it. I'd thought my offer to tell the police that Mabry had stayed outside had mollified him, but now I wasn't sure.

I ran my hand down his chest, coming to rest on his belt buckle. I wanted to forget all about Lauren and the vacuity that had shaped our lives for the past sixteen years. I wanted him to empty me of everything but the feeling of the cool pillow against my forehead and his hands on my hips. But Warren slid my head off his thigh and stood without a word. He picked up the wine bottle and our glasses and carried them into the kitchen.

I heard water running and glass clinking against the porcelain and then his footsteps on the stairs. When I went into the kitchen, I found one wineglass upside down in the drainer and another untouched, pink dregs floating in the bottom of the bowl. He'd washed his glass and left mine in the sink.

16

October had come and gone before I realized that I was avoiding Sean at work. It had started as instinct, a passive merge into the track of my inclinations rather than a conscious choice. If I saw him coming down the hall, I would turn to the nearest staircase, telling myself that it was the quickest route back to my classroom. When we both had cafeteria duty, I managed to stay on the other side of the room, migrating toward a rowdy table whenever he seemed to be coming my way. He must have picked up on it, because he never popped into my classroom to crack jokes and remind the kids that the principal was their P-A-L, as he did with some of the other teachers. It seemed we kept our distance by mutual agreement, and I liked it that way.

Could things have turned out differently with us if I hadn't been such an asshole? he'd asked that night at the Hideout, and I could admit now that the answer was probably yes. We might not have stayed a couple, but we would have kept in touch. After Lauren's disappearance, we could have helped each other. I wasn't naive enough to believe I could have saved him from addiction, but in those years when he was in and out of rehab, perhaps I could have been a support, some kind of stable, steady presence to set against the chaos.

Maybe we'd had a chance at that again when we'd come back into each other's lives this summer, but I'd chosen Warren instead, and I knew the old Sean would have found that unforgivable. I was convinced that he'd find some way to make me feel his resentment, so I ducked him when I could, right up until Warren and I broke up.

Break up was how I thought of it, though the words were never said—no *I need some space*, no *I guess we jumped into this too quickly*. When Warren went upstairs without me after the visit from the detective, I walked back to my mom's house in the dark and hadn't seen him since. The story of the diamond earring, short on details, was covered on the front page of the local newspaper the next morning, and when I found an excuse to drive down Blue Ridge Road after school, I saw that the driveway had been blocked off with police tape. Lauren's disappearance might not have been a national story, but the locals remembered it just fine, and now everyone had an opinion. "Somebody beat the shit out of her," I heard Glenda Morris saying as I walked into the teachers' lounge, echoing my own thought. "You got to hit a woman pretty hard to make her earring pop out."

I waited for Detective McRae to make some kind of public statement, but weeks went by and no new stories appeared. Tender_Medusa didn't respond to my private message, and Warren never apologized, his name moving farther and farther down on my list of recent texts.

In certain ways, I realized, he was a lot like Connor Mack. They were both good-looking athletes in a town where little else was needed for social success. Boys like that were never encouraged to develop any kind of fallback capacities. It was true that I'd always thought of Warren as a nice guy, but it wasn't hard to be nice when everything came easy. Even Lauren's disappearance hadn't done him much damage; he'd come out of it with local-celebrity status, the most eligible grieving husband in the tri-county area.

Sean and Warren had grown up with the same privilege, but Sean had always been second best, tarnished brass to the golden boy. It was still hard to imagine forgiving him for what he'd done to me back then, but I began to wonder if I was giving enough credit to the man he'd become. What if, all these years later, he really had changed?

◆ ◆ ◆

WHEN I'D GOTTEN MY ACCEPTANCE LETTER FROM FLETCHER COLLEGE, Sean had been the first person I called, even before I tried my mom at the house she was cleaning that day. "I have news," I said. "Can we go up to Bearwallow?"

I gathered there had been a time when Sean and Warren had a key to the house, but that had all ended after the Halloween party when Lauren had to be taken to the hospital for hypothermia. Now we had to be content with hanging out on the grounds, which was almost as good. I'd never told Sean the whole story about my strange friendship with his grandmother, but I was sure he could see how much I loved even the smallest details about the place—the uneven brick paths, the smells of boxwood and whitewash, crepe myrtle crowding the steps of the old spring house.

"Did Lauren call you?" he asked when we'd shaken out the fleece blanket that smelled of weed and pizza cheese and lain down flat on our backs, inches apart.

"About what?"

He raised his eyebrows. "They got engaged yesterday."

I shrugged. "That's good, I guess." Lauren and I weren't exactly on the outs—I still saw her when she came back to Tyndall—but I knew she was mad at me. She'd wanted me to apply to the college she attended in Richmond, but I was already getting calls from coaches at out-of-state schools and had made excuses. With her unerring instinct for what others most wanted to hide, she'd seen that I thought I could do better than she had done, and that was something she couldn't forgive.

"I thought they'd break up," Sean said. "Being at different schools."

I said nothing. There might have been a time when Lauren had wanted more out of life, but it didn't shock me to learn that she'd made the safe choice. If she bet on her own future, she had no guarantee of success, but if she chose Warren, she couldn't fail. In Tyndall they would always be at the top, preserved at their best like a bride and groom on top of a cake.

I was surprised to find I could think so dismissively of them. Three years ago, I had hated and envied Lauren in equal measure. "That's not why I wanted to talk," I said.

I told him about Fletcher, describing the campus on the Eastern Shore of Virginia, only two miles from the beach. It wasn't my dream school—I'd hoped that a soccer scholarship would let me afford one of the New England colleges I'd read about in novels, where everyone wore Bean boots and went skiing on the weekends, but Fletcher had offered four years of free tuition with room and board plus a stipend for books, and I couldn't pass that up. Besides, the place had its charms. The old library was full of nooks and crannies to curl up in, and the snack bar had a frozen yogurt machine.

I reached for the half-empty Bud Light stuck in the grass and turned to Sean expectantly. There was just enough light in the sky for me to catch his expression, somehow surly and blank at the same time. "What's wrong?"

"I got my last rejection today," he said. "Unlucky number eight."

My stomach lurched like when you miss a step on the stairs. "But you were wait-listed at Tech," I said faintly. Virginia Tech had been his safety school. Sean's dad had gone there and sometimes gave money to the athletic department.

He took papers and a baggie from his lap and spread them on the blanket between us. "You don't need to worry about me or anything. I'm fine."

"You could work for a year," I said. "Or there's the two-year college in—"

He gave a short laugh. "I don't know why I thought I wanted to go in the first place. Tech is just a bunch of dumbass jocks and engineering nerds."

He passed the joint, and I took one hit and then another until Sean said, "Hey," and snapped his fingers. I lay back on the blanket and—

breathed in the chill mountain air, listening for the animals I was sure I could hear moving at the edge of the yard. Maybe tonight was the night I would finally see one of the bears for which the house was named—rearing up out of the brush, outlined by the moon.

I saw the spark of the roach arc overhead like a shooting star, and then Sean's face appeared above me. He put a knee on either side of my body and bent to kiss the side of my face, then my lips. I tried to relax. This was part of my plan, wasn't it? But my Nicola necklace had gotten tangled, and the brim of Sean's baseball cap was hitting me in the nose.

"Stop," I whispered, but he didn't, his hand fumbling with the snap at my waist. His pelvis moved against mine, and now his hand was inside my jeans, pushing my underwear to the side. Sean was my friend, I told myself; he must think I wanted this or he wouldn't be doing it, and maybe he was right, maybe I did want it, there was probably never a perfect time for this sort of thing. Then I felt the tip of his cock against my hip and jerked my whole body out from under him. "What?" he groaned as he rolled off. "Jesus, what's wrong?"

"I thought I smelled something," I said.

The dry grass was singed, but there was no fire. Listening to the squeak of Sean's boot soles as he stamped out the smoldering roach, I drew my hood up over my head and pressed my face to my knees. I was fine, I told myself sternly, like a mother reassuring her child even while she checked for blood. I was absolutely fine. Nothing had even happened to me.

I WASN'T INVITED TO LAUREN AND WARREN'S ENGAGEMENT PARTY AT THE Ballards' beach house. At school, Sean and I stayed away from each other, and I spent lunch in the library reading in a chair by the big windows. I went back to the books Mrs. Ballard had given me, *Jane Eyre* and *Wuthering Heights*. They read differently to me now than they had when I was in middle school. Heathcliff was emo as hell, and I couldn't understand why Jane wanted to be with some forty-year-old dude with anger issues.

After graduation, I got a job at Sam's Videos. There was only one other employee, and it surprised me to learn that she went to Fletcher; no one had mentioned it when I'd applied. Then again, I'd barely known Erika when she was in Lauren's class back in high school. She was one of those girls who clearly didn't give a fuck what anybody thought of her, which I found both impressive and intimidating. She wore baby-doll dresses over flared jeans, with three silver hoops stacked in the cartilage of her right ear. Her dark hair was almost as long as mine, and though she never wore makeup, she had enviably clear skin with a hint of pink that seemed to come and go as she breathed. She was pretty, I realized now—not in the way that counted in Tyndall County, but maybe that didn't matter anymore.

"You'll like Fletcher," she said as we restocked the dirty videos in the back room. "There are some hoity-toity full-tuition types running around, but most of the kids are pretty decent. Make sure you ask to live in Burgess House. It's the best dorm on campus, honestly, I don't know why they let the freshmen live there."

I half listened as I scanned the cover of *Home by Midnight*, which showed a split image of an actress wearing a schoolgirl outfit on one side and a black leather miniskirt on the other. I knew that if I told Erika what Sean had done, she would be furious. I could already script her words in my head: *Fuck that piece of shit. He better not show his face in here or I'm throwing the complete Orson Welles right at his stupid head.*

But the truth was that I wanted him to come. I wanted to hear the bell ding over the door and see him standing there in his baseball cap and sunglasses, sheepish and contrite. If he'd tried to explain, I would have listened. If he'd apologized, I would have forgiven him. The longing I felt was so intense, so ungovernable, that I almost mistook it for love.

I WAS STILL WAITING FOR THAT APOLOGY. HE'D COME CLOSE THAT NIGHT at the Hideout, but not close enough. By the standards of the time, Sean might not have been much better or worse than most of the guys

I'd known back then, but surely he'd learned enough about consent in the intervening years to realize that his actions were wrong. Was it too much to ask for him to simply acknowledge that he'd crossed a line?

On the other hand, shouldn't his actions count for something too? In the years we'd been apart, he'd finished school, married, become a father. He seemed to have mended things with his family, even if there was still some tension with Warren. I respected his manner with the students, and I'd heard that he'd cut the dropout rate in half since becoming principal. The next time I met him coming in from the faculty parking lot, I hung back and held the door.

The upper half was glass, and I could tell he'd already seen me and put on the ironic half-smile that was different from the smile he used with the students. This smile said that we both knew this pretense of being grown-ups was only a fun game we were playing, and we were the same kids as ever underneath.

"Nicola," he said, giving a sarcastic bow, a showy sham of chivalry. He was dressed like a principal, in a blue button-down, khakis, and a repp tie, with the addition of unnecessarily cool aviator sunglasses that hid his eyes. Back in high school, I'd had a suspicion that he'd modeled his whole persona on Matthew McConaughey in *Dazed and Confused*, and he still looked like he was constantly on the verge of crooning "All right all right *all right*."

"Heading out?" he asked. "Big plans tonight?"

"You know it," I said, hefting my bag full of papers. "Where are you coming from?"

"Meeting with the superintendent," he said, turning to walk with me. "I dropped my keys when I was passing your car and noticed that your tires were low. There's an air pump at the Seven-Eleven on Montrose—I could follow you there if you want, or you could ask Warren to take a look."

Did that mean Warren hadn't told him we weren't seeing each other anymore? "I know how to put air in my tires," I said, more snappishly than I'd intended.

Sean put up his hands to block a flurry of imaginary punches, but he was smiling. "Hey, what are you doing right now?" he asked. "I have to ride out to Jessi's place and bring her some files. She's been home with her kid for a couple of days. Why don't you come along?"

I fingered my necklace, pressing the sharp points into the pad of my thumb. "Okay," I agreed. "As long as we don't stay too late."

Sean winked. "I'll have you back by curfew," he said. "Cross my heart."

I'D FEARED THE AWKWARDNESS OF BEING ALONE WITH SEAN, BUT IT WAS A classic autumn afternoon in the mountains, the sky blue as hard candy, and the combination of the weather and the joint he lit up before we turned out of the parking lot put us both in a good mood. I was surprised to find that he still kept a packet of Zig-Zags and an Altoids tin in his glove compartment, but I wasn't going to ask again about his recovery. If he'd decided that weed and beer didn't count, that was his business.

"What's your relationship with the cops these days?" I asked, hanging my elbow out the window. "Like what does it say that the high school principal can ride around high as a kite in no fear of a ticket?"

Sean shrugged. "I'm not high as a kite. This is just to take the edge off. Anyway, the cops spend all their time at that speed trap by the interstate."

He turned on NPR, and as we drove out of the city, he told me that the superintendent wanted to extend next year's calendar into June to allow for snow days. "I told her what with climate change, we can't be expecting blizzards like when we were kids," he said. "Virginia is subtropical now. We might as well be Florida."

His mention of Florida reminded me of what Warren had told me months ago about Sean's divorce. "Are you going to see your son over the holidays?" I asked.

He looked at me with surprise, though I couldn't tell if it was because of the change of subject or that I'd remembered he had a son. "I'll go down there for a week over Christmas."

"It must be hard," I offered tentatively.

He plucked the joint from between my fingers. "Yeah, it's not good," he said. "I don't want to speak ill of his mother, but she'd definitely like me to see him as little as possible, and she's got good lawyers to back her up. It doesn't help my case that I've been to rehab three times. At this point I think he sees me as some weird guy who shows up to play mini-golf with him a couple of times a year."

"I'm sorry," I said. It felt inadequate, but what else was there to say? I looked out the window and saw we were passing the empty lot of what had once been Kyle Plastics, the old metal buildings now rusty and swagged with kudzu. "Do you think Warren and Lauren would have stayed married if she hadn't gone missing?" I asked.

"Not a chance," he said. "Lauren was a restless person. Nothing was going to make her happy."

It occurred to me that Sean had probably known Lauren better than I had in the years before her disappearance. Clearly they'd partied together, since they'd been drinking at lunch the day Lauren left Mabry in the hot car. I felt a prickle of jealousy, though I wasn't sure exactly who I was jealous of or why. "If she was so restless, why did she get married at twenty-two?" I said. "Nobody put a gun to her head."

As soon as I heard the words out loud, I could see that they were in spectacularly bad taste, given that someone probably *had* put a gun to Lauren's head the night she disappeared. But Sean didn't seem to notice my faux pas. "She wasn't as sure of herself as you thought," he said. "That was a front. That's how it seemed to me, anyway."

I took the joint from him and cranked back my seat. This conversation reminded me of something else about Sean that I'd forgotten: he was perceptive about people, keenly aware of the human being under the social conventions. Back in high school, he'd seen through guys like Jason Mack and Luke Barlow when everyone else seemed to think they were cool. That sensitivity was what had convinced me to look past his class-clown persona in the first place.

He cleared his throat. "Speaking of high school stuff," he said, "I was a dick to you back then. I could say I thought that was how I was supposed to act, but that's not an excuse. With the position that I'm in now, I don't want you to assume that I'm the same person I was in those days. To be honest, it disgusts me."

It was what I'd wanted to hear, and yet I found myself with no idea how to respond. "Connor Mack collects nude pics of girls and shares them with his friends," I said. "Don't ask me how I know. I just thought you'd want to look into it."

Sean raised his eyebrows. "Okay," he said. "Thanks for the tip."

Just before the road pitched up the side of the mountain, he pulled off on a dirt lane beside a sign that read *Willow Creek Farm.* In other parts of the country, it might have been the name of a subdivision, but here it seemed to be an actual working horse farm, with a chestnut mare and a roan trotting up to the fence to watch the car roll by. "This is beautiful," I said. "I didn't know Jessi lived so far out."

Sean took the last hit and dropped the roach in a Coke can. "It's for her son," he said on a strangled inhale. "He does equine therapy, and the owner gives him free lessons in exchange for Jessi helping out with the horses."

I wanted to ask Sean for more details about the son, but I didn't want him to think I was gossiping. After all, it wasn't like Jessi and I were friends; in fact, we'd hardly spoken since the day we'd hung out in her office. We smiled and nodded when we saw each other in the halls, and I told myself that our failure to seek each other out didn't mean anything—we were simply busy adults on parallel tracks—but now I wondered if I had been a coward. I didn't want to face the shame and guilt that came over me like stomach flu whenever I thought of Jessi, and for a moment I wished I hadn't come.

She was waiting on the steps of the house, a one-and-a-half-story log cabin so neat and well kept that it looked more like a vacation rental than a place where a real person would live. Jessi looked different too.

When I'd seen her at the faculty meeting, my only thought had been that she wasn't as pretty as I'd remembered, but that had been a shortsighted judgment. She had aged, but not necessarily in a bad way. She looked strong and capable, her face bare of makeup and her long graying hair pulled back in a thick ponytail like a horse's mane. There was something about her that reminded me of my mother, I thought, and I realized my palms were sweating, the way they did on a plane right before takeoff.

"Thanks for bringing this shit," she said, holding the door for Sean, who was carrying a stack of files. He staggered to the table, pretending that his arms were about to give out from the weight, and slapped them down on a placemat stitched with the image of a moose.

Jessi hadn't asked me to come in, but I took advantage of the open door and slipped in behind Sean. Inside, the cabin looked even more like a showplace, all honey-colored wood, plaid blankets, and ceramic wildlife-themed knickknacks. I wondered if this was a rental and Jessi was just staying here temporarily, or if this was her actual design aesthetic.

I heard a door close at the back of the house and a boy emerged, maybe eleven or twelve but so tall that he had to hunch a little to get through the door. I'd taught a handful of college students on the autism spectrum, and I recognized his way of holding his body, along with the gaze that didn't quite settle on any one face. His skin was several shades darker than Jessi's, but he had the same shiny raven-colored hair falling to his shoulders.

"Hello," he said. His voice sounded stiff, as if he'd rehearsed the word in his mind before he said it out loud.

"Hey, buddy." Sean stepped forward to clap him on the shoulder, and the boy didn't flinch as I'd expected. "This is my friend Nicola. She works with me and your mom. How are you feeling today?"

The boy sketched a quick wave in her direction. "Are we getting pizza?" he asked his mom, who was leaning over the table thumbing through the files.

"Why don't we take a walk out to the paddock real quick?" Sean asked. "I want to see that new bay you've been telling me about. Maybe I'll do a little bareback riding."

"You're not allowed to do that," the boy said, and Sean stared at him, feigning incredulity. "It's not healthy for the horses," he went on as they walked outside. "They're used to restraint. That's what makes them comfortable." I could hear Sean arguing on the way down the steps, asking how he knew, had anyone ever actually *asked* the horses?

Jessi took two Miller Lites from a mini-fridge under the counter. "He's good with kids," she said. "The more difficult they are, the better he is with them. It's a real gift."

I took the beer she handed me and followed her out to the back porch. "It's still pretty much the last thing I would have predicted," I said. "Sean becoming an actual grown-up."

"He was an idiot in high school, but who wasn't?" She sat in one of the Adirondack chairs and put her feet up on a low table that seemed to have been placed for that purpose. Gesturing at the mountains with her beer, she said, "He probably told you about the view."

He hadn't, but I could understand why she'd mention it. Rolling green fields in the foreground ended at a line of flame-colored oaks and maples that ran along the Campbell River. On the other side, the mountains pitched up, their crests backlit against the sky, which had gone from hard blue to the light, milky shade of an Easter egg as the sun declined. I was pretty sure that one sharp peak to the right was the backside of Bearwallow Mountain.

"How is your son doing?" I asked, phrasing the question carefully to allow her to tell me as much or as little as she chose. "Sean said you'd been home for a couple of days."

She didn't answer right away. Following the line of her gaze, I saw that they'd appeared beside a fence in the distance. Sean was talking, gesturing with both arms, and the boy nodded seriously as if filing the information away for future reference, his hair swinging into his eyes. "He has bad anxiety and OCD sometimes," Jessi said finally. "It can be hard to get him out of the house. I had to take him out of the middle school last spring because of bullying. He goes to an alternative school in Ewald now. Sean was a big help getting it all squared with the district."

I cast about for the proper response. It wasn't *I'm sorry*, I was pretty sure about that, but what else was there? "Nicola, why are you here?" Jessi asked, working her nail under the label of her beer. "If you have something to say, spit it out."

I was startled enough to blurt out the plan I'd been meditating on during our drive over from the high school. "I want to talk to your brother," I said. "I was hoping you could put me in touch with him."

"You want to talk to Matt?" She peeled off a long strip of the label and laid it carefully on the wide arm of her chair. "Why?"

I reminded myself to slow down, to tread carefully. "I was the one who pointed the cops toward your dad," I said. "Sometimes I wonder if maybe they didn't follow up on other leads because they were so focused on him."

Jessi blew air through her lips. "It wasn't your fault. You told the police what you saw. They were the ones who ran with it."

"It made sense at the time," I said. "Lauren keys a twenty-thousand-dollar truck, and the next thing you know, she turns up missing. When the police told me your dad was the prime suspect, I didn't think to question them."

Even after all my hesitation, I'd managed to say the wrong thing. "It didn't make any fucking sense," Jessi snapped. "Dad hadn't been in trouble since he was a teenager. Why would he up and kill somebody for no reason?"

I thought but didn't say that Lauren and I had given him plenty of reasons. "I understand how you feel."

Jessi wouldn't look at me. "My mom and dad were happy together," she said. "I didn't pay much attention at the time because I was just a kid, but I look back now and I can see how good they were for each other. Happy marriages are rarer than people think." She stared out at the view, her cheeks hollowing as if she were sucking on something sour. "After he died, she tried to keep going, but there was nothing holding her up anymore."

"What happened to her?" I was sure I knew the answer: she'd moved away, or died of grief.

"She lives with Matt and his wife," Jessi said. "She helps take care of the kids, but she's changed. You can just be having a regular conversation, and all of a sudden she'll say she's tired and has to lie down."

A few strands had come out of her ponytail and blown against the side of her face. Her eyes looked bright, though I couldn't tell if she was tearing up or if it was just the wind. Where would Jessi have ended up if Lauren hadn't disappeared? There was no way to know for sure, but I felt confident that it would not have been Tyndall County.

"Matt's the assistant football coach at Ewald," she said. "You can meet me at the game if you want, and I'll introduce you, but I can't promise he'll talk to you. He doesn't put up with any shit."

I assured her that I didn't want to give him any shit, I just wanted to ask a few questions, but she waved my words away. We finished our beers and I went inside to pee, and when I came out, Sean and Jessi's son were back from the paddock. The boy looked windblown and content, with fresh color in his cheeks.

"Dale was telling me that he got a ninety-four on his math test," Sean was saying. "I told him the highest grade I ever got in math was an eighty-five, and that was because I got extra credit for memorizing the first ten digits of pi."

Jessi looked happy too, I thought as we said goodbye, the weight on her shoulders lifted for a moment. I felt guiltier than ever when it occurred to me that both Warren and Sean had apparently managed to stay friendly with her over the years when I, once her best friend, had abandoned her without a backward glance.

But that wasn't what I was thinking about as Sean and I climbed into his car and drove out past a pair of galloping chestnut colts, their coats shining with sunset light. It made me almost angry to think of the burden that Jessi had placed on her son's shoulders before he was old enough to know better. It wasn't enough that he was built to stick out like a sore thumb in a town where Warren Ballard was the ne plus ultra of manhood. On top of all that, she'd gone and named him Dale.

17

It stood to reason that nobody wanted to believe their father was a murderer. I'd watched enough documentaries about serial killers to know the wives and children often persisted in doubt to the point of absurdity. No one wanted to admit that they had lived with a killer, passed him the butter, shared the same roll of toilet paper. If your father was a monster, then you were the monster's child, and nothing else about you mattered.

That wasn't what I'd heard from Jessi. Denial did something to the face and the vocal cords; you could see and hear it, the same way you could fear or hatred. Jessi had been straightforward, the facts of the matter beyond question from her perspective. She probably hadn't hesitated to name her child after a man whom most of the town considered a murderer, because it was clear to her that most of the town was wrong.

But I didn't want to bring any of this up at the football game. Whether she believed it or not, nothing would make me happier than to be assured that Dale Westcott was innocent, since that would mean that my mistakes had no connection to Lauren's disappearance.

IT HAD BEEN A LONG TIME SINCE I'D BEEN TO A FOOTBALL GAME. IN HIGH school, I'd occasionally made it to one of the home games to cheer for

Sean, even though I could never remember which of the little numbers on the field belonged to him. Now, as I *sorry*'ed and *excuse me*'d over the knees of burly, ornery-looking men in camo and Carhartt jackets, I was surprised to feel tears prickling the corners of my eyes. It was the snare drum, I decided. It got to me, stirred something in the blood. It was the stadium lights, which made the dark outside seem darker, and the smell of clean winter air with a tinge of bonfire smoke. It brought the feelings that had been stirring in me up to the surface. It made me believe that I was on the verge of a revelation, everything falling neatly into place.

Or maybe that feeling had more to do with the notification that had popped up on my phone as I made my way over to Ewald that night. Tender_Medusa had finally responded to my private message, and when I saw what she'd written, I almost drove off the road:

Nicola Bennett, are you serious?

Hahaha

It's Erika ☺

I didn't answer right away. I'd driven the rest of the way in a daze, taking deep breaths to ease the buzzy feeling in my chest. I tried to remember the last time I'd in touch with Erika—was it before or after I finished grad school and took my first job at a tiny little ag school in Nebraska? For a while we'd written emails, the long, detailed letter-like emails that no one seemed to write anymore. It was weird to see her using emojis, but it didn't surprise me to know she was on Reddit. Erika had always liked trivia; she was one of those people who could tell you that it takes seven hundred grapes to make one bottle of wine or that the unicorn is the national animal of Scotland.

It did surprise me, at least a little, to see her on the Lauren Ballard page. Erika had never cared for Lauren. "She's Frankenstein's Barbie," she'd said once, and I knew exactly what she meant—Lauren as a kind of monster of perfection, a plastic doll with her mother's credit card. It was a cruel and limited view of her character, but there was something to it just the same.

Erika and I had broken up before Lauren disappeared, but she was still living in Fletcher then, and I'd gone to her for comfort. She'd done everything a friend could do—made me eat, passed me boxes of tissues—but she'd done it all with a curious sense of reserve that made it clear she was holding back her real opinions. Only once, after two vodka tonics, had she said what was on her mind: "I mean, it's pretty obvious that one of them did it."

We were sitting on the porch of her rental house, watching a trio of sunburned frat guys lug a disemboweled couch out to the curb. "One of who?" I asked.

"One of the Ballards," she said, enunciating carefully. "Probably Warren. Who else would have a motive?"

"Dale Westcott—" I began, but she waved it away.

"Most of us have to take responsibility," she said. "And then there are the people who don't. Somehow they just skate through life never having to pay for anything they do." She swept her arm out from her body in a stagy gesture. "I couldn't stand Lauren, but it fucking sucks that nobody is going to answer for this."

I'd started crying again then, the tears dripping off the end of my nose into my drink. Erika sighed, but she didn't take my hand or pat my shoulder, as I'd hoped she would. "Come on, I'll walk you back to the dorm," she'd said finally. "Maybe we can sober up on the way."

She'd left Fletcher later that year, and while we'd stayed in contact for a time, we'd never discussed Lauren again. Knowing Erika, it made sense that the lack of resolution in the case would have continued to bother her. Stories were supposed to have endings. Questions were supposed to have answers. I didn't agree that Warren must have been involved with Lauren's murder, but I shared Erika's frustration. What kind of world did we live in when someone could abduct a woman in the middle of the night and escape unscathed for sixteen years?

But I had no idea what to say to her now. If I followed up, I'd have to tell her that I was back in our hometown, my academic career having devolved into a one-semester sub position at our old high school. She already knew that I'd started the r/LaurenBallardDisappearance page, and that was embarrassing enough. If she knew I was in Tyndall, sleeping with Warren and going to football games with Jessi, she'd think I'd given up on adulthood, and maybe she'd be right.

I'd made it to the middle of the bleachers before I saw Jessi seated at the far end, dressed more fashionably than I'd ever seen her, in dark-washed jeans and a black sweater, with an accordion file of papers open on her other side. Did she go anywhere without taking paperwork along? "There's Matt," she said, pointing to the Ewald sidelines. "With the headset. The kid he's talking to is my nephew."

Matt Westcott didn't look like his dad; he was taller and broad-chested, with a dark beard clipped close. His attention was focused on the field, but he must have felt my eyes on him because he looked up, frowning in my general direction. I blushed and turned away, as if I'd been checking him out because I found him attractive. "Did you tell him I wanted to talk?"

"Well, I didn't want to spring it on him." Jessi paused, and I felt that she was enjoying my discomfort. "He said you had some fucking nerve."

I tried to fumble through the reasons why I thought it was important that Matt and I have a conversation, but she interrupted me. "Honestly, I don't understand why you're still so interested in this stuff," she said. "I'm sorry for anybody who gets themselves murdered, but let's tell it like it is. Lauren was a terrible person."

I poked at an empty straw wrapper with the tip of my shoe. "She could be a bitch, all right, but she was more than that," I said. "She was complicated."

"Complicated my ass." Jessi took a thermos from her bag and unscrewed the cap with a deft twist. Somebody scored a touchdown then, and I was grateful for the roar of the crowd that allowed us to drop the subject.

For the next hour, I watched Matt Westcott instead of the game. Sometimes he huddled with the head coach, and sometimes he roamed the sidelines, clapping and shouting encouragement. In the fourth quarter, one of the Tyndall players made an illegal hit on Westcott's son, and he got so mad he tore off his headset and threw it on the ground. One side of the stands cheered and the other booed. I couldn't be sure without a program, but I thought the kid who'd hit him might have been Connor Mack.

When I tuned back in, the Tyndall Lions were trotting to the field and listlessly taking their positions to run out the last ten seconds on the clock. Apparently we'd lost, sixteen to seven. The stands were already half empty. I'd thought that Jessi might walk away without a word, but when she started down the bleachers, she waved impatiently for me to follow.

She headed first for her nephew, grabbing his chin and planting a cheek kiss that he tolerated with a bashful smile. When Matt saw her, he sauntered over and threw one arm around each of them. "Glad you made it," he said to Jessi, and paused, looking at me as if trying to place my face.

Jessi nudged me forward. "This is Nicola Bennett. We used to be friends."

Used to be. In that moment I wanted nothing more than for a hole to open in the grass and swallow me up. "Nice to see you again," I said to Matt, my voice sounding unnaturally high. "Do you have a minute to talk?"

He sighed and crossed his arms over his chest, looking as if there were a thousand things he'd rather do. "A minute, but that's it. I'll see you in the locker room," he said to his son, and the boy nodded and jogged away. Jessi had already disappeared in the crowd on the field.

Matt and I fell into step toward the parking lot. "I want to apologize," I said.

This seemed to get his attention, and he slowed his pace. "For what?"

"Lauren Ballard," I began. "Maybe if I'd stopped her from keying the truck, things would have been different. I don't know what your dad did or didn't do, but I feel like I set the whole thing in motion, and I'm sorry."

I'd told only half the story, but Matt grimaced as if I'd already said enough. "Did you interrogate my father?" he said. "Did you beat down our door in the middle of the night to search our house and scare my mother half to death? No, you didn't. So I'm not sure what you're apologizing for."

A group of tipsy-looking middle-aged men in Ewald jackets approached us, cheering and hooting, reaching out to clap Matt on the shoulder. He smiled but in a way that made it clear he wasn't going to stop to talk. Somehow we'd already reached the edge of the parking lot, where the lights were so bright they made me squint. "What do you think happened to your dad on the lake?" I blurted out before he could walk away.

Matt stopped short. "What do you mean? He drowned."

Had the explanation that immediately struck me really never occurred to him? "People said—" I began, but stopped myself before I mentioned the rumors about the sleeping pills. "I mean, didn't you ever think he might have done it on purpose?"

He looked away, flexing his right hand in a gesture that made me want to step back. "My dad wouldn't have killed himself," he said. "Jessi and my mother needed him. *I* needed him. I just kept telling him to hold on until I got home from Fort Bragg, and I'd handle things."

"Fort Bragg?" I repeated. Clearly I'd missed something. "I thought you were deployed when Lauren disappeared."

"No," he said. "I was on leave. Here, let me show you something." Before I could process what he'd just told me, Matt reached into his pocket and pulled out his phone, flipping through the photos app. "I don't know how well you knew my dad," he said. "He was on the water every chance he got. He didn't care if he caught anything, he just liked being out there watching the world wake up."

The picture he held out then showed Dale in an old metal rowboat, wearing sunglasses and a Redskins cap, the ends of his walrus mustache nearly touching the corners of his mouth. Matt cleared his throat. "The second the police called him a person of interest, it was like everyone could just say whatever they wanted about him," he said. "But Dad was a real person. You can't turn him into a villain just to make the details fit."

Though I was pretty sure the *you* was rhetorical, a scalding blush set my cheeks on fire. I wanted to look at the photo again, but Matt stuffed his phone back in his pocket.

"The whole thing was so stupid, anyway," he said. "Everybody knows who did it, even if they won't say it out loud. I know Warren told people he was out of town, but my mom saw his car up at Bearwallow that morning. She remembered it because it was parked next to one of those compact excavators. The ones you can rent from John Deere."

This didn't make any sense. If there was one thing I knew about Lauren's disappearance, it was that Matt Westcott was in Germany and Warren was in North Carolina, and now Matt was telling me that neither of those things were true. "Warren had an alibi," I said.

Matt shrugged. "Well, then somebody else had his car. I wouldn't believe it, though. That whole family's full of shit."

We'd reached my old Toyota, parked in a shadowy corner away from the lights. "Did you tell the police about that?" I asked. "About your mom seeing Warren's car?"

"Of course we did, but they were never going to look at the Ballards," Matt said. "Be careful what you stir up around here, Nicola. Nobody's going to thank you for it. Not even me." He slapped the trunk of my car, but it felt less like a friendly goodbye than a *Get the fuck out of here.*

I placed my hands on the wheel and took a few deep breaths. It was no wonder that Matt resented the Ballard boys. They were the other kind of Southern man—the kind who took their cars to the mechanic instead of putting them up on blocks in the driveway; the kind who played football because they got misty-eyed about teamwork and brotherhood and not for the scholarship money. I'd never heard anything about Warren being seen at Bearwallow the day of Lauren's disappearance, and it sounded like a rumor, like the blood on the dashboard that he swore had never been there in the first place.

I'd come to the game tonight hoping that Matt would be able to convince me of his dad's innocence. The fact that Dale now seemed so much less likely a suspect should have come as a relief, and yet I felt a prickling on my scalp, a sense that something wasn't right. What Matt had just told me shifted him into the picture in place of his dad. He'd admitted that he hadn't been out of the country at the time of Lauren's disappearance, and he clearly had no love for the Ballards. Could he have been so affronted by the damage to his truck and the memory of what happened to Jessi that he'd set out to even the score?

I set my purse in my lap and felt around for the keys hidden among a confusion of hairbrushes, chargers, tampons, and dried-out tubes of lip gloss. My fingers brushed a piece of paper, folded around an object I couldn't identify by touch. I knew before I opened it what the paper would say, in letters made to look like dripping blood: *NO ONE WANTS YOU HERE.*

But the object inside wasn't a knife, as I'd thought at first. It was a straight razor, the case removed, the blade sharpened so finely that when I touched it, blood beaded on the pad of my thumb.

I PUT THE RAZOR AND THE NEW LETTER IN MY UNDERWEAR DRAWER. From time to time I'd take them out and turn the blade this way and that, examining my cut-up reflection: sliver of eye, slice of cheek. The name of a German blade maker was scripted along the side, and I found the same model on eBay for $150.

There was no way to know who had put it in there or when. At school I kept my purse snugged up under the legs of a plant stand so I wouldn't trip when I walked around the room. It would have been easy for a student to slip something in there without my knowledge. Even though I'd found the letter at the game, that didn't necessarily implicate the Westcotts. Matt and Jessi seemed more like the type to stick a razor blade in your face than to slide it into your purse.

I didn't call the police. I knew they'd say the same thing about the razor that they'd said about the cinderblock: I was being pranked, probably by a student. To them, the dead cat had been a bad joke, not a threat, and I wasn't so sure they were wrong. Of course, it was theoretically possible that Lauren's killer was here in town and knew I'd been asking questions, but it didn't make sense that he'd come after me. I wasn't trying to solve her murder. I wasn't a detective. I wasn't even an amateur Web sleuth like the ones on the Reddit thread, spending my time poking around databases and poring over photos of skeletal remains.

Years ago Lauren had said that I wasn't the kind of girl to become a victim, and I still thought she was right. It might give me a sick thrill to imagine myself in the place of the missing and murdered women I read about, but I also counted on certain fundamental differences between us. I'd never had the sense of being marked out for a tragic destiny. I was neither especially interesting nor especially unlucky. Somehow, in spite of everything, I couldn't make myself believe that anything truly terrible could happen to someone like me.

18

It took me another week to reply to Erika, and when I did, I was surprised to find that we had to go through the usual rusty chit-chat: *How are you?* and *Pretty good, you?* We didn't follow each other on social media, but her Instagram was public and I'd occasionally creeped her posts, just as I'd done with Warren before I moved back to Tyndall. I knew that Erika was living in California and married to a woman who worked at an animal rescue. Most of their pics featured dogs and sometimes their son, a solid curly-haired toddler with the surly expression of an out-of-work Teamster. I didn't feel jealous when I looked at those pictures, but I did feel ever more self-conscious about the direction my life had taken.

Over the course of that first week, Erika told me about her job working for a production company that made training modules for universities—*It's not the French new wave, but hey, at least it's film*—and sent pictures I'd already seen online: Erika and her wife, Lollie, posing with a giant prize-winning gourd at the local farmers' market; the boy, whose name was Tobias, pumping his legs in a baby swing with a sun-splashed ocean vista in the background. Erika said that her parents had left Tyndall and moved to Oklahoma to be closer to her brother, who had seven children. *Seven, can you believe it? And before you ask, no, they're not in a cult, just incredibly fertile.* When the conversation at last turned to me, I tried to answer her questions without offering additional information. Yes, my last full-time teaching gig had ended in the spring. No, I didn't have a contract for my book yet. *So where are you now?* she asked finally.

I waited two whole days before opening the app again, and when I did, I saw she'd sent three question marks as a follow-up. *I'm actually in Tyndall*, I wrote before I could change my mind. *My mom died in the spring and I came back to sell her house.*

I'm so sorry, she wrote back immediately. *I always liked your mom.*

That surprised me, since I was pretty sure it wasn't true. I'd never told my mom that Erika and I were dating, but she'd seemed to sense something, and when she visited me at Fletcher, she was even more standoffish with Erika than with other people.

That was around the time Susan and my mom had stopped speaking, and though I'd cherished a fantasy that the conflict originated with my mom defending me from Susan's homophobia, I had to admit that it wasn't the most plausible explanation. My mom believed everything her pastor said about homosexuality, and I was far from sure that she would have stuck up for me if I'd told her the truth. I knew it had bothered Erika that I'd never come out to my mom, and bothered her more that I didn't see it as a problem. After all that, it was strange to hear her saying the conventional things about my mother's death, but maybe age had softened her.

I thought the conversation might end there. It was true that I'd been less than forthcoming, but Erika didn't know that. I'd told her just as much as I told the old acquaintances I ran into at Kroger or the bank, and maybe that was enough. Now we could say *Great seeing you, so good to catch up*, and then go our separate ways.

But then she asked the question I'd been dreading most of all.

Do you ever miss us? Don't get me wrong, I'm happily married, but do you ever think about how things could have gone differently?

It was so close to the question Sean had asked on the night we met at the Hideout that for a moment I felt dizzy. How had I ended up in a situation where all the important people from my past were popping in to ponder the road not taken? What was next, the ghosts of Lauren and my mother wafting in at the stroke of midnight to queue up play-back video of all my past mistakes?

I debated for two days on how to respond, and then I told her the truth. *Yes*, I wrote. *I think about that all the time.*

I HADN'T PLANNED TO HANG OUT WITH ERIKA AT COLLEGE. I'D LIKED HER well enough when we'd worked together at Sam's Videos, but she was a senior while I was a freshman, and I couldn't imagine that we'd have much to do with each other. That was before I found out that she'd been assigned as the resident adviser in Burgess House, which meant she had a double to herself, as well as the only DVD player and window-unit air conditioner in the whole dorm.

In those first weeks, I worried that I'd chosen the wrong school. Maybe I should have taken out loans to attend one of the New England colleges, the ones with dorms like Gothic castles and snow-dusted pine groves along frozen rivers. Though located on the opposite side of the state from Tyndall, Fletcher was disappointingly familiar. The town was so small that you could see from one side of downtown to the other. The only restaurant/bar didn't have a single vegetarian entrée, and despite the ever present odor of disinfectant, the tables always felt sticky. Burgess House turned out to be a redbrick box that looked like a doctor's office, and my roommate was a girl named Becky from Richmond who on the first day announced her plans to move out as soon as she pledged Delta Zeta. I formed tentative friend-ships with a couple of the other non-sorority types on the hall, and we migrated down to Erika's suite on the first floor.

Erika always allowed the group to vote on the first movie, which was usually a comedy or the kind of blockbuster action flick in which hatchet-faced men jumped from the top of one building to the next, but for the second feature, she pulled out one of the art house films she ordered from a catalog. Often I was the only one left by the time the credits rolled at the end of *Double Indemnity* or *Breathless* or *The*

Killing of a Chinese Bookie, struggling to stay awake as disjointed images of strippers and European skylines flashed like the flickers of a dream.

Even when we found ourselves alone, Erika and I never talked about Tyndall. It was as if we'd agreed to pretend that we'd never met before, which was fine with me. I had every intention of reinventing myself in college. In my first semester, I was taking 400-level seminars on Shakespeare's comedies and nineteenth-century women writers. I was determined to be such a standout in class and on the field that neither my coach nor my professors would ever guess I couldn't afford gas money for a weekend trip to Norfolk.

Erika hadn't changed at all since high school, but I found that my perception of her had. I began to notice little details about her, like the way she always sat with her legs folded, almost in a lotus position. Though her features were sharp, she had the lushest lips I'd ever seen, as if she'd gotten one of those celebrity collagen treatments.

One night I fell asleep during the second movie. A few other girls had stayed to watch *The Golden Coach*, but when I woke, the room was empty and I was curled up on Erika's bed, which she'd made by pushing two single beds together. When I turned, I found that she was asleep on her back, her arms flung up as if she were falling in a dream.

At least I'd thought she was sleeping. "How did you like the movie?" she asked, eyes closed.

"Umm." I remembered something about a circus and maybe bullfighting. "It was good."

"What about the part with the flesh-eating eels?"

This didn't sound right. "Well," I said hesitantly, "it was a little violent."

Erika snorted. "That's from *The Princess Bride*, you idiot." She swatted at me and I swatted back, and then somehow I was lying with my head pillowed on her outstretched arm. My heart was beating so loud I was afraid she could hear it.

We kissed for a long time, until my mouth felt bruised, but I didn't try anything else, didn't unbutton her shirt or let my hands roam over her body. I didn't know what to do with a girl, and the whole thing might easily have stopped there. I might have sneaked back to my room and climbed into my single bed without incident. Becky probably had no idea I'd been gone. The next day, going down the long row of hot dishes in the dining hall, Erika and I would have avoided each other's eyes, just as Sean and I had done after the night at Bearwallow.

But Erika knew what to do. She took off my clothes as if I were a doll and used her hand and her mouth to make me come. It happened again the next night and the one after that. Every night I waited for the other girls to leave the room, and then she laid me on my back and did things that made fireworks explode behind my eyes. Then, after a double feature of *Face/Off* and *Last Year at Marienbad*, she raised herself on her elbow and said, "Does it bother you that I'm older than you?"

"What?" I mumbled. My body was still pulsing, and I felt mildly annoyed that she hadn't waited until the next morning to say whatever she had to say.

"The power dynamic," she said with a tinge of impatience. "I just wouldn't want anyone to think I was taking advantage."

I frowned, trying to put my thoughts in order. Erika was only three years older than I was. At Fletcher, as at Tyndall, the senior boys regularly went after the freshman girls, and no one ever seemed to have a problem with it. "I don't know what you mean by power dynamic," I said. "Come here."

Though I'd been attracted to girls before Erika, my fantasies had never gone any further than I'd gone with Jessi Westcott. When I'd thought about what surely came after the kissing and touching, it had struck me as faintly disgusting, like picking up my roommate's dirty underwear from the bathroom floor. Now, though, I was the one who kissed her and slid my fingers into the waist of her pajama bottoms to ease them over her hips. What I'd felt for Sean was a light squall in the face of this great storm that left me pale and shivering, over and again undone.

◆ ◆ ◆

I DIDN'T SEE LAUREN WHEN I WENT HOME FOR CHRISTMAS THAT YEAR, AND hardly gave her a thought until I got a letter on the pink stationery that I couldn't believe she still used. She'd heard that I was staying in Fletcher for the summer, and she wanted to visit. She was getting married in August, and this was her *last chance*, she wrote, underlining the phrase three times.

Erika listened patiently as I anguished over my reply, but soon I noticed her suppressing a sigh whenever I brought up Lauren's name. "Look, I don't care one way or the other," she said. "I always thought she was a bitch, but if you want to see her, that's fine. If you don't want to see her, tell her not to come."

I crumpled Lauren's pink letter. I'd never told Erika what had happened with Jessi Westcott, never explained what I owed Lauren after I'd inadvertently ruined her life. "It'll be fine," I said. "She can be fun. You'll see."

I COUNTED DOWN THE DAYS UNTIL LAUREN'S ARRIVAL, CONSUMED NOT by anticipation but by queasiness and dread. She'd emailed that she'd be there on Friday at five, and at 5:06 she pulled into the driveway of the rental house that Erika had found on the working-class end of downtown Fletcher. Lauren wore cutoffs and an over-size blue T-shirt that made her look less high-maintenance than I remembered. In Tyndall she'd been an archetype; here, she was simply a girl.

She was supposed to stay a week. I worked daytime shifts at the coffee shop downtown, and after work Lauren and I drove down to the weedy public beach to catch the sunset before ending the night at Charlie's, the only bar in town. I'd made friends with the bartender, a bearded local who winked at my fake ID and sometimes rolled his eyes over the heads of the out-of-towners as if we shared a secret.

Lauren never mentioned her wedding. I'd gotten my invitation, *Mrs. Richard Kyle requests the honor of your presence* on heavy embossed card stock, and I'd wondered if Lauren had come to ask me to be a bridesmaid, but the subject never came up. Instead she seemed perfectly content to follow me around town, enthusing over Fletcher's dinky historic district and charming everyone she met. Back in Tyndall, Lauren had called Erika a fuzz bumper, but this week she'd thanked her for putting her up and even complimented her new nose ring. Perhaps she regretted her past behavior, having learned that things were different in college, where two girls could walk around the quad holding hands without anyone batting an eye.

Once I asked Erika what she and Lauren did all day while I was at work, and she shrugged. "She mostly sleeps. I've never seen someone sleep so much. Do you think she might be depressed?"

"No," I said immediately. "What would she have to be depressed about? Her life is perfect. It always has been."

Erika made a face. She was lacing up a pair of vintage Frye boots that were a half-size too small and always made her grouchy. "Nicola," she said, "your naïveté is truly breathtaking sometimes."

ON THE LAST NIGHT, ERIKA AGREED TO COME OUT WITH US. SHE'D BROUGHT home a bottle of vodka from her catering job at the golf club, and we pre-gamed in the backyard before heading out to the bar. Like everything else about Lauren's visit, the drinking we did that week seemed lighthearted, shorn of even the possibility of consequence. At the bar Lauren ordered us tequila shots that we took out on the deck, downing them under the eye of the fading sun.

Later it was too breezy on the deck and we moved inside, to a table crowded between a trio of drunk bikers and a party of rowdy locals celebrating the birthday of someone named Sheila. I saw Erika stiffen when the bartender, delivering the next round, placed his hand briefly on my shoulder. For the next hour, she sipped a single glass of red wine and said little. Lauren chattered on, but she was different too.

Something within her had become barbed and dangerous, and I felt myself flinching in anticipation.

Three drinks in, we decided to play darts. The board was old and scarred, encased in a wooden cabinet with the initials of old winners scratched on the panels. Erika couldn't hit the side of a barn, but I'd spent hours playing with Sean in the Ballards' basement, and Lauren and I kept the game going, finally tying the score at twenty-eight. I was about to close out and go for the bull's-eye when Lauren said in my ear, "So, are y'all in it for the long haul or are you just experimenting?"

I took my shot and hit the nine. "What do you mean?"

When I turned around, I saw that she was smiling. *Butter wouldn't melt in her mouth,* my mother used to say. "I'm just asking," she said. "Have you ever heard the term *lesbian until graduation*? I think the same thing happens in prisons."

Erika stood up from the table. "I'm leaving, Nicola."

Obediently I slid my darts back into the leather case and put my hand out for Lauren's, but she held them away from me. "I want to stay. Just leave the door unlocked."

I tried to talk her out of it, but she wouldn't budge. The bartender, cleaning glasses, studiously ignored us, but I could tell that he and Lauren were aware of each other, like two animals circling in the dark. Erika took my hand and tugged me toward the exit. Lauren could take care of herself, she'd tell me later as I lay sleepless in our bed. "You're not her keeper," she'd say.

She was wrong, I thought: I *was* Lauren's keeper. I was responsible for and to her, and now I was going to have to call Warren and explain that I'd let her go off with some near-stranger whose last name I didn't even know. I imagined the call I'd have to make to the police, and then I saw myself shamed out of Fletcher, the target of whisper campaigns and pointed stares. We had a very active chapter of Take Back the Night, and I knew that rule number one was never leave a drunk friend alone.

At six in the morning, I was on my way to the kitchen to make coffee when I heard the door on the screened porch creak open. Lauren slid in sideways and winked at me. She looked exactly the same as she had the night before, skin glowing, not a hair out of place. "Where the fuck have you been?" I whispered.

She smirked. "None of your business."

I wanted to yell, but tears came to my eyes instead. "You ruin everything. Why are you like that?" I asked, choking back a sob. "It's not fair."

"What are you talking about?" She shucked off her parka and hung it on one of the pegs. "Hey, what do you think Erika would say if I wanted to move in for a while? I can pay a third of the rent, and I don't need a bedroom. I can sleep on the couch."

It was the last thing I'd expected. "What about the wedding?"

She met my gaze and I noticed that the skin around her eyes and nose was faintly pink, as if she'd scrubbed it with a tissue. "People cancel weddings all the time," she said. "It's not the end of the world."

I tried to picture what it would mean to cancel this one—deposits forfeited at St. Philip's and the country club; a designer dress hung in the closet of her childhood bedroom, never to be touched. And those were only the material repercussions. Warren would be brokenhearted, I was sure.

I couldn't deny that seeing Lauren brought down a notch would scratch some petty itch in my psyche, but her willingness to besmirch her perfect image made me suspicious. What did she plan to do if she didn't marry Warren Ballard? And how would I explain to Erika that Lauren intended to camp on our couch for the foreseeable future? "You'd have to apologize," I said. "Erika's really mad about last night." What Erika had actually said was *That girl is a grade-A bitch and I can't fucking believe you didn't stand up for us*, but I was not going to tell Lauren that.

"I'm pregnant," Lauren said, sitting on the steps. "I flushed my pills down the toilet."

It was the last thing I'd expected. "So you were *trying* to get pregnant? Why would you do that?"

"I honestly don't know." She braced her elbows on her knees and cupped her face in her hands. "I think I just wanted to see what would happen."

I sat on the step below hers. "Well, it's not rocket science," I said. "Jesus, Lauren, you've been drinking like a fish all week."

Lauren shrugged. "It doesn't matter. I don't think I'm going to have it. I thought maybe you'd go to the clinic with me."

"I guess," I said. "I mean, if you need me to."

Then I set about trying to talk her out of it. I told her she should go home. I told her that Warren loved her and they'd make a beautiful family. When the sun was up, I took her into the kitchen and made her coffee and a bagel that she tore into pieces instead of eating. Finally she looked up and the old poise was back, her eyes shining like a blade. "Forget it," she said. "I'm fine. I don't know what I was thinking."

WHEN MY NICOLA NECKLACE WENT MISSING, I DIDN'T THINK TO CONNECT it to Lauren's visit. I didn't wear the necklace at Fletcher anyway; the last I'd seen it, it had been stuffed in a jewelry pouch with the imitation pearl earrings I'd worn to graduation and some old Bakelite bracelets I'd found at a yard sale. The pouch's zipper stuck, and it was easy to imagine the necklace falling out as I carted it from the dorm to our summer rental. I felt a pang of regret for my mom's sake, but then again, she never had to know.

When I thought about it now, I realized it was no wonder that Lauren had wanted revenge. I'd told myself that she chose Warren and early motherhood, but that wasn't true, or at least not entirely. What if I'd taken her to Planned Parenthood? What if I'd given her permission to stay with us for a while? Maybe it would have given her time to imagine a life that didn't revolve around babies and starter homes and the same faces at football games and charity galas year after goddamn year.

Lauren and I had made each other's fates. Erika and I had broken up not long after her visit, and though Erika had lingered in Fletcher for another year and a half, the connection between us was never the same. I knew she'd lost respect for me when it turned out that I cared more about other people's opinions than I did about her, and I couldn't really blame her. In the years since, I'd occasionally dated women, but only in the enlightened college towns where I landed for temporary teaching appointments, and even then the relationships had never lasted longer than a month or two. If I hadn't been willing to go all in for Erika, I certainly wasn't going to do it for anyone else.

Lauren and I had destroyed each other. She'd planted the seed of disloyalty in me, and then I'd turned around and packed her off to Warren like a package COD. Even now, all these years later, I still didn't know which one of us was worse.

19

I decided to let the rest of my time in Tyndall play out, like the last seconds of a tennis match when even the announcers have stopped paying attention. I'd do my job, such as it was. I'd be friendly with Sean and Jessi but not too friendly. I would not, would not, would not talk to Warren, no matter what.

It wasn't what Matt had said at the football game that was bothering me. Warren had told me himself that the police had processed his car, checking for blood, and that didn't seem like the kind of thing someone would lie about. It was true that Warren and Sean benefited from their family name, and the cops might have been inclined to let him go with a warning if caught speeding in a school zone, but I was pretty sure that even the Ballard laissez-faire wouldn't extend to covering up a murder.

But Warren didn't need to be a murderer to be a shitty boyfriend. I knew his character now in a way that I hadn't six months ago. I knew him the way Lauren must have known him, and I could see the flaws that might have made her want to crash on my couch indefinitely rather than going home to marry him. I was so determined to cut him out of my life that I deleted his number from my phone, and so when he finally called, I simply stared for a few moments before I found the presence of mind to press accept.

◆ ◆ ◆

THE WINDOWS WERE DARK WHEN I ARRIVED, BUT THE DOOR OPENED immediately in response to my knock, as if he'd been waiting behind it. He wore basketball shorts and a Georgetown Hoyas T-shirt with a coffee stain near the collar, and his hair was mussed, his chin prickly with stubble. He certainly hadn't dressed up for me, but then again, he didn't have to. At the sight of his face, I felt the familiar mutinous jolt in the pit of my stomach.

Lucky II nosed between Warren's legs and bumped his snout against my fist, wiggling joyously. "Hey," Warren said, sounding startled, though he was the one who'd called me. "Want a drink? I have bourbon. Ginger ale, water."

"No, thanks," I said, turning my body to keep a careful distance between us as I passed into the living room. He'd been tying flies; pliers, tweezers, and a weird hook thing with a spool of thread at the end were laid out on the coffee table. "Where's Mabry?"

"Susan has her for Thanksgiving."

"Why don't you spend it together?"

Warren ran a hand through his hair, which needed a trim. "I'm not a big fan. Never liked turkey."

"Same." When I was growing up, my mom and I never did holiday meals. She said it was too much trouble for just two people, and I'd inherited the sense that cooking all day just so you could spend the whole night doing dishes was an incomprehensible waste of time.

"I wasn't expecting to hear from you," I said, perching on the edge of the leather club chair and angling my knees toward the heat of the wood-stove. "Isn't it a little strange to get an offer on a house today?"

"It's unusual, but I think they really want an answer ASAP." He pronounced it like a word instead of an acronym, a habit that always annoyed me. "It's that family who drove down on Tuesday. One-seventy-five with twenty percent down, no contingency, sixty-day close. Apparently it's going to be their country getaway." He leaned forward to pick up the long-handled tool from the coffee table.

"Seriously?" I said. "They think a town of two thousand people is the country?"

"When you're from D.C., maybe it is." He wrapped the thread around a fishhook, intent as a jeweler. "Anyway, it's a full-price offer. What do you want me to do?"

Though the thought of not having a home to come back to filled me with mild panic, I had no reason to say no. "Take it, I guess."

He went out on the porch to call the buyer's agent, and I made no effort to listen. Through the window, I watched him pace, gesturing with his free hand. He looked more animated now, more like the old Warren, as if the prospect of a deal had excited him. I poured out the feathers that he'd been attaching to the flies and sorted them into piles by color.

"She's sending me the contract," he said as he stepped back in, rubbing his hands. "Damn, it's cold out there." He sank onto the couch, the expectant pleasure lingering on his face. "I'm glad you stopped by. I've missed you, Nicola."

I didn't respond. Picturing Warren on Thanksgiving, I'd imagined him in a creased button-down and his best dad jeans, making pumpkin tiramisu in tiny ramekins while music played from the Bose speakers on the counter. Somehow it was a relief to find that he preferred to spend the holiday mildly drunk, tying next season's flies in an empty house, but I still didn't know where to start. "Why didn't you call?" I asked. "If you missed me, you could have just said so."

"I don't know." He laughed a little, though I wasn't sure what was funny. "I should have, I guess. I'm bad at this kind of thing."

I didn't have to ask what kind of thing. I thought of the girlfriends between Lauren and me, the ones who didn't stay for breakfast. With a few of the high school classmates who'd asked me about Warren when I first moved back, I'd caught a whiff of jealousy, and for the first time I found myself wondering how many of Tyndall's soccer moms he'd bedded and ghosted. Maybe it wasn't loyalty to Lauren's memory that had kept him single all this time. Maybe he simply didn't know how to have a relationship.

Suddenly I wanted to put him on the defensive, even though I already knew he'd deny everything. "I heard something about you," I said finally, picking out one of the orange feathers and turning it in my hand. "Somebody told me that you were here in Tyndall the weekend that Lauren disappeared. People saw your car."

He sighed, an out-of-place smile still on his lips. "Yeah, I was here," he said. "I dropped Mabry off with my parents at the beach and then drove back to Tyndall. I told the cops about it the same day I reported Lauren missing."

My hand hurt, and I realized that I'd squeezed my thumb and forefinger hard enough to crush the feather into a ball. "You told me they processed your car. You said that a forensics team went over it and there was nothing."

"They did," he said. "I didn't say I killed her. I just said I was here."

He stood and walked into the kitchen, and I watched the muscles in his back move as he reached to take down the bourbon from the built-in liquor cabinet. It was the good stuff, an artisanal Virginia blend that my mother never could have afforded. Warren set the bottle and two heavy cut-glass tumblers on the table with a clunk. "There are a lot of things you don't know," he said.

HE'D FOUND THE ENVELOPE IN LAUREN'S PURSE NOT LONG AFTER THEY were married. The letter inside was missing, but he saw that the return address belonged to a neighborhood of million-dollar houses in the West End of Richmond.

Lauren had been secretive about her life at college. On the weekends, she'd always insisted on coming to him in Charlottesville rather than him visiting her. She said it was because she hated Burwell, but when she told Warren that she didn't want to go to the spring formal, he had to wonder if she was telling him the whole truth. Lauren loved dances, and the fact that she didn't like her classmates should not have been reason enough to forgo the pleasure of showing up late and half-drunk in a skintight cocktail dress.

When they married and moved back to Tyndall, he'd overheard occasional late-night whispered phone calls and caught a glimpse of emails that she deleted as soon as she saw him looking at the screen. Once somebody sent her a bouquet of lilies on a day that was nowhere near her birthday or their anniversary. She claimed they were from her mom, but when Warren found a reason to mention them in front of Susan, she looked at him as if she had no idea what he was talking about. Now suddenly Lauren wanted to drive up to Richmond once or twice a month, sometimes staying overnight, sometimes only for a couple of hours. She said she was seeing friends, but what friends?

Then he found the letter. The return address said Taylor Vaughn, and the name alone filled Warren with righteous contempt. "But it wasn't what I thought," he said.

I took another sip of the bourbon and tried not to cough. "What do you mean?"

Instead of answering, he reached for his phone and typed the name into Google. I wasn't surprised that the first result was for the website of a white-shoe law firm with offices in Richmond and D.C., Vaughn & Barclay. I'd been picturing a stereotypical upper-middle-class WASP, a grown-up version of Connor Mack, and so far, everything fit.

But when Warren clicked on the banner titled *About*, it wasn't what I'd imagined at all. For one thing, Taylor Vaughn was a woman. For another, it was a face I'd seen before—the face of the girl from the photo in the Nine West box. The awkward, homely teenager who had leaned against the brick wall beside Lauren, the bones of her clavicle visible above the gaping collar of her oversize T-shirt. She had cleaned up nicely: her hair was cut in an asymmetrical style that flattered the sharp angles of her face, and the glare of a surly adolescent now looked fierce and confident. It was a look of a woman you would trust to—I skimmed the bio below the photo—*provide an aggressive and effective defense for our valued clients.*

I tried not to let the recognition show on my face. Warren didn't know that I'd stolen the photo, much less the connection I'd just made:

Teevee, Taylor Vaughn. From what he'd said to Detective McRae, he'd never thought much about who might have taken the arty photos in the Nine West box. "So you think Lauren was having an affair with a woman?" I asked.

"No," he said. "I think she gave her money. And I think Taylor stole it."

On her twenty-first birthday, Lauren had come into an inheritance that her father had set up through a family trust. Though Susan already gave her a substantial allowance, that money came with the assumption that she'd keep her mother happy, while this was twenty-five thousand dollars with no strings attached. After they were married, Warren had suggested that they invest it together, but Lauren demurred. A friend had suggested that they buy some property together, and she wanted to look into it before she made a decision.

"I'm not going to lie, it pissed me off," Warren said. "My dad owned a brokerage. Why was she going to a stranger for investment advice? When I finally got access to her bank accounts after she disappeared, that twenty-five thousand dollars wasn't anywhere. I remembered Taylor Vaughn's name from the letter, and I looked up her holdings online. She'd paid one-fifty in cash for a house in Jackson Ward right around the time that Lauren went missing." He scratched at his stubble. "I tried to talk to Taylor a few times. Once I even went to the house. I was polite and all—I didn't make a scene or anything, but she wouldn't let me in."

"So you think Taylor killed her?" I asked, leaning over the table to pour myself another shot. "To cover up the theft?"

Warren was quiet for a moment, and then he shook his head—reluctantly, I thought. "From what I can tell, Taylor doesn't need to steal twenty-five thousand dollars. I think she just wanted to fuck me over. I mean, she only got one side of the story. I'm sure Lauren told her all kinds of things."

"So you came back to town that day to follow her," I stated. "Because you thought she was up to something."

He shrugged. "I didn't know what I was looking for. I didn't know if Lauren was meeting Taylor or if it was something else—if maybe she was seeing another guy. After I dropped Mabry at the beach, I drove back in time to follow you to the river that morning. Then I went up to Bearwallow to wait. I was going to stake out the house on Blue Ridge Road that night and wait for somebody to show up, but I accidentally fell asleep and didn't wake up until two o' clock in the morning. When I finally got there, the lights were off and Lauren's car was in the driveway. I waited for a while, but I didn't see anything and decided I'd just been paranoid. I drove back to the beach and that was that."

He moved his chair an inch closer, and suddenly our knees were touching. "I'm lucky I'm not in prison," he said. "I think the only reason the police went easy on me is they didn't believe I could really be that stupid. If I was going to kill my wife, I would have done a better job of covering my tracks."

Though it wasn't the point of the story, I couldn't help being stunned by what he'd revealed about the investigation. The police knew that Warren was in town and still didn't consider him a person of interest. Even if I was still pretty sure that he had nothing to do with what happened to Lauren, I'd learned something new and troubling about the Ballard family. It wasn't just that Warren had never been a real suspect. It was that he never could have been a real suspect, not even if he'd been found standing over his wife's bloody body with a carving knife in his hand.

And where did that leave me? Should I use what he'd told me as an excuse to stomp out? In all our private messages, I'd never told Erika about my fling with Warren earlier in the fall—not because the relationship had ended but because I was embarrassed to admit that it had happened in the first place.

"I feel weird saying that I believe you," I said. "Because you really haven't given me any reason to. You lied, and you were kind of a dick the last time we saw each other."

Instead of answering, he leaned forward, and I was tipsy enough not to pull away. He was so good at this—first the long kiss, fingers gently tugging on the hair at the back of my neck; then the slight tinge of consensual roughness as he pulled me into his lap. Now my skirt was around my waist, and part of me wanted to ask wouldn't Mabry be back soon, shouldn't we go upstairs, but then he shoved my underwear out of the way and pulled me down on him and I wasn't thinking of anything at all.

I'd come back to Tyndall wanting to prove that I wasn't implicated in Lauren's death, but later, lying in Warren's bed, I admitted to myself that I didn't really want her found, alive or dead. I didn't want to see Warren, Mabry, and Susan consumed by the horror of imagining her last hours. I certainly didn't want her hauled back to the light after a decade and a half in some psychopath's basement. I could imagine nothing worse than Lauren coming home to find that I'd had sex with her husband in the living room with the blinds wide open, for once in my life wholly incapable of giving a damn what the neighbors thought.

20

The next few weeks were a daydream. I came over after work and drank wine at the kitchen island while Warren made soup with white beans and escarole. On weekends, we drove farther into the mountains and browsed outdoor Christmas markets in adorable tourist towns. We hiked to the overlook on Bearwallow Mountain and took a selfie against a backdrop of winter branches. We went out to the new Thai place that had been written up as a weekend destination in *The Washington Post*, and the locals we passed as we walked to our table smiled and nodded, not just at Warren but at me too. When we went for a walk on the new greenway along the Campbell River, we could hardly go a quarter mile without someone coming up to ask Warren how his parents were doing or to wax poetic about a pass he'd made against Logan County in 1996. Sometimes I'd hum "Glory Days" under my breath just to make him blush.

I'd always thought that Warren and Lauren looked like they'd stepped out of a magazine, but now it was as if I'd fallen into the full-page ad with the new grill and the checkered picnic blanket. Now I was the woman with the quilted vest and furry boots, throwing a stick for an adorable lunk of a black Lab. It was a strange feeling, not unpleasant but vaguely unreal, as if I were playing a part in a play. On the other hand, maybe this was the realest I had ever been.

At times I felt a sense of trepidation that quickened my heartbeat. I'd tried to tell myself that the red letters and the dead cat were just childish pranks. I'd never even told Warren about the razor that had shown up in my purse at the Ewald game. I hadn't wanted to believe that anyone could see me as a threat, but what if I was wrong? What if it wasn't my interest in Lauren's disappearance but my mere presence in Tyndall County that had pissed somebody off?

Weeks ago Warren had raised the possibility that Lauren was out there somewhere, keeping tabs on the family she'd abandoned. It defied logic to imagine her skulking around her hometown slipping notes under my windshield and blades into my purse, and yet deep down I believed that I was due some kind of reckoning. It wasn't only that I had moved in on Warren. I had slipped into another woman's life, and surely some cosmic punishment would be meted out for my willingness to abandon every ethical principle for Sunday-morning made-to-order omelets and good dick.

Then I got the text from Erika. *Just wanted you to know,* she'd written. *They found Opal Yarrow's body.*

THE YARROW FAMILY HAD MOVED AFTER OPAL'S DISAPPEARANCE, TO A tiny town south of Richmond. The church where the service was held, St. Rose of Lima, had clearly been built in the sixties and could have been a high school gym if it weren't for the image of the saint on the front. She smiled mildly and held one hand against her chest, positioned as if she'd just finished zipping up a blue graduation robe.

I took a seat in the third row from the back and watched the other guests file in: old women; teenage boys looking uncomfortable in ties and button-downs; young mothers holding babies. How many of them had known Opal, and how many had come because they knew the family, or simply for the spectacle of the thing? The group of people who would feel her loss after this long would be small: parents, certainly; siblings; maybe a few friends.

I was surprised to spot a face I knew. It was Malik Walker, who was in my second-period AP with Connor and Mabry. He was hard to miss; almost a head taller than the group of women clustered around him, he stood straight in his black suit, his eyes roving around the room until they settled on me with a startled look. He raised his hand—a quick wave, funeral-appropriate—and I nodded back.

But maybe it shouldn't have been a shock to see Malik here. The Black population in Tyndall and Ewald counties numbered in the low single digits, and it made sense that the families would know each other. Though Opal had disappeared right around the time Malik was born, he would have grown up hearing about her, probably as much or more as he heard about Lauren Ballard. He would have heard about how little attention the police had paid to the original report, insisting to Opal's parents that she'd just run off and would be back when she felt like it. For Malik, she might have been a warning, Exhibit A in his family's cautionary tales.

A photograph I remembered from some of the news articles had been placed on an easel at the front of the church, under a nearly life-size crucifix. I kept looking from one to the other, from Opal's braids and fat cheeks to Jesus' anguished face. Feeling queasy, I checked my phone, and a white woman beside me turned to give me a dirty look. She had a high ponytail and a spot of red on each cheekbone that looked as if she'd colored it with crayon. I stared right back at her, and she turned around with a small sniff.

I didn't listen to the sermon. The priest was young and good-looking, and probably adept at keeping his audience's attention under normal circumstances, but I could tell he hadn't known Opal. "When a young soul is taken from us, the saints mourn with us," he intoned, and I discreetly glanced down at my text app.

After Erika and I had switched from private messages to texts, our contact had dwindled to once or twice a week. I thought that was probably a good thing in most ways, especially now that I was back together with Warren. A little nostalgic flirtation was one thing, but I couldn't let myself feel any more than that for a woman who was happily married and lived nearly three thousand miles away. Still,

I was sure she'd want to hear about Opal's funeral, so I typed out a quick *This is so sad, her family looks devastated.* Next were more hymns, and I was thinking about checking my phone again when a woman stood and walked to the lectern.

I could feel everyone sit up straight. This woman could have been an age-corrected version of the picture on the Missing posters, tall now and poised, dressed in a black suit that looked as if it had been professionally tailored. Even without the program, I would have known that this was Jennifer Yarrow, Opal's twin.

"No one can understand what it's like," Jennifer said. She paused, her hand to her throat, and when she started again, her voice was thick. "The last time I saw Opal, we were playing hide-and-seek and she was running down the street to hide. I was supposed to count to sixty and then go find her, but I never saw her again."

She described how she'd waited at home for her sister, at first only a little worried but later in full-blown panic. None of the scenarios that were offered made any sense. Opal would not have jumped in a car with strangers. She would not have gone anywhere without telling Jennifer. "I knew right away that something had happened," she said, her whole body held so rigid that I was afraid she might buckle at the knees.

She didn't tell the rest of the story. How, just weeks ago, a developer had bought an abandoned house a block away from where Opal's family had lived back then. How they'd found a chest freezer in the basement, the old-fashioned kind that locked when the lid closed. How, when they lifted the lid, they'd found the mummy of a girl wearing pink sneakers and a tattered and faded Minnie Mouse T-shirt. Looking at her sister's face, I was certain that her family was just as tortured by the thoughts of her last moments as Lauren's family could ever be. That small child alone in the dark, unable to scream or to breathe.

Jennifer started sobbing, and a man with a red carnation in his lapel stood to escort her back to her seat. The organist launched into another hymn, and my stomach heaved. Maybe I didn't belong here. Maybe what I thought of as empathy was nothing more than a greedy feeding on someone else's catastrophe.

After the final hymn, I would have made a quick exit, but the man at the end of the row ushered me into the line of people waiting to express their sorrow to Jennifer and the rest of the family. Malik was just a few steps up the aisle, and as I approached, he moved away from the women he was talking to. "Hey, Ms. Bennett," he whispered, maintaining his sorrowful expression. "I didn't expect to see you here."

In a student body notable only for its general torpor, Malik had stood out to me for both his intelligence and his sweetness. This year's star quarterback, he had a GPA that put him in the running for valedictorian, and he held down a part-time job at Kroger after school. Sometimes he lingered after class to talk about the paintings I'd put up. It turned out that he admired the Dutch masters for the same reason I did, their tangibility and specificity: an orange was an orange, a nose was a nose. Last week he'd told me he'd been accepted to The Citadel with a full scholarship. He was beaming, shy with pride, but he added that he'd still have to pay for books and travel, and money was tight.

As one of the few students of color in the senior class, Malik had far more in common with Jessi Westcott than with me, and yet I understood this part of his life—the desperate drive to scrape together enough dollars to make it out of Tyndall County. The next time I'd seen him in the checkout line, I'd tried to slip him a twenty palmed around a honeydew, but he told me they weren't allowed to accept tips.

The man behind Malik was watching me carefully, clearly trying to determine what business I might have with his son. I didn't think it was the right time to introduce myself, but I smiled in what I hoped was a reassuring way. "Did your family know Opal?" I asked Malik.

"Yeah, my parents grew up in Ewald. How about you?" he said politely, but the line was moving into a more congested part of the church, where an older woman clutching a clump of tissues to her face was openly weeping. I put a finger to my lips and shrugged as the crowd bore me away.

When only three people separated me from Opal's family, I exited the line, directing my path so anyone paying attention would think

I was heading for the bathroom. Beside the women's room, I found a door to the parking lot and punched the gold bar, letting in a shivery draft and the smell of snow.

As I buttoned my coat, I looked back at Malik. He'd bowed his head over the woman with the tissues, who clutched his arm like a life raft. Aimed up and out of Tyndall County, he was the antonym of the poor child locked in her makeshift coffin. The crying woman looked up at him with a hungry hopefulness, and I felt as if I'd trespassed on something intensely private.

In the face of real grief, I saw the inadequacy of what I'd felt for Lauren. I had missed her unpredictability, her vivid boldness, but what I'd missed the most was what her presence had done for me, transforming the monotony of the everyday into something bright and thrilling. Even the fact of her vanishing had been converted to suit my purposes. I wanted to know why she'd disappeared. I wanted an ending, and the lust for narrative coherence that had driven me now seemed as contemptible as bidding for a serial killer's dried-out toothbrush on eBay. If Lauren was still out there somewhere, she had every right to be furious with me.

In the parking lot, wind spun snowflakes through the air and kicked pellets of gravel against my ankles. The smell of exhaust churned my stomach. Turning my body away from the mourners, I threw up in the dead grass beside my car—a sudden, desperate retching, a sour taste in my mouth that wouldn't go away.

21

For the first time I understood where I'd gone wrong. My insistence on seeing Lauren as the Girl Who Had Everything had made it impossible for me to ever know her. Judging by the secrets she'd kept, Warren and Susan hadn't had a clue who she really was either, and Sean had been too fucked up to pay much attention to anything outside his own head. That left one person who might be able to tell me about the real person under that shiny surface: Taylor Vaughn.

After Warren had shown me her picture, I'd googled her myself and pored over the results. I'd learned that she'd gone to St. Catherine's School, like Mrs. Ballard, and then to Burwell, graduating with Lauren's class in 2000. I signed up for both alumni newsletters, but among the bits of news on weddings and babies and promotions, there was never anything about Taylor Vaughn. On social media, I found her tagged in the background of a few pictures from regattas and charity luncheons, but no matter how far back I went, I couldn't identify partners or ex-partners or even close friends. As a lawyer, Taylor was probably cautious about putting her personal business on the Internet, and I had to admire how thoroughly she'd managed to stay out of sight.

Before Warren had mentioned it, I hadn't realized that you could research someone's real estate holdings online, but now I found that the house Taylor owned in Jackson Ward had nearly doubled in value since 2003. She also owned two rental properties near downtown, along with a house worth nearly $2 million on Demeter Avenue that I assumed was her primary residence. When I plugged the address into my phone, I saw that it was only fifteen miles from the town where Opal's service had been held.

In economic terms, it might as well have been the distance from here to the moon. The houses in Taylor's neighborhood were the size of elementary schools. Burwell College sat right in the middle, the declining sun turning the buildings a brittle bright orange. A few students walked back and forth on the dead grass, hunched over the books in their arms.

Taylor probably did pretty well for herself as an attorney, but this neighborhood required money that went back generations, piles and piles of it. Still, even the mansions of the neighbors didn't prepare me for the sight of 743 Demeter Avenue, which made me take my foot off the gas and idle there in the middle of the road, gaping as if I'd never seen a house before.

It was a contemporary, at least six thousand square feet, all glass and stucco, like something Frank Lloyd Wright might have built for the Kardashians. In this neighborhood of redbrick and Colonial Revivals, it clearly had been designed to make the neighbors clutch their pearls, and I found myself wondering how Warren would have written the listing description. He would have said: *This stunning modernist home features luxurious finishes throughout.* It was *exquisitely appointed and impeccably maintained*; it was *the house your friends will envy.*

Lauren certainly would have envied it. At first I'd been surprised by her friendship with Taylor Vaughn, too odd-looking to be even an effective foil, but when I saw the house, everything clicked. Burwell was only a mile away, and it was easy to imagine Lauren swinging by here on a run or executing a pretend-spontaneous drive-by. How her jaw must have dropped when she saw where the girl she'd probably dismissed as an awkward rando had grown up. Beside this place, even the nicest homes in Tyndall—even Bearwallow—looked small and old-fashioned, frumpy relics of a forgotten time. I knew without hesitation that Lauren had wanted this for herself, and that whatever relationship she'd had with Taylor would have had a sense of envy at its heart, the canker in the rose.

"SO WHY DIDN'T YOU KNOCK?" SEAN ASKED.

I gave him a look. "Like I'm going to just go up to the door and say, 'Hey, I think we had a mutual friend sixteen years ago'? She'd think I was a crazy person."

"Maybe, but what's the alternative? Keep driving by until you see her taking out the garbage and then do a meet-cute?"

"I doubt she takes out her own garbage," I said. "You should see this place, Sean. She probably has a personal assistant to wipe her ass."

I'd told Sean about Taylor out of a sense of desperation. Though Erika and I had reconnected on the Lauren Ballard Reddit page, I was afraid that borderline-stalking Lauren's college friend might strike her as a bit over the top, and I certainly couldn't talk to Warren. That left Sean as my only possible confidant. I wasn't looking for the answers to Lauren's disappearance, I told him. I could see now how my adolescent self-absorption had made me oblivious even to the people I thought I'd known best—Lauren, Erika, my mother—and I hoped that talking to Taylor would give me the perspective I'd lacked back then.

"You could do one of those candygrams," he said as we started down the stairs. "Remember that old *Saturday Night Live* skit with the shark?"

I was about to tell him he was the only person I knew who still quoted *Saturday Night Live* when I heard a voice from the landing on the first floor. I knew the cadence and the tone: Jessi's son, Dale. I prepared to press myself against the wall and wait them out. I hadn't slept well the night before and I just wanted to go back to Warren's and take a nap while he made dinner, but of course Sean had other plans.

"Hey there!" he yelled, his voice echoing in the empty stairwell. "I hear congratulations are in order."

I had no idea what he was talking about, but when we reached the bottom, I saw that Jessi was trying to bite back a smile. "Coach Nye just announced that he's retiring at the end of the month," she said to me. "I guess that means I'm next in line."

"Right now?" I asked. "Why not wait until the end of the year?"

"He's had some health problems." Jessi shrugged, dispensing with the usual show of performative sympathy. I couldn't blame her; I had seen enough to guess that Coach Nye dumped most of the work on her shoulders while continuing to enjoy the higher rank and bigger salary.

"So you'll get promoted? That's great!" I said, and then looked around guiltily and said it again in a stage whisper. "I mean, *that's great.*"

She laughed, a real lowdown chuckle that surprised us both. "We'll see if he goes through with it," she said. "I always thought he was the type to die with his boots on."

"No, it's a done deal," Sean assured her, hefting his messenger bag. "You didn't hear this from me, but the board wants him out. They're sick of the complaints from parents when he tells some girl she's too pretty for college."

Out of the corner of my eye, I saw that Dale had moved closer to the window looking out on the courtyard. He pressed his nose to the glass, staring at either the concrete patio furniture, or the ashtray full of sand and cigarette butts, or possibly the birdfeeder, where a pair of nuthatches twittered in circles. Any kid would have wanted to distance himself from an adult conversation as dull as this one, but something about the tension in his body worried me, and I wondered if Sean or Jessi had noticed. Before I could alert them, Dale shouted, *"No!"* and punched the glass—once, twice—before rearing back and headbutting the window with all his strength.

Jessi screamed. Sean leaped forward, but she elbowed him out of the way and pulled Dale back from the glass, both of them collapsing on the floor of the stairwell.

Pounding footsteps sounded on the other side of the hall doors. When the custodian wrenched them open, Jessi was holding her hand to her mouth, her face a mask of blood. I stood there and watched, thinking about how tired I was and how now I'd have to wait to see if they were okay before I could go home. That was what I remembered later—how, while Sean crouched beside Jessi and the custodian bent over Dale, I'd simply frozen, useless as tits on a bull and unable, even in this moment of crisis, to think of anything but myself.

JESSI REFUSED TO LET US CALL AN AMBULANCE. "INSURANCE WON'T COVER it," she mumbled, holding the side of her face as we helped her to her feet. Still, it was clear that Dale needed a doctor—the gash on his head was at least an inch wide and bleeding freely—and when the paper towels the custodian gathered from the men's room did nothing to stop the flow, she agreed to let me drive them to the emergency room with Sean following. In my car, Jessi sat in the back with Dale, holding his hand while he kept his eyes closed. There was a smear of blood on the headrest, but I decided not to say anything about it.

At the admittance desk, Jessi told us we could leave. "Thanks for your help, but we'll probably be here for a while," she said, her eyes on the nurse typing Dale's information into a computer. "I can call somebody to pick us up."

I'd expected Sean to insist on staying, but his gaze flickered between us, uncertain. "I'm supposed to FaceTime with my kid at five."

I heaved an internal sigh, but there was no getting around it: someone had to stay. "I'll wait," I said, patting Jessi's shoulder, which seemed to stiffen under my hand.

An hour later, I regretted my words. Jessi was back somewhere in the bowels of the hospital, and I'd finished every moderately interesting article in last July's issue of *Vanity Fair*. Warren had already texted me twice, but I hadn't responded. Finally, when I was beginning to consider leaving a note at the desk telling Jessi to call if she needed anything, she walked heavily into the waiting room and fell into the chair beside me. "He's fine," she said. "The doctor has to stitch him up and thought he might be calmer if I stepped out."

For the first time I could see the profound toll that years of exhaustion had taken on her body. She slumped as if pulled toward the ground by a force stronger than gravity. "Did the nurses look at that bruise?" I said, touching the side of my own mouth in the place where her skin had turned a mottled purple.

She shook her head. "I'm fine."

"Do you know what upset him?"

"Birds," she said, so matter-of-factly that I stopped myself from laughing just in time. "He loves birds, all kinds. He can identify every species native to America by plumage and call. He saw a squirrel stalking those nuthatches and it set him off."

"He must have a warm heart," I said, but Jessi scoffed.

"He's not Dr. Dolittle," she said. "He's an autistic kid who can't control his impulses, and now he's going to have a two-inch scar on his forehead for the rest of his life."

I turned back to the *Vanity Fair*, rolling it into a tube like a pretend telescope. "What about his dad?" I ventured when Jessi stayed silent. "Does he help out at all?"

She looked at me with surprise. "He died of lupus when Dale was two. You didn't know?"

Clearly I had never asked—not Sean or Warren, not Jessi herself. I stammered through my condolences, which Jessi waved away, looking down to fumble in her purse. She pulled out her cigarettes, but I put a hand on her arm before she could rise from her seat. I was so tired of secrets, and I might never have a better time to confess than right now, when she was distracted by her son's condition and maybe inclined to be sympathetic. "I have something to tell you," I said. "I was the one who spray-painted your locker in high school. I thought Lauren would be blamed and then she'd leave you alone. It was stupid. I'm sorry."

The shock on her face told me that she hadn't seen this coming. At times I'd wondered if she guessed the truth, but I knew now that it had never once occurred to her that the betrayal that had altered the course of her life had originated with her best friend. "Well, shit," she said, so loudly that the old lady nodding in the far corner jerked awake and shot us a scolding frown. "That one backfired, didn't it?"

"I'm sorry," I said again, but Jessi wasn't listening. She shook her head, smirking.

"Wow," she said. "All this time I blamed myself a little bit. Because Lauren was right about me and Warren. He called after that Halloween party and asked if he could pick me up. We drove down to the river and fooled around in his Jeep. It happened a few times, actually."

I felt a burning in my chest that was half rage, half humiliation. "I don't know why you think I'd care about that."

Jessi leaned closer. "You know what I heard about you?" she said, her voice soft, almost friendly. "I heard that you and Erika Callaghan were together in college, and you dumped her and broke her heart. I had a friend at Fletcher, and she said you told her that it was just easier being with men."

I didn't remember the conversation, but it sounded like something I might have said back then. With Erika, I'd never been able to shake the fear in the back of my mind—fear of popular girls who viewed lesbians with the squeamishness they usually reserved for the fetal pig in biology class; and fear of the nameless boys in pickup trucks who passed us late at night, looking for an excuse to release the corked-up rage they carried in their bodies. If I'd stayed with Erika, it would have meant accepting those fears as a condition of life. At the time, the decision had seemed practical, but now Jessi was calling me a coward, and she was right.

"I don't even understand what you're doing back in Tyndall," Jessi went on, the scorn on her face mingling with disbelief. "You went to *Yale.* You've had opportunities that most people can't even imagine, and this is where you end up? Substitute teaching and sleeping with Warren Ballard?"

Hurt compressed my body like a lead apron. "What do you want me to say?" I asked, raising my voice enough to make the woman in the corner shoot us another look. "This isn't how I wanted things to turn out. I've made a lot of mistakes, and I'm sorry." For a moment it felt like I was apologizing to everyone: Jessi, Erika, even Lauren.

Jessi only rolled her eyes. *"I don't care,"* she said, giving each word its due emphasis. "I don't care about Lauren Ballard. I could give a shit whether she's dead in a ditch or living in Bermuda. I don't think about Warren unless I run into him in the checkout line. I don't care about you either," she said, almost as an afterthought. She turned away, her eyes searching the room. "Get out of my face, would you please?"

I DIDN'T TELL WARREN WHAT HAD HAPPENED WITH JESSI. I DIDN'T TELL him how I'd gathered myself up like a box of broken china and hobbled out of the lobby to my car. No one had ever looked at me with such contempt, and the worst was that I had no doubt I deserved it.

I couldn't fall asleep that night. Warren slept warm, and even in winter he often threw off the blankets in the middle of the night, leaving his body exposed down to the knees. In the glow of the hallway light, I watched the pulsing vein in his neck. It was always a surprise how vulnerable people were in sleep, even the ones who revealed almost nothing of themselves during the daylight hours.

All this time I'd told myself that I couldn't picture Warren as a murderer, and if I couldn't imagine it, it must not be true. But I'd never imagined him as a cheater either, and look where we were now.

On the nightstand, my phone lit up with an email notification. I grabbed it and slipped out of bed, tiptoeing to the landing. I was wearing a blue Tyndall Lions shirt that Warren had kept since high school, and I pulled it over my knees for warmth.

It was the Burwell College class of 2000 alumni newsletter, inexplicably automated to send at midnight. I opened the message and scrolled listlessly until my eye caught on a box at what would have been the bottom of the second printed page. *You are cordially invited to a Holiday Open House at the home of Taylor Vaughn. December 14, 6:30 p.m. 743 Demeter Avenue.* I realized that I'd been unconsciously fingering a hole in the hem of Warren's T-shirt, widening the tear by poking my finger through it. Now I could fit two fingers in, forcing a jagged rip in the fabric.

That was when I heard it—a thunk on the front porch. I leaped to my feet, and my phone tumbled from my hand through a gap in the railing. *"Warren,"* I hissed, trying not to wake Mabry, but there was no sound from either of the closed bedroom doors.

Warren didn't own a gun, and he didn't keep a baseball bat by the front door like people in movies. There were knives in the kitchen, but to get there, I'd have to go down the stairs and circle around to the back of the house. If I wanted to call the police to tell them that whoever had broken the window and left the dead cat on the porch was back, I'd have to retrieve my phone from the living room first. I was frozen, my toes curling with fear, when I heard another thunk, and a face appeared in one of the little panes of glass beside the front door. Connor Mack.

All at once, I wasn't afraid. I was angry.

Before Connor spotted me, I retreated to the bathroom and grabbed Warren's old bathrobe from the hook, shrugging it over my shoulders like a coat as I ran down the stairs. Even through the frosted glass, I could tell that Connor was unsteady on his feet, and when I opened the door, he almost fell on me.

I'd thought he might be hurt, but he was only drunk, the yeasty scent of cheap beer enveloping him like a cloud of cologne. "Ms. Bennett," he said, trying to leer but failing to muster the energy. "Fancy seeing you here."

"Shut the fuck up, Connor," I said, and hauled him into the kitchen, depositing him in the chair at the head of the table. He slid down on his spine, using a hand to prop his head. "Why are you here?" I demanded. "Got another dead cat in the back of your car?"

He looked up at me with what seemed to be genuine alarm. "A dead what?"

"Were you going to egg the house or something?"

"I don't know what you're talking about." He lowered his face into his hands. "I just wanted to see Mabry."

I was pretty sure no sixteen-year-old could lie that well when wasted out of his mind. I let my voice soften by a single degree. "Are you okay? Did you take anything? Other than alcohol?"

He shook his head.

"How much did you drink?"

He held up six fingers and then, after consideration, added another: seven beers.

"Were you partying by yourself, or are your buddies around somewhere?"

"Went home," he mumbled. "Adam and Malik and them."

I filled the kettle and pulled a mug from the shelf beside the sink. "What do you like in your tea?"

"I don't like tea."

I ignored him and opened two packets of English breakfast. I had done this before, not for a high school kid but for the college students who had shown up at my door in my various postings around the country, drunk or high and usually crying. Even though I was just passing through, the misfits always found me, and whether or not I said the right things, they seemed grateful simply to be taken in. These were the purest relationships in my life, and I thought of them with more affection than most of the people I'd slept with.

But this was the first time I'd have to counsel and comfort a student I felt no connection to—in fact, one I actively disliked. "You can stay for a few minutes, but you have to keep your voice down," I said, leaning against the counter. "I know he seems like a nice guy, but if Mabry's dad finds you here, he will absolutely beat your ass."

That seemed to sober him. He ran a hand over his face and said without much conviction, "I'm fine. I can go now."

"You're not driving until you drink your tea," I said, and held out my hand for his keys, which he slapped into my palm with a token show of reluctance. I put them in the pocket of the bathrobe and made his cup, stirring in a diabetes-worthy quantity of sugar and two tablespoons of half-and-half. He was still a kid, after all.

He took a sip and grimaced. "She turns it on and off," he said without looking at me. "First she's saying how much she cares about me, and then the next day she's all over some other dude."

I didn't have to ask whom he meant. "She told me you broke up."

"We've broken up like ten times. Then she texts me and it's like . . ." He put a hand to his neck, simulating a collar yanking him to the side. "I fucking hate it."

"You could say no," I suggested, but he shook his head vehemently.

"You don't understand."

"You know Mabry's leaving at the end of this year," I said. "She has to. She'd be miserable otherwise. I think the best thing for both of you is just to move on. Then, if you pick things up later, you'll know it's meant to be."

I didn't really mean the last part, and he seemed to know it. He took a long swallow that probably scalded his mouth and stood up, holding the table to steady himself. "I'm sorry if I scared you," he said. "I shouldn't have come over here."

For the first time since I met him at the front door, he looked me in the eye. At school, his dead-eyed smirk had led me to think of him as a twenty-first-century Patrick Bateman. I had blamed him for the broken window and the cat in the banker's box, but now I wasn't so sure. I remembered what Mabry said the day we'd had lunch at Rio Bravo: he was an asshole, but not that kind of asshole.

"If Mabry says she cares about you, I'm sure she means it," I said. "I've gotten to know her better in the last month or so, and she's a good person underneath it all."

He gave me an unreadable look. "You won't tell her I was here, will you?"

"No chance." I mimed zipping my lips.

I watched from the front door as he walked with heavy steps to the Audi SUV parked at an angle in the drive. I wasn't worried about him getting home at this point; Stephanie lived only three streets away, and Connor had fourteen milligrams of caffeine plus a hefty dose of embarrassment to help him make it there. I *was* worried about whether anything I'd said about Mabry was actually true. It was all too easy to imagine her dumping Connor like a sack of potatoes on her way out the door, and I certainly wouldn't blame her. After all, Lauren probably should have done the same thing.

I drew the collar of Warren's bathrobe around my neck. Back in the kitchen, I pushed Connor's chair in to the table and put the kettle on again. I already knew I wouldn't get to sleep. I still didn't like Connor Mack, but I was ninety-nine percent sure now that he hadn't been the one to slip the razor in my purse and launch a cinderblock through Warren's window. Despite the police's theory, none of my other students seemed like good candidates, which left me with two questions: who was after me, and what in the hell did they want?

22

All through the night, I went over the possibilities. If the pranks didn't have anything to do with my job, they must be personal in some way, so next I had to ask who had reason to hate me. There were Jessi and her brother, of course. There was Sean, assuming that he'd been harboring a secret bitterness since I'd chosen Warren over him. There was Susan, who probably resented me for moving into her daughter's place. There was Warren, and there was Lauren herself, if I accepted Warren's theory that she'd faked her own death and somehow circled back to Tyndall County.

For months I'd been telling myself that since I meant no harm, no one could really want to hurt me, but both of those propositions seemed less and less certain. I'd done harm, whether I'd meant to or not. And people hurt each other for all kinds of reasons.

Crashing Taylor Vaughn's Holiday Open House would do nothing to answer these questions. Like my taste for true crime, my curiosity about Taylor was prurient and pointless, devoid of social value. I wanted to see for myself what had made Lauren want to befriend a girl so unlike the rest of her circle. I was sure it had something to do with Taylor's money, and I had to wonder if Lauren's decision to put her trust fund into real estate had represented a route into that richer, rarer world. The Ballards might have been the elite of Tyndall County, but I could tell even from my brief glimpse of her house that Taylor Vaughn was something more than that.

I still didn't like Sean's suggestion that I knock on Taylor's door, but if I showed up at the Open House, she'd have no way of knowing that I didn't belong there. I even came up with a fake name: Rebecca Sanderson, class of 2002. I decided to make Rebecca a history major and did a quick scan of the faces on the department website just in case someone asked me about Professor So-and-so's seminar on France Under the Old Regime.

But nothing went the way I'd planned. When I turned in to the driveway, I saw that a Burwell shuttle bus had been parked under the portico, which meant the real alumni had left their cars at the school and arrived as a group. Then, as I was rushing to get out of the cold, my heel caught on an uneven slate and I pitched forward on my hands and knees. Gravel raked my palms. A light went on behind the door, and before I could get to my feet, I felt a hand on my elbow. "Oh my God," a woman said. "Can you stand up?"

"It's nothing," I said, though I knew that wasn't true. My right shin stung so sharply that tears sprang to my eyes. I blew on my scraped palms and tried to muster a game smile.

The woman helping me to my feet had to be Taylor, though she hadn't introduced herself yet. Like her house, she was all angles and expensive finishes, the adolescent gawkiness long refined away. She wore a red silk dress with a matching jacket, and her hair fell against the side of her face like a black wing. As she helped me toward the door that looked like it belonged in a cathedral rather than a private home, I could see a blur of people moving in the far recesses of the foyer.

The weather had turned sharply cold that day and I'd underdressed, choosing high-waisted navy silk pants, now torn, and a thin white sweater. Now that the shock of my fall had worn off, I was shivering again, and the lamplit hall behind the door looked warm and inviting. I let Taylor pull me in, her grip surprisingly strong on the underside of my arm.

"I think I have Band-Aids," she said. "Let me find you a place to sit and I'll look."

"Please don't go to any trouble," I said. How could I get her to go away before she realized that I had no reason to be here?

The guests mingling in the two-story hall looked at us from the corners of their eyes, assessing the situation in the way of well-bred people in their Sunday best. Taylor grabbed two glasses of champagne from a passing tray and led me toward the stairs, and I had no choice but to follow her. As soon as she left me to look for Band-Aids, I would sneak back down the stairs and out the front door.

The house looked more livable than it had from the street. There were plants everywhere, pots of violets on racks by the windows and jungly-looking things hanging from the ceiling, and the furniture was surprisingly unmodern, with big plush armchairs and leather couches that made me want to sink down and take a nap. Birds twittered in the background, and I wondered if the sounds came from a recording or if one of the many doorways led to an actual aviary. The art was what I would have collected if I'd had the money. There was a painting by David Wojnarowicz that looked like a cartoon printed on newsprint, and a little sculpture by Annabeth Rosen that I could swear I'd seen at a gallery in New York. Though I'd sworn not to draw any more attention to myself, I couldn't help telling her, "You have a beautiful home."

Taylor looked around as if she'd never seen it before. "I grew up here, believe it or not. My dad bought the place in the sixties for peanuts. It was somebody's dream house, and then the money fell through and he swooped in. Both my parents died while I was at Burwell, and I thought I'd sell, but I never did."

I didn't believe her about the house costing peanuts, even in the sixties. At the top of the stairs, we came into an open living area with a wall of windows and a lit fireplace at one end, the ceiling crisscrossed with high white beams. Taylor deposited me on a white couch, placing my champagne on the glass coffee table. The noise of the party had receded and I could hear the crackle of the fire, which was made of real wood and threw off a pleasing warmth even in the cavernous room. "Thank you," I said. "Sorry about this."

Taylor shrugged. I got the distinct impression that she was bored by apologies and conventional politeness, a quality I had always admired, especially in women.

I rolled up my pants leg and couldn't help wincing when I saw the damage. The scrape wasn't deep, but it was long. It looked as if someone had taken a cheese grater to my skin. "That looks pretty bad," Taylor said, but when I looked up, she wasn't looking at my leg. She was staring at my face. I realized now that I hadn't given her my fake name, and she hadn't asked.

"I'll find the Band-Aids," she said, and disappeared behind one of the doors opening on the atrium.

This was my chance to escape. If I could manage to shuffle down the stairs, I could probably make it out the front door before she noticed I was gone. But my knee was throbbing in time with my heartbeat now, and if I got caught, how would I explain what I was doing limping around her house? The best strategy was to play it cool and make it back to the party as soon as I could. I picked up an interior design magazine and flipped past pictures of outdoor kitchens and pool cabanas while I nervously sipped my champagne.

The party noise downstairs had died to a murmur, and I wondered if they'd moved out to the grounds. Before I'd finished my glass, Taylor was back, followed by a dark-haired older woman carrying a tray with a cup of water, cotton balls, antiseptic ointment, a bottle of ibuprofen, a washcloth, and about three dozen assorted Band-Aids. The woman was wearing a gray uniform with a white collar, like a maid in a movie, and she kept her eyes demurely lowered. She set the tray on the coffee table beside my glass. "Thank you, dear," Taylor said. From TV, I knew that this was how one dismissed servants, and the maid immediately took the hint, trotting noiselessly down the stairs.

When she was gone, Taylor picked up her champagne and settled back on the couch, looking at me with a hectic glimmer in her eye that might have been tipsiness or something else. "You look so familiar," she said. "I'm sure we've met before."

This was the time to turn into Rebecca Sanderson, but my confidence had deserted me. The look in Taylor's eye told me she already suspected something. She'd ask me what dorm I had lived in or who my favorite professor had been, and she'd see right through me. I'd never been a good liar. "I didn't go to Burwell," I said.

She leaned forward. "Are you a reporter? Because I can get security up here quicker than spit."

"No," I assured her. "I'm Nicola Bennett. I was a friend of Lauren Ballard's."

I'd expected her to be surprised, but she had one of those faces that didn't show much. She paused, eyes narrowing, and sipped her champagne before she spoke. "So you're Nicola. I heard a lot about you from Lauren, but you don't look the way I pictured you. I thought you'd be a little more avant-garde, I guess."

I didn't want to ask what she'd heard, and it seemed both rude and indiscreet to reveal that Lauren had never mentioned her existence. "How did you know each other?"

"She lived across the hall from me," she said, leaning back. "I knew who she was before then, of course. Lauren was hard to miss. Almost as soon as we met, I asked if I could photograph her."

I tipped out two pills from the bottle of ibuprofen, swallowing them with the last of my champagne. "I saw some of your photos," I said. "It was a series, kind of like Cindy Sherman. Do you still do photography?"

"Now and then, but not seriously." Taylor's lips had curled into a half-smile, but her eyes looked absent. "I always knew I was going to go to law school, but Burwell had a great darkroom. It was a good time to indulge my passions before the real world caught up to me."

As if some silent alarm had been triggered when I set down my champagne, the maid appeared at the top of the stairs with two more glasses and a tray of mini crab cakes. I smiled to thank her as she set them down. "You and Lauren must have been close," I said.

"We were close," Taylor agreed, but she seemed to be speaking carefully, measuring her words. "I cared about her, and she confided in me. I never understood why she married Warren. She could have done something better than turn herself into a fucking Stepford wife."

This seemed unfair. "But she was pregnant."

"She had an appointment at the clinic here about a month before the wedding," Taylor said, stroking her bare leg. "Then she asked me to cancel it. She never told me why, but I can guess."

I'd dabbed the antiseptic ointment on a cotton ball and was just about to press it to my skin, but then I paused. All this time I'd thought I was the reason Lauren hadn't gone through with an abortion, but now Taylor was telling me that she'd volunteered to help and Lauren had shut her down. "Why?"

"*War*-ren." Taylor slowed the name down, separating the syllables. "I think he threatened her. He could be intimidating. He showed up here once after she disappeared, yelling and beating on the door. I almost called the police."

This wasn't how Warren had described their encounter to me. "I thought he came to see you about the money," I said. "The twenty-five thousand dollars that Lauren gave you. He said he just wanted to ask you about it, but you wouldn't let him in."

She looked indignant. "Damn right I wouldn't let him in. He was drunk and screaming. My gardener had to come out with a machete to get him to go away." She reached for her glass, the color rising in her cheeks. "Anyway, Lauren didn't give me any money. Maybe Warren kept it. Maybe he made up the whole story to deflect attention from himself."

I peeled the backing off one of the extra-large Band-Aids. It occurred to me now that Taylor wasn't the only one who'd bought property in 2001. Warren must have signed the contract on the house on Lovell Avenue around the same time.

Taylor was still looking at me, and I had the niggling feeling she was remembering something that Lauren had told her about me— some slight or criticism that she could finally judge the truth of. "She was jealous of you, you know," she said. "I think that's why she strung me along in the first place."

The sticky tab had stuck to itself and I had to choose a new Band-Aid. I felt that I was struggling to keep up with the pace of the conversation. What did Taylor mean by *strung me along*? Did she mean that Lauren had flirted with her and that she'd done it because of me—because of my relationship with Erika? "So you think Warren hurt her," I said, "and you've just been sitting here all these years waiting for someone to show up at your door so you could tell them about it?"

"Fuck you," she shot back, but it was the way a friend would say it, almost playfully, with a heavy emphasis on the first syllable: *fuck* you. "I told the police, for what it was worth. I don't know anything about Dale Westcott, but I know Warren was never really investigated. And he should have been."

I killed the second glass and then wished I hadn't. "Did you ever think that she might have run away? There were sightings. That cashier at the gas—"

"There were sightings all over the country," Taylor interrupted. "People will say anything to get themselves on TV. I understand why you'd be reluctant to point the finger at Warren, though. As long as you don't set him off, I'm sure he can be an appealing guy."

There was something malicious in her gaze. I felt a sudden scalding certainty that she knew everything about me, and all her courtesy had been a ploy. "I have to go," I said. "Thanks for the Band-Aid."

Taylor had leaned over to stoke the fire. As she poked at the logs, a spark leaped out and landed dangerously close to the toe of her satin shoe. "It was nice to meet you," she said negligently, as if she wanted me to know that she didn't really mean it.

The maid was standing at the top of the stairs as if she'd been waiting for us. I thanked her for the help, but she didn't answer or make any move to get out of my way, and finally I had to turn sideways to squeeze past her, navigating the stairs with my hand on the wall. Though I'd taken Connor Mack's keys to stop him from driving drunk a couple of weeks ago, I had every intention of doing so myself now.

The foyer was empty. Safe on the threshold, I turned to face Taylor, steadying myself against the doorframe. "You said Lauren told you about me. What did she say?"

She crossed her arms over her chest. "She said you were the most gullible person she'd ever met in her life."

"Okay," I said. The cold outside was bracing, and I tried not to stumble on my way down the slate walk. This time I knew they were watching me through the window, and I didn't want them to see how much it hurt.

23

Taylor had said that the sightings of possible Laurens meant nothing, and probably she was right. Unless Lauren had been abducted and held against her will, there was absolutely no way to explain how she would have ended up in Bark River, Michigan, or Elephant Butte, New Mexico. Knowing her, Lauren would have hightailed it for Kauai or some beach town that wasn't in any of the guidebooks, where she could pay a shirtless young man slathered in coconut oil to bring her mai tais.

Still, I realized when I left Taylor's that I was only five miles from the town of Meadowbrook, where a gas station attendant claimed to have sold Lauren a newspaper in the days after her disappearance. It was only seven thirty p.m., and I thought the drive across town might sober me before I got on the interstate for home.

As soon as I found a parking spot facing the pumps, I wondered why I'd bothered. I stared at the gas station, which was gratuitously pretty, with gingerbread trim and willow trees lining a swollen creek. I had no desire to go in and ask questions. I knew the name of the attendant who claimed to have seen Lauren—Roger Scanlon—but an Internet search had told me that he was dead. Dead as in dead end, another one.

But maybe I hadn't come here because I wanted to see the place where some bored cashier had pretended to spot Lauren Ballard for the shits and giggles of inserting himself into a police investigation. Maybe I'd come here because I wanted to avoid going home to Warren, who even now might be glancing at the clock, wondering when I'd be back from the out-of-town shopping trip I'd mentioned at breakfast that morning.

He'd told me a different story about the visit to Taylor's house. He said that he'd shown up looking for information about his missing wife; that he'd been polite and respectful and Taylor had simply refused to open the door. If Taylor was telling the truth, then he'd lied. Just like he'd lied about his relationship with Jessi Westcott. Just like he'd lied about being in town on the night Lauren disappeared.

I had to admit the version of Warren that Taylor Vaughn had described was frighteningly plausible. It was easy to imagine him pounding on her door, demanding the missing twenty-five thousand that he believed was his by rights. I'd never caught more than a glimpse of his quick-tempered, vindictive side, but I knew that Warren was a businessman, and if he thought he was owed something, he would find a way to collect.

THAT WEEK THE DECEMBER COLD DEEPENED, THOUGH THE SKY STAYED brilliantly blue. The weather report said that a polar vortex had dipped down from Canada, and day after day, the temperature refused to budge over twenty degrees.

After my visit to Taylor's, I'd gone home to my mom's house. I had nearly a month until the closing date, and I'd told Warren that I wanted to pack up a few things in the basement, but the truth was that I just wanted time to think.

Watching true crime, I'd felt nothing but pity and contempt for the girlfriends and wives of murderers. They always seemed so stupid, wringing their hands and whimpering that he couldn't have done it, he was home with them all night. I refused to be one of their number, these women so blinded by love that they couldn't see the man in their bed for what he really was. Leaving for work on

Monday morning, I kept my head down, which might have been why I was halfway across the lawn before I noticed a woman at the front of my car, tucking a manila envelope under the wiper blades.

Blood rushed to my head as I thought of the cat, the razor, the red letters. The woman spotted me and tottered back, so unsteady that I worried for a moment she would fall. It was Susan Kyle, dressed in fur boots and a long black velvet cape that made her look like a witch. "I just wanted to leave this," she said across the hood of the car.

"Susan," I said, breathing hard. "You scared the shit out of me. Come inside."

She hesitated, but after a moment she nodded and followed me to the door. I checked my phone: 7:32. If I got rid of her in the next ten minutes, I could make it in time for my first class.

In the living room, I watched her take it all in—new windows, bamboo flooring, eggshell paint replacing the prison gray my mother had favored. "This must have cost a pretty penny," she said, sitting heavily on the old ottoman. "What on earth would your mother say?"

I wanted to tell her that I was making over a hundred thousand dollars on the sale and could well afford the renovations, but I was afraid she'd have some snide comment about not spending my windfall all in one place. "What can I do for you, Susan?" I asked instead.

She unbuttoned the cape and let it fall around her, pooling on the ottoman. Underneath she was dressed normally, in wool pants and a sweater, though the sweater appeared to be inside out.

"I felt it when Lauren died," she said. "The night she disappeared, I woke in the middle of the night with my heart beating like a jackhammer. I didn't even know she was missing yet, but later I understood. That was the moment she was killed." She turned to me, her blue eyes a washed-out shade that made me wonder if she'd started a new medication. "You couldn't understand, because you don't have children. When you're a mother, there's a part of your mind and body that is always conscious of your child, and then you know when something goes wrong. It's like when your foot falls asleep. That part of me went numb, and it's been numb ever since."

"I understand," I said, even though she'd just told me I didn't.

She was still staring at me in that unnerving way, as if my face were a window she could look through. "You were always jealous of her," she said, leaning so close that I could smell her stale breath. "You wanted what she had, and now you have it. Congratulations."

Her earrings were missing, I noticed—the four-carat diamond studs that she'd worn as long as I'd known her. Was that another sign that she was deteriorating? Then I thought of the diamond that Mabry had found on the floor at Blue Ridge Road and felt a sudden chill.

"So you think I killed Lauren," I said as gently as I could manage. "Is that what you're trying to say?"

"No." Susan reached over and took my hand, and the gesture surprised me so much that I let her keep it. "I don't think you had anything to do with what happened to Lauren," she said. "I just came to give you this."

But I refused to take the envelope she held out to me. I'd already guessed what was in it: a piece of loose-leaf paper, folded in half and covered with bloodred ink. Of course it had been Susan tormenting me with the red letters over the past months. She hated me, of course she did. What mother could stand to watch another woman take over her daughter's life?

But could I really imagine Susan dropping a straight razor into my purse or chucking a cinderblock through Warren's window? She kept shoving the envelope at me, and the corner, sharper than I'd expected, stuck me in the arm.

"You must have figured out by now that your mother made up that story about Charlie Smalls," she said. "We argued about it. Eventually she got so mad that she cut me off completely. I told her she should tell you the truth, and now I'm going to do it for her."

I opened the flap with an eerie sense of calm. Inside were half a dozen newspaper articles from the Fayette County, West Virginia, *Tribune* dated between April and May 1983: "Charges Dropped Against Three Local Men." The defendants were accused of raping a local woman at a Memorial Day picnic. They claimed the sexual contact had been consensual, and no one could be found to corrobo-rate the woman's story that they'd dragged her into the bushes.

The men were shown in school picture–sized photos below the headline. One had a droopy mustache like Dale Westcott's. I didn't recognize any of the names.

I read the articles twice, then folded them neatly and put them back in the envelope. This was my history, I thought—these three men whom I knew now I'd seen once before, in the mutilated photo I'd found in my mother's drawer. I felt suddenly light-headed and wished I could put my head between my knees. "Why didn't she tell me about this?"

Susan gave a short laugh, loose skin wobbling beneath her chin like a turkey wattle. "She said you didn't need to know. She said you'd grow up thinking you were different from other kids, and she didn't want that for you. I said it wasn't fair to you, but you know your mother. You couldn't tell her anything."

I wanted to protest. I'd been thirty-six when she died—plenty old enough to handle a traumatic backstory. "What happened to the men?"

Susan shook her head. "I don't think she had any idea. She never went back to West Virginia. She wouldn't even talk to her family. When she first moved to Tyndall, a lot of people were wary of her, you know. The women were suspicious of a girl who showed up pregnant and wouldn't say much about her past, but I stood up for her. She re-minded me of myself in some ways. When she started her business, I convinced the other families in Laurel Heights to hire her, and I never regretted sticking my neck out. It might not have been easy, but it was the right thing to do."

I was still gaping at this self-serving speech when I realized she wasn't done. "Well, I do regret one thing," she went on more tentatively. "I regret telling Lauren."

"You told her what happened to my mom?"

Big shiny tears trembled behind her lashes. "Just before she went to visit you at Fletcher, she told me she was pregnant. She wanted to have an abortion. I told her how your mother had chosen to give you the gift of life even though you'd come into the world in the worst possible way. Then I told her she'd never see another dime from me if she went through with it."

With my free hand, I reached down to rub at a scuff mark on the bamboo floor. This explained so much: why Lauren had asked for my help, why she'd been so desperate for a place to stay, and why, finally, she'd gone back to Warren. Just like Taylor, Susan was telling me that I'd been far less central to Lauren's decision-making than I'd supposed. "But wasn't she supposed to inherit from her father's trust?" I asked.

Susan scoffed. "Not enough for her tastes. I paid for their house," she said, sticking out her pointer finger as if making a list. "I paid for that BMW. I bought all the furniture, all her clothes. Jim Ballard wouldn't do a thing for them after Warren graduated. He said he needed to earn his keep. Warren would have been happy to go on living like a college student, but Lauren deserved better than that. She deserved everything." The tears were spilling now, leaving silver trails like the tracks of tiny snails. "She wasn't perfect, I know that. But I wanted to make sure she always knew how loved she was."

I would have risen to get her a tissue, but she'd squeezed my hand even harder, and I couldn't pull away. She looked around for something to wipe her face and, finding nothing, mopped her streaming eyes and nose with the sleeve of her velvet cape. "At least there's Mabry," she said. "That's my only comfort. At least she'll have everything Lauren never got to have."

24

'd never been a crier, but on the way to school, I pulled over in the McDonald's parking lot and sobbed into my hands until I realized that the girl in the drive-through window was craning her neck to get a better look. The clock on the dashboard read 7:48. I ran a wet finger under my eyes to remove splotches of mascara and made it to school just as the bell rang, then taught two classes in a row before I had a chance to catch my breath.

Third period had been canceled for an assembly that I had no plans to attend. My eyelids felt as if they were stuck to my eyeballs, and my throat was so sore that I worried I might be getting sick. When the last student filed out, I locked the door, pulled down the shade that was never supposed to be pulled down, and grabbed the mostly empty vape pen I'd brought from Washington State. It wasn't the first time I'd used it at school, but it was the first time I'd done it before the sound of students' voices had faded from the hallway. I had done my best for the young minds of Tyndall County, but I was all out of fucks to give.

On my phone, I googled the three men from the articles that Susan had given me. Two of them were dead: one had been murdered by a neighbor in a property dispute back in the eighties, and the other had died of lung cancer three years ago. The third lived in Logan County, only half an hour away. According to his Facebook page, he was married with three wonderful children, worked as a bus driver, and loved Jesus, America, and the Pittsburgh Steelers, in that order. He didn't look anything like me.

One of these men was my father. Though it had been years since I'd fantasized about Charlie Smalls coming back to claim me, I realized that I'd always pictured him as a good person. I'd imagined that he probably felt some regrets about his short-lived relationship with my mother and might have reached out to her if he'd known how. If he ever found out I existed, he'd be flabbergasted but also moved. In secret moments of yearning, I'd seen us sharing a meal at some out-of-the-way restaurant/gas station that served the best fried chicken in three counties. We'd chat shyly about our lives, like strangers, and after that we'd exchange Christmas cards. We might never be close, but we'd share some cherished corner of the other's mind, like the longing for a beloved place that could never be revisited.

All that was gone now. Reading about women dumped in reservoirs or buried in the desert, I'd played with the idea of being the victim of violence, but my mother had actually experienced it. I would never know what had led her to keep the cut-up photograph of her rapists, but I imagined that it must have been some kind of token—a reminder of how far she'd traveled and why she was never going back.

After all these years, I had no way of telling which of the headless men was my father, and I wasn't about to hunt down their descendants and pester them for DNA samples. I was better off as an orphan, as my mother surely must have known.

What Susan had told me had altered my vision, like a filter that turns the world askew. I knew why Lauren had chosen not to have an abortion, and I was certain that it wasn't because my mother's story had moved her to empathy, no matter what Susan thought. Lauren hadn't gone on with the pregnancy because she'd had a pro-life epiphany and realized that fetuses were people too. Once she'd made the impulsive choice to flush her pills, all future decisions had been taken out of her hands. I'd refused to help her; so had Susan. The only person left was

Taylor Vaughn, and as loaded as Taylor was, she probably wasn't prepared to support Lauren for the rest of her life.

Even though my own life was the one in question, it was clear to me that my mother could have made a different choice and been perfectly justified. She'd been hurt, and she'd decided to make a life for me out of that hurt and guard it like a fortress. She had kept me safe when so many other girls had not been safe. Other mothers had done worse.

I closed the search and tried Erika's number. Though we texted at least once or twice a week, neither of us had ever suggested talking on the phone. It was only desperation that led me to call her now, and just before the phone clicked over to voicemail, I realized that of course she wasn't going to answer; it was only seven thirty a.m. in California. The message was an automated one that read back the number you'd dialed in a robot voice, and I hung up before the beep. *Hey can we talk later?* I texted instead. *I just heard some weird news.*

I hesitated a moment and then plunged forward. I'd seen what secrets could do, and from now on I was going to tell the whole truth about myself. *Also I've been sleeping with Warren Ballard since I moved back to town. Until recently, that is. Things have been kind of chilly lately.*

Anyway I kind of need someone to talk to. Sorry for blowing up your phone!

We'd never enabled read receipts, so I had no way of knowing if she'd seen the messages. I stowed my phone in my bag and reached for a tissue, dabbing the tender skin at the corners of my eyes. Maybe confiding in Erika was a bad idea. She might think I was overreaching, presuming on the evidence of a few catch-up texts that we'd established some kind of friendship. Already I felt embarrassed, but what was the alternative? I had no one else.

The assembly ended at ten-forty-five, which gave me about fifteen minutes to clean myself up and set out the books for my next class. As I crossed to the cabinet where I kept my stack of Norton anthologies, my gaze fell on a backpack leaning against the bookshelf in the corner of the room. It was a red Lands' End with a monogram: CGM. Connor Mack.

I knew I shouldn't open it. He'd be back any minute now, trying the knob and knocking on the glass. Quickly I unzipped the largest pocket and stuck my hand in, pulling out two binders covered with William & Mary stickers. When Connor joined a fraternity, he would be one of those guys who never took off the letters.

Underneath I found a notebook with ENGLISH on the cover and flipped it open. Interspersed with notes in his surprisingly neat cursive were drawings of gargoyles and airplanes, and one of a generically beautiful girl with long, straight hair who might have been Mabry. On the second-to-last page was a caricature of me that showed far more skill than the girl and the gargoyles. He'd caught the way my eyebrows went up when I talked. My mouth was twisted in a rictus as if I'd been frozen midword, and a bubble coming out of my mouth said, *A bildungsroman is blah blah blah education.* Though the drawing wasn't flattering, it somehow made me like him a little bit more. He'd been paying more attention than I'd thought, and he'd even spelled *bildungsroman* correctly.

I hadn't found his phone, and I wondered if he had it with him, even though the students weren't supposed to carry them during school hours. In the little front pocket, I palmed a wallet that held Connor's driver's license and library card and a Visa in the name of Jason Mack. Next came two red pens and a long snake of condom packets—meaning that he was having lots of sex or that he wanted to be very prepared, just in case?—and Mabry's school picture in a plastic protector sleeve. She was wearing a blue crewneck sweater, and she looked sweet and winning, her looks as misleading as her mother's had been at that age.

There was one more pocket that I hadn't checked, the middle-sized one between the front pocket and the main cavity. I felt something heavy shift as I pulled the backpack toward me. I unzipped it and peered inside and then sat back on my heels. I didn't have to reach in and touch it to confirm what I already knew: I was looking at a gun.

25

Stephanie Gilliam Mack stomped into Sean's office and took a seat without acknowledging my presence. She was wearing cream-colored wool slacks, a hunter-green silk blouse, and high-heeled boots, and her long, thick hair cascaded over her shoulders as if she'd just had a blowout.

Jason entered behind her. He looked exactly like I'd pictured the grown-up Jason Mack: tall and broad, padded with muscle now rather than fat. His suit might have been bespoke, and his hair was swept back from his face in a stylish mane that made him look like a TV patriarch. Jessi had said he was a financial analyst, and so far, everything fit. He took a seat on the opposite side of the room from his ex-wife and nodded at me, his lips curling in a sharkish smile that made me want to smack him in the mouth.

"I called our lawyer," Stephanie said to Sean, pointedly ignoring both Connor and me. "This looks to me like illegal search and seizure."

"That term only applies to the police," Sean said with more gentleness than I thought was appropriate given the circumstances. "The school has a right to know what's in a student's belongings when he's on school property."

"But why was she looking through his backpack in the first place?" Stephanie said, her voice rising in pitch. "Do teachers just rummage through students' things whenever they get the opportunity? Is this some new policy that I'm unaware of?"

Sean looked at me, and I saw that I was actually expected to answer. "Can you please explain why we're talking about me?" I asked, cringing inwardly when I realized that my voice was trembling. "He had a gun, and I found red pens too. He's the one who sent me those letters."

Connor shifted in his chair. "What is she talking about?" Stephanie asked Sean.

"Nicola has been the victim of pranks in recent months," Sean explained. "She thinks that Connor might be responsible."

Connor let out a puff of breath. I looked over at him, but he tucked his chin into his chest and didn't speak. "Where did you get the gun, Connor?" Sean asked.

For a moment I thought he wasn't going to answer, but then he raised his head and said, "From my dad. He showed it to me when I was at his place last weekend, and I stuck it in my backpack while he was out."

Jason passed a hand over his face as if he hoped he might wake up somewhere else. "Well, it's not illegal," he said finally, when he realized that everyone was waiting for his response. "I have a permit. I didn't know he'd steal the fucking thing."

It seemed to me that we were all taking this very calmly. Before Jason and Stephanie arrived, Sean had left the room to talk to the superintendent, but there seemed to be no thought of evacuating the school. Now Stephanie was staring at the gun on Sean's desk as if it were a mud pie that a toddler had brought her from the garden. She straightened and put on a bright smile. "Sean, I know that you have real problems to deal with. Of course I'm not saying that the gun isn't something we need to address, but let's not blow this out of proportion."

Sean looked suddenly tired. "I would prefer that we save this discussion for the police," he said. "And your lawyer, if you think you need one. Is that all right with you, Connor?"

"I want to apologize," Connor said.

Sean nodded as if he'd expected this all along. For the first time I understood that what he'd said was true: as surprising as it might be to everyone who had known him back in the day, he was damn good at his job. "All right," he said. "Who do you want to apologize to, and for what?"

Watching Connor squirm, I was caught between the hope that he would spill it all and the impulse to shout out to him not to do it, to wait for the lawyer. "To you," he said. "And to my parents. But mostly to Ms. Bennett."

Even Jason looked nervous. "Connor, stop talking."

"Dad." Connor's voice was less tentative than I had expected. "Mom, it's okay. I did it. I wrote that letter. I want to talk to the police."

Perhaps I should not have been surprised by the look of scorching hatred that Stephanie gave me then. From her point of view, I was the problem: I had poked my nose in where it didn't belong, and now Connor Mack's future lay in ruins. "Sweetheart, don't say anything else," Stephanie said. "Our lawyer will be here in just a minute. Do you remember Mr. Musgrove, from Mommy's birthday party?"

Connor was staring at his shoes and didn't appear to hear. "What was the gun for, Connor?" I asked. "Were you going to shoot me? Or your classmates?"

"What?" When he met my eyes, he looked dazed, all the cockiness stripped away. "No, of course not. I mean, I was thinking about shooting my . . ." His voice trailed off, and he rubbed his eyes vigorously.

"You said you wrote the letters," I pressed on. We could circle back to the suicidal ideation later, but first I needed to hear from him exactly what he'd done.

"I wrote one letter," he said. "I made it look like it was written in blood, and I put it under your windshield wiper. I did it for Mabry."

I looked at Sean and saw that he was frowning, lines I'd never noticed before cut into the skin on either side of his mouth. "Connor—" Stephanie said with a desperate note in her voice, but his face didn't flicker.

"She hated you," he went on. "She always thought that her mom might come back someday, but she couldn't as long as you were here." He rested his elbows on his knees and bent his head. "I did it for her," he said again, "and now she's sneaking around with Malik behind my back. She's a fucking bitch."

The room went so still that I could hear the rush of hot air through the vents. *Lysistrata*, I thought. Mabry had cut Connor off until he did what she wanted, and then she'd turned around and started dating someone else. I'd had no clue about her and Malik, but it made a certain kind of sense. He was as bright and promising as Warren had once been, and Mabry, like her mother, had always believed she deserved the best.

The receptionist knocked on the door. "The police are here," she said to Sean with a hint of suppressed excitement. "They're waiting in the conference room."

Connor stood up. His face was serious, and with his shoulders back and his hands folded at his waist, he had a dignity that made him look like a different person from the smirking frat boy in training I'd met in the classroom. He was on the point of throwing it all away—football, college, all the advantages and connections that would have followed—and he wore it easily, as if none of it mattered. I thought of Lauren on the diving board at Bearwallow, poised to cast her body into the frozen pool.

Stephanie followed him, throwing a last singeing glance at me over her shoulder. Poor Stephanie, I thought. She'd modeled her life on Lauren's—marrying at the same time, having a baby at the same time—and look what it had gotten her: an ex-husband she hated and a troubled, unhappy kid who would be lucky to avoid jail time. Jason slunk out last. I wondered if he ever ran into Jessi Westcott when he was in town, and if so, whether they spoke to each other. If she'd been here, I was pretty sure she would have aimed a kick right at the seat of his Italian wool pants.

When the door closed behind them, Sean fell back into his chair. "I hope the police confiscate his phone," I said. "Did you tell them about the revenge porn?"

He didn't respond. "I'm going to find someone to cover your classes for the rest of the day. The police will want to talk to you after they're done with Connor. You can wait with Nancy," he said, gesturing at the outer office where the receptionist was probably pressing her ear to the door.

"He'll be expelled, right?"

"That's just the beginning. But I'm sure Jason and Stephanie have a good lawyer." Sean rubbed his forehead as if trying to wipe away the early stages of a headache. "Nicola, I'm afraid this is going to get lost in the shitstorm that's about to come down on us, but you shouldn't have been in that kid's backpack. It's unethical, and it's against our policies."

I could hardly believe it. "You're going to get on my ass after what he did?"

"I know you hate him, and for good reason. He's a piece of shit, but that's not an excuse." Sean reached to straighten a framed photo that had been knocked sideways by the slamming door. It showed a blond boy with a sunburned nose and a sweet smile, one side of his mouth lifted higher than the other. "I know you don't give a fuck about this job," he said, looking at the picture rather than at me. "I just wish you'd been a little better about hiding it."

AFTER MY INTERVIEW WITH THE POLICE, I WALKED DOWN TO THE LOUNGE and made myself grade papers while I eavesdropped on the teachers gathering in little buzzing groups. They seemed to assume they'd narrowly escaped a mass shooting, and I could tell this was the narrative that would take shape going forward. My involvement didn't seem to be general knowledge, and no one tried to pull me into their conversations. They weren't going to waste good gossip on me. I'd always been an outsider, and my time was almost up.

They'd put together one part of the puzzle that I hadn't thought of yet: the smashed trophy case must have been Connor's handiwork too. "I *knew* it," Glenda Morris repeated, the appliqués on her Christmas sweater bobbing with every nod. "You could see it all on that smug face of his. Bet that little bitch helped too."

Mabry, she meant. Glenda might be right, but I would have bet every penny in my savings that Mabry would never be held responsible for any of it. She was a Ballard, after all.

Susan had said it herself: Mabry could have everything. Born at her grandmother's behest and kept alive only by the intervention of the mailman who'd spotted her in Lauren's locked car, she had proved her good luck before her first birthday. With two wealthy and doting families behind her, plus more than enough talent to set her on a trajectory for success, she had every chance of making her dreams come true. I'd been cheering her on from the sidelines, and all the time, while I took her to lunch and marked comma splices in her application essays, she was secretly plotting her revenge.

It wasn't the hostility that shocked me so much as the childishness. All these years she'd held on to the fantasy that Lauren might return and slip into her old life just as easily as slipping on an old pair of shoes. From Mabry's perspective, I was the only thing standing in the way.

And what about the diamond earring she'd supposedly found in the house on Blue Ridge Road? How far would she go to get people talking about her missing mother? Connor said that he hadn't put the dead cat on the porch or the razor in my purse, but he couldn't speak for Mabry.

I gave up on grading and pulled up photos of the three red letters on my phone, comparing and contrasting. Now that I knew what to look for, I noticed subtle differences between the September letter and the other two. The drops of blood were larger on the second and third letters, less realistic, made with less skill. The paper was different too, I realized. The first letter had been written on regular loose-leaf paper, the later ones on college-ruled, with smaller lines.

Connor had told the truth: he had written the first letter but not the others. That meant the person who had written the later letters must have heard about the first and decided to imitate it. I made a mental list of the people I'd told about the letters—Warren, Sean, Jessi, the two officers. And Mabry.

But I had to admit that the list wasn't exhaustive. The people I'd told could have passed on the news of the first letter to an unknown number of others. I looked suspiciously at the teachers gathered around the coffeemaker. I knew they didn't like me, but did they dislike me enough to try to drive me out of Tyndall for good?

The snow started in the afternoon and fell hard, and by the time I made it out to the parking lot, half an inch had settled on my car. When I checked my phone, I had a text from Warren wanting to know if I'd heard about Connor and reminding me that we had the final home inspection the next day. *Also Mabry still hasn't heard from Juilliard. Do you know anything about admissions? Is it normal to wait this long?*

Erika hadn't responded to my text about wanting to talk, but she'd laughed at the one about sleeping with Warren. *Lol not surprised,* she wrote. *He always liked younger women.*

I didn't respond to either of them. The snow was thick enough that my wipers could barely keep up, and as I turned onto Montrose, it occurred to me that I didn't remember seeing a shovel in my mom's garage. The parking spots in front of the hardware store were all taken, but I managed to snag the last of the heavy-duty shovels with a metal arm, along with a ten-pound bag of rock salt. I wheeled them out to my car, the cart sticking in the slush, and was loading everything into the trunk when a dingy old Jetta pulled up beside me. It was Sean. He rolled down his window, and I saw that he was wearing a pair of fuzzy blue earmuffs.

"Hey," he said. "I'm sorry about this afternoon. I didn't mean to come down on you like that. You want to come over for a beer and talk it out?"

I snickered and pointed to the earmuffs, and he pulled them off, looking sheepish. "I pulled these out of lost and found," he said. "I didn't even bring a coat today."

"You look like Cookie Monster. I'll come over," I said before I could give myself time to think. He looked surprised but pleased.

Sean said he had to run into the grocery store for a few things, and I needed wine and coffee. Malik was working the ten-items-and-under line, and I went to his register while Sean got stuck with a sour-looking old woman on the other end of the checkout area.

"Hey, Ms. Bennett," Malik said with the sweet smile that for the first time struck me as a bit theatrical, even calculated. "How about this snow, huh?"

Was it you? I wondered. After moving on from Connor, had Mabry convinced Malik to do her dirty work? Somehow it was hard to picture. He was a smart kid, and he had a lot to lose. "Hi, Malik," I said. "Are you worried about getting stuck here? It's coming down pretty hard."

"No, my uncle's picking me up," he said, palming the bag of coffee beans and tossing it in the air. "He's got a plow on his truck."

I watched Sean move to the register, where the old woman glared down at a tomato as if it had insulted her. He caught my eye and winked. Sean was the only person I'd ever known who winked at people as a regular thing, and I was surprised I didn't hate it. I felt newly grateful for how well he'd handled the situation with Connor, and I could forgive him for snapping at me when I thought about how much stress he'd been under. As soon as he'd seen that gun, he must have imagined the worst-case scenario—students covered in blood, the rat-a-tat-tat of bullets echoing in the stairwell.

Nestling the coffee into the brown plastic bag, Malik whispered, "Hey, do you think Principal Ballard has a girlfriend?" I felt my back stiffen. "I was checking him out the other day, and he was buying lady stuff," Malik went on. "Pink razors, deodorant. Tampons. Weird, right? Somebody told me his wife left town a while back."

"Weird," I agreed. As far as I knew, Sean did not have a girlfriend. I decided to ask him about it as we crossed the parking lot. "Hey, Malik said—"

"Whoa," Sean interrupted, grabbing my arm to keep me back from a car fishtailing in the slush. The driver waved apologetically as his tires gained traction, and Sean returned the wave: no harm done.

But the touch of his cold, wet hand on my bare skin had jarred me, and the half-formed fantasy that had played through my mind in the checkout line vanished like headlights reflected on a wall. I couldn't explain the sense of repulsion that came over me then. It felt like my body was warning me back from him, and for once I was going to listen.

I made something up. I said I had cramps, bad ones. They'd been coming on all day, but now I could barely stand up, I told him, holding my stomach and wincing for dramatic effect. I counted on him getting embarrassed, the way some men do when you mention periods, but he just looked concerned. "Let me at least follow you home," he offered, but I said no, that was silly; I was only half a mile from my house. I would take a shower and a couple of ibuprofen, and I'd be fine in the morning. I walked to my car as quickly as I could, afraid he'd see that what I wanted most of all was to get away from him.

I drove like an old lady, slowing even for green lights, until I saw Sean turn off on Alexander Street. I took a deep breath and told myself that what I was thinking couldn't possibly be true, but still I couldn't shake the image in my mind: fingers reaching around cracked plywood, curling toward the light.

26

When Sean and I watched horror movies in high school, I was always the one who made fun of stupid things the characters did. Why would they try to find the killer themselves instead of calling the police? What kind of people heard a creepy cackling and went down into the dark basement instead of hauling ass out of the house? It strained credibility. In real life, the survival instinct would win out over curiosity every time.

But now, when I reached for my phone to call Detective McRae, I stopped myself. If I told her that I thought Sean and Warren had kept Lauren imprisoned on Bearwallow Mountain for the past sixteen years, she would treat me like one of the psychics who called up to say they'd had a vision of a body buried near water.

This was why no one in horror movies went to the police: they didn't want to be laughed at. They didn't want to be disbelieved or branded crazy, and I wasn't above those considerations. I needed to see for myself before I asked for anyone else's help. I needed proof that Lauren was really there.

A SINGLE PAIR OF HEADLIGHTS FOLLOWED ME UP THE MOUNTAIN. THE car was too far away to qualify as tailgating but close enough to make my hands sweat on the steering wheel. At every curve, I hoped it would fall back or turn off on one of the side roads, but then the lights would swing into place behind me again.

At least the snow had slowed to flurries, and the road was mostly clear. I drove past the entrance to Bearwallow and pulled into a trail-head parking lot. The car that shot by was a dark SUV that looked nothing like Sean's Volkswagen.

I knew the way even in the dark—I had roamed these woods both alone and with Sean, and I knew every deer path, every hollow tree— but I hadn't accounted for the disorienting effect of a night without moonlight, black as a locked room. Even with my phone flashlight, I couldn't see more than two feet in front of me. I could hear snow sifting through the branches, but I didn't feel cold until the tip of my shoe caught on a root and I pitched forward, landing on my hands and knees in freezing slush. My palms, not yet healed from the fall at Taylor Vaughn's, tingled as if I'd been stung.

My teeth were chattering by the time I came in sight of the house, looming at the end of the long driveway, a thicker and more structured darkness. I'd lost my hat in the fall, and my hair was wet. At least I knew where the extra key was, under a loose slate on the patio outside the conservatory.

Frozen grass squeaked underfoot and something scurried in the shadows, a rat or a mole. I fumbled the key and dropped it in a patch of leaves. I scrabbled around on my hands and knees and thought about giving up, but then my fingertips brushed cold metal.

The house wasn't much warmer on the inside. After shutting the door behind me, I stopped and listened for any sound, and for a moment I thought I heard something, a faint rustling or thumping from an upper story. I peeled off my wet jacket and set my jaw to stop my teeth from chattering, then inched forward until I felt the reassuring solidity of the banister knob at the bottom of the stairs.

I'd stopped shivering, but I was still cold. As I climbed the next flight, I found myself tracing the wainscoting with my fingertips, and I thought of the men forced to build this house for Warren's great-great-grandfather in the years before the Civil War. The wild backwoods of the Blue Ridge, fifty miles from any settlement, must have looked like the ends of the earth as they hauled rocks and stacked timber in the freezing cold or burning heat. Surely their spirits had gotten into the bones of this house, keeping company with the old family ghosts.

Some people thought there was a limit to what human beings were capable of, at least among the upper classes. Babies weren't intentionally left alone in hot cars. Women weren't locked in attics. But I had never been upper-class, and I knew that Christelle's hand reaching through the crack in the plywood was real, and the ghosts of the enslaved were real, and Lauren was real. Susan said that she'd felt the moment when her daughter died, but I was just as sure that I'd felt her presence, the pulse of her existence, hidden but perceptible, like wires humming in an empty house.

Suddenly I stumbled, and as I righted myself, I thought I heard the front door click shut. I paused, frozen in a crouch, but there were no other sounds. I made myself slow down and take the final stairs one step at a time, pausing to listen for footfalls below me. The air smelled of dust and a dim echo of the perfume worn by Mrs. Ballard, another of the old house's flitting ghosts.

By the time I got to the third story, my eyes had adjusted enough to make out the shapes of the doors, white rectangles in the dimness. Mrs. Ballard's room was the second on the left. The crystal knob turned too easily, and for a moment I thought it was going to come off in my hand, but then the door swung open. All the furniture had been moved out, the curtains pulled closed. The carpet was like a snow-covered field, and I thought of a girl I'd read about who had gotten off a bus in Montana and disappeared into the woods, never to be seen again.

There was something in the carpet—one of Mrs. Ballard's silver bobby pins, the old-fashioned kind with a rhinestone on the end. I picked it up and slipped it into my pocket.

The closet stood empty, a few hangers swinging in the dark. I shone the beam of light over the wood panels and ran my fingers along the edges, searching for a button or a lever. I thought about going down to the garage to see if I could find a machete or an ax. I was breathing high in my chest, almost panting. Even after all my caution, there was always the possibility that I'd been followed. Would Warren and Sean hurt me if they found me here? It terrified me to realize that I didn't know the answer.

That was when I heard it. It wasn't anything as obvious as the creak of a door or the sound of footsteps on the stairs. It was the sound of a held breath, a pause sustained. A waiting.

27

I looked around for something I could use as a weapon. A hanger? Could I get behind him and somehow fit the triangle part over his head like a garrote? It was too late; the door was opening. All I had was my phone, and I threw it and then launched myself at the body in the doorway. We fell together, my shoulder hitting the wood with such force that I could feel it in my skull.

The man gave an *oof* as I punched him in the stomach, but he was stronger, and he rolled on top of me and pinned my arms at my sides. I spat in his face, then threw him off and scrabbled backward into a corner.

"Nicola? What the hell is going on?" Sean said with what struck me even in my agitation as genuine confusion. "Why are you attacking me?"

"Did you follow me?"

"Follow you? What are you talking about?" He wiped off the spit with the back of his hand. "Warren put in one of those doorbell cameras last year. The image comes to my phone, but I couldn't tell who it was in the dark, so I decided to come up myself instead of calling the cops." He braced his back against the wall, rubbing his knee. "This is why you bailed on me? So you could break into my grandma's house?"

"I thought—" I said, gesturing to the closet. I couldn't bring myself to finish the sentence.

"You thought what?" Sean asked, and even in the dim light I could see his eyes flicker in the same direction. "How did you even know about that?"

I didn't answer. Sean crossed the room, limping a little, and disappeared into the darkness of the closet. He switched on a flashlight and then stuck his head out, beckoning me to join him. "A couple of years back my dad got all excited about this, thinking the house must have been a stop on the Underground Railroad," he said. "Turns out he was wrong. Anyway, I spent a lot of time up here with him and the historian he hired."

He shone his flashlight through the gap. The pantry-sized room was empty. It was dirtier than the rest of the house; the cleaners clearly hadn't been up here. I glimpsed roses on the wallpaper and a layer of dust on the floor. On the far wall was the little lozenge-shaped window I'd spotted from the lawn.

"They never did figure out what it was for," Sean went on, playing the light over the walls. "The historian said the architect was into adding false walls and secret passageways—for fun, I guess. I know my grandmother used to hide from her dad in here. He was an alcoholic. You should see the letters from his wife."

"I asked Warren about it," I said. "Your grandmother had told me about a room on the third floor I knew I'd never seen before, but he said he didn't know what I was talking about."

Sean laughed, the sound harsh enough to make me jump. "That's because Warren never listens to a word anybody says," he said. "Why didn't you just ask me about it instead of rushing up here by yourself?"

Briefly I considered trying to bluff, but I couldn't think of a single response other than the truth. "Malik saw you buying women's things. Like pink razors. Women's deodorant. I thought maybe someone was up here."

He still didn't get it. "Someone who?" He held the flashlight sideways, illuminating my face without blinding me, and after a moment he gave a low chuckle with even less humor than the first. "Lauren?" he said. "You thought I'd been keeping Lauren in captivity? For Christ's sake. That stuff was for my neighbor. She's in a wheelchair, and sometimes she asks me to do her shopping."

"Your neighbor." I had met her once, a sweet frail-looking woman who'd asked me if I'd been saved.

The words of apology were on my lips when I looked at his face, lit by the flashlight beam. Something I saw there gave me pause. I knew all the nuances of Sean's expressions, and I could see that he wasn't irate or offended, as I might have expected. He was nervous, and I thought I knew why.

The tire tracks. I could still picture them, deep muddy ruts gouged out of the overgrown lawn. I'd thought at first that the police might be able to match them to the tread on Dale Westcott's truck, but when I never saw them mentioned in the coverage of Lauren's case, I'd stopped thinking of them as a clue. They were just another dead end, a detail that led nowhere.

Or maybe not. I'd made fun of Sean for how he never seemed to put on his brakes in time, always bumping into curbs and flower beds. "You were there," I said. "The night she disappeared. Weren't you?"

He said nothing, but then—so slightly that it might have been a trick of the light—I saw him nod.

IT STARTED IN HIGH SCHOOL. ONCE WHEN WARREN WAS IN BED WITH THE flu, Sean had driven Lauren home from a party, and they'd fumbled into a drunken kiss when he reached over to open her door. It happened two or three times after that, but always with enough space between to convince him he wouldn't do it again. He made up his mind to avoid situations where he and Lauren might end up alone. After all, he wasn't an animal, at the mercy of his instincts. All he had to do was say no.

But how did you say no to Lauren? She was irresistible, and the worst part was that she knew it. One weekend at the beach house, she walked into his room while he was changing out of his swim trunks. Sean expected her to apologize and turn to leave, but instead she stepped forward, and before he could move or say a word, she dropped to her knees, tugged his cock from his waistband, and took it into her mouth. The room was mostly dark, but the bathroom light illuminated the tops of her breasts, the wet of her mouth sliding over him. He was so guilt-ridden that he spent the rest of the trip in his room, faking a hangover. A confession would have eased his mind, but if he'd told Warren about the blow job, Sean knew he'd end up telling him about the kissing too. That would be the worst part—not that it had happened, but that he'd let it happen more than once.

Besides, he thought, what right did he have to bring misery to others? Surely it had all been a drunken mistake. It was impossible that Lauren really liked him, unthinkable that she'd prefer him to Warren. It would be cruel to ruin her life just to relieve his own conscience.

Then he stopped thinking about it, because Warren and Lauren were off to college. He was happy when they called to tell him they were engaged, and happy when they decided to move back to Tyndall. When he remembered what had happened, he told himself that was high school stuff. Bringing it up now would make three people unhappy and do no good at all.

Still, he renewed his pledge never to be alone with Lauren, and he stuck to it until the night she showed up at his apartment soaking wet, crying her eyes out. Mabry was only a month old, but Lauren already had her body back. Her ass was as tight as a bed at basic training.

She and Warren had fought, she told Sean, and he'd locked her out of the house in the rain. What could Sean do then but invite her in and give her a towel and an old pair of sweats while he threw her clothes in the dryer? Lauren had a bottle of red wine in her bag, and between that and her wet hair bringing back that night at the beach house— still, if he wanted to be honest, the most memorable erotic experience of his life—even he wasn't surprised when they ended up in bed.

At first he tried to believe that it was simply another mistake, a slipup by two people whose attraction was powerful enough to overrule even the sincerest resolutions. The more he thought about it, though, the stranger the circumstances seemed to him. He couldn't imagine Warren locking a stray dog out in the rain, let alone his wife. And what were the chances that Lauren would just happen to have a bottle of wine in her bag? Had she set him up? But why? What kind of game was she playing?

He decided to keep his distance. He refused their invitations to dinner and dropped out of the rec football team that he and Warren had joined together. He was partying a lot then, and he knew that Warren would assume he was too busy with his new friends to have time for his big brother. But he didn't move his spare key from under the dead geranium on the front porch. He must have known there would be a night when Lauren would let herself in and crawl in beside him. They were nearly silent, and the next day he could almost pretend it was a dream. That was how he would have preferred to keep it. If he was going to betray his brother, let it be in the dark.

I slid down the wall, wondering if the chill setting into my bones was an effect of his story or an early stage of hypothermia. "And where was I in all this?" I asked. "I mean the high school part."

Sean sat beside me, and I watched him consider for the first time how it might feel for me to hear about clandestine blow jobs and Lauren's military-grade ass. "I didn't want you to know about it," he said. "I mean, I liked you too. You were the rational choice, obviously, but I couldn't stop thinking about her. I told myself she was the only one who didn't judge me."

Now it was my turn to laugh. "Jesus, Sean. Lauren judged everybody."

"Right," he said. "Well, I was fucked up."

My fingertips were numb and stayed that way no matter how many times I tapped them against my knees. I knew the story Sean was about to tell would be full of self-serving excuses. He'd try to convince me that the murder had been an accident, some combustible combo of anger, substance abuse, and bad timing, but none of that would change the fact that he'd taken a life. He'd killed his brother's wife, his niece's mother, and then he'd set about rehabilitating himself, eventually persuading half the county that he was the better of the Ballard brothers.

Including me. Despite some reservations, I'd believed in the new Sean. Now I knew he was worse than I'd ever imagined, and I could feel my body start to shake, a secret tremor.

He shifted restlessly. I thought he might try to take my hand, and I tucked it under my leg. "I didn't kill her," he said. "I mean, maybe I did. I'm not sure."

WHEN WARREN AND LAUREN MOVED BACK TO TYNDALL, SEAN WAS WORK- ing as a manager at the pet food store in the mini-mall by the interstate. He flattered himself that it was the perfect job for his lifestyle. He could stay out all night and go to work fucked up and no one even seemed to notice.

The change in perspective he'd experienced since giving himself over to a constant state of intoxication felt revelatory. Sometimes he found himself mistrusting the solidity of everyday objects. He'd walk back into the same room two or three times to make sure a chair was still there. Once, after two days of not sleeping and adding some mushrooms to his usual regimen, he had a vision of God peeping out of the inside of a tree. God had come to explain that everything in the universe was connected, and that music was a language invented to allow people from different times and places to communicate. When he sobered up, it all seemed embarrassingly corny, but he couldn't shake the feeling that he'd glimpsed something real.

He didn't tell his friends that Lauren was a big part of the reason he stayed high. He didn't want to think too much about what he was doing. For six months or so they couldn't leave each other alone, meeting at dinky hotels by the interstate or driving out to the woods to fool around in the back of his car. He loved to kiss the keloid scar on her arm. He loved everything about her, even the damaged bits.

Then she cut it off. She refused his calls, wouldn't answer emails. There was no explanation, and he lost it a little, stopped going to work. For a few days, he didn't eat. Keeping the extent of his broken- ness from Warren was even harder than keeping the secret of the affair. He avoided his brother, circling the block when he saw his car outside the liquor store.

By the night of August tenth, he'd had enough. Warren was at the beach house with Mabry, and Sean knew that Lauren thought he was out of town too, visiting friends. If he showed up at the house, he might be able to take advantage of her surprise and at least get a foot in the door.

She was angry at first, but not as angry as she could have been. Pretty soon they were grabbing at each other. She wanted to suck him off on the couch, but paranoia was one of the side effects of the cocktail of drugs he was on, and he couldn't get hard. He tried to pick her up to carry her to the bedroom, but her foot caught a glass sitting on the end table and swept it onto the floor, shattering it into pieces. They were both laughing so hard that they could barely stumble up the stairs, where he shucked his shirt and kicked off his boots in the hall.

He'd dreamed about her body for months, even when he was with other girls, but the sex wasn't as good as he'd anticipated. He finished too quickly, and as long as he worked on her, she didn't come. It began to seem to him like intentional stubbornness, like she was trying to make him feel bad, and finally he stopped trying. That was how the fight started.

"He'll be back soon," Lauren said. "Sometimes I wish he'd just die. I want it to be painless but quick, like an embolism."

Sean folded his arms behind his head. He didn't like hearing her talk that way about Warren, but he wasn't in a position to complain. "Why don't you just leave him?"

She scoffed. "I'd never get custody. They'd find out about us, and people already think I'm a shit mom."

He winced. He'd heard about the car incident when Warren had shown up at his door to yell at him for letting Lauren drive drunk. Sean had been a little insulted that, even after that, Warren didn't seem to suspect that anything was going on between his brother and his wife. It was as if he couldn't imagine Sean as a worthy rival. "Are you sure you'd want custody?" Sean said. "Maybe Warren would be the better one to raise her anyway."

He could feel Lauren go rigid, even her skin shrinking away from him. "What's that supposed to mean?"

She was about to kick him out, and he didn't want to go yet. "I'm sorry," he said. "I didn't mean that."

But it was too late. "Fuck's sake, I don't have time for this," she said, pulling her dress over her head.

He followed her to the landing. If he couldn't fix things between them, he wanted to hurt her, since even hatred was better than contempt. "Well, you seemed to enjoy it," he said. "Nobody made you spread your legs."

As soon as she turned around, he had second thoughts. Lauren was dangerous when she was mad. She moved in close, her lips curling in an expression that was more like a snarl than a smile. "I could say you did," she whispered. "I could call the police right now and tell them you raped me."

He had seen her fake-cry before, but he'd forgotten how good at it she was. Actual tears leaked from the corners of her eyes, her lips trembling as she cast her eyes up and moaned, "I thought I could trust him, Officer. I never thought he'd do something like this."

Sean felt the urge to punch her, and to stop himself, he balled his fists at his sides. "I wouldn't put it past you," he said. "Anybody who would leave her kid to die in a hot car probably wouldn't flinch at a fake rape charge."

She smacked him. There was no sound like in the movies, but his cheek burned as if she'd held a lighter to his skin. "You're disgusting," she hissed. "No wonder Nicola would rather eat pussy than be with you. Why don't you buy a blow-up doll and stop following me around?"

She still looked beautiful to him then—that was the worst part— even when he happily could have driven her face into the wall. Her hair was wild and her makeup smeared, and he saw her bouncing on the balls of her feet like before she'd jumped into the frozen pool. When they'd gotten home that night, Warren had said, "That girl's going to ruin my fucking life," and Sean had said, "Yeah, probably."

"You know your brother can't stand you," Lauren said. "He thinks you're pathetic. That's why he doesn't go down to the beach when you're there."

That was the worst thing. To hear that Warren too despised him, even without knowing that Sean was sleeping with his wife. "You might as well start Mabry in therapy now," he said. "That kid's going to grow up hating your guts."

Lauren's face twisted. She turned toward the stairs as he tried to grab her, already regretting what he'd said, how far he'd taken what never should have been a fight in the first place. Her foot caught on the boot he'd left on the top step, and she fell.

Maybe it was the drugs, but it seemed to take an impossibly long time for her to reach the bottom of the stairs. He felt every impact in his own body while he stood powerless, unable to move. It was like a prank video, he thought. It could not be real—limbs and elbows sticking out at funny angles, Lauren upside down and then right side up again. She would pop up at the end, sober and sore, rubbing her ass with a wince. But toward the bottom, she stuck out a foot, trying to stop herself, and that turned her body at an angle that sent her crashing down, curled like a potato bug.

He'd heard the clang of bone on metal, but didn't know what it was until he got down there. She lay crumpled on her side. There was blood on her hair and blood on the floor; beside her, the cast-iron doorstop that he vaguely remembered once being in his parents' house: a simpering baby with a pink bow in her hair and a silly smile.

For a moment he was sure she was dead. Then he saw her chest fluttering with her breath and relaxed, but only a little. The gash on her head looked bad, long and deep with blood seeping out like pie filling. One of her earrings had come out in the fall. He tried his best to clean up. He went upstairs and neatly made the bed, as if covering up the fact that they'd had sex was the important part.

He had to get out of there. Lauren would wake up eventually, and she'd be glad that he'd decided to leave her. She would come up with some kind of explanation for Warren. She was good at things like that. He took the doorstop but forgot about the broken glass and the washcloth he'd used to dab at the cut on her head.

"As soon as I got home, I fell asleep," he said. "I guess it was a stress reaction. I woke up at three in the morning, and right away I knew I'd made a mistake. I was sure she was lying there in a coma or dead. I drove there going eighty—it was amazing that I didn't get stopped." He picked up the diamond-headed bobby pin I'd dropped and twiddled it between his fingers.

I wondered if he realized he'd missed Warren by a matter of minutes. "So you got rid of the body," I said.

Sean shook his head. "She wasn't there."

This didn't make sense. "What do you mean?"

"She wasn't there," he said again. "I don't know what happened—if she was dead and Warren got rid of the body, or if she just walked away. I honestly have no idea."

In the days to come, he'd waited to be arrested, but no one even questioned him. He had no idea if the detectives knew he and Lauren had been sleeping together, but he felt reassured that the police weren't ever going to investigate him or his brother. "I'm not asking you to understand," he said. "I know I let Jessi's dad take the fall for me. I've spent the last ten years trying to make it up to her, for whatever that's worth."

I couldn't stand to listen to him justify himself. "Did you ever think about what it was doing to Mabry not to know what happened to her mother?"

Sean let his head fall back against the wall. "Sometimes I managed to convince myself that it wasn't real. I'd go whole years feeling like it was some weird nightmare I'd had. Then you came back to town." His eyes met mine, and without the easy smile I'd grown accustomed to, he looked like a different person. "I was sure you were going to put it all together," he said. "I did everything I could think of to get you to back off."

"The letters," I said.

He nodded. "Not the first one—that was Connor—but the cinderblock and the razor, and the cat. I found it in a shed up here at Bearwallow. It was already dead, if that makes any difference. I didn't want to hurt anyone. I just wanted you to stop asking people about Lauren."

I wanted to leave, but I couldn't make myself move. I suddenly felt too tired to lift my arms. "You're shaking," Sean said with a tenderness that made me faintly nauseated. "What's wrong?"

"Sean, you have to go to the police," I said. "You have to tell them what you did. For Mabry and Warren's sake."

"I know," he said. "I will. It's weird, but I feel so relieved now. You don't know how long I've wanted to tell you the truth."

Before I could move away, he reached out and touched the side of my face, tracing his finger down the line of my jaw. In that moment I saw all the Seans I'd ever known—the smartass kid who teased me about my E.T. eyes; the shy, cocky boy spraying himself with a hose after he'd chased me down outside the high school; the Green Man, leaning to kiss me on the roof. There was a time when I'd imagined that this house could be our house, the frozen flowers in the garden brought to life again, but I knew the truth now. Nothing here had ever belonged to me.

28

I woke from a dream of my mother. *Get up*, she demanded, shaking the side of my bed, and I could tell from the tone of her voice that she was disappointed. I'd always been too accommodating, and now look where I'd ended up.

Then she was gone and I could hear birds outside the window. As long as I kept my eyes closed, I could pretend I was waking up in Warren's bed on a Sunday morning, feeling the vacant spot beside me and knowing that he'd sneaked downstairs to make my first cup of coffee. I tried to sink into it—the warmth of the sun on my closed eyelids, the luxurious emptiness of the big white bed.

But something was off. For one thing, the bed was smaller than Warren's. The window to the right was in the wrong place, and the sky was still dark. I was wearing a pair of blue-flowered pajamas that were normally bunched at the bottom of my drawer. Out of the darkness, a figure emerged and moved toward me. I tried to find the breath to scream, but all that came out was a high whine, like a scared animal.

"Nicola," he said. "Shh. It's just me."

Warren switched on the bedside lamp. His face was bleary, his cheek marked by the zipper of the pillow he'd wedged between the back of the chair and the wall. "I just got to sleep."

What was I supposed to say, *Sorry for waking you*? "Why am I in my mom's room?"

"You were pretty out of it when we got back from the hospital," he said, yawning. "I didn't want to just dump you on the futon."

I had a dreamy memory of a nurse poking and prodding and a tall man frowning at me as if I'd done something wrong. Warren rubbed his eyes with the heels of his hands. "The doctor's name was Dr. Hard, can you believe that? Paul Hard. I looked him up on the website just to make sure I hadn't heard it wrong. You kept falling asleep when he tried to ask you questions."

"Hmm," I said, not wanting to let on that I didn't remember that at all. I eased myself out of bed and grabbed a pair of yoga pants and a long-sleeved T-shirt from the dresser. Warren stayed at a respectful distance, looking at nothing in particular, as if the body he'd seen naked a hundred times now repelled or embarrassed him.

When I was dressed, I shuffled down the hall to the bathroom. I looked like a walking corpse. Shadows pooled beneath my eyes, and mascara was smeared along my cheekbones like day-old eye black. While I wound my hair into a bun and washed my face, I watched Warren in the mirror. He was sitting on the edge of the bed with his hands folded between his legs, and even the circles under his eyes couldn't spoil his looks.

Sean had said he'd left Lauren bleeding and unconscious at the bottom of the stairs, and he didn't know what happened after that. If he was telling the truth, that left only two possible options: either she'd gotten up and walked away without a car or a wallet, or someone else had come along and finished her off. Someone like Warren.

He must have a pretty good idea of what Sean had told me, and now I was alone with him, in the middle of the night, on a block that my mother had chosen for its dearth of nosy neighbors. I'd never believed that the Ballard brothers were capable of violence, but I'd been wrong before.

I used the wall for balance on the way back to the bedroom. "Where's Sean?" I asked. I had a vague memory of him dropping me off at the hospital, but I didn't think I'd seen him after that.

Warren sighed. "I talked to him about an hour ago. He went to the police station, but they didn't charge him—not yet, anyway. He left a message for the superintendent to tell her he's stepping down."

I found myself wondering who the acting principal would be. Probably Glenda Morris; from what I'd heard, she'd been eyeing the job for years. "Do you think he killed Lauren?" I asked.

Warren stood and walked to the window, twitching the curtain aside. "It never crossed my mind before today," he said. "I can't imagine Sean hurting anybody."

But if I had to accept that people were different from what I'd believed them to be, Warren should have to accept it too. "He was sleeping with your wife," I said.

"I know that, Nicola." He picked a sock off the floor and turned it in his hand. "I want to talk to you about something else," he said. "I kept something from you. I was pretty sure that Connor and Mabry were responsible for the pranks, and I should have told you. I'm sorry."

I felt as if I'd swallowed an ice cube. I'd been prepared for half a dozen different confessions, but I'd never expected this. "The night we found the dead cat," Warren said, "something woke me up, and I went out on the landing. Mabry was standing there in her pajamas, looking out at the lawn. She said she'd heard a noise, but later I wondered if she'd gotten Connor or some other boy to smash the window. When we heard you coming out, I shoved her back into her room so you wouldn't see her."

That was why he'd lied to the police, I thought. That was why he'd told them he was in bed with me when I knew he hadn't been. "I thought there might be something wrong with her," he said. "What happened with Lauren—I thought it broke her and it just took a while to see the effects. I wanted to keep her safe. That's always your instinct as a parent, to protect your child."

He threw the sock toward the hamper. "She got into Juilliard, by the way. We got the email yesterday."

I could hear the pride in his voice, absurd but unmistakable. Under normal circumstances, I thought, Warren might have been a good father and a decent husband, and no one ever would have known that he harbored this capacity, like the latent marker of some debilitating disease. Even now, I wasn't sure he understood that his desire to protect his daughter by any means necessary was a dangerous thing. Mabry had never learned accountability, and I had to wonder if her talent would be enough to keep her going in a world where no one gave a damn that she was a Ballard.

He looked up and flashed a rueful version of his cover-boy smile. "I hope you'll forgive me," he said. "I'd like us to see a counselor, someone who specializes in blended families. With you coming into our lives so quickly, there are a lot of things that we never talked through."

I sat down suddenly in the armchair beside the bed. After all that had happened in the past twenty-four hours, he still thought I'd come running when he crooked his little finger. "I'm not staying in Tyndall," I said. "I can't, Warren."

His smile vanished like a light switching off. "You don't mean that."

For a moment, I almost regretted my decision. Even if it was supremely arrogant of him to assume I'd want to continue the relationship, I still felt bad about breaking his heart. "I don't want to hurt you," I said. "But no matter what happens with Sean, I could never feel at home here. I shouldn't have come back in the first place."

"But what would you do?" he asked. "You don't have anywhere to go."

I didn't want to admit that I had no idea. "I don't think we're good for each other," I said. "You're not the person I thought you were."

He looked as if he could hardly believe what he was hearing. "So *I'm* the problem? You've built your whole existence around never having to commit to anything or anybody. You think what happened to Lauren gave you permission to live your life the way you wanted to, but all it gave you was an excuse to treat people like shit."

The blow landed just as he intended. I could feel it high in my chest, an ache that eclipsed all the lesser aches in my body. "At least I cared that she was gone," I said.

Before I could register what was happening, he was leaning over me, gripping the arms of my chair. "Aren't you afraid to be alone with me right now?" he whispered. "Sean said that when he left, she was still alive, right? So what happened to her?"

"That's what I'm trying to figure out," I said, trying to keep my voice even. I was nearly eye-level with his crotch, and I saw that he was half-hard.

"What if I've been lying to everybody?" he said in a soft, almost tender tone that made me sick to my stomach. "What if I found her at the bottom of the stairs and knocked her on the head again just to make sure?"

I wasn't going to let him see my fear. "Did you?"

He was smiling when he put his hand to my throat. There was no squeezing, not yet. "You're right, I wasn't sorry that she was gone," he said. "You have no idea how difficult it was to act all grief-stricken in front of the police and the reporters, when inside I couldn't have been happier. That drama teacher we had in high school, he said that the only reason he cast me in *Becket* was because I looked good with a crown on. Joke's on him, I guess. Turns out I'm the greatest actor of my generation."

I remembered that drama teacher, a small bald man in glasses who clearly thought he was meant for better things. The comment about the crown had gotten around at the time, and I'd agreed that Warren had been wooden in the play, thrusting out his arm like a staff as he asked the crowd to rid him of this troublesome priest.

No matter what Warren said, I couldn't imagine him physically finishing Lauren off—shooting her or cracking her on the head a second time with the iron doorstop. But could he have gotten someone else to do it? Maybe he and Sean had been in it together, or maybe he'd called an old football buddy, one of those guys who got teary-eyed reminiscing about that come-from-behind win against Logan County in the '96 playoffs.

Warren's thumb pressed against my windpipe, and I found I couldn't speak. I tried to signal him with my eyes that he needed to let go, this wasn't a joke anymore, but his face was avid, greedy, transformed by an expression that reminded me of the moments just before he came. I remembered the advice my mom had given me—if a man tried to hurt me, kick him right in the balls—but the angle of Warren's body made it impossible for me to raise my leg. Maybe I'd been wrong, I thought. Maybe Warren was perfectly capable of violence, and this was how I found out, in the last moments of my life, that I'd underestimated him all along.

I nudged my heel back against the broken chair leg. Nothing happened, so I kicked again, harder, and this time it worked: the leg collapsed and I fell to the side, Warren's hand dislodging from my neck. His body pinned me down, but I scrambled out from under him and ran to the bathroom, clutching my throat.

As soon as I'd locked the door, I wrapped my fist in a towel and punched the mirror. I'd seen this in a movie once, and I was surprised when it worked, the glass shattering into large shards in the porcelain sink. I grabbed the sharpest one and sank into a crouch, waiting for him to break down the door. I wasn't going to wait for him to attack this time; I would go right for the jugular.

But there was no sound—no footsteps, no breathing. I counted to four hundred, and then opened the door a crack, confirming what I already knew. Warren was a practical man underneath it all, and he'd always had a sense of when to cut his losses. Killing me would have only caused more problems. He was Grieving Husband Warren Ballard, and he had a reputation to uphold.

29

I was stuffing a few stray items of clothing into my one suitcase when Detective McRae knocked on the door.

I didn't want to invite her in, so I threw on my coat, wrapped a scarf around my neck, and stepped out on the porch, hugging myself against a stiff breeze. She was dressed differently than I'd ever seen her, in an expensive-looking black suit with a necklace made of gumball-sized blue beads. "I saw the police report," she said. "Do you have a minute to talk?"

I let the reluctance show on my face. "The new owners are doing a final walk-through tomorrow."

She followed my gaze to my old Toyota, which was packed to the gills, a pair of mustard-yellow throw pillows smushed up against the back window. "Glad I caught you, then," she said. "What if we take a walk? The elementary school is letting off two hundred balloons for the two hundredth anniversary of the founding of Tyndall County, and I think we could see it from the park down the street."

There was definitely something different about her, I thought. Her tone of voice, the way she had done her hair, even her expression seemed to have changed, and it put me on edge. I followed her meekly to the end of the block, but before we made it to the park gate, I stopped and folded my arms across my chest. "I'm not pressing charges against

Warren," I said. "I never should have called in the first place. I just wanted you to know what kind of guy he is, not that it'll make any difference."

I'd hoped that my outburst would right the balance between us, but she simply ignored me. "The balloons are supposed to start at eleven thirty," she said, her gaze ranging over the concrete picnic table and the weedy brown lawn littered with cigarette butts. "We couldn't have missed it, could we?"

"Maybe the principal's giving a speech," I said as I followed her to the table. I could remember standing out on that asphalt courtyard with the giant chalk map of the fifty states, waiting for Field Day, my knees trembling with excitement as some adult droned into a microphone. While we watched, a few balloons floated up above the tree line—kids who had let go too soon.

McRae took a pack of cigarettes from her bag. What was it about her that had changed? I made a mental list: the brown hair that she'd worn in a ponytail last time was hanging loose; she wasn't wearing earrings and had on little makeup, only a slash of the nude lipstick that Southern women of every race and class kept in their bag at all times.

But that wasn't it. It was the way she carried herself. The searching eagerness that had so annoyed me was gone.

Finally I decided I couldn't stand the silence. "So did you crack the case?" I asked. "Who killed Lauren Ballard?"

I thought she'd resent my smartass tone and refuse to answer, but I'd guessed wrong again. "Well, the smart money's on Sean," she said. "He can't prove that she was alive when he left. It seems pretty damn convenient that someone else would come along and finish what he started. On the other hand, why place himself at the scene if he killed her? He didn't have to confess at all."

It was true, I thought. He could have bluffed his way out of it, as the brothers had done so many times before. "You're wrong," I said. "It was Warren." I loosened my scarf and showed her the bruises on my neck. "I saw the look on his face—I know what he's capable of."

We both looked up as a white van passed the park gate, cruising slowly to the end of the block before turning at the cul-de-sac. McRae rolled her eyes. "Reporters," she said. "As it turns out, you're a pretty important part of this story."

It was what I'd been waiting to hear for sixteen years, but now her words made my stomach drop. The article in the Tyndall paper had reported that Sean had first confessed to *an unidentified woman*, but I knew I wouldn't stay unidentified for long.

McRae took a drag and tilted her head to the side, a dubious gesture that I couldn't quite read. "I just want to be clear that when it comes to pressing charges, you don't really have a choice in the matter," she said. "If the state decides to charge Warren with assault, you can't leave town. You'll be a witness. And if we charge either or both of them with Lauren's murder, we'll need you for the trial."

My hands itched, and I raked my nails across each palm in turn. "But you're not going to charge him," I said, "are you?"

"With assault?" She shrugged. "Not my call, but no, I don't think so. It's hard to make a case without a cooperative witness, and there's a lot of public sympathy for Warren right now. But, if I wanted you to stay in Tyndall, I'd have other ways. I could arrest you, for example."

"What?" I could barely get the word out. "You think *I* killed Lauren?"

A robin swooped up into a poplar as if it had been spooked. Without warning, the sky was full of balloons—mostly the yellow and blue of the Tyndall Lions but with grace notes of green, red, and purple. "You were the first person on the scene the next morning," McRae said, her eyes fixed on the balloons. "You destroyed evidence at a crime scene. You should have been a suspect from the beginning. Also, looking back at the case files, I'm pretty sure that your mom lied about your alibi. She said she checked on you every hour, but why would she? You were eighteen years old, not a newborn."

"I wouldn't have killed her," I said, my voice stronger now. "I had no reason to. Lauren was a bitch sometimes, but that's not a reason to murder someone."

A slight wrinkle appeared between McRae's eyebrows. "You're free to leave," she said after a moment. "But we'll talk again."

Even as relief washed over me, I felt, perversely, that I wasn't ready for the conversation to end. "Can I ask you one thing?" I said. "It's probably none of my business, but I've been wondering. How did you end up in a shithole like Tyndall County?"

Her expression didn't change. "I was born here," she said. "I was two years behind you in school. I guess I didn't make much of an impression."

It was the last thing I'd expected. "I used to watch the girls' soccer practice," she went on. "My mom worked in the cafeteria, and sometimes I had to wait for her. My maiden name was Richards, Colleen Richards. McRae is my wife's name."

"I'm sorry, I don't remember," I said, but as I spoke, a picture drifted back to me—a little girl sitting on the bleachers while Lauren and Jessi and I waited for Coach Scott at the picnic tables. A girl a few years younger than us, with scraggly brown hair and a dirty yellow backpack.

But that girl had been poor. That was the word I would have used at the time—not disadvantaged or low-income but dirt-poor, poorer than me. The kind of girl, like Jessi Westcott, whom people might overlook or, worse, see as disposable.

The hair-twirling, eager-to-please version of McRae had all been an act, I saw now. It might have been meant for Warren rather than for me, but I'd been fooled too. Clearly I was even worse than I'd thought at seeing through the mask to the real person underneath.

"Well, good luck to you," McRae said, dropping the cigarettes into her purse. "I'm sorry things didn't turn out better here, but at least you sold your house."

As we rose to leave, one last blue balloon floated up out of the trees. The child must have been holding on too hard, I thought. A teacher must have knelt beside her and unknotted the string that had bitten white lines in her fingers. The teacher might have been impatient, but I understood the child's reluctance to absorb this early lesson in disappointment. Why would the world give you a beautiful thing in the first place, if you were just going to have to watch it disappear?

30

I spent my last day in Tyndall tying up loose ends. Movers came and carted what was left of my mom's stuff to Goodwill while I deposited the check from the realty company in my checking account. Months ago Warren had told me that he was going to apply his commission to the closing costs, but he'd apparently changed his mind and charged me six percent instead.

I was hunting in my purse for the extra key when I found the discharge paperwork from the hospital. I flipped through it, and at the bottom of the second page, in a welter of scientific terminology, I saw the words *hCG detect*. The word sounded familiar, and after I googled it, I drove straight to the hospital and told the nurse at the desk that I had to see Dr. Hard.

I thought I'd communicated the urgency of the matter, but I waited in the lobby for almost forty minutes before he called me back to his office, a windowless room hardly bigger than Jessi's converted storage closet. "The nurse said you had a question about your paperwork," he said, looking not at me but at the ornate wooden clock on his desk.

I pulled the papers out of my purse and pointed to the line in question. "This means pregnant, right?" I asked. "But I'm not pregnant. Am I?"

"The hormones in your urine indicate that you were a few days ago," he said, tapping a pen against his blotter. "But they can stay in the body for days or weeks. Without an ultrasound, there's no way to know if the fetus is viable. The nurse should have gone over all this with you before discharge."

I tried to take it in. I was pregnant, or had been pregnant; he wasn't sure which. "But wouldn't I know?" I asked. "If I'd miscarried?"

He looked at me for the first time, brows drawn together over his bulging eyes. "It can take some time for the tissue to be expelled. We can do an ultrasound now, if you'd like."

"No." I pushed my chair back so quickly it made a shrieking sound on the tile. "I have to go. I mean, I have plans. I'll go to the doctor in a day or two."

Walking out of the hospital, I was in such a daze that I nearly smacked my nose on the glass doors. The timing worked: Warren and I had sex on Thanksgiving and then pretty much constantly until Opal's service in mid-December. I hadn't noticed any symptoms, but four weeks was not a long time.

Until I made it to a doctor's office for another test, the thing inside me was Schrödinger's baby, suspended between being and non-being. I had no idea what I would do then, but I did know one thing: even if I was still pregnant, it was none of Warren's business. My mother had kept the circumstances of my birth to herself for nearly forty years, and it was far from the worst thing that had happened to me. I could make my own money, and I wouldn't have asked Warren for child support in any case. What good would it do him to know that he had a child hundreds or thousands of miles away, a child for whom he would never be anything but a name on a birth certificate?

If I was pregnant, the baby belonged to me. I might be making it right now, out of the blood and flesh of my own body. I was not a good person, I had proved that over and over, but it didn't necessarily follow that I wouldn't be a good mother.

THE IDEA OF CALIFORNIA HAD COME TO ME IN THE HOURS AFTER WARREN left. A skeptical young officer I'd never seen before had stopped by to take the report on the assault, and when he was gone, I sat on the front steps and tried to make a plan.

I had to get out of town, and not just because my right of occupancy was about to expire. I'd spent the past decade and a half trying to find a place for myself in Lauren's story, but I hated the idea of people shoving cameras in my face, demanding to know whether Sean had killed her and what he'd done with the body. God knows I didn't have any answers.

But where would I go? I couldn't get another teaching job—not in the middle of the year and not without a recommendation from my principal, who clearly had other business to attend to. I had a few friends scattered around the country who might take me in, but I shrank from the idea of having to explain myself. I wanted to rest. I wanted to sleep until noon and eat when I felt like it and not think about Lauren or the Ballards, not ever again.

At least I had plenty of money. Even after Warren's cut, the funds from the sale of the house plus my savings could keep me going for several years if I lived frugally. The next question was where to go, and I was surprised to find that I already had an idea. Erika lived on the Central Coast of California, in a little beach town called Los Osos that looked like paradise, at least on Instagram. It was less expensive than Los Angeles or San Francisco, and yet the area was populous enough that I was pretty sure I'd be able to find a job. Though I'd hated the little third-rate college in Washington where I'd taught before moving back to Tyndall, I'd loved living on the West Coast. Surely there were worse places to hole up while I recovered and waited to see what would happen next.

I called Erika as soon as I got on the interstate, but again the call rolled right to voicemail. *I know this is kind of weird,* I texted, *but I think I'm going to be in your area for a few days and I was wondering if you wanted to grab lunch or a coffee? Just give me a call back when you can!*

INDIANA, ILLINOIS, MISSOURI. BIRDS SKIMMED ALONG THE SHOULDER OF the interstate, in and out of the ditches swamped by winter rains. At a gas station, I saw a man covered in tattoos and found myself thinking of the *Resurgam* on Sean's arm: *I will rise again.* Like Lady Lazarus, eating men like air; like the balloons at Tyndall Elementary, vanishing into a stainless sky.

There was one thing that was still bothering me: what McRae had said about arresting me. I was pretty sure it had been just a tactic, but it bothered me to realize how plausible it sounded. She was probably right that my mom had lied about my alibi, claiming to have checked on me throughout the night when she'd done no such thing. If I had killed Lauren, my mother would have helped me bury the body with no questions asked.

But I hadn't killed her, and I hadn't prompted Dale Westcott to kill her either. Whatever happened to Lauren, I was ninety-nine percent sure it had nothing to do with me, and it was time to let go—time to stop worrying over a question that would probably never have an answer. Even if they did find the body, it was unlikely that either Sean or Warren would admit culpability. Sean might talk a good game about what a relief it was to tell the truth, but surely he'd lawyered up by now. If he had additional information about Lauren's fate, he'd probably keep it to himself.

When I pulled over at the rest stop in Feldspar, Missouri, the parking lot was deserted, the inside empty except for a gray-haired cleaning woman humming along to canned Christmas music. On my way out, a brightly painted building at the bottom of the hill caught my eye. It was small and weathered, a shed or a small barn, with a picture I couldn't make out on the side.

I stepped carefully down the hill littered with straw wrappers and soda cans and picked my way across a ditch where a rusty tricycle lay half-submerged in brown muck. It wasn't a lost masterwork of primitive art after all but just another Virgin Mary, one of many you could see on walls or makeshift grottoes throughout the Midwest. Though her head was bent demurely, her mouth was luscious, rounded and pink as the dimple in a peach. It surely wasn't the artist's intention, but something about her made me think of the femmes fatales in the old noir films that

Erika sometimes made me watch back in college—plushy and curved, the prototype of femininity that no real woman could ever match.

I took a picture and sent it to Erika. *Midwest folk art! Are you free for a sec?*

But the text turned green instead of blue, and after a moment a little red exclamation point popped up: *not delivered.* I pressed her number with my thumb. I worried that maybe her unresponsiveness had been a sign that she didn't want to talk to me anymore, and when I hadn't gotten the hint, she'd blocked me. That was embarrassing, and hurtful too. After all, she had no way of knowing that I was driving in the general direction of California for her sake alone. I'd never let on how our online flirtation had thrilled me. I was determined to turn over a new leaf, and I had tried not to dwell on my unfounded fantasy that she and her wife might not be happy together. I felt bad enough about myself without adding homewrecking to my list of vices.

But even before the automated voice came on to tell me that the number was no longer in service, I knew it wasn't just that Erika had decided she didn't want to have lunch with me. It was far worse.

I always liked your mom, she'd said.

Warren always liked younger women.

I'd registered in the moment that those lines didn't sound like Erika. My mom had always given her the cold shoulder, and she'd hardly spoken to Warren that I remembered; how could she know what kind of women he liked? But it was hard to interpret tone in a text, and a few odd moments hadn't seemed significant, until they did.

At that moment I knew what had happened to Lauren. I *knew.* I'd tried to make myself into the protagonist, but all the time I'd been a secondary character, moved from here to there at the author's whim.

A truck blasted by on the interstate, air brakes wheezing. Though part of me wanted to drive straight to the nearest airport and hop a flight, I knew this too: wherever she'd been, she was already gone.

31

Forty yards out from the beach, Lauren cut the motor and drifted. As soon as she felt the bottom scrape sand, she jumped out and pulled the skiff up on the beach. The child was looking away, over the windy rustle of the bay, hair whipping behind her like a flag. Between her feet she held the backpack, stocked with saltines and bottled water. Lauren had forgotten sunscreen, but luckily neither of them burned.

"I'm going to look for my rosebush," Hazel said, and waited for Lauren to nod approval before she ran off along the beach, her head ducked against the brisk wind off the Atlantic.

Lauren had lucked into the job as a nanny for the Harbisons at exactly the right moment. Her landlord in California had recommended her to his chief counsel, who was on the hunt for emergency live-in childcare after the last nanny had left without notice. Lisette Harbison had mentioned during their first meeting that the family would be spending the holidays at their house on an island off the coast of Virginia, and she asked if Lauren would consider joining them. The island was only a short ferry ride from the Eastern Shore, where Lauren had visited Nicola at college, and the symmetry of this return to her home state had pleased her.

At first she stayed wary, on the lookout for the hidden domestic tensions that might have convinced the last nanny to pack up without warning, but the job was close to perfect. Hazel was the only child, a solid, precocious nine-year-old so unconcerned with appearances that you could hardly believe she'd grown up in Malibu. Lisette was a typical stressed fast-talking lawyer, but she was nice enough when something happened to remind her of Lauren's existence. She flew in on weekends, but the resident parent at the rambling, unpretentious house was her husband, a quiet painter who treated Lauren with a humorous courtesy blessedly free of sexual undertones. She had the third floor of the house to herself, a skinny suite of rooms with floor-to-ceiling vistas over the Chesapeake Bay.

Most mornings, she and Hazel set off in the family boat for neighboring Potato Island, which had been home to a small settlement descended from Scottish dissenters before being abandoned in the 1940s. It was Hazel who had found the rosebush, the last reminder of what probably once was a flourishing garden. A weathered picket fence enclosed a plot of land on the highest ridge, where the apple trees had died long ago, leaving bleached branches twisted like a broken spine. Only the rosebush still grew, producing brash, magnificent blossoms that would have won prizes at any flower show. Some trick of the Gulf Stream had kept it blooming into December.

In storms, the ocean swamped the small island and the sandy remains of the town's foundation, intent on taking this last slip of land back to itself. On other visits, Lauren had found buttons made of bone, arrowheads, an ivory comb. She kept them. Probably they belonged to the state, but no one would ever know.

WHEN SHE LOOKED BACK AND TRIED TO FIGURE OUT WHERE THINGS HAD gone wrong for her in California, she felt pretty sure that it all started with the Boyfriend.

One morning in August, he'd clomped across the bedroom floor in his thick-soled hiking boots and woken her out of a deep sleep. It wasn't immediately clear whether he'd disturbed her intentionally or was simply being his usual inconsiderate self, but from the satisfied look on his face as he perched on the end of the bed, Lauren suspected he'd done it on purpose.

"Hey, I'm going to head out," he said, patting her foot through the layer of blankets. "I just wanted to say goodbye."

Lauren found herself wishing he'd just left her a note on the kitchen table, but he was a sentimentalist at heart. Now that he was leaving, he clearly wanted to pretend that theirs had been more than a transactional relationship: on her side, good sex and a warm body to put between her body and the cabin's floor-to-ceiling windows; for him, a free place to stay.

"I'll call you when I get to Alaska." He reached to caress her cheek, something she couldn't remember him ever doing before. She felt a momentary impulse to jerk away but repressed it in time. If she hurt his feelings, he would want to stick around and talk about it.

"Happy trails," she said, and briefly worried that this sounded too lighthearted—a flip dismissal of whatever he'd decided they'd meant to each other—but he only smiled gently and leaned in to kiss her on the forehead.

"Take care of yourself, Rachel," he said, and he was gone, those monstrous hiking boots thunking dully on the cedar boards of the porch. A moment later, she heard his Forester roar to life in the driveway. Back when they couldn't keep their hands off each other, she'd given him five hundred dollars toward the down payment after he told her he needed a four-wheel drive for the muddy roads of the mountain spring. That was before he'd ever mentioned Alaska or the friend he was visiting there, who, as far as Lauren could tell, lacked both a name and a gender. She hadn't raised any objections, but she'd put a BB in his valve stem cap as a parting gift. If all went well, it should cause a flat before he made it as far as Salinas.

When the sound of crunching gravel receded into the distance, Lauren turned off the lamp and tried to go back to sleep. The bedside clock said 6:47, which meant she'd have to be up in an hour to get ready for her nine o'clock yoga class. Behind the glass wall, light stole over the rims of mountains, the tops of the pines flaring like birthday candles.

Since there was no chance of sleeping, she rolled over and grabbed her laptop, checking Reddit and then her email. Yesterday there had been an update on a case she'd been following for years: a nineteen-year-old named Terry Standish who'd disappeared while hiking in New Mexico, whose backpack had just been found in the woods. She skipped the thread about a girl spotted on a beach in Greece who people thought could be a missing three-year-old from Houston named Sarah Belle Ivers. There were at least three new Sarah Belle Ivers posts a week, while there were other cases that hardly anyone seemed to care about. What was the calculus that led some stories to catch and hold the public imagination, while others sank without a trace?

No matter what the Redditors thought, Lauren felt certain that Sarah Belle Ivers was dead. She had a sense about these things, and she was almost always right. The girl might be buried in a field or in a forest, her bones cooling under layers of fallen leaves, but she was dead. Lauren would have put money on it.

SHE'D NEVER MEANT TO STAY SO LONG IN ONE PLACE. WHEN SHE'D LANDED the waitress job at Nepenthe, the rest of the staff had assured her that it was impossible to find a rental, and she might as well resign herself to commuting like the rest of the plebes. This she'd been willing to do, in theory—the tips were fabulous at Nepenthe; something about the dizzying view made people free with their cash—but then she met the Big Man. He'd developed a dating app called Bucket that allowed users to anonymously rank their hookups, and he owned a five-acre spread just north of Pfeiffer Big Sur State Park. He would rent her the guest cabin for six hundred a month, provided she agreed to vacate the premises any time his daughter felt like coming for a visit. At first this provision had worried her, but the daughter worked for the UN in New

York and seemed uninterested in visiting her dad. Possibly, Lauren thought, she was embarrassed by his association with Bucket, refuge of dirtbags the world over.

Everyone at Nepenthe assumed that Lauren was sleeping with him, but she wasn't. She looked ten years younger than her actual age, and she didn't need to fuck a squash-playing Jeff Bezos lookalike for a place to stay. In fact, no sooner had she settled into her new life in the guest cabin than she met the Boyfriend, who was busing tables at another cliffside restaurant while he worked on his novel and looked like a Dutch prince masquerading as a beach bum. The Boyfriend had come to Big Sur because Henry Miller had lived here, although he was self-aware enough not to praise Miller in her presence.

She'd always known that the relationship could not be serious. She pretended not to know that the Boyfriend got the occasional check from home, and he pretended not to know about her true-crime obsession. Lauren couldn't have said exactly why she wanted to keep that part of her life secret; perhaps it was simply hard-won experience. These days she liked a relationship to be a sort of emotional fan dance, based on the principle that what was hidden was always more provocative than what was revealed.

That was why she was surprised to find herself feeling a little hurt by the Boyfriend's departure. After all, finding a new partner would not be a problem. Men liked her face and the long dark hair she wore in a dancer's bun, and they liked her body, curves and all. People expected yoga teachers to be whip-skinny supermodels, but she'd given up worrying about her weight years ago. When they'd first met, the Boyfriend had compared her body to ancient fertility statues, and she'd taken it as the compliment he'd intended it to be.

She was five minutes late for her first yoga class at Cooper Point Inn, and the activities manager gave her a dirty look, but Lauren smiled brightly as she breezed into the studio, where three middle-aged sisters from Tucson were giggly from the mimosas at breakfast and hadn't noticed that she was running behind. She taught three classes in a row, then stopped at the overpriced gas station and convenience store where she bought milk and bread when she didn't feel like making the trek all the way to Carmel. One of the waiters from Nepenthe was filling up at the pumps, and when Lauren said she might go for a walk at Pfeiffer Beach, he asked if she'd mind taking his dog. He'd been called in early to work, he explained, and didn't want to leave him in the car. The dog was a big blue-eyed husky with tufted eyebrows that made him look like a good listener. She loaded him in the back and drove down to the beach, where they played Frisbee until she ran into a pair of massage therapists who invited her to their barbecue. They'd lucked into a job as caretakers for a money guy from L.A., and they had the passcode to his sauna. They also had peyote, and Lauren spent the afternoon lying on a lawn chair under the redwoods with the dog's head on her lap. When she reached for the Boyfriend's name, it seemed to dance out of her reach, like a dried leaf on the wind.

By the time she returned the dog and made it back to her cabin, it was after ten, and her depression and sense of menacing dread returned when she saw one of the Boyfriend's flip-flops lying on its side next to the recycling bin. It was the drugs, she reminded herself sternly as she made a cup of lemon-ginger tea and drew a bath. All she had to do was get herself to bed and then to sleep. She always felt better in the morning.

While the water ran, she sat at the kitchen table and checked the Lauren Ballard Reddit page. She didn't let herself post often enough to draw attention, but every once in a while she'd throw in a comment about Opal Yarrow or the girl found in the Campbell River just to point the Web sleuths in the wrong direction. Some racist dipshit had replied, and she also had a private message from a user named *ngb4379: Hi, my name is Nicola Bennett. I saw that you said you grew up in the Tyndall County area, and I'm just wondering if we know each other?*

32

People in the online crime community often said that the best way to catch a person who had disappeared voluntarily was to try to get a handle on his hobbies. Did he love baseball? Stake out the local games. Was she a passionate philatelist? Hang around the yearly conference. People couldn't stop doing the things they loved, they said, but Lauren begged to differ. You could break even the strongest habit if you had a good enough reason. A smoker could switch to chewing tobacco; a rock guitarist could develop a taste for opera; a soccer player and runner could take up yoga. In most cases, it wasn't the activity that drew people as much as the fact of a hobby. If you knew that somebody might be looking for you, you could switch things up, find a different vehicle for your obsession, and no one would ever be the wiser.

The problem was that she'd never thought of true crime as a hobby. It had all started with the tabloid news show she used to watch with Nicola and her mom, with its sexy-stern hosts and stories of girls snatched off the school bus or abducted from their childhood bedrooms. By the time she was in high school, she knew the names of all the most famous victims: the Beaumont children, Etan Patz, Suzy Lamplugh. The ones where the explanation was insultingly obvious—where blood spatter was found in the family home or clothes washed up on a nearby beach—didn't interest her. Her favorite was the case of David Lang, who in 1880 was seen crossing a field near Gallatin, Tennessee, when he suddenly disappeared. His wife and children thought he might have fallen into a sinkhole, but when they reached the spot where he was seen last, there was no sign of him, not a button, not a scrap of cloth. Some sources argued that the tale was apocryphal, an Ambrose Bierce legend that was then reported as news, but she thought it was too good a story to not be true.

Maybe it was cruel of her to pretend to be Erika Callaghan, but it was also embarrassingly easy. She pored over Nicola's and Erika's posts going back years and confirmed that they'd never liked or commented on each other's photos, making it unlikely that they were in touch offline. Then all Lauren had to do was screenshot some of Erika's pictures and pass them off as her own. Of course, she could have made up the name of some imaginary Tyndall resident who had graduated ten years before them or ten years after. But she wanted to talk to Nicola, and there was no possible way to do it except in the disguise of someone she cared about. Lauren didn't want anything from her—just to pretend, if only for a few moments, that she still had the kind of friends you could really talk to. The kind of friends who would open their hearts to you, and trust you to do the same.

LESS THAN A WEEK AFTER SHE'D STARTED COMMUNICATING WITH NICOLA again, she came home and found her landlord sitting on her steps. He looked like he hadn't slept or shaved in days. "I'm selling," he announced before she even reached the porch. "But don't worry, you won't have to be out next week or anything. My agent says that properties like this can take a long time to find a buyer."

Properties like this: meaning a thirty-million-dollar spread on the side of a cliff in one of the most beautiful places in the world. "Come on in, let's talk about it," Lauren said.

That was what he wanted—to talk while she listened—and like most rich men, he was so accustomed to getting what he wanted that he couldn't fathom the idea of anyone saying no. Lauren cut up some apples and put them on a plate with cheese and crackers, a good hostess, while he told her why she would soon have no place to live.

His marriage was breaking up. She decided not to mention that he had never told her he was married, that she'd never seen him wearing a ring in the two years she'd known him. "She wants this place," he said. "But tough shit. Her name's not on the deed. Even if I have to give her half my assets, I'm not giving her this fucking house."

While he talked, she was thinking over her own options. She hadn't made enough friends to find another rental, and she was sure as shit not going to commute from Carmel. Clearly this was a sign that it was time to move on. She'd managed to save some of the money but not a lot—definitely not enough to start from scratch tomorrow. She would have to make a plan.

When the Big Man asked if she had wine, she said no, but it turned out that he had a case of a Paso Robles red zin in the back of his car. The drunker he got, the more he talked. He had given his son a quarter of a million dollars to start an organic pet food company. *To learn the value of money*, he said, but now the son wouldn't return his calls.

"I don't know what to do," he said. "I feel like he's daring me to get the lawyers involved." He was stretched on the rug, bare feet under the coffee table. "Speaking of which, have you heard from that guy? The one who went to Alaska?"

Lauren wondered how he could possibly think this was a *speaking of which*. "I got a postcard a few weeks back," she said. "He got a job in a bike shop."

"He wasn't good enough for you," the Big Man said. "I love your tattoo sleeves, by the way." He was pointing to the severed head of Medusa. The tongue and lips were red, with green snakes curling around the skull. "Are they symbolic or something?"

She didn't know what he meant by *symbolic*. Did he think the word was a synonym for *meaningful*? "Not really," she said. "I had a friend in L.A. who does beautiful sleeves. He said he'd give me a discount if I let him do whatever he wanted."

"So is your family in L.A.?"

Before she could answer, she felt something on her leg. It was a toe, sliding up and down the smooth skin on the inside of her calf. It gave her goosebumps, but not in a good way. "Okay if I crash here tonight?" he asked, clearly no longer interested in her family history. "I'm never going to make it down that road in the dark."

"I'll drive you," she said with an encouraging smile. "You know you'll be more comfortable in your own bed."

"You've been drinking too."

"I only had half a glass." It was actually a glass and a half, but he'd had four and surely hadn't been counting.

Lauren thought she'd made a good argument, but the Big Man wouldn't move. She prodded and coaxed. He'd closed his eyes and lay with his hands crossed over his chest like a corpse. She got down on her knees and gave him a little shove, just to see if she could roll him on his side, but he had half a foot and nearly a hundred pounds on her, and he wouldn't budge. As she sat back on her heels, wondering what to do next, a long nasal breath that could have been a snore issued from his mouth. Had he passed out, or was he faking?

She could have called the police. But it would take them an hour to get there, and then what if they refused to get involved? He was the property owner, and she didn't even have a formal lease.

She washed the wineglasses and brushed her teeth, making as much noise as possible, but he didn't stir. Around two in the morning, she heard the knob of the locked bedroom door rattle, and her whole body tensed, her toes knotting. She didn't get back to sleep until the sky whitened behind the blinds. She must have slept through the car starting, because when she finally dragged herself out of bed, he was gone.

He wouldn't forgive her for this, Lauren thought, and not just for locking her door and denying him the comfort of her bed. He wouldn't forgive her because he'd behaved like the lonely asshole he was, and she'd seen it. She wasn't surprised when she got the email late that evening: she had to be out by the end of December.

◆ ◆ ◆

AS IT HAPPENED, SHE SPED THAT UP BY MORE THAN A WEEK.

She was in the convenience store, picking up a loaf of bread and a bottle of Malbec, when the report came on CNN. *Mountain Love Triangle.* The sound was off, but the blond anchor's mouth moved as they flashed a picture of Sean in a suit and then the old cheesecake headshot of her in the wedding dress that wasn't even hers.

Lauren left the store and drove to the parking lot of the public library, the one place in town where you could get reliable free Wi-Fi. Her hands were trembling, and sweat slicked the small of her back. She googled *Lauren Ballard Virginia* and read enough to assure herself that Sean had confessed, then closed the browser on her phone and deleted the search history. She told herself that the case would not have much longevity in the press. There was nothing to give it staying power: she hadn't been a teenager, like Natalee Holloway, or pregnant, like Laci Peterson. Within weeks, something more shocking would come along, and Lauren would be forgotten.

But that wasn't enough to keep her safe. The brief fever of media attention virtually guaranteed that somewhere, in Newfoundland or Perth or Miami, an amateur would get interested in the disappearance of Lauren Ballard. Lauren had come across plenty of these online, and she knew that for them the coldness of the trail was a draw, not a deterrent. For all she knew, one of these armchair detectives might turn out to be ex–law enforcement, with sophisticated tools and strategies at their disposal. Just because no one had ever followed her trail to an end didn't mean it couldn't be done.

33

In her least favorite class at Burwell, Introduction to Political Science, they'd studied the social contract. As she understood it, the theory was that people mostly behaved themselves in return for the protection of the police and the government, but that was straight-up bullshit, in her opinion. It wasn't true that everyone in society agreed to respect the rights of others. There were people in the world who would deliberately go right just because you wanted them to go left, and who cared no more for civil society than they did for the spotted owl.

But after what happened on August 10, 2001, she thought she finally got what that professor had been going on about. People lived their lives based on what they thought others were capable of. They assumed that the neighbors would continue to behave as they expected them to behave, but sometimes a crack appeared in the veneer of moral constraint and widened until it ate up the whole world.

ON THE NIGHT OF HER DEATH, SHE WOKE UP ON THE FLOOR.

It was dark, and she could hear water dripping. When she tried to raise herself on her elbows to look around, the pain in her head went off like a bomb.

Sleep. A phrase from another class she'd taken in college floated into her brain: *Death's second self, that seals all up in rest.* The guy behind her had muttered that Shakespeare didn't make any fucking sense, but she had aced the quiz that day. It wasn't hard. Death's second self was night and the sleep that came with it.

In her old life, sleep had been recreation, a pool to dive into and surface from refreshed. This was different. Shakespeare was right: sometimes sleep was a dark well, death repeated again and again. It was black and final, a casket lid closing with a click.

WHEN SHE WOKE THE SECOND TIME, THE PAIN HAD EASED A LITTLE. SHE got on her knees and then wobbled to a standing position. The clock on the end table said 10:54. She felt something wet on her head and dabbed at it with a washcloth she found on the floor. It was sticky. Blood.

Sean had been here. Had he pushed her down the steps, or had she fallen?

She dragged herself to the couch. She'd gotten enough concussions playing soccer to be able to recite the list of doctor's recommendations— rest, limit activity, avoid mental exertion—but she had to exert herself at least a little to figure out what to do next. Warren and Mabry wouldn't be back until morning. Should she go to the hospital? She didn't think she could drive. She could call someone to take her, but when she'd found her phone, she couldn't remember how to find Nicola's number or even her mother's. The only number that came to mind was Taylor Vaughn's, which she'd memorized one night when she was partying downtown and had to call Taylor for a ride back to school.

She was so tired that the walls seemed to be moving, contracting and releasing like the muscles of the heart. Taylor would let her sleep, would take her back to Richmond and put her to bed in the guest room with the pillow-top mattress, and she couldn't imagine anything she wanted more than that.

"I'm leaving right now," Taylor said, and hung up. The parking lot was still dark when she arrived, the silver Audi cutting its lights before sliding into the parking space in front of the house. Taylor had brought bottled water and a thick cashmere blanket, and Lauren was asleep in the backseat before they made it out of the mountains.

SHE WOKE IN A ROOM DARK AS A CAVE, WITH ONLY A THIN SEAM OF LIGHT visible under the lip of the blackout curtains. The clock was a fancy gilt thing with hands instead of numbers, and she had to switch on the bedside lamp to read it. Seven fifteen. It could have been a.m. or p.m.

The pillowcase was smeared with blood. She put her hand to the cut on the side of her head, and as if on cue, it began to throb. She started crying. Part of her brain registered that it was an embarrassing sound, but she couldn't stop herself. She'd fallen back into the bed, and now Taylor was there, holding her the way she might have held a child.

As the heaving of her chest eased, Lauren could feel the tightness of Taylor's arms, her knobby feet tangling with her own feet. Lauren wore nothing but a bra and underwear, and now she could smell herself—a thick, rank scent like the sludge at the bottom of a trash can. She sat up, back against the headboard. "I don't know what to do," she said.

Taylor rolled onto her back. She was fully dressed in a white silk blouse and a cute yellow skirt that, even in her distress, Lauren wanted for herself. "I gave the maid the week off," she said. "I can make breakfast. I'm not much of a cook, but I could do eggs."

Breakfast: so she'd slept for a whole day. "Don't you have to go to class?"

Taylor shrugged. "I can play hooky."

Lauren shook her head, trying to clear it. Taylor was acting like she'd come for a weekend getaway. "I should go home. I can call Warren to pick me up."

Their eyes met, and after a pause, a small smile twitched the corner of Taylor's mouth. "You can do anything you want."

What she wanted right then was a shower. The water that ran down her shoulders and chest to pool at her feet was first deep red, then pink, and finally clear. The cut on the side of her head still hurt, so she cleaned around it, soaping the clotted mass of hair and massaging it with her fingers. Why had they left that doorstop with the baby's face at the bottom of the stairs, anyway? She'd always hated that thing. It reminded her of Nicola, with that stupid dimple.

She'd made the right decision, coming to Taylor's. Taylor would do anything for her. Lauren had kissed her for the first time out of curiosity and a petty sense of rivalry with Nicola, who inexplicably had managed to do so many things that Lauren herself had never experienced. She'd allowed it to continue because she enjoyed the sense of being someone's muse, and because it was useful to have people around who would do anything you asked.

After the shower, she dried with the plush bath sheet from the heated rack and wrapped her body in a white cotton robe. In the kitchen, a plate of fried eggs and a bagel were waiting on the island beside a carafe of French-press coffee the color of mud.

How long had it been since she'd eaten? Hadn't she read somewhere that people who'd been without food for a long time had to take it slow to prevent stomach cramps? She couldn't convince herself to care. She ate every bite and ran her finger around the plate to catch the last traces of runny yolk.

When her plate was clear, she wouldn't have minded going back to bed. She propped her chin on her hand and stared out the window at the backyard, where giant old-growth oaks waved in the dappled sunlight.

Taylor hadn't said a word since Lauren came downstairs, but she could see the top of her head above the rim of the living room sofa and hear the busy tap-tap of fingers on a keyboard. Lauren waited for a pause and then raised her voice to ask, "Would you look at this thing on my head?"

Taylor complied. Her touch was generous and kind but somehow detached, self-protective, as it had been the two times they'd slept together. "I don't think you need stitches," she said. "You're going to have a big-ass bruise, though."

This was such a minor detail that Lauren couldn't bring herself to respond. "Are they talking about me on the news?"

"Not yet."

She closed her eyes, enjoying the feeling of Taylor's cool fingertips against her jaw, their faces only inches apart. If Lauren let her, Taylor would take charge and arrange everything. "Should I call Warren?" Lauren asked.

"If that's what you want."

Her eyes snapped open. "What else can I do? I mean literally. Do you want me to stay in your guest room forever?"

"Well, that's not exactly what I was picturing." Taylor moved to the other side of the island and filled a glass at the tap. "Not that I wouldn't love to have you."

Her brain seemed to be moving more slowly than usual. Maybe it was trauma and exhaustion, or maybe it was simply being with Taylor, who always seemed to be several chess moves ahead of everyone else.

Taylor took her time answering the unspoken question, draining her glass of water and setting it beside the sink. "You always said you wished you could start over," she said. "Here's your chance."

Gradually she understood: Taylor was offering to buy her a fake identity. "My dad had this client who got arrested for fraud," she went on. "He moved to Texas and assumed the identity of a man who had died in a car accident. He even got married and had kids. When he got caught, I was working as a paralegal, and he told me all about how he did it. It's not as hard as people think. It is expensive, but I can keep the money you put into the Jackson Ward house and we can call it even."

Lauren picked up her coffee mug and put it down again. "They'll come looking for me."

"The police? No, they won't. You think Sean is going to go straight to the station and report that the girl he maybe killed isn't there anymore? Unless the Tyndall cops are a fuckload better than I think, it'll be a missing person case. And missing person cases are hard to solve."

Lauren knew that already. She thought of Suzanne Lyall, Amy

Wroe Bechtel—all the missing girls and women who had never been found.

It was true she wasn't happy in her life in Tyndall. Looking back, she partly blamed Stephanie Gilliam, who had started the whole thing by telling Warren that it would be *so super-cute* if he asked Lauren to the Valentine's dance. At the time Lauren had her eye on a boy named Trevor Bland, who had grown up to be an investment banker in Chicago with a dog-faced wife and a second home in St. Barts.

There were so many other lives she could have lived if she'd just been smart enough to stay away from Warren, or at least avoided pregnancy. In Tyndall County, social capital meant having the right husband and the right house in the right neighborhood, and Lauren had signed on to that moronic vision of the good life before she knew what she was doing. Fucking Sean had been nothing more than an act of desperation, and now here she was, sitting in Taylor's kitchen with a gaping head wound and no idea what to do next.

"I have a husband and a baby, Taylor," she said. "I can't just leave them. And what about my mom?"

"You can't stand your mom."

That was true. She held Susan responsible for pushing the relationship with Warren, living vicariously through Lauren's success in the town where she'd always be an outsider.

She said no, of course. She said no several times, elaborating on all the reasons why she couldn't do what Taylor was suggesting. Later she thought that if Taylor had argued with her, everything might have been different. But Taylor had simply sat with her legs thrown over the arm of the chaise longue, her eyes flicking absently over the lush green lines of her lawn, her face so blank that anybody could have told she was bored.

On the fifth day, Taylor told her that the police had called. "Some detective," she said.

Lauren sat up straight. "Why does he want to talk to you?"

Taylor seemed unconcerned. "Warren gave him my name, probably. Don't worry. I'm a great liar."

They were waiting for the driver's license, birth certificate, and social security card that Taylor had ordered to be sent via courier. They
had agreed that the twenty-five thousand dollars she'd given Taylor
in cash when they bought the rental property would cover it, though
Lauren suspected that Taylor was spending far more than that.

The day of the police interview, she spent the whole afternoon on
the edge of the living room sofa, jumping up whenever she heard a car.
When Taylor finally walked through the front door, Lauren felt her
body go limp with relief. Taylor gave her what was probably supposed
to be a once-over, but she was clearly exhausted, the ogle only half-
hearted. "Look at you," she said, flopping into an armchair. "Like the
housewife I always wanted."

Lauren perched on the coffee table. "What happened? What did he
ask you?"

"How would I describe our relationship. When did I last talk to
you." She crossed her legs at the ankle. "He asked me about some guy
named Dale Westcott."

Dale Westcott? At first she drew a blank, and then it came to her:
Jessi Westcott's dad. Why on earth did the detective want to talk
about him? "So you don't think he picked up on anything? He didn't
seem suspicious?"

Taylor had closed her eyes, the strain of the past week finally visible
on her face. "I told you," she said without opening her eyes. "I'm a great
liar."

HER NEW NAME WAS RACHEL MONROE. SHE'D BEEN BORN IN LINCOLN, NE-
braska, the oldest child of John and Deborah Monroe, who'd divorced
when she was four. Rachel had gone to Lincoln East High School and
then to the University of Nebraska, where she'd planned to major in
journalism but had dropped out after a semester because of financial
problems. Taylor made her memorize these facts, drilling them into
her while combing the brown dye into her hair. They'd decided that
Rachel was a brunette.

Later she embellished the story, adding a younger brother who died of the flu at eleven months, precipitating the divorce, and a parental kidnapping by her estranged father. Though Taylor told her not to keep records, Lauren wrote Rachel's backstory in a marbled composition notebook that she kept in the zippered front pocket of her suitcase, adding tastes in movies and music, names of elementary school friends. Wasn't there some acting technique where you had to learn everything about a character before you portrayed them onscreen? She'd never been a success in the high school drama productions—even Warren was a better actor—but this would be different. This wasn't a performance; this was her life.

Her documents were supposed to arrive in a week. She spent a whole day fantasizing about Hawaii, but Taylor opposed that idea, arguing that in a place where people came and went, a lingering stranger would draw unwelcome attention. "You should go to a city," she said. "Chicago, San Francisco. Somewhere you won't stand out."

"San Francisco," she repeated. Like every East Coast kid, she'd grown up dreaming of California. "Why not? I'll go there."

FOR TWO WEEKS LAUREN EMERGED ONLY AT NIGHT, DARTING OUT FOR A quick sprint around the neighborhood in Taylor's running shoes, which pinched her toes. Though it was against the strict rules that Taylor had set, sometimes she ran all the way to Meadowbrook, where she bought a newspaper and read it in the parking lot before tossing it in the dumpster.

The *Post-Dispatch* had run a story about her every day for the past week. On Sunday it was an in-depth article on the first page of the state section, but since then it had diminished in size from three columns to one. Then one night, the story was gone. She flipped through the section three times, telling herself that she must have missed it. For a moment she felt like throwing up, but maybe she shouldn't be surprised that interest had died so quickly. People wanted resolution, and as long as she stayed away, there could never be answers.

She bent forward and put her head between her knees. The lights in the parking lot felt sticky on her skin. She would go inside and ask the attendant to call the police. She would tell them exactly what had happened that night. Anything was better than existing in this in-between, this suspension between two possibilities.

She spat on the asphalt and threw the paper in the trash. The next day she got on a plane for San Francisco, newly baptized as Rachel Monroe.

34

For the first six months, her life was quiet and almost happy. She found a job waitressing at a Mediterranean restaurant and rented a room in an old Victorian from an anthropologist couple whose first names she could never remember. She had recurrent headaches that were probably related to the concussion, but lying down in a dark room usually made them go away. At work she was popular with the other servers, but she avoided partying with them after she found that her Southern accent came out when she drank. When they started calling her Miss Scarlett, she quit and found another gig, this time dancing at a bar near the Ferry Building.

She never heard from Taylor. That was something they'd agreed on before she left Richmond. "You've got to stay out of trouble," Taylor had warned her. "And you've got to stay away from anybody who might look like trouble. If you get caught up in something, it won't take the police long to figure out that there's no record of your existence before 2001."

Sometimes on her way to work at the bar, she stopped by the library. She liked mysteries and thrillers, the higher the body count, the better. After she picked up a new stack of books, she would log into a computer and look up the latest coverage of her disappearance. She always waited for the machine that faced a wall so no one could look over her shoulder.

At first there had been a rash of sightings. The attendant at the gas station where she'd bought all those newspapers had gone to the police, as had a few people at the airports she'd passed through, but then the case had been eclipsed by the tragedies in New York and Washington. When the police identified a person of interest, only the Tyndall paper bothered to give his name: Dale Westcott.

Several weeks later, there was news of the accidental drowning. She sat for a minute staring blankly at the screen, feeling a tingling in her fingertips. She couldn't believe her luck.

SHE'D BEEN IN SAN FRANCISCO SEVEN YEARS WHEN SHE MET HER HUSBAND at a burlesque club where she was bartending. He was not the type to ask lots of questions about the past. He worked as a promoter for a slate of bands in the L.A. area, and she understood early on that he wouldn't be faithful to her. It hurt at first, but when you were keeping as big a secret as she was, you could give only so much of yourself to another person.

The lead singer of one of her husband's bands took her to get her first sleeve, covering up the chickenpox scar on her arm. The next day, she filed for divorce. Short-lived as the marriage was, she found that she was grateful to her ex for helping her fill in the outline of the new person she'd become. She was Rachel Monroe Black now, one step further from Lauren Ballard.

WHEN NICOLA TOLD HER SHE WAS SLEEPING WITH WARREN, LAUREN WAS surprised but not particularly upset. It was inevitable, now that she thought about it: two lonely people brought together by a shared loss. Plus, Nicola had always wanted to be her.

Her lack of indignation made her realize just how much she'd changed in sixteen years. She'd been a bad person back then, mean and sneaky and even cruel. She'd done stupid stuff, like sleeping with Sean and stealing Nicola's necklace, but she hadn't done everything she'd been accused of. She hadn't vandalized Jessi Westcott's locker. She'd never been sure who had, though she suspected Stephanie Gilliam and Jason Mack. Also she hadn't fucked that bartender, the one she'd met when she visited Nicola at Fletcher. They'd stayed up all night doing coke and talking, but he hadn't even tried to kiss her. She'd felt insulted at the time, and had left him a note calling him a limp dick before she'd sneaked out in the morning.

She'd been an awful mother too. It was amazing there was nothing wrong with Mabry, given the way Lauren had treated her body during pregnancy. After the birth, Lauren found that she felt nothing when she heard the baby cry—certainly none of the overwhelming love and desire to protect that she'd been told about. Mabry was the spitting image of Warren; everybody said so, and if you didn't love your husband, how could you love the child who looked just like him?

If she'd been honest with the doctors, they might have diagnosed her with postpartum depression, but she knew it was worse than that. She wasn't sad or anxious; she simply wished she'd never gotten pregnant in the first place. She tried to do what was expected, of course, and no one seemed to notice that anything was wrong except Warren, who started calling the local daycares to see if anyone would take a baby under six months old.

Then she'd done the worst thing. On that hot June day, she'd known that Mabry was in her carseat when she turned her back and walked into the house. The baby had been crying all the way home—wailing inconsolably, as she often did when she sensed that she was alone with her mother. Lauren had drunk nearly a bottle of wine at lunch with Sean, and all she wanted to do was lie down on the couch. She told herself that she'd go back in five minutes and get her daughter, but then she let her head sink down to the pillow. She woke a quarter of an hour later to the mailman's shouts and the hope—brief, hardly conscious— that the baby was already dead.

When Sean had said that Mabry would be better off without her, he was absolutely right. There was something missing in her, or something broken, a cog that didn't spin. It wasn't just a comfortable lie that she told herself to ease the guilt of running away. She'd been a terrible mother and a terrible wife, and she would have destroyed both her husband and daughter, one way or another, if she'd gotten the chance.

The amazing thing was that it really was possible to reinvent yourself. She'd shed not only her identity but her personality too. *Wherever you go, there you are*, the Buddhists said, but that was a lie. Wherever you went, there was someone new—someone you'd never even known existed.

BUT THIS TINY ISLAND STRANDED IN THE ATLANTIC COULD BE ONLY A temporary refuge. Eventually the Big Man would figure out that she was the one who had placed the ad on Craigslist offering his property for rent. She'd left a set of keys she'd stolen from the housekeeper for the new tenants, who had moved in while he was out of town and were now refusing to leave, claiming squatters' rights. So many of his household staff hated him that the suspicion hadn't yet fallen on her, but it was only a matter of time. She was thinking Thailand or maybe Costa Rica. She'd feel safer in a place where few questions would be asked.

"Rachel!" Hazel shouted from the ridge, waving something over her head. "Look what I found!"

Lauren started up the rise, pushing back the sawgrass that whipped at her legs. When she got to the top, Hazel smiled and held out her find: a watering can that had once been copper but was now an oxidized blue-green. "Can I take it home?"

"Sure." Lauren watched as the girl knelt beside the rosebush and carefully tilted the spout over the roots, realizing at once that Hazel wasn't just pretending to water the flowers. "Sugar, did you fill that can up in the ocean?"

Hazel heard the warning in her voice and looked up. "Yeah."

"That's okay," Lauren assured her. Hazel liked taking care of things, and if some of her efforts didn't work out as planned, at least her intentions were good. In her old life, Lauren would have had nothing but contempt for this kind of idiot hopefulness, but now she thought it was kind of cute.

"Smell this one," Hazel said, pinching the stem carefully between thumb and forefinger. "This is my favorite."

She bent and let Hazel lift the rose to her face. At first she'd worried that being around another little girl might remind her of the daughter she'd lost, but it didn't bother her at all. She had no unplumbed regrets. Maybe she was a sociopath, the accusation that Warren had sometimes thrown at her in the heat of an argument, or maybe she had one of the other disorders that were only slightly less damning: narcissism or borderline. It was possible that he'd been right, and the innate selfishness she'd been aware of her whole life was a deep sickness, a pathology, but it didn't matter now. People wanted you to feel guilty. They wanted you to feel like you owed them something, but that was just manipulation. She wasn't responsible for anyone's suffering. She was happy, and perhaps the worst thing about her was that she didn't feel bad about it, not even a little bit.

The scent of the rose was like strong red wine, so heady and rich that her knees nearly buckled. Even now, forced again to make a new start out of nothing, she knew how fortunate she was. She was free, released from obligation and expectation. She was what every girl wanted to be.

Acknowledgments

Like a lot of writers, I make it through the frustrating times, when it feels like a book is never going to come together, by writing my acknowledgments page in my head. Now that I'm actually writing it, I'm terrified that I'm going to forget one of the people I've been mentally thanking for the past four years. If I did leave someone out, please forgive me and know that your name is inscribed on the acknowledgments page in my heart.

I can still remember exactly where I was and what I was doing when I answered the first call from my agent, Denise Shannon. I felt so fortunate to be working with her then and still do. Similarly, I knew from my first conversation with Sarah Stein, my editor at Harper, that she understood exactly what I wanted in *The Good Ones* and how I could make it better. I couldn't imagine a more thoughtful, insightful, and enthusiastic guide through the editing process, and I'm forever grateful. Thanks to my film/TV agent, Shari Smiley, for her advocacy and invaluable guidance.

Thanks to my UK editor, Hannah Wann of Little, Brown UK, and my UK agent, Judith Murray of Greene & Heaton, for their hard work and excitement about this project, and for welcoming me on my visit to London last year. Heather Drucker and Katie O'Callaghan at Harper are phenomenal at what they do and fantastic champions for writers, and I feel so fortunate to be on their team. Thanks to Robin Bilardello for designing the cover of my dreams. Thanks also to David Howe at Harper, Claire Dee at the Denise Shannon Literary Agency, and Elora Sullivan for teaching me how to social media. Thanks to Laura Dillon Rogers for taking lovely author photos that make me look one hundred percent more put-together than I do when I'm actually writing.

Maybe it seems counterintuitive given their subject matter, but crime writers are the nicest, most welcoming people in the world (and also surprisingly fun and hilarious). Thanks to Ace Atkins, Samantha Bailey, Darcey Bell, Allison Buccola, Amy Jo Burns, Kirstin Chen, May Cobb, Shawn Cosby, Eli Cranor, Katie Gutierrez, Angie Kim, Danya Kukafka, Laura McHugh, Sara Flannery Murphy, Hank Ryan, Alex Segura, Chris Whitaker, and so many others. Thanks to Dwyer Murphy at CrimeReads for supporting my work and the community as a whole. Thanks to all the booksellers out there, especially Flannery Buchanan at Bluebird Bookstop. I grew up blowing my allowance at independent bookstores and still can't imagine life without them.

Thanks to my family: the Pennocks, the Walkers, the Longfellows, the Schultzes, and everyone in St. Louis, especially the Tracys and the Murphys. Charlie Cline is a great friend, coparent, and creative brainstorming partner. My mother, Mary Welek Atwell, is the reason I'm a writer, and the best role model anyone could ever ask for.

I'm lucky to have much better lifelong friends than the ones in this novel. Special thanks to the JBS—Norm Ash, Diane Brookreson, Sarah John, and Sabrina Rose-Smith—and to Cindy Lindstrom Marich, for twenty-plus years of Frank Talk. Thanks to Carroll Ann Friedman, Liam Buckley, and the community at Ashtanga Yoga Charlottesville for helping me stay sane so I can keep writing books.

Thanks to my colleagues and friends at VMI, especially Emily Miller; Rob, Christina, and Grace McDonald; my pals in Cohort 15, Catharine Ingersoll and Michelle Iten; and Henry Wise. I can't imagine a place where the work of writing and reading would feel so vital or so important. Thanks to the cadets I'm privileged to teach, especially the one who really got the *Jane Eyre* tattoo. Thanks to Thorpe Moeckel, Julie Pfeiffer, Lisa Radcliffe, and the rest of the Hollins University

English department, and to the amazing staff at the Virginia Center for the Creative Arts, for the priceless gift of a quiet workspace while this book was in the final stages of revision.

Nearly every word of this novel was written between four and seven o'clock in the morning. Thanks to my children for being good sleepers, along with their many other wonderful qualities, and thanks to my stepchildren, who are some of the bravest and strongest people I know, and have made my heart grow at least three sizes.

In the past year, I've asked a lot of writers who are also parents how they kept writing during the pandemic. No one has a definitive answer, but we all know it has a lot to do with the teachers and daycare workers who kept educating our children under difficult circumstances and rarely get the support and respect they deserve. Thanks to the educators, especially the incredible, dedicated staff at the Virginia Institute of Autism.

Finally, this book is for Keith, who knows all the reasons why.

About the Author

POLLY STEWART grew up in the Appalachian Mountains of Virginia, where she still lives. She graduated from Hollins University and has an MFA in fiction and a PhD in British literature from Washington University in St. Louis. Her short fiction has appeared in literary collections and journals, including *Best New American Voices*, *The Best American Mystery Stories*, *Epoch*, and the *Alaska Quarterly Review*. Her nonfiction has appeared in the *New York Times*, CrimeReads, and *Poets & Writers*, among other publications.